TRAITOR GENERAL

As THE FATE of the Sabbat Worlds campaign balances
on a knife-edge, the success of the Imperial crusade
rests with one high-ranking officer, captured by the
dark forces of Chaos.

Colonel-Commissar Ibram Gaunt leads a hand-
picked strike team deep behind enemy lines to track
down a captured Imperial officer who holds
strategic knowledge of Warmaster Macaroth's entire
battleplan. Their mission is simple: stop him from
revealing his secrets to the enemy – whatever the
cost. With their lives forfeit, Gaunt and his team are
the key to a mission that will bring either death or
glory!

Dan Abnett comes out with all guns blazing as he
throws Gaunt and his elite stealth team into the very
heart of darkness in this awesome novel, which
begins a new story arc called *The Lost*.

A WARHAMMER 40,000 NOVEL

TRAITOR GENERAL

Dan Abnett

For Mrs Abnett.
XDX

A BLACK LIBRARY PUBLICATION

First published in Great Britain in 2004.
Paperback edition published in 2005 by BL Publishing,
Games Workshop Ltd.,
Willow Road, Nottingham,
NG7 2WS, UK.

10 9 8 7 6 5 4 3 2

Cover by Adrian Smith

A CIP record for this book is available from the British Library.

ISBN 13: 978 1 84416 113 3
ISBN 10: 1 84416 113 7

Distributed in the US by Simon & Schuster
1230 Avenue of the Americas, New York, NY 10020, US.

Printed and bound in Great Britain by
Bookmarque, Surrey, UK.

See the Black Library on the Internet at
www.blacklibrary.com

Find out more about Games Workshop
and the world of Warhammer 40,000 at
www.games-workshop.com

IT IS THE 41st millennium. For more than a hundred centuries the Emperor has sat immobile on the Golden Throne of Earth. He is the master of mankind by the will of the gods, and master of a million worlds by the might of his inexhaustible armies. He is a rotting carcass writhing invisibly with power from the Dark Age of Technology. He is the Carrion Lord of the Imperium for whom a thousand souls are sacrificed every day, so that he may never truly die.

YET EVEN IN his deathless state, the Emperor continues his eternal vigilance. Mighty battlefleets cross the daemon-infested miasma of the warp, the only route between distant stars, their way lit by the Astronomican, the psychic manifestation of the Emperor's will. Vast armies give battle in his name on uncounted worlds. Greatest amongst his soldiers are the Adeptus Astartes, the Space Marines, bio-engineered super-warriors. Their comrades in arms are legion: the Imperial Guard and countless planetary defence forces, the ever-vigilant Inquisition and the tech-priests of the Adeptus Mechanicus to name only a few. But for all their multitudes, they are barely enough to hold off the ever-present threat from aliens, heretics, mutants – and worse.

TO BE A man in such times is to be one amongst untold billions. It is to live in the cruellest and most bloody regime imaginable. These are the tales of those times. Forget the power of technology and science, for so much has been forgotten, never to be re-learned. Forget the promise of progress and understanding, for in the grim dark future there is only war. There is no peace amongst the stars, only an eternity of carnage and slaughter, and the laughter of thirsting gods.

'TOWARDS THE CLOSE of 774.M41, the nineteenth year of the Sabbat Worlds Crusade, Warmaster Macaroth seemed to be consolidating the victories he had finally secured after several desperate years of tactical brinksmanship. The leading edge of the Crusade host had at last toppled the fortress world Morlond, and was now driving onwards into the Carcaradon Cluster and the Erinyes Group, to wage what Macaroth had declared, with typical arrogance, would be the final phase of the war against the archenemy overlord ('Archon'), Urlock Gaur.

'Crucial to the prosperity of this advance was the fact that the savage attempts by two of Gaur's warlord lieutenants to bisect the Crusade force at the Khan Group had failed. Enok Innokenti's assault on Herodor had been repulsed, and Innokenti himself slain. Anakwanar Sek's counter-strikes had been denied at Lotun, Tarnagua and, most particularly, Enothis.

'But Sek and his forces remained a threat to the Crusade flank. In retreat, the magister's host had seized a tranche of worlds in the margins of the Khan Group, and dug in. Macaroth charged the Fifth, Eighth and Ninth Crusade Armies to annihilate the warlord's disposition in that region.

'Macaroth may have underestimated the scale of this endeavour. The war to dislodge Sek raged for *several years, and saw some of the most massive and bloody battles of the entire Crusade. However, documents recently declassified by the Administratum reveal that one of the most vital actions during that period was undertaken on a far less monumental scale...'*

– from *A History of the Later Imperial Crusades*

PROLOGUE

THE LAST OF the daylight was fading, and the fields of windflowers beyond the mansion walls had turned to violet shadow. From the terrace, in the evening cool, it was possible to see the redoubts of the Guard camps on the far side of the river, the elevated barrels of the defence batteries sticking up into the pale sky like thorns.

Barthol Van Voytz set his drink down on the terrace wall, and adjusted his fine, white gloves. They were loose. He'd lost weight since he'd last worn them for a formal occasion like this. He yearned for battlefield armour, not this ill-fitting dress uniform, starched and heavy with medals. Tomorrow, he told himself, tomorrow he could put on his wargear. Because tomorrow at oh-five thirty Imperial, the war to retake Ancreon Sextus would begin in earnest.

'My lord? The chamberlain wonders if they might begin serving dinner.'

Van Voytz turned. Biota, his chief tactical officer, stood behind him attentively. He too was gussied up in white, formal dress regalia.

'You look like a game-bird's behind in the moonlight,' said Van Voytz.

'Thank you, lord general. You are no less splendid. What shall I tell the chamberlain?'

'Are we all here?' asked Van Voytz.

'Not quite.'

'Then tell him to wait. If we're going to do this, we're going to do this right.'

They wandered back up the stone terrace together, and went in through the glass hatches. The banquet hall appeared to have been made of gold. Hundreds of yellow glow-globes lit the long room, casting everything in a golden light. Even the white cloth on the long table and the flesh of the men present seemed to be gilded.

There were forty places set at the table, and Van Voytz counted thirty-eight officers in the room. They clustered in groups, stiff in their formal attire, filling the room with the low murmur of their conversations. Van Voytz noted General Kelso of the Crusade Eighth Army, and Lord Militant Humel of the Ninth, mingling with the other regimental leaders and senior officers.

Luscheim had been killed on Tarnagua, so now Van Voytz had command of the Crusade Fifth Army. He felt the honour was overdue, and hated the fact that it had taken the death of his old friend Rudi Luscheim to make his promotion possible.

'Can we not begin, Van Voytz?' Kelso asked grumpily. He was a squat, elderly man with heavy jowls, and his brocaded dress uniform made him look even wider than he actually was.

'We're not all here yet,' Van Voytz replied. 'If we're going to endure the indignity of a formal staff dinner to mark the eve of war, we might as well make sure everyone suffers.'

Kelso chuckled. 'Who are we missing, then?'

'The commissar and commanding officer of the Tanith First, sir,' Biota said.

'Well, I suppose we could take our seats at least,' Van Voytz conceded.

Kelso gave a signal, and the assembled officers began to move to their places at the long table. Servitors passed among the company, charging glasses.

The outer door opened, and two men entered. One was a tall fellow, dressed in the uniform of an Imperial commissar. The other wore the black number one issue of his regiment.

'At last,' said Kelso.

'Gentlemen, please,' Van Voytz said, pointing the newcomers to their seats. The Tanith officers crossed to the places reserved for them.

'A toast, I think. Van Voytz?' Kelso suggested.

Van Voytz nodded and rose to his feet, glass in hand. The distinguished company rose with him, chairs scraping back.

Van Voytz considered his words for a moment. He looked across the table at the commanding officers of the Tanith regiment: Commissar Viktor Hark and Major Gol Kolea.

Van Voytz raised his glass and said: 'To absent friends.'

ONE

ON THE SIX hundred and fourth Day of Pain, the two hundred and twenty-first day of the Imperial Year 774, Gerome Landerson left his place of work at the sounding of the carnyx horn. The horn signalled the change from day-labour to night-labour.

He was weary, hungry and drenched with sweat. His arms and spine ached from swinging a hammer, and his hands were so numbed from the constant impacts that he could no longer feel his fingers. But he did not trudge towards the cookshops or the washhouses with the other day-labourers from the Iconoclave, nor did he begin the long walk back to the consented habitats along the river wall of Ineuron Town.

Instead, he walked west, down through the fractured arches of the town's old commercia. Markets had once thrived there – the daily cheaps of foodstuffs, grain, livestock, instruments – and the licensed mercantile houses had once raised their lavish silk tents and displayed the gewgaws and trinkets of their trade.

Landerson had always loved the commercia for its flavour of the faraway. He'd once bought a small metal plaque with an engraving of an Ecclesiarchy templum on Enothis just because it had travelled so far. Now the faraway seemed even more remote and unreachable, even though it was his business tonight.

The commercia was a ruin these days. What remained of the vast roof vault was smoke-blackened and rotten, and the rows of metal stalls where the traders had congregated for the daily cheaps were twisted and corroding. On the rubble-strewn ground, a few furtive dealers lurked by oilcan fires, bartering luxuries like marrowbones and bent cutlery for ration coins and consent wafers. Every time there was a hint of an excubitor patrol passing nearby, the scavengers melted away into the shadows.

Landerson walked on, trying to rub some life back into his soot-caked hands. He left the commercia via the wide flight of white marble steps, steps still riddled with the black boreholes of lasfire, and began down the Avenue of Shins. That wasn't its real name of course, but the yoke of oppression bred black humour in the conquered. This had been the Avenue of the Aquila. Long and broad, it was lined on either side by rows of ouslite plinths. The statue of an Imperial hero had once stood on each. The invaders had demolished them all. Now only splintered stone shins rose from the proud feet planted on those plinths. Hence the name.

Talix trees, tall and slender, grew along the outsides of the avenue. At least two had been decapitated and remade into gibbets for the wirewolves. There was no point trying to avoid them. Landerson walked on, trying not to look up at the skeletal mannequins hanging limply from the axl-trees on their metal strings. They creaked, swinging slightly in the breeze.

Daylight was fading. The sky, already hazy with the perpetual canopy of dust, had taken on a sheen as if a fog were closing in. To the west, the furnaces of the meat foundries glazed the low clouds with a glow the colour of pomegranate flesh. Landerson knew he had to hurry now. His imago consented him only for activity during daylight.

He was crossing the square at Tallenhall when he smelled the glyf. It stank like a discharged battery pack, an ionized scent, the tang of blood and metal. He huddled down in the overgrown hedge by the tangled iron railings and watched. The glyf appeared in the northern corner of the square, drifting like a balloon eight metres up, slow and lazy. As soon as he had located it, he tried to look away, but it was impossible. The floating sigils, bright as neon, locked his attention. He felt his stomach churn at the sight of those abominable, intertwined symbols, his gorge rising. At the back of his mind, he heard a chattering, like the sound of swarming insects rubbing their wing cases. The imago in the flesh of his left arm twitched.

The glyf wavered, then began to glide away, out of sight behind the shell of the town library. As soon as it was gone, Landerson sank onto his hands and dry-heaved violently into the burned grass. When he closed his eyes, he could see the obscene symbols shining in meaningless repeats on the back of his eyelids.

Unsteady, he rose to his feet, succumbed to a spell of giddiness, and slumped against the bent railings for support.

'Voi shet!' a hard voice barked.

He shook his head, trying to straighten up. Boots crunched across the brick dust towards him.

'Voi shet! Ecchr Anark setriketan!'

Landerson raised his hands in supplication. 'Consented! Consented, magir!'

The three excubitors surrounded him. Each was two metres tall and clad in heavy buckled boots and long coats of grey scale armour. They aimed their ornate las-locks at him.

'I am consented, magir!' he pleaded, trying to show them his imago.

One of them cuffed him down onto his knees.

'Shet atraga ydereta haspa? Voi leng haspa?'

'I… I don't speak your–'

There was a click, and a crackle of vox noise. One of them spoke again, but its coarse words were obscured by a rasping mechanical echo.

'What is your purpose here?'

'I am consented to pass in daylight, magir,' he answered.

'Look at me!' Again, the barbarous tongue was over-laid with augmetically-generated speech.

Landerson looked up. The excubitor leaning over him was as hellish as any of its kind. Only the upper half of its head was visible – pale, shrivelled and hairless. A drip-ping cluster of metal tubes and pipes sprouted from the back of its wrinkled skull and connected to the steaming, panting support box strapped across its back. Three huge, sutured scars split its face, one down through each eye socket – in which augmetic ocular mounts were now sewn – and the third straight down over the bridge of a nose from which all flesh had been debrided. A large brass collar rose in front of the face, mercifully obscuring the excubitor's mouth and most of the nasal area. The front of this collar mounted a wire-grilled speaking box, which the excubitor had switched to 'translate'.

'I… I look upon you, and I am graced by your beauty,' Landerson gasped as clearly as he could.

'Name?' the thing snapped.

'Landerson, Gerome, consented of day, b-by the will of the Anarch.'

'Place of industry?'

'The Iconoclave, magir.'

'You work in the Breaking House?'

'Yes, magir.'

'Display to me your consent!'

Landerson lifted his left arm and drew back the sleeve of his torn workcoat to reveal the imago in its blister of clear pus.

'Eletraa kyh drowk!' the excubitor said to one of its companions.

'Chee ataah drowk,' came the reply. The sentinel drew a long metal tool from its belt, the size and shape of a candle-snuffer, and placed the cup over Landerson's imago. Landerson gasped as he felt the thing in his flesh writhe. Small runes lit up on the shank of the tool. The cup withdrew.

The third excubitor grabbed Landerson by the head and turned it roughly so as to better examine the stigma on his left cheek.

'Fehet gahesh,' it said, letting him go.

'Go home, interceded one,' the first excubitor told Landerson, the machine words back-echoed by the alien speech. 'Go home and do not let us catch you out here again.'

'Y-yes, magir. At once.'

'Or we will have sport with you. Us, or the wirewolves.'

'I understand, magir. Thank you.'

The excubitor stepped back. It covered the grille of its speaking box with one hand. Its brethren did the same.

'We serve the word of the Anarch, whose word drowns out all others.'

Landerson covered his own mouth quickly. 'Whose word drowns out all others,' he repeated quickly.

The excubitors looked at him for a moment longer, then shouldered their massive las-locks and walked away across the overgrown square.

It was a long while before Landerson had recovered enough to get back on his feet.

* * *

IT WAS ALMOST dark when he reached the abandoned mill at the edge of the town. The dimming sky was lit by fires: the burning masses of the distant hives and the closer glows of the ahenum furnaces that powered the town's new industries. On the wide roadway below the mill, torches were bobbing and drums were beating. Another procession of proselytes was being led to the shrines by the ordinals.

Landerson tapped on the wooden door.

'How is Gereon?' asked a voice from within.

'Gereon lives,' Landerson replied.

'Despite their efforts,' the voice responded. The door swung open, revealing only darkness. Landerson peered in.

Then he felt the nudge of an autopistol muzzle against the back of his head.

'You're late.'

'I ran into trouble.'

'It had better not have followed you.'

'No, sir.'

'Step in, nice and easy.'

Landerson edged into the darkness. A light came on, in his face.

'Check him!' a voice said, as the door swung closed behind him.

Hands grabbed him and hustled him forward. The paddle of an auspex buzzed as it was passed up and down his body.

'Clean!' someone said.

The hands withdrew. Landerson squinted into the light, resolving his surroundings. A dank cellar of the old mill, figures all around, flashlights aimed his way.

Colonel Ballerat stepped into the light, holstering his pistol.

'Landerson,' he said.

'Good to see you, sir,' Landerson, replied.

Ballerat moved forward and embraced Landerson. He did so with only one hand. Ballerat's left arm and left leg had been ripped away in the foundries. He had a crude prosthetic that allowed him to walk, but his left arm was just a nub.

'I'm relieved you got the message.' Ballerat smiled. 'I was beginning to worry you hadn't.'

'I got it all right,' Landerson said. 'Dropped into my food pail. It was difficult getting away. Is it tonight, sir?'

Ballerat nodded. 'Yes, it is. They're definitely down. We need to make contact so we can move to the next stage.'

Landerson nodded. 'How many, sir?'

'How many what?' Ballerat asked.

'I mean… what sort of numbers, sir? Disposition? What sort of size is the liberation force?'

Ballerat paused. 'We… we don't know yet, major. Working on that. The key thing right now is to make contact with their recon advance so we can lead them in.'

'Understood, sir.'

'I'm sending you, Lefivre and Purchason.'

'I know them both, sir. Good men. We served in the PDF together.'

Ballerat smiled. 'That's what I thought. So you know the area well. Rendezvous is an agri-complex at the Shedowtonland Crossroads. Contact code is "Tanith Magna".'

Landerson repeated the words. 'What does that mean, sir?'

Ballerat shrugged. 'Damned if I know. A Guard code. Ah, here they come.'

Lefivre and Purchason approached. Both were dressed in the ragged, scrabbled-together remnants of PDF combat gear. Lefivre was a short, blond man with a scrappy beard. Purchason was taller, leaner and dark-haired. Both shook hands with Landerson. Both carried silenced autorifles.

Another member of the resistance hurried over with a
set of fatigues, equipment and weapons for Landerson.
Crouching, Landerson began to sort through the stuff.

'That can wait,' Ballerat said. 'We have to strip you out
first, son.'

Landerson nodded and rose to his feet. Ballerat led
him into an adjoining chamber that stank of animals,
chyme and dung. The air was warm and heavy. Landerson could hear grox snorting and farting in the gloom.

'Ready?' Ballerat asked him.

'I'd just like to get it over with, sir,' Landerson said. He
pulled up the sleeve of his left arm.

Several other men appeared and took him by the
shoulders, holding him tight. One offered him a bottle
of amasec. Landerson took a deep swig. 'Good boy,' the
man said. 'Helps dull the pain. Now bite on this. You'll
need it.'

Landerson bit down hard on the leather belt that was
pushed into his mouth.

The chirurgeon was a woman, an old lady from the
habs. She smiled at Landerson, who was now pinned by
four men, and poured more amasec over the imago.

Landerson felt it squirm.

'They don't like that at all,' the chirurgeon muttered. 'It
numbs them. Makes them sleepy, dull. Makes them easier to withdraw. Steel yourself, boy.'

She produced a scalpel, and quickly slit open the huge
blister on his forearm. It popped, and viscous fluid
poured out. Landerson bit down. It hurt already. The
coiled black thing in the meat of his arm, now exposed,
fidgeted and tightened in the sore, red cavity. He tried
not to look, but he could not help it.

The chirurgeon reached in with long-handled tweezers.

She began to pull. Most of the glistening black grub
came away in the first tug, but the long, barbed tail, dark
and thorned like razor-wire, resisted. She pulled more

firmly and Landerson bit down harder, feeling his flesh tear. The grub began to squirm and wriggle between the tips of the tweezers. Agony pulsed down Landerson's arm. It felt like a barbed fishing line was being drawn out down an artery.

The chirurgeon doused the wound with more alcohol, and yanked hard. Landerson bit through the belt. The whipping grub tore free, jiggling at the end of her surgical tool.

'Now!' she cried.

One of Ballerat's men had already slit open the haunch of one of the grox in the stalls. The old woman stabbed the twitching grub into the wound, and then, as she released it, clamped the wound shut with a wadding of anaesthotape and bandage.

She held it tight, fighting as if something was trying to get out from under the wadding.

'We're all right,' she said finally. 'I think it's taken.'

Everyone fell silent for a few long minutes, listening intently for the sound of an excubitor alarm or worse. Landerson realised he was shaking hard. The old woman beckoned to one of the men to hold the wadding tight to the animal's flank, and came over to Landerson to bind his wound.

She cleaned it carefully, sealed it, bandaged it, and then gave him a shot of painkillers and counterseptic agents.

Landerson began to feel a little better, though he was slightly distressed to note an odd sensation of absence. All those months, longing to be rid of the foul, twitching thing under his skin, and now his body seemed to miss the imago.

'Are you feeling all right?' Ballerat asked him, emerging from the shadows.

'Yes, sir,' Landerson lied.

'I'd like to give you more time to recover, but we don't have it. Set to move?'

Landerson nodded.

Ballerat showed him a crumpled, hand-drawn map. 'Take a moment to study this. Memorise it, because I can't let you take it. This is the route I suggest you follow. These are the times and locations of the patrols we know about.'

Landerson studied the information hard, looking away from time to time and then back at the map to test his recall. Then Ballerat handed him an envelope, and Landerson glanced inside.

'What's this for?' he asked.

'You never know,' the colonel replied. Landerson put the envelope inside his jacket.

'Right,' said Ballerat, nodding Lefivre and Purchason over to join them. 'Rendezvous is set for twenty-three fifteen. Find out what they need from us and do your best to provide it. Contact with us is via the usual methods. We'll be staging a diversion event about forty minutes prior to rendezvous that should draw surplus attention away from your zone. Any questions?'

The three men shook their heads.

Ballerat couldn't make the full sign of the aquila, but he placed his right hand over his heart as if he were. 'Good fortune, and for the sake of Gereon, may the Emperor protect you.'

THE NIGHT WAS cool and damp. Landerson had almost forgotten how it felt to be outside in the dark. They made good progress out of Ineuron Town, smuggling themselves through the western palisades, and then headed out across the old ornamental park called the Ambulatory. The lights of the town flickered behind them, and once in a while they heard distant horns and kettle drums.

The bloodiest phase of the battle for Ineuron Town had been fought around the precincts of the Ambulatory and the ground, now fully overgrown, was littered with machine debris and pathetic scatters of human bone. The three men made no sound. Ballerat hadn't picked them for this mission simply because of their local knowledge. All three had been in the ranger-recon brigade of the PDF.

Halfway across the Ambulatory they had to take cover behind a thicket of juvenile talix trees as a patrol went by: two half-tracks, blazing with hunting spotlights, the lead one resembling an ice sled because of the long string of fetch-hounds straining ahead of it on chains. The animals growled and rasped, pulling at their harnesses. They were trained to scent imagos and also human pheromones. The last thing Landerson and his companions had done before leaving the mill was stand under a crude gravity shower that soaked them with scent-repellers.

The patrol moved away. Landerson signalled the other two men forward. He used the sign language fluently, like his last ranger-recon mission had been the day before. But he noticed that his left arm felt curiously light. Had the old woman got it all out? Or was there some piece of the grub still inside him, yearning for–

Landerson dismissed the thought. If even a scrap of the imago had been left behind, corposant would be crackling over every gibbet in the town and the wire-wolves would be gathering.

They left the Ambulatory, and picked their way through the silent ruins of the tiered hab blocks that ran down the slopes of Mexley Hill. This suburb was an agriculture district, marking the point at which the heavy industry of the inner conurbations gave way to the farm-land disciplines of the town's rural skirts. Behind the habs, strips of crop fields were laid out across the hillside and over into the next valley. Landerson could smell silage, plant rot, and the distinctive perfume of canter-wheat. But the crop, unharvested, had gone over, and the smell was unpleasantly strong, with a sickly tinge of fer-mentation.

Purchason stopped dead and signed a warning. The trio melted into cover behind the yard wall at the rear of one of the habs.

Thirty metres away, a glyf hung, almost stationary, above the lane.

In the dark, the glyf was even more terrifying than the one that had passed Landerson by in daylight. Its coiled, burning symbols seemed to writhe like snakes, forming one unholy rune then another, bright against the night sky as if they were written in liquid flame. Landerson could hear it crackling like a log fire. He could hear the thick, nauseating insect noise. This time, he managed to look away.

He was suddenly aware of Lefivre next to him. The man was shaking badly. Glancing round, Landerson saw that his companion had his eyes locked on the infernal glyf. Tears were trickling from eyes that refused to blink. Landerson reached out quickly and took Lefivre's weapon just moments before it slithered out of the man's nerveless hands. In the half light, he could see Lefivre's jaw working and his adam's apple bobbing. Lefivre's lips were pinched and white. He was fighting not to scream, but it was a fight he was about to lose.

Landerson clamped his hand over Lefivre's mouth. Realising what was happening, Purchason grabbed Lefivre too, hugging him tight to keep him upright and pin his arms. Landerson felt Lefivre's mouth grind open, and squeezed his hand tighter, fighting back a cry as Lefivre's teeth bit into his palm.

The glyf trembled. The insect noise increased, purring, then sank away. The glyf drifted off to the north, hissing over the shattered roofs of the hab terrace and then away across the park. Landerson and Purchason maintained their grip on Lefivre. Ten seconds later, five excubitors ran past along the lane, heading towards the town. The glyf had found something, and now the patrol was drawing in. After a few minutes, they heard the dull bark of las-locks discharging.

Some poor unconsented, no doubt, hiding in the rambles of the park.

Landerson realised he was now unconsented too.

He took his hand away. Blood pattered onto the stony path. Lefivre slumped over, panting like a dog. In his terror, he'd lost control of his bladder.

'I'm sorry… I'm sorry…' he gasped.

'It's fine,' Landerson whispered.

'Your hand…'

'It's fine,' Landerson repeated. His hand really hurt. Lefivre had bitten a large chunk out of his palm. Now he smelled of blood, Lefivre smelled of piss, and they all stank of the sweat the tension had engulfed them in.

Landerson wrapped his hand in his neck cloth, and prayed they would not meet any fetch-hounds.

IT WAS ALMOST twenty-two thirty when they reached the Shedowtonland Crossroads. Left untended and unirrigated, the paddies had dried up, and now great areas of fertile land were reduced to caked mud mouldering with neglected, blighted crops. The air was ripe with mildew and corruption.

Thunder rolled in the distance, out beyond the agriculture belt, out in the untamed swampland of the Untill. Once, those miasmal regions had been seen as danger zones. Now, post intercession, they seemed safe compared to the populated areas.

They skirted wide round the bulky prefabs of the agricomplex and then turned back into them, weapons ready, long suppressor tubes fixed. They crept through the shadows, between immobilised tractor units and dredge-harvesters in the low garages, and on past iron pens where swine had been slaughtered and left to decompose. More than once they disturbed carrion mammals feeding on refuse, local fauna lured out of the

swamps by the scent of decay. Squalling, the small creatures bushed their tails up and started off into the
darkness.

Lefivre was still spooked. He swung his gun at every
last forager.

'You gotta calm down,' Landerson whispered.

'I know.'

'Really, friend. Deep breaths. I can't have you jump-
ing.'

'No, major. Of course not.'

Apart from the foragers, there were rats everywhere.
Everywhere in the Imperium, Landerson imagined. The
starships of Holy Terra had spread many things across
the galaxy – faith, colonists, technology, civilisation –
but nothing so comprehensively or so surely as the
indomitable *rattus rattus*. Before the Intercession, he had
heard learned men joke that the Imperium was actually
forged by rats, and humans were just along for the ride.
On some worlds, the accidentally imported rat had over-
mastered all other life forms. On other worlds, they had
interbred and created monsters.

The three men completed a circuit check, and found
nothing except some sickening runes daubed on the
outer fence that might have been charged to become
glyfs. Landerson didn't want to risk it, so he doused each
one he found with the flask of consecrated water that
had been issued as part of his kit.

Purchason helped. Lefivre held back. He didn't want
to look at the marks. He didn't want his mind to lapse
that way again.

They reached the main buildings. It was twenty-two
thirty-seven. Pretty much on cue, they heard a boom
from the town behind them. A fiery glow slowly rose
into the sky. Then a buzzing filled the air. In the valley
below them, they saw glyfs floating like ball lightning,
drawn to the commotion.

The colonel's diversion was underway.

'Emperor protect you,' Landerson muttered.

Landerson checked the main door. It was unlocked. Weapon braced, he crouched his way in as Lefivre pushed the door open. Purchason stood to his left, rifle raised to cover.

The prefab hallway was dark. There was an intense smell of dry fertilizer. Rats scurried.

Landerson signalled Lefivre to watch the door, then he and Purchason swept up the hallway, covering each other door by door. The place was deserted. Chairs and tables were overturned, agricultural cogitators smashed, seed incubators and nursery racks destroyed.

There was a dim light ahead. Cautiously, they prowled on, signing to each other, weapons set. The light was coming from a central office area. A single candle, guttering on a desk.

Landerson glanced at Purchason. Purchason shook his head. He had no idea what was going on either.

They slid inside. The room was empty apart from broken furniture and the desk with the candle. The windows were locked. There was only one door.

'This is the place,' said Landerson as loudly as he dared.

'What the hell's that candle about? Are they here already?'

Landerson looked around for a second time. 'I don't know,' he whispered. 'Go check on Lefivre.'

Purchason nodded and slid back out into the hallway. Landerson stood by the desk, his weapon aimed at the doorway. A minute passed. Two. His hands began to sweat.

He heard a faint noise.

'Purchason?' he called quietly.

The candle suddenly went out. An arm locked about his body, pinning his weapon. He felt a blade at his throat.

'Say it now and say it right,' said a voice in his ear.

'T-tanith Magna…'

The grip released.

Landerson turned in the darkness, terrified.

'Where are you?' he gasped.

'Still here,' the voice said, behind him again. Landerson switched round.

'What are you doing?' he breathed. 'Show yourself!'

'All in good time. You got a name?' The voice was behind him yet again. Landerson froze.

'Major Gerome Landerson, Gereon PDF.'

There was a click of tinder sticks and the candle on the desk relit. Landerson swung round to look at it, gun raised. The candle fluttered, solitary. There was no sign of whoever had lit it.

'Stop it!' Landerson said. 'Where are you?'

'Right here.' Landerson froze as he felt the cold muzzle of a weapon rest against the back of his neck. 'Put the gun down.'

Landerson gently placed his silenced rifle on the desk.

'How did you get in?' he whispered.

'I was here all the time.'

'But I searched the room–'

'Not well enough.'

'Who are you?'

'My name is Mkoll. Sergeant of scouts, Tanith First-and-Only.'

'Could you take the gun off my neck?'

A man appeared in the candlelight in front of Landerson. He was short, compact, shrouded in a camouflage cloak that seemed to melt into the darkness. 'I could,' he said softly, 'if it was my gun. Ven? Let the poor guy off the leash.'

The pressure of the gun-muzzle went away. Landerson glanced round and saw the second man. Just a shadow in the extremity of the candlelight. Taller than the first, a murmur of a shape.

'W-what are you?' Landerson stammered. 'Ghosts?'

By the light of the single candle flame, Landerson saw the eyes of the man calling himself Mkoll crinkle and glint. A smile. That was the most unnerving thing of all, for clearly this was a face unaccustomed to smiles.

'You could say that,' Mkoll said.

TWO

THEY LED LANDERSON back into the yard. The amber glow in the sky was still bright and defined. He could feel the distant agitation of the enemy on the night air, like the balmy pressure of a closing storm.

Lefivre and Purchason were on their knees facing the stockade fence, hands behind their heads. A third soldier in black stood watch over them.

'Bonin?' Mkoll asked.

'These seem to be the only other two, sir,' the third soldier replied.

'Three of you, is that correct?' Mkoll asked.

'Yes,' said Landerson. He heard the muffled click of a vox-com. 'One, this is four. Move in,' Mkoll said quickly. Then he glanced at the tall man. 'Mkvenner? Take Bonin and secure the perimeter.'

Mkoll's two comrades moved off and disappeared into the darkness at once. Then other shapes loomed, detaching themselves from the night. At least a half-dozen figures. The tallest strode right up to Landerson and looked him up and down. He was a lean, powerful man dressed in black boots and fatigues, a black leather jacket, and a dark camo-cloak wrapped tightly around his throat and upper body. There was a pack on his back, and a soot-dulled bolt pistol strapped across his chest in a combat rig. Under the brim of his plain, black-cloth cap, his face was slender and sharp.

'Which one is the leader?' he asked.

'I am,' said Landerson. He froze as he felt the man Mkoll lean close to his ear. 'Under the circumstances, I advise you not to speak unless we give you permission,' Mkoll said.

Landerson nodded.

'Say to him what you said to me,' Mkoll instructed.

'Tanith Magna,' Landerson said quietly.

'Tell him your name.'

'Landerson. Major Landerson.'

'And address him as sir,' Mkoll added.

'Sir.'

The tall man in the cap made the sign of the aquila and then saluted. 'Major,' he said. 'My name is Gaunt. I have command of this operation. You're in the right place at the right time and you've given the correct code, so I'll presume for the moment you're the man I've come to see. You've been instructed to meet us by the commander of the Ineuron cell.'

Landerson swallowed. 'I have liberty to discuss certain things, sir. They don't include the possible activities, movements or even existence of any resistance cells.'

'Fair point,' said Gaunt. 'But the next stage of our business involves establishing contact with a colonel called Ballerat, or any of his chief officers.'

'Regard me as such, and then we'll review,' Landerson replied.

A man appeared at Gaunt's side. He was shorter than Gaunt, but a little more robustly proportioned, as dark as Gaunt was fair. There seemed to Landerson something sleekly cruel about the man's face.

'Want me to beat the crap out of him, sir?'

'Not at this stage,' Gaunt replied.

'Just to loosen his tongue, you understand.'

'Wouldn't want you to get your hands dirty, Rawne.'

The man smiled. It was not a little chilling. 'I wouldn't. I'd get Feygor to do it.'

'Full marks for delegation. Now step off, Rawne.'

The man shrugged and walked away. Landerson could see the others now, quite plainly. There were seven of them, apart from Mkoll, Rawne and the commander, all dressed in black camo-gear and packs. Most of them were tattooed. A large, rough-looking man hefted an autocannon; a slight, older fellow carried a marksman's weapon. The four other troopers had lasrifles. The seventh, Landerson realised, was a female. She too was clad in pitch-black combat gear, but the only weapon she carried was a compact autopistol in a holster.

Gaunt looked at Landerson. 'Major, in your estimation, how long can we remain here safely?'

'Another thirty minutes would be pushing it.'

'Do you have secure fall-back positions?'

'I know a place or two where we could avoid the patrols.'

'And they're safe?'

Landerson stared at him. 'Sir, this is Gereon. Nowhere is safe.'

'Then let's get on with this,' Gaunt said. 'Doctor. Check them out, please.'

The woman moved forward, pulled off her pack and produced a small narthecium scanner. She began to play it across Landerson.

'Lily of Thrace,' said Landerson.

'What?' she asked, stopping and looking at him.

'Your perfume. Lily of Thrace. Am I right?'

'I haven't used perfume or cologne for three weeks,' she said firmly. 'Part of the mission prep–'

'I'm sure you haven't,' said Landerson. 'But I can still smell it. That, and counterseptics, and sterile rinse. The fetch-hounds would have you in a second.'

'That's enough,' said Mkoll. The woman shook her head at the scout and stared at Landerson. 'These… hounds. They'd detect my scent even though I have been scrupulous not to use anything that might give me away?'

'Yes, mamzel. You're too clean. All of you.'

'These hounds would find me because I don't smell like shit, like you?'

'Exactly, mamzel. Gereon gets in the pores. Into the flesh. The smoke, the dust, the taint.'

'Speaking of taint,' the woman said, reading her scanner. 'You have elevated B-proteins and a high leucocyte count. What exactly has been bonded to your metabolism?'

Mkoll immediately raised his rifle and aimed it at the side of Landerson's head.

'I'm going to show her my arm,' Landerson said, very aware of the gun barrel pointing into his ear. He raised his left sleeve and revealed the bandage. 'The archenemy brands all citizens with an imago. I've had mine removed, so have Purchason and Lefivre. Can they get up, by the way? I'm not really happy with the way you're depriving my men of their liberty at this point.'

'Want me to get Feygor?' Mkoll muttered.

'No,' said Gaunt. 'Is he clean, Curth?'

'Clean is a strong word. In so many ways,' said the woman. 'But… yes, I'd say so.'

'Check the other two. If they're clean, get them up. Major Landerson, walk with me.'

Gaunt led him back into the prefab, down to the room where the candle still burned.

'Have a seat,' he offered.

'I'll stand, sir.'

Gaunt frowned, and sat down himself.

'What is your rank, sir?' Landerson asked.

'Colonel-Commissar.'

Landerson felt his heart skip slightly. 'I see. You're very cautious.'

'I'm landing a mission team on a Chaos-held world, Landerson. Do you blame me?'

'No, sir, I suppose I don't. How did you reach the surface?'

'I don't think I'm going to tell you that.'

'Uh huh. Can you tell me your force disposition?'

'I shouldn't do that either, not until I trust you a little better. But you can count.'

'I've counted a dozen of you.'

Gaunt said nothing. The candle fluttered.

Landerson nodded to himself. 'The advance party. I understand that. I also understand you're not going to tell me anything about the main force, where they're concealed, what armour they've got, but–'

'But?'

'At least tell me when it's going to start.'

'When what's going to start, major?'

'The liberation, sir.'

Gaunt looked up at him. 'Liberation?'

'Yes, sir.'

Gaunt sighed. 'I think,' he began, choosing his words, 'I think perhaps the understandably tortuous lines of communication between the Gereon resistance cells and Guard Intelligence have been even less adequate than we'd hoped.'

'I don't understand,' said Landerson.

'Twelve mission specialists, major. Twelve. You've seen them all, you've counted them yourself. We're not the advance. We're it.'

'Sir?'

'No one else is coming. We're not meeting here tonight to pave a way for a triumphant liberation army.

Your priority is to link with my team and get us underground so we can achieve our mission parameters.'

Landerson felt a slight buzzing in his head. A dizzi-
ness. He pulled a chair out from the table and sat down
heavily.

'I don't understand,' he repeated. 'I thought–'

'I realise what you thought. I'm sorry to disabuse your
hopes. We're all that's coming, major. Now I need you to
do your part and get us inside. Can you do that?'

Landerson shook his head.

'Is that a no?'

'No, no.' Landerson looked up. 'I just… it's not what I
was expecting. It's not what anyone was… I mean, we
assumed. The colonel said… I…' He tailed off. 'What
mission?'

'I'm not going to tell you that either, Landerson. Not
even going to hint until I know you better. Even then,
maybe not. I'm as scared of what you might be as you
are of what I might be. Let's not fight about it. Right
now, I need you to do as you were instructed so we can
get on. I can tell you that I need to establish face contact
with Ballerat, or his proxy, or with the leader of another
cell in the Ineuron Town region. I can also tell you that,
unless any senior resistance contact can inform me otherwise, I'm going to need a clear and secret line of
deployment to the Lectica heartland. And I can tell you
that my mission parameters were given to me directly by
Lord General Barthol Van Voytz of the Crusade Fifth
Army, as ratified and instructed personally by Warmaster
Macaroth himself.'

'This is so much shit,' snapped Landerson, rising.

'Sit down.'

'This isn't what we need! This isn't what Gereon was
waiting for–'

'Sit. Down.'

Landerson turned to face Gaunt, his fingers curled like
hooks, tears in his eyes. 'You come here with this crap?

Some half-arsed stealth mission that you can't breathe a word of? Screw you! We've suffered! We've died! Millions have died! Do you know what those bastards have done to us?'

'Yes,' said Gaunt quietly.

'I don't bloody think so! The invasion? The slaughter? The extermination camps? The things they buried in our flesh to keep us tame? The foul propaganda they blast from the speakers every hour of the day and night? The few of us left who can think straight, the bloody few of us, risking our lives every day to keep the resistance alive! A raid here, a bombing there, comrades massacred, dragged off for interrogation or worse! What kept us going, do you suppose? What the hell kept us going?'

'The thought of liberation.'

'The thought of liberation! Yes, sir! Yes screw-you sir! Every day! Every day for six hundred and four days! Six hundred and bloody five now! Days of Pain! We have a calendar! A bloody calendar! Six hundred and five days of pain and death and torment–'

'Landerson–'

'Do you know what I do?' Landerson asked, wiping his mouth, his hands shaking. 'Do you know what the bloody ordinals make me do? I am consented to work in the Iconoclave! Do you know what that means?'

'No,' said Gaunt.

'It means I am allowed to go to what was the town hall for twelve hours every day and use a sledgehammer to break up any symbols of the Imperium that the bastards drag in! Statues... plaques... standards... insignia... I have to pound them to scrap and rubble! And they allow me to do this! They permit me! It's seen as a special honour for those of us consented to do it! A perk! A trustee's luxury! Because it's that or file into the maws of the meat foundries and, you know, somehow I'd rather splinter a statue of Saint Kiodrus into chippings than be dragged off there!'

'I understand–' Gaunt began.

'No, you don't!'

Gaunt raised his black-gloved hands. 'No, I don't. I don't begin to understand what that's like. I don't begin to understand the pain, the misery, the torment. And I certainly don't understand the choices you've had to make. But I do understand your disappointment.'

'Yeah?' laughed Landerson, bitterly.

Gaunt nodded. 'You wanted us to be your salvation. You thought we were the front markers of a crusade force come to free you. We're not, and I can understand why that hurts.'

'What do you know?'

'I know I left a world to Chaos once.'

'What happened to it?' Landerson asked quietly.

'What do you think? It died. But the few men I saved from it have now spared a thousandfold more Imperial citizens from suffering than I would have managed if I'd stayed there.'

Landerson stared at the candle flame.

'Some of those men are with me here tonight,' said Gaunt. 'Look, major. This is the Imperium of Man. There is only war. It has edges and corners, and all of them are hard. If I could save Gereon, I would, but I can't and that's not why I'm here. Gereon must continue to suffer. In time, there may be a liberation effort. It's not for me to say. Right here, right now, I have a mission. Its success is important to Lord General Van Voytz, to Warmaster Macaroth, and to the Imperium. Which means it's important to the God-Emperor himself. What I have to do here is bigger than Gereon.'

'Damn you to hell.'

'Very likely. But it's true. If my team fails here, we're talking about the possible failure of the entire Sabbat Crusade. One hundred inhabited systems, Landerson. Would you like them all to end up like Gereon?'

Landerson sat down again.

'What,' he whispered. 'What do you want me to do?'

'I'd like you to–' Gaunt paused and put his hand up to the micro-bead vox plug in his ear. 'Beltayn, this is one. What do you have?'

He listened for a moment, then rose to his feet. 'We'll have to finish this later, major,' he said.

'Why?' asked Landerson, getting to his feet too.

'Because something's awry.'

OUTSIDE, EVERYONE HAD disappeared. Landerson felt a slight rise of panic, but Gaunt strode out into the yard. As if conjured by some sorcery, Mkoll appeared from nowhere.

'Report?'

'Movement on the road. Perimeter is secure.'

'Have we made them?'

'I'm waiting for Mkvenner and Bonin now, sir,' Mkoll whispered.

'Where are the–' Gaunt paused. Landerson knew he'd been about to say prisoners. 'Where are the major's associates?'

'Varl's moved them to the shed there,' Mkoll pointed.

'Take the major to join them,' Gaunt instructed.

'I can be more use here,' said Landerson.

'Major, this is n–'

'Do you know what you're facing?'

Gaunt breathed deeply. 'All right, with me. Stick close. Do exactly what Mkoll and I tell you.'

They headed for the gateway. Landerson realised that two of the visitors – the man with the marksman's rifle and the devil who'd offered to beat him up – were concealed by the fence stakes, wrapped in their camo-capes. He didn't see them at all until he was right on them.

Landerson ducked low and tucked in behind Gaunt and Mkoll as they went up the ditch to the road wall.

The vox pipped. Mkoll listened and replied softly.

'Two carriers, coming this way. Ven counts twenty-
three heads. Dogs too, in a chained pack.'

'Standard mechanised patrol,' whispered Landerson.
'It wasn't on my expected schedule.'

'They know we're here?' asked Gaunt.

'I doubt it, sir. If they knew there were insurgents at
this location, they'd have beefed up the numbers. We
staged a diversion in the town tonight to distract from
this meeting, but there was always the chance they'd step
up the patrols as a consequence. The enemy is not stupid.'

'That's been my experience too,' said Gaunt darkly.

'You don't want an open firefight with a patrol,' Lan-
deron said.

'Delighted to see you grasping the meaning of the
phrase "stealth mission",' said Gaunt. 'We need to peel
out and find a back door. What's that way?'

'Agricultural land. Field systems. Too open.'

'That way? Over there?'

'Open ground for about five hundred metres, then
woods.'

'We'll take the woods,' said Mkoll.

Gaunt nodded.

'Make it fast,' said Landerson. 'Once the fetch-hounds
have your scent – and they will get your scent – we're
screwed.'

'Let's get going,' said Gaunt, and Mkoll turned and
simply vanished into the night. Landerson followed
Gaunt back down the ditch to the gate.

'Up and out that way, Rawne,' Gaunt said. 'Lead them
out. Head for the woods.'

'On it.'

'Larks?' Gaunt said, turning to the marksman.

'Sir?'

'You'll be out last with Ven. Cover us. But remember
engagement rules. Keep your finger off that trigger unless
there's no other choice.'

'Yes, sir.'

'The Emperor protects, Larks,' Gaunt said and moved Landerson into the yard. Purchason and Lefivre were coming out of the shed escorted by two of Gaunt's troopers.

'I request you return our weapons,' said Landerson.

'I will, if you promise not to use them,' Gaunt said.

'Still grasping that meaning, colonel-commissar.'

'Good,' said Gaunt. 'Varl?'

One of the troopers came over. His broadly grinning face was smeared with filth.

'Fall on your face?' Gaunt asked.

'Pig dung,' said Varl. 'I fething hate dogs. I'd rather they smelled you first.'

'Your loyalty knows no beginning, Varl. Give these men back their weapons.'

'Sir.'

Landerson immediately felt more confident with his muzzled autorifle back in his hands. He followed Gaunt and the others to the perimeter fence, climbed it, and dropped into the waste ground beyond. They all started to run towards the dim treeline half a kilometre away.

The ground was rough and scrubby, thick with ground vine and fronds of cupwort. Landerson glanced back. Beyond the fence and the silhouette of the agri-complex, he saw the twitching radiance of lights on the road.

He should have been looking where he was going. The loop of ground vine yanked his ankle and he went down on his face.

'Get up, you clumsy gak!' a voice hissed at him, and Landerson was pulled to his feet. It was the other trooper who'd been guarding his men with Varl. He was a she.

'Move it or I knife you and leave you!' the female trooper snarled.

Landerson ran after her.

They reached the trees. The thick canopy cut out what little ambient light the night sky provided. It was as dark as the void. The woman made no sound as she moved through the knee-deep vegetation. Landerson felt like he was making as much noise as a charging foot patrol.

'Down!' she said.

He got down. There was silence, apart from the breeze in the leaves, and a distant engine note coming from the agri-complex.

As his eyes adjusted, Landerson saw Gaunt's team was all around him, in cover, weapons raised.

'How long before your point men pull out?' Landerson whispered.

'They already have,' said Gaunt. Landerson realised the marksman and the tall, thin scout were with them. How in the name of Holy Terra had they done that?

They heard the sound of dogs on the night air. Eager, frantic, whining and howling.

Landerson knew that sound.

'They've got the scent,' he whispered, his heart sinking.

'Feth!' spat Gaunt.

'Lily of Thrace, I suppose,' said the female medic.

Landerson shook his head. 'No. Blood. Blood is the one thing they fix onto more than anything else.' He held up his hand. His fall had torn the bandage off the bindings, and blood was weeping again from the bite in his palm.

'I'm sorry, sir.' He rose to his feet. 'Get your men away. I'll draw them off.'

'No,' said Gaunt.

'It's me they've scented. I–'

'No,' Gaunt repeated. 'If they've got us, they'll be on us all night, no matter how heroic and stupid you decide to be. We'll end this quickly here and get clear before anyone comes looking for a missing patrol.'

'You're mad,' said Landerson simply.

'Yes, but I'm also in charge.' He looked round at the mission team. 'Straight silver. Let the dogs come and do them first. Then switch live and take out the rest. Understood?'

A whispered chorus of affirmatives answered him.

'For Tanith. For the Emperor.'

The sound of the dogs grew louder. Down by the agri-complex, an engine revved and a section of the outer fence stoved out and collapsed, driven down by the front fender of a large half-track. Its spotlights blazed out across the waste ground. Around it, through the gap, the unleashed hounds dashed out.

They were big. Some kind of semi-feral mastiff breed sired in the holds of the archenemy fleet. A dozen of them, each one so thickly muscled it weighed more than an adult human male. They could hear their paws thumping on the rough ground, hear their slavering growls.

Gaunt slid out a long silver dagger dulled with soot.

'Let them in,' he whispered. 'Let them come right in…'

The first bounding animal crashed through the tree-line, heavy and stinking with spittle. Landerson heard it barking, heard it–

Whine. A meaty thump. An interrupted whimper.

The next came, and then the next. Two more frenzied dog-voices suddenly stilled away in pathetic squeals.

Then the rest. The other eight. One came in through the tree trunks right for Landerson. He saw its dull eyes, its gaping, wretched maw, the fleshy, drooling lips bouncing with the impact of its stride. He gasped out and raised his weapon.

Two metres from Landerson, as it began the pouncing leap that would bring him down, it jerked sideways in the air. Using his lasrifle like a spear, Mkoll wrestled the hound to the ground on his bayonet. It howled and writhed. He put a foot on its distended belly to free the blade, and lanced it twice more.

Around him, Landerson heard a quick series of dull, wet impacts, like ripe fruit being hacked by a machete. One human cry of pain.

A moment's pause.

'All done?' Gaunt asked, wiping dog-blood off his warknife.

'Clear. They're done,' Mkvenner replied from nearby.

'Everyone all right?'

'Fething dog bit me!' complained Varl in a whisper.

'Must've liked the idea of pig for dinner,' replied the female trooper who had dragged Landerson up.

'Imagine my surprise that he didn't go for you then, Criid,' Varl said.

'That's great. Talk some more so the enemy knows where the feth we are,' said the man Gaunt had called Rawne.

'Here they come,' said Mkoll, his voice just loud enough to be heard.

'Safeties off,' said Gaunt. 'Mkoll. Circle the scouts round to the right and pincer. Brostin, Larkin? The transports. Ana? Keep your head down please.'

'But–'

'Keep it the feth down! Everyone else. On my word. Not a moment sooner. That goes for you too, major. You and your men.'

'Yes, sir. Lefivre? Purchason? Don't shame me, you understand?'

Landerson looked back across at the fence. Both half-tracks had moved out through the collapsed section and were advancing across the rough ground at a slow lick, searchlights sweeping. He saw a dozen excubitors dismounted alongside them, walking forward, las-locks raised.

'Looking for their fething pooches,' muttered Varl.

'Noise discipline!' Rawne snapped.

The patrol came closer.

'Not yet….' Gaunt whispered. 'Not yet… let the foot troops get into the trees.'

So close now. Searchlight beams washed in through the trees, dappling off the shrubs and low boughs. Landerson could smell the spice and sweet unguents of the excubitors. There was no way they could take them all. Two to one, not counting the vehicles.

He raised his autorifle to his shoulder.

He saw the first excubitor enter the hem of the trees, a lanky black shape, las-lock right up to aim. He could hear the knock and thump of the bastard's respirator box.

The excubitor disappeared. It had bent down. It had found one of the gutted fetch-hounds.

'Voi shet tgharr!' the excubitor yelled, rising.

'Now,' said Gaunt. His bolt pistol banged and the excubitor flopped backwards violently.

The edge of the woods went wild. Lasfire streamed out between the trees, shredding the low foliage. It was suddenly so bright it was as if the sun had come up.

The noise was extraordinary. Landerson saw at least four of the excubitors cut down in the opening salvo. He started to fire, but the air was suddenly thick with smoke wash and water vapour from the burst foliage.

The patrol began to answer, charging and firing weapons into the hail of fire from the woods. The half-tracks gunned forward. A heavy bolter on the top of the closest vehicle began to flash and chatter. Small trees in the woodline were decapitated and deep wounds tore the trunks of the more mature trees.

'Larks! The lights!' Gaunt yelled.

The sniper close to Landerson sat up and fired his long-las, reloading and refiring with amazing precision. The searchlights on the vehicle rigs exploded one after another like cans on a shooting gallery wall, spraying out glass chips and stark thorns of shorting electricals. Another sniper round took the head off one of the excubitors manning the lamps.

Landerson saw Gaunt striding forward, shouting to his men though the roar of the intense combat drowned him out. He had a compact bolt pistol in each hand and was firing both of them. What Landerson had taken to be a single chest holster had evidently been a doubled pair.

Shots screamed through the trees. Branches exploded Landerson could smell wood pulp and sap, fyceline and blood. He crawled to the nearest trunk and tried to get a better angle.

'Brostin!' Gaunt yelled. 'Nail that first track!'

The big, rough-looking man calmly advanced with his massive autocannon cradled like a baby in his arms. He dropped the long telescope monopod to brace and then let rip, feeding ammo on a belt from one of two heavy hoppers strung to his hips.

The half-track plating buckled and twisted. This Brostin seemed to be aiming for the main chassis of the vehicle rather than the upper crew compartment. Why the hell would he be aiming for the most heavily armoured section, the engine bearing, the–

The half-track ignited like a fuel-soaked rag. Flames gushed out from underneath it and wrapped it in a cocoon of fire. The steady flow of armour-piercing rounds had ruptured the deep-set fuel tank. Landerson saw two excubitors, swathed in flame, tumble screaming out of the crew well.

'Holy Throne of Earth…' Landerson mumbled.

'He's got a thing about fire, our Brostin,' said the man next to him. It was the sniper. Larks. Larkin. Something like that. He had a face as lined and creased as old saddle leather. 'Plus, he's ticked off he wasn't allowed to bring his precious fething flamer. Whoop, 'scuse me.'

Larkin raised his long-las, panned the barrel round and snapped off a shot that destroyed the head of another excubitor.

Pincer fire suddenly ripped in out of the right-hand quarter. Lasrifles on rapid, but devastatingly precise. Some of the excubitors tried to turn and were smacked off their feet. Landerson saw a chest explode, scale-mail pieces flung out. A las-lock was hit as it fired and blew up in a crescent of torched energy. Another excubitor was hit in the head and stumbled blindly across the wasteland like a jerking puppet until another shot put him down. Mkoll, Mkvenner and Bonin appeared out of the dark, coming in from the side, firing from the chest.

The last of the excubitors went down. The second half-track tried to turn and reverse. A tube-charge spun in from Rawne – a long, precise throw – and blew it apart.

Landerson lowered his weapon. He was breathing hard and his mind was reeling. How long? Thirty, forty seconds? Less than a minute. A whole patrol slaughtered in less than a minute. How… how was that even possible?

'Cease fire!' Gaunt yelled.

The area was bright with the burning wrecks of the vehicles.

'Douse them?' Varl asked Gaunt.

'No, we're out of here. Now.'

'Into the woods!' Rawne shouted. 'File of two, double time! That means you too, Varl, feth take your dog bite! Come on! Keep our new friends with us!'

'Stick with me,' the sniper said to Landerson. He smiled reassuringly. 'Stick tight. The archenemy's not found a thing yet that can kill Hlaine Larkin.'

'Right,' said Landerson, hurrying after him. For an older man, the sniper could move.

'What's your name?' Larkin called back over his shoulder.

'L-Landerson.'

'Stick tight, Landerson. The woods await.'

'The woods?'

He heard Larkin laughing. 'We're Tanith, Landerson. We like woods.'

THREE

THEY HAD REFUSED, from the very start, to refer to him by his name or rank. He was pheguth, which his life-ward told him meant something like 'one that commits base treachery' or 'one for whom betrayal has become a way of life', only less flattering. It was a slur-word, a taboo. They were letting him know what they thought of him – vermin, filth, the lowest of the low – which was rich coming from them.

And it was fine by him. He knew what he was worth to them. Calling him a pariah was the worst they could do.

'Awake, pheguth,' commanded his life-ward.

'I'm already awake,' he replied.

'And how is your health this morning?'

'I'm still pheguth if that's what you mean.'

The life-ward began to open the chamber shutters and let in the daylight. It made him wince.

'Could you leave that for now?' he asked. 'I have a headache, and the light hurts my eyes.'

The life-ward closed the shutters again, and instead lit the glass-hooded lamps.

'This is because of the transcoding?' the life-ward asked.

'I would imagine so, wouldn't you?'

His life-ward was called Desolane. It (for he had not yet been able to determine its gender with any conviction) was two metres tall, lean and long-limbed. Its slender, sexless body was sheathed in a form-fitting suit of blue-black metal-weave that had an iridescent lustre, like the filament scales of a bird's wing. Around its shoulders, a gauzy black cloak drifted rather than hung. It was light and semi-transparent, like gossamer or smoke, and moved with Desolane's movements even though it did not seem quite attached to the life-ward. The smoke-cloak almost but not quite concealed the pair of curved fighting knives sheathed across the ward's thin back.

Desolane had been the pheguth's constant companion now for six months, ever since his transfer to the custodianship of the Anarch and his removal to Gereon. The pheguth had begun to think of the life-ward as human, as far as that term would stretch, but this morning it was especially hard to ignore the xeno-traits, particularly the way Desolane's long legs were jointed the wrong way below the knees and ended in cloven hooves.

And Desolane's face. He'd never actually seen Desolane's face, of course. The polished bronze head-mask had never come off. Indeed, it looked like it was welded on. It fitted around the ward's skull tightly, smooth and featureless except for four holes: two for the eye slits and two on the brow through which small white horns extended.

The eyes themselves, always visible through the slits, were very human, watery blue and bright, like a young Guard staffer the pheguth had once had in his command. So very human, but set far too low down in Desolane's face.

'Do you wish to eat?' it asked.

'I have little stomach for food,' he answered. He wondered how Desolane ate. The bronze mask had no mouth slit.

'The transcoding?'

He shrugged.

'We were warned that the transcoding process would unsettle your constitution,' said Desolane. Its voice was soft and pitched on a feminine register, which the pheguth decided was the reason he couldn't determine the life-ward's precise gender. 'We were warned it might make you… sick. Should I fetch a master of fisyk to attend you? Perhaps a palliative remedy could be manufactured.'

He shook his head. 'We were also warned that I should imbibe nothing that might interfere with the transcoding process. I imagine that if a safe palliative existed, I would have been offered it already.'

Desolane nodded. 'A drink at least.'

'Yes. A cup of–'

'Weak black tea, with cinnamon.'

He smiled. 'You know me very well.'

'It is my job to know you, pheguth.'

'You tend to my every need with perfect decorum. I've had personal adjutants who've taken less care of me. It occurs to me to wonder why.'

'Why?' asked Desolane.

'I am a senior branch officer of your sworn enemy's armies and you are – forgive me, I'm not entirely sure what you are, Desolane.'

'You are pheguth. You are atturaghan–'

'That's something else I don't want to know the meaning of, right?'

'You are enemy blood, you are flesh-spoil, you are of the Eternal Foe and you are the most shunned of those that must be shunned. I am a sept-warrior of the Anarch, trophied and acclaimed, consented and beloved of the High Powers, and the winds of Chaos have breathed into me splendid magiks by which I have achieved the rank of life-ward, so as to stand amongst the Anarch's own huscarls. Under almost every circumstance, my duty and choice would be to draw my ketra blades and eviscerate you.'

'Almost every circumstance?'

'Except this one. This strange one we are in.'

'And in this circumstance?'

'I must attend your every need with perfect decorum.' The pheguth smiled. 'That still doesn't tell me why.'

'Because it is what I have been ordered to do. Because if one harm comes to you, or you suffer for one moment, the Anarch himself will scourge me, bleed me ceremonially, and eat my liver.'

The pheguth cleared his throat. 'A fine answer.'

'You do so love to taunt me, don't you, pheguth?' said Desolane.

'It's the only pleasure I get these days.'

'Then I'll allow it. Once again.' The life-ward walked towards the door. 'I'll bring your tea.'

'Could you release me first?'

Desolane stopped by the chamber door and turned back.

'Of course,' it said, producing the keys from under the smoke-cloak and unshackling the naked man from the steel frame.

AN HOUR LATER, Desolane escorted him out of the chamber and down the long, drafty steps of the tower. The pheguth was dressed in the simple beige tunic, pants and slippers that his captors issued him with every morning.

In the long basement hall at the foot of the steps, where Chaos trophies hung limp in the cloying air, the pheguth turned automatically towards the chamber set aside for the transcoding sessions.

'Not that way,' said Desolane. 'Not today.'

'No transcoding today?'

'No, pheguth.'

'Because it makes me sick?'

'No, pheguth. There's something else to do today. By the order of the Plenipotentiary.'

'What's going on?' he asked.

Two antlered footman came up, las-locks slung over their stooping shoulders. One carried a dagged foul-weather cloak of selpic blue rain cloth.

'This may be added to your garments,' said Desolane, taking the cloak and handing it to the pheguth.

He put it on. He could feel his pulse racing now.

Desolane led him out into the daylight of the inner courtyard. The bulk of Lectica Bastion rose like a cliff behind them. At a barked command, a waiting squadron of excubitors shouldered arms and announced their loyalty to the Anarch. One of the foot-men scurried forward and opened the side hatch of the transport.

'Where are we going?' asked the pheguth.

'Just get in,' said Desolane.

THEY DROVE FOR an hour, down through the steep cliff passes away from the bastion, onto a highway that had been repaired after shelling. The squadron of excubitors escorted them in their growling half-tracks. Deathships, fat-winged and freckled with gunpods, tracked them overhead.

'There is a function,' said Desolane, sitting back in one of the transport's ornate seats.

'A function?'

'For which your presence is required.'

'Am I going to like it?' he asked.

'That hardly matters,' the life-ward replied.

They passed through some burned-out towns, through tenement rows of worker hab-stacks that the enemies of the Imperium had turned their meltas on. Finally, the cavalcade drew to a halt on the head road of a massive dam that curved between the shoulders of a craggy mountain range. The daylight was cold and clear, and water vapour hung like mist.

About three hundred battle troops stood in files along the dam top, weapons shouldered. Several pennants fluttered in the wind. As he dismounted from the transport, pulling the cloak around him for warmth, the pheguth saw the waiting group of dignitaries. Ambassadors, stewards, division commanders, warrior-officers, chroniclers, all attended by their own life-wards.

And the Plenipotentiary Isidor Sek Incarnate himself.

'By the Throne!' the pheguth gasped as he saw him.

The troops and excubitors in earshot cursed and ruffled, some spitting against ill-omen.

'Try not to say that,' said Desolane.

'My apologies. Old habits.'

'This way.'

Desolane walked him down to the waiting group. There was some back-and-forth formal ceremony involving Desolane and the other life-wards. Challenges were shouted, antique oaths and ritual insults, a drawing and brandishing of weapons.

Isidor waited until the performance was done, and then beckoned to the pheguth.

He'd met Isidor twice before, once on arrival on Gereon, then again the night before the transcoding sessions had begun. Isidor Sek Incarnate was a short, plump human male wearing long black robes and a grey cowl. His pale, hairless face presented a permanent expression of disdain. He was the Anarch's instrument of government on Gereon.

There was nothing about him that was at all intimidating or frightening, and that's why he terrified the pheguth. This little man was surrounded by monsters – a veritable minotaur held a black parasol over his head deferentially – and massive Chaos Marines paid him fealty, yet there was no visible clue to his source of power. He was just a little man under a parasol.

'Welcome, pheguth,' the Plenipotentiary said. His voice was like a sharp knife slicing satin.

'Magir magus,' the pheguth responded as he had been rehearsed, bowing.

'There are two persons I would like you to meet,' said the Plenipotentiary. 'You will be spending a lot of time with them in the next few months.'

'What, may I ask, about the transcoding, magir magus?' he asked.

'That will continue. Transcoding you is our foremost agenda. But other issues will grow in importance. Otherwise, there is no point keeping you alive. Meet these persons.'

'Of course, magir magus.'

Isidor made a signal. Something vast and vaguely female crawled forward. She was immense and swollen, like the effigies of the Earth Mother early humans had fashioned, so morbidly obese that all the features of her face had vanished into folds of skin except her loose mouth. A wide-brimmed Phrygian hat perched on her scalp and swathes of green and silver fabric enveloped her bulk and flapped loose in the wind. Four midget servitors, squat and thick, clung around her lower body in the folds of her gown, to support her weight. Two hooded life-wards, both women, both skeletally thin, walked beside her, their long fingers implanted with bright scalpels.

'This is Idresha Cluwge, Chief Ethnologue of the Anarch,' said the Plenipotentiary. 'She will be interviewing you over the coming weeks.'

'I...' he began.

The female slug spoke. A barbaric clutch of conso-
nants burst from her fat mouth like a burp. Immediately,
her two female life-wards translated, in chorus.

'This is the pheguth, Isidor? How intriguing. He is a
little man. He looks not at all like a commander of soldiers.'

'I'd like to say you don't look like an ethnologue,' said
the pheguth. 'Except that I have no idea what one of
those is.'

The female life-wards hissed and raised their blade-
fingers towards him.

'Oh, have I erred on the protocol front?' the pheguth
asked dryly.

'Show respect, or I will slay you,' Desolane warned
him.

'He'll eat your liver...'

'I'll take that chance. The chief ethnologue is a person
of consequence. You will evidence respect for her at all
times.'

'Just playing with you, Desolane. Can she at least tell
me what an ethnologue is?'

'It is my duty to learn in all detail about the life and
culture of the enemy,' the life-wards said in unison the
moment the female thing had stopped burping out
more noises.

'I'm sure it is,' said the pheguth.

'All will become evident,' said the Plenipotentiary. He
nodded, and a second figure stepped forward. 'This is
the other person I wish you to greet.'

The man was a warrior. The pheguth recognised that at
once. Straight-backed, broad, powerful. He wore a simple coat of brown leather, insignia-less army fatigues and
steel-shod boots. His head was bald and deeply,
anciently scarred. Ritually scarred. The warrior took off
one glove and held out an oddly soft and pink hand to
the pheguth.

'I believe this is how one warrior greets another in your part of the galaxy,' he said in clipped, learned Low Gothic.

'We also salute,' said the pheguth, shaking the man's hand.

'Forgive me. I can clasp your hand, sir, but I cannot salute you. That would result in unnecessary liver-eating.'

The pheguth smiled. 'I didn't catch your name, sir,' he said.

'I am Mabbon Etogaur. The etogaur is an honorific.'

'I know,' said the pheguth. 'It's a rank name. The Guard had pretty damn good intelligence. It's indicative of a colonel rank or its equivalent.'

'Yes, sir, it is. General, actually.'

'It's a Blood Pact rank.'

Mabbon nodded. 'Indeed.'

'But you present to me unmasked and your hands are clean of rite scars.'

Mabbon pulled his glove back on. 'You appreciate a great deal.'

'I was a general too, you know.'

'I know.'

'And you're going to be talking to me?'

Mabbon nodded.

'I look forward to it, sir. I wonder if at some point we might explore the meaning of the word "pheguth".'

Mabbon looked away. 'If needs be, that might happen.'

The pheguth looked back at the Plenipotentiary.

'Are we done?' he asked.

'Not even slightly, pheguth,' the magir magus replied. 'Nine worlds in the Anarch's domain lack water sources. They are parched, thirsty. Today, here, we conduct a ceremony that will access Gereon's resources to aid them. The process has already been done at four sites on the planet already. I wanted you to oversee this one.'

'Another test of my resolve?'

'Of course another test. Wards, bring the cylinder.'

With Desolane and the minotaur at their heels, the Plenipotentiary led him to the wall of the dam overlooking the vast reservoir beyond.

'Eight billion cubic metres of fresh water, replenished on a three-day cycle. Do you know what a jehgenesh is?'

'No, magir magus, I don't.'

Isidor smiled. 'Literally, a "drinker of seas". That's quite accurate. It leaves out the warp-fold part, but other than that...'

Two goat-headed servants clopped up to the wall, and held out a glass canister in which about three litres of green fluid sloshed. Deep in the fluid suspension, the pheguth could see something writhing.

Isidor Sek Incarnate took the cylinder and handed it to the pheguth. 'Don't be misled by its current size. It's dormant and infolded. Released into the water, it will grow. Essentially, it's a huge maw. On one end, flooding in, this water source. The jehgenesh is a warp beast. The water that pours into its mouth will be ejected through the holy warp onto another world. The arid basins of Anchisus Bone, for example.'

The pheguth gazed at the cylinder in his hands. 'This is how you plunder?'

'It is one way amongst many.'

'But this is why so many worlds we find have been drained?'

The Plenipotentiary nodded. 'The drinkers swallow water, also fuel oil, promethium, certain gas reserves. Why would we conquer worlds if we didn't actually use them? I mean, literally, use them?'

The pheguth shrugged. 'It makes perfect sense. What do I have to do?'

'Unscrew the lid. Release it.'

'And prove I am loyal?'

'It's another step on the way.'

The pheguth turned the steel cap of the canister slowly. He felt the warp-thing inside writhing, agitated. The lid came off. There was a smell... like dry bones. Like desert air.

'Quickly,' said the Plenipotentiary. 'Or it will drink you.'

The pheguth up-ended the canister, and the green water poured out into the reservoir, along with something slithering and coiled.

'Two days,' said Desolane. 'Then it will grow.'

'I'd like to go back to the bastion now,' the pheguth said, turning away from the lake.

FOUR

Gaunt opened his eyes. It was early still, and only a thin suggestion of light bled through the woodland canopy. In the violet twilight of the forest, it was cold and damp, and dawn mists fumed like artillery smoke.

They'd found the glade late the previous night and had bedded down to steal a few hours' rest. Gaunt had settled into a half-waking doze, more meditation than actual slumber, ready to snap alert at the slightest cue. He got like that during intense combat rotations. Sometimes true sleep would elude him for days or weeks at a time, and he survived on these snatches of subsistence rest. 'Sleeping with one eye open,' that's what Colm Corbec had liked to call it.

It was at times like this – the quiet, tense interludes – that Gaunt missed Corbec the most.

He realised his awakening had been triggered by a shadow next to him. Gaunt looked up. It was Mkvenner. The tall scout was standing so still he seemed to be part of the tree behind him.

'Ven?' Gaunt whispered.

'Everything's fine, sir,' Mkvenner replied. 'But it's time we were waking. Time we were moving.'

Gaunt got to his feet, his joints stiff and aching. A campfire was a luxury they couldn't afford. Nearby, Beltayn, Varl and Larkin were huddled up, drinking soup through the straws of self-heating ration packs. Brostin was still asleep close to them, bundled up under his camo-cloak with his arms around his autocannon.

'Wake him up,' Gaunt told Beltayn, and his young adjutant nodded.

Tona Criid sat against a large, sprawling tree root further up the slope. She was cleaning her lasrifle and keeping watch over the three locals. They were curled like children in the underbrush, slumbering deeply. Gaunt took three ration packs from his own kit and handed them to Criid.

'Wake them in a few minutes,' he told her, 'and give them these. Make sure they eat properly.'

'All right,' she said simply, not commenting on the fact that Gaunt was giving away some of his own precious supplies.

'Did you get any sleep?' he asked.

Her hands fitted the lasrifle sections together, wiping each one with a vizzy cloth. She didn't even have to look at what she was doing.

'Not much,' she admitted.

'In the night. Anything?'

She shook her head.

'That's good.' He paused. 'He'll be all right. All of them will. You know that, right?'

'Yes, sir.'

'Because you trust my word on that?'

'Because I trust your word, sir,' she said.

Tona Criid's lover was a Tanith trooper called Caffran. Both of them were excellent soldiers, amongst the very best in Gaunt's regiment. Competition for a place on this mission had been gratifyingly fierce. Gaunt had been forced to turn down many fine Ghosts he would have loved to bring along. Both Criid and Caffran had qualified easily for the final cut. It had been a hard choice, but Gaunt had accepted he could take one or the other, so he'd switched Caffran out in favour of Feygor, Rawne's adjutant.

Criid and Caffran had two kids in the regimental entourage, waifs they'd rescued from the urban wastes of Vervunhive. He couldn't and wouldn't risk both parental proxies on a mission that the Departmento Tacticae officially rated 'EZ' – *extremely hazardous/suicidal.*

Gaunt made his way on up the slope. He couldn't see Mkoll or Bonin, but he knew they were out there, invisible, covering the perimeter.

Rawne and Feygor sat with Ana Curth, the team's medicae, in the shadow of a moss-skinned boulder. She was giving them both shots using a dermo-needle from her field kit. Curth was technically a non-combatant, but she had guts and she was fit and it was essential they had a medicae with them. Gaunt knew he'd have to look after her, and he'd asked Mkoll to keep a special eye out for her safety.

Curth had voluntarily undergone intensive field training for the mission, and Gaunt was already impressed with the discipline she displayed. She'd been the only viable choice for the medicae place anyway: Dorden, the regiment's chief medic, surpassed her in ability, but he was too old and – after the grievous injuries he'd taken on Herodor almost a year before – too frail for this kind of operation.

'Everything all right here?' Gaunt asked, joining them.

'Dandy,' said Murtan Feygor. Rawne's adjutant was a rawboned rogue whose voice came flat and sarcastic from an augmetic voice box thanks to a miserable throat wound he'd taken on Verghast. He was a mean piece of work, vicious and disingenuous, but he was a devil in combat. He'd made Gaunt's cut because Gaunt figured his relationship with Rawne would work better if Rawne felt he had a crony to complain to.

Major Elim Rawne had become Gaunt's number two following the death of Colm Corbec. Rawne was darkly handsome and murderous. There had been times, especially in the early days, when Rawne might have sheathed his silver Tanith warknife in Gaunt's back the first chance he got. Some among the Tanith – a precious few, these days, and getting fewer all the time – still blamed Gaunt for abandoning their homeworld to its fate. Rawne was their ringleader. Hate had fuelled him, driven him on.

But they had served together now for the best part of nine years. A kind of mutual respect had grown between the major and the colonel-commissar. Gaunt no longer expected a knife in the back. But he still didn't turn his back on Rawne, nevertheless.

'Feygor's showing signs of the ague,' Curth said, cleaning and reloading her dermo-needle. 'I want to give everyone a shot.'

'Do it,' said Gaunt.

'Arm please,' she said.

Gaunt rolled up his sleeve. This was to be expected. The ague was a broad and non-specific term for all kinds of infections and maladies suffered by personnel transferred from one world to another. A body might acclimatise to one planet's germ-pool, its pollens, its bacteria, and then ship out on a troop transport and plunge into quite another bio-culture. These changes required adjustment, and often triggered colds, fevers, allergies, or simply the lags and fatigues brought on by warp-space transfer. Gereon was going to make them all sick. That was a given. Potentially, they might all get very ill indeed, given the noxious touch of Chaos that had stained this world. It was Curth's primary job to monitor their health, treat any maladies, keep them fit enough to see out the mission. Treating wounds and injuries they might sustain was entirely secondary to this vital work.

She gave him the shot.

'Now you,' Gaunt said.

'What?'

'You're looking out for us, Ana. I'll look out for you. Let me see you self-administer before you go to the others.'

Ana Curth glared at him for a moment. Even annoyed, even smeared with dirt, her heart-shaped face was strikingly attractive. 'As if I would jeopardise this operation by failing to maintain my own health,' she hissed.

'As if you would withhold preventative drugs because you decided others needed them more, doctor.'

'As if,' she said, and gave herself the shot.

Gaunt rose, and drew Rawne to one side.

'What's the play?' Rawne asked quietly.

'Unless I hear a good reason, the same as before. We use our contacts to penetrate Ineuron Town and contact the resistance cell. We've got to hope they can give us what we need.'

'Right,' said Rawne.

'You have concerns?'

'I don't trust them,' said the Tanith.

'Neither do I. That's why I've disclosed as little as possible.'

'But you've told Lanson–'

'Landerson.'

'Whatever. You've told him there's no liberation coming.'

'I have.'

Rawne took off his cap and smoothed his hair back with one gloved palm. 'They're jumpy. All three of them. Fething dangerous-jumpy, you ask me.'

'Yes, strung out. I noticed,' said Gaunt.

'They've had things in them too.'

'The implants, you mean? Yes, they have. They call them imagos. It's the archenemy's way of tagging the populace.'

'And the marks on their faces.'

Gaunt sighed. 'Rawne, I won't lie. I don't like that either. The stigmas. The brands of the Ruinous Powers. Makes me very uneasy. But you have to understand, these people are Imperial citizens. They had no choice. To remain active, to keep the resistance running, they had to blend in. They had to submit to the authorities. Take the brand, play along.'

Rawne nodded. 'Troubles me, is all I'm saying. Never met anyone or anything with a mark of Chaos cut into its flesh that wasn't trying to kill me.'

Gaunt was silent for a moment. 'Major, I doubt we'd find a man, woman or child on this world that hasn't been scarred by the archenemy. This is intruder ops, nothing like anything we've ever faced. The point is, sooner or later we're going to have to trust some of them. If not trust them, then work with them at least. But your point is well made. Consider operational code Safeguard active from this time. Command is "vouch-safe". Tell Feygor, Criid and the scouts.'

'All right then,' said Rawne.

'But only on the word, and it had better be mine, you understand me? These people, and any others we meet, are to stay alive unless there's a fething good reason.'

'I hear you.'

'Look at me when you say that.'

Rawne fixed Gaunt's eyes with his own. 'I hear you, sir.'

'Let's round up and move out. Ten minutes. Make a personal check that Curth's given everyone a shot of the inhibitors.'

Rawne saluted lazily and turned away.

'I'VE BEEN DISCUSSING things with my men,' Landerson said. His eyes were still puffy from sleep. 'We're uneasy.'

'We're all uneasy,' Gaunt said.

'You're telling me you want us to get you into Ineuron Town?'

'Yes.'

'And broker contact with the cell there?'

'Yes.'

Landerson paused for a moment. 'I'd like you to reconsider this, sir. I'd like you to think again.'

Gaunt looked at him. 'I'm not sure I know what you mean.'

'Gereon requires liberation, sir. We're dying. I don't know what your intentions are here, sir, but whatever they are, it's not what we want or need. I'd like you to reconsider your mission, perhaps even withdraw if necessary. I'd like you to contact your forces and coordinate a full counter-invasion.'

'I know you would,' Gaunt said. 'We've been over this. Last night, I thought you understood—'

Landerson reached into his shabby jacket and produced an envelope. 'I'm authorised to give you this, sir.'

'What is it?' asked Gaunt.

'An incentive, sir. An incentive to get you to aid us in the way we need aid. Right now.'

Gaunt opened the envelope. There were twenty hand-drawn paper bills inside, each one notarised and issued to the value of one hundred thousand crowns. War money. Bonds that promised to pay the bearer the full stated amount once Imperial rule and monetary systems had been re-established.

Gaunt put the bills back in their envelope.

'I wouldn't for a moment describe this as a bribe, Landerson. I know we're not talking in those terms. But I can't accept this. There are three reasons. One: I have no way of withdrawing now or making contact with my superiors. I can't coordinate any kind of deal. Two: even if I could, there is no deal to coordinate. At this time, my lord general, who I am privileged to serve, has no means or manpower to orchestrate the sort of mass operation you're talking about. There will be no liberation, because there are no liberators to achieve it. Three – and this is the one I need you to truly understand – my work here is more important than that. More important, it pains me to tell you, than the lives of every citizen currently enslaved on this world. And that's the up and down of it.'

Gaunt handed the envelope back to Landerson. Landerson looked as if he'd been slapped.

'Put them away, and let's not speak of it again. Now, I'd like you to get my team into the town and get us face to face with your cell leader.'

A few metres away, in the treecover, Feygor glanced round at Brostin.

'You see that?' he whispered.

Brostin nodded.

'The bonds, I mean?'

Brostin nodded again. 'I ain't blind, Murt.'

'Did you see how much he just turned down?'

'A real lot,' said Brostin quietly.

'Feth yes! A real lot.'

Brostin shrugged. 'So what?'

Feygor looked back at the envelope Landerson was tucking away in his jacket.

'I'm just saying, is all,' he muttered.

A FILMY SHEEN of sunlight filled the air. Through the mists, they made their way along the limits of the woodland into the dykes and ditches of the Shedowtonland pastures. The day seemed opaque. Gereon's parent star was hot and white, but the atmosphere was dirty with ash and particulates, and it deadened the pure light down to a tarnished amber.

Landerson had told Gaunt that the town was about two hours' walk away by road, but the roadways were not an option. He mentioned patrols, and other hazards that Gaunt made a mental note to quiz Landerson about when the opportunity came. So they stuck to the watercourses and the overgrown embankments of the agricultural landscape. The going was slow, because the ditches were choked with weed. Horrors lurked there too in the foetid, slippery ooze. Vermin, again in great profusion, and wildly swarming insects. On two occasions, they were forced to turn back and find a new route because the dyke path ahead was blocked by a buzzing mass of insects, the overhanging vegetation bent over by the weight of their molten, dripping numbers. It had been common for farmers in this region to use entomoculture techniques. Specially reared and hybridised swarms were employed seasonally to pollinate the field systems. Unmanaged since the invasion, these hive populations now roamed feral.

There were other horrors too. Rat-gnawed skulls bobbed and rocked in the pools, yellowed bones jutted from the mire. War dead had been dumped here, or refugees had fled here and died lingering, famished deaths as they hid from the patrols.

They walked for three hours, in virtual silence except for the occasional verbal or manual instruction. The mists began to burn off as the heat of the day increased, but the sky above, glimpsed through the overhanging brambles and gorseweed, slowly set into an arid, baked strata of yellow and ochre cloud, like the ribbed sands of an open desert. It was as if the touch of Chaos had caused the atmosphere to clot and fossilise.

Mkoll held up his hand and everyone stopped dead. A moment's pause.

He looked back at Gaunt.

'Did you hear that?'

Gaunt shook his head.

'A horn of some kind. Not close, but clear.'

'That's the town,' Landerson whispered. 'The carnyx sounding a labour change. We're close. Within a kilometre.'

They continued for another ten minutes, down a particularly dark and overhung stretch of marshy ditch. Then Mkoll signalled again, this time adding the gesture that ushered them low. Everyone hunkered down, Beltayn pulling down Lefivre, who seemed slow to understand.

Mkoll, a shadow in the gloom, signed to Gaunt and indicated Bonin. Gaunt signed affirmative. The two scouts slipped away ahead of the group.

They waited for five minutes. Six. Seven. Gaunt distinctly thought he caught the sound of a combustion engine, a passing vehicle.

Then he heard two flicks on the vox-channel.

Gaunt waved the group on slowly. Their boots were sticking in the sucking black muck, and it was hard to walk without slopping the water. Landerson and his comrades seemed particularly inept. Gaunt saw Rawne's look. He shook his head.

Mkoll and Bonin were waiting for them at the end of the ditch, where it opened out into an overgrown morass, some kind of pen or farming yard. The broken, peeling shapes of four large bunker silos faced them, festooned with climbing ivy and brightly flowered merrymach. Beyond the silos, a stand of trees followed the line of a track.

'There was a patrol,' whispered Mkoll. 'But it's gone by now.'

'Let's get out of sight,' said Gaunt, and they hurried across the squelching morass into the nearest of the silos. It was dark and dusty inside, with a noxious, yeasty smell. The grain reserves heaped up against the backboards were rotten, and they all tried to ignore the weevils writhing through the mass. Mkoll sent Mkvenner and Bonin outside to cover the approach, and Larkin up onto the grain mound to take a firing position from the open slot of the feeder chute.

'You know where we are?' Gaunt asked Landerson.

'Parcelson's agri-plex. West of the town. This is where I should leave you.'

'I beg your pardon?'

'You want me to make contact for you? Then I have to get into the town and make arrangements. You stay here and–'

'No, we won't,' said Gaunt flatly.

Landerson glanced away in frustration. 'Do you want my help or don't you?'

'It would be good.'

'Then listen to me. I can't get a dozen people into Ineuron without having somewhere to hide them at the other end. It doesn't work like that. I have to slip in, make contact, and then bring you all in.'

Gaunt thought about it. 'Fine, but you're not going alone. Mkoll and I are coming with you.' Something in Gaunt's face made Landerson realise there was no room for negotiation.

'All right,' he sighed.

'How long will this take?'

'We should be back by tomorrow. Arrangements take time. Things will need to be checked. Remember, you're asking me to make contact with people who don't want to be found.'

Gaunt nodded. He called Mkoll and Rawne over to him and took them to one side. 'I'm going with Landerson to arrange a handshake. Mkoll, you'll be with me. Rawne, you're in charge here. Keep everyone low and contained. Move only if you have to.'

'Got it.'

'Landerson's guys are in your care. If they're not still breathing by the time I come back, you'd better have a feth of a good reason that can be vouched for by Mkvenner and Curth.'

'Understood,' said Rawne.

'If we're not back by this time tomorrow, figure us as dead and move on. The mission will be yours then,

Rawne. Don't come looking for us. Get out and get it running, try and establish contact of your own. I suggest you use Landerson's men to get you to another town and try somewhere fresh. If Mkoll and I don't come back, Ineuron's probably a dead end.'

Rawne nodded. 'Codes?' he asked.

'Code positive… "Silver". Code negative… How about "Bragg"?'

'Works for me.'

'Go tell the others,' Gaunt said, and Rawne moved off.

'Sir–' Mkoll began.

'Save it, old friend,' Gaunt smiled.

'Save what? You don't know what I was going to say.'

'You were about to tell me that this was a job for the scouts, and that I should stay here.'

Mkoll almost grinned. He nodded.

'This is not the normal order of things,' said Gaunt. 'We're all front-line here. Right?'

'Sir.'

'Unless you have some concerns about my abilities?'

'None whatsoever, colonel-commissar. But if this is a stealth insertion, I'm calling the play. Ditch your kit. Bare minimum. And switch one of your bolt pistols for the auto I gave you.'

'Agreed,' Gaunt said.

Gaunt took off his pack and went through it, transferring a few essential items into his uniform pockets. He took one of the bolt pistols out of his holster rig and slipped it, along with half his bolt-ammo allowance, into the pack. Then he gave the pack to Beltayn's safe-keeping.

Except for Larkin, none of the team was armed with their usual weapons. Ordinarily, the Tanith Ghosts carried mk III lasrifles, finished with solid nalwood stocks and sleeves, with a standard laspistol and silver warknife as back-up. For this mission, it had been decided they needed to be light and compact. They'd swapped their rifles for hand-modified versions of the so-called 'Gak' issue weapon: wire-stocked mk III's supplied to the Verghastites in the regiment. The wire stocks made the weapons lighter, and could be folded back to make them significantly shorter. The special modifications had also shortened the muzzle length, strengthened the barrel, and increased the capacity of the energy clip. These were insurgence weapons, tooled for commando work, with the power and range of a standard lasrifle but about a third less overall length. The Ghosts had kept their trademark warknives, of course, but the laspistols had also been ditched in favour of compact autopistols. These pistols lacked the stopping power of a lasweapon, but a lasweapon was hard to keep muffled and it was impossible to keep flash suppressed. Each autopistol had a fat drum silencer screwed to the muzzle.

Gaunt checked the fit of the suppressor on his auto, slipped four spare clips onto his coat pocket, then cinched the weapon into the adjustable holster he'd taken the bolter from.

One item remained for consideration: the long, flat object, wrapped in camo-cloth, that Gaunt had strapped across his shoulder blades. Reluctantly, he removed it and handed it to his adjutant.

'Look after this,' he told Beltayn.

'I certainly will, sir.'

'If I don't come back, give it to Rawne.'

'Yes, sir.'

GAUNT, MKOLL AND Landerson left the silos, and followed the rutted track down to the edge of the trees, turning west through the thickets and saplings that had flourished along the edge of the road. It was hot and dusty, and the sunlight had a strange, twisted quality that unsettled Gaunt. So many worlds he'd been to in his career, some Imperial, some wild, some touched by the archenemy of man. But he had never been to a world before where the archenemy held total sway. It was more distressing than any battle zone, any fire field or bombarded plain. More distressing than the pandemonium of Balhaut or Verghast or Fortis.

Here, he suspected everything. The mud on the path, the starving birds in the silent trees, the wild flowers glittering along the verges. He noticed the way the hedges and thickets were browning and dying, slain by the atmospheric dust. He noticed the pustular livestock shuddering in spare fields. The twitching vermin in every gulley and ditch. The very perfume of the place.

Gereon was not a world that could be trusted in any detail. It was not a world where Chaos could be fought back or displaced. Chaos owned every shred of it.

And how long, Gaunt wondered, before it owned him and his men too? He'd read his Ravenor, his Czevak, his *Blandishments of Hand*. He'd read a double-dozen treatises from the Inquisitorial ordos as recommended by the Commissariat. Chaos always tainted. Fact. It infected. It stained. Even into the most sturdy and centred, it seeped osmotically and corrupted. That was an ever-present danger on the battlefield. But here… here on what was by any measure a Chaos world… how long would it take?

Before departure, Gaunt had spoken to Tactician Biota, a man he trusted. Biota had reckoned – in consultation with the Ordo Malleus – that Gaunt's men had about a month.

After that, no matter what they felt or thought about themselves, they would most likely be corrupted beyond salvation.

The thought made Gaunt wonder again about Gerome Landerson.

THEY HUGGED THE roadside thickets as traffic approached. Motorised transports, growling in towards the town. An excubitor patrol that left them cowering in a foul-smelling gutter for fifteen minutes. A convoy of traders, and a line of high-sided carriers laden with grain drawn by puffing traction engines.

'Vittalers,' Landerson said of these last. 'Food supplies from the midland bocage. They've maintained crop production up there, because the land is easily harvested. Grain is needed to supply the cookshops. The working population must be fed.'

Ineuron Town now lay below them, a pattern of habs and derelict mills, towers, ruined stacks and snail-horned temples that, Gaunt knew without asking, had been desecrated and reordained to god-things whose very murmured name would make him weep.

They faced the western palisades, a towering shield wall that circuited the western hem of the town. There were two gates, well guarded, accessed by metal-frame bridges that spanned the deep, murky ditch at the foot of the wall. In cover, in the leached undergrowth, Gaunt took out his scope and played it over the scene. The palisade was solid, but in poor repair, patched after the invasion. Excubitor teams sentried the gates. On the fighting platforms of the wall itself, he could make out troopers of the occupying force, glinting in the dead light like beetles as the weary sun caught their polished, form-fitting green combat armour.

Beyond the wall, inside the town, he saw distant manufactories, pumping black smoke into the air.

'What are those?' he asked.

'The meat foundries,' Landerson replied.

'Where they–?'

'Yes, sir.'

'Right,' said Gaunt, and stowed his scope. 'How do we get in?'

'The same way I got out,' said Landerson. 'The vittalers.'

Landerson and his comrades had hopped on an empty, outbound wagon the night before. Now they had to stow away on a laden one.

The excubitors helped them. At the wall gate, the sinister guardians were checking tariff papers, stigmas and imagos carefully, and the long convoy of high-sided carriers had come to a standstill, tractors panting. Mkoll led them down to the roadway and, after checking both ways, hurried them over to the tail gate of the rear wagon. They monkeyed up the tailboards and dropped over into the grain piles.

'Bury yourselves!' Mkoll snapped, and they wriggled down into the moving mass of loose grain, spading it over their backs with open hands.

The carrier started to roll forward again, its traction engine puffing. Another halt. Steam hissed. More checks ahead. Then they were shunting forward again, and the shadow of the gate-mouth fell across them.

Choking in loose grain, Gaunt listened hard. A challenge, an exchange of voices. The gurgling rasp of the excubitor voices. Questions.

Then a rattling of chains and the sniffling whine of hounds.

More orders, shouted.

They're searching the carriers, Gaunt realised. They're looking for scents. The hounds. The fetch-hounds.

His hand closed around the grip of his holstered autopistol and he thumbed the safety off. There were loose kernels of grain and chaff in his nostrils now. He felt a sneeze building.

Gaunt clamped his mouth shut. His throat constricted with the pressure. His eyes teared up. He tried not to breathe. Dust tickled his larynx.

A shouted order. A sudden jolt. They were moving again.

The panting chuff of the tractor was so loud that Gaunt risked a cough. Across the grain heap, Mkoll raised his head and glared at him.

They were in. Feth, they were in!

Landerson was already getting to his feet, the grain pouring off him like sand in a glass.

'What are you doing?' Mkoll hissed. 'Get the feth down!'

'No time!' said Landerson. 'Trust me, we can't wait until we roll into the market. There's only one section of roof low enough to exit on and it's coming up fast!'

They scrambled up and got to the left-hand side of the carrier. Below, narrow low-hab streets hurtled by. Gaunt looked back. On the palisade, the guards were visible... looking outwards.

'Where?' Mkoll asked.

'Here! Quickly! It's coming up!' Landerson urged. He pointed. A low roof section, two metres lower than the wagon's side, badly-tiled.

'There! That or nothing else!'

They swung their legs over the edge of the wagon's side, hands gripped to the lip. The street, five metres below, rushed past. Certain, broken death: a mis-jump, a glancing fall against the gutterwork...

'Now!' Landerson cried.

They jumped.

IT WAS ALMOST balmy now. The amber sunlight baked the soil, and clouds of drowsy insects murmured around the silos.

Rawne slithered down from his check on Larkin. Varl, sitting in a corner, looked at him.

'How do you think they're doing?' he asked.

Rawne shrugged.

MKOLL FOUND A grip and held it. The impact had all but winded him. The old tiles were rotten, and they shredded under his fingertips. He dug in with his knife and got a good purchase. He looked back.

Gaunt had landed well. Landerson had slipped, and was sliding back down the low roof, scrabbling for a hand-hold.

Gaunt stabbed his own knife home, then threw out the end of his camo-cape to Landerson. The man grabbed it and his slide ceased.

'Help me,' Gaunt grunted.

Mkoll edged back down the roof, and threw his own cape out to Landerson. Between them, Gaunt and Mkoll dragged Landerson up to join them. 'My thanks,' he gasped.

'How do we get in?' Gaunt asked.

'Skylight on the far side.'

THE BUILDING WAS an old scholam primer. They dropped down into the gloomy interior, and walked past half-sized desks and alphabet murals. Gaunt paused briefly and gazed at the scatter of tiny wooden building blocks and forgotten dolls.

Landerson led them to the back exit, out into a dingy alley that led back along a series of rents and low-habs. Filthy water gurgled down the central gutter.

'Where to?' Gaunt whispered.

'Just shut up and follow me,' Landerson replied.

They chased him through a series of gloomy vacant lots and under the rough timber scaffolding that had been erected to shore up the sagging wall of a manufactory.

At the corner of the aged building they stowed themselves in cover and waited until Mkoll gave them an all clear.

Then they sprinted across the cobbled thoroughfare and ran down the stone steps beside a public water syphon.

The air was dank. Landerson headed on through the dim blue shadows until he reached a chainlink fence.

'We're blocked,' Gaunt started to say. Landerson shook his head, and took off his coat, wrapping it around his hands so he could grab the filaments of razorwire knotted into the fence without ripping his palms open. He hefted hard and a section lifted away.

'Through. Now!' he barked, and Mkoll and Gaunt ducked under the partition. Landerson followed, and settled the section back in place. He put his coat back on. It had a number of fresh tears.

He beckoned them. They jogged down a low pavement, flanked on either side by the plaster-finished walls of public buildings, and then across a small yard where a dried-up fountain stood forlorn. A left turn, another alley, and then up a flight of worn stone steps to the next street.

Mkoll hushed them back hard.

They clung to the mossy wall and watched the steel-shod feet of an excubitor patrol stride past on the street level.

Mkoll put his silenced pistol away again and nodded them on.

'We have to cross here,' Landerson said.

Mkoll nodded, and took a look out. The side-street, cobbled and shadowed, was empty.

'Go!' Mkoll said.

They darted across the street and into an adjacent alley. Ten metres down from the alley mouth, there was a door of heavy wood, painted red.

Landerson waved the Ghosts back. He knocked once.

A slit opened.

'How is Gereon?' a voice asked from inside.

'Gereon lives,' Landerson replied.

'Even though it dies,' the voice responded.

Landerson stiffened abruptly and turned away from the door. He started walking back towards Gaunt and Mkoll.

'What's the matter?' asked Gaunt.

'Move. Move,' Landerson whispered urgently. 'It's not safe.'

They began to hurry away.

The red door opened wide and an excubitor stepped out, its las-lock raised to fire.

Mkoll spun around, dropped to one knee and fired three shots with his silenced autopistol. It made a *phut! phut! phut!* noise.

The excubitor slammed backwards as if it had been yanked back by a rope.

'Run!' said Mkoll.

FIVE

GAUNT STARTED TO run, but heard Mkoll's weapon spit again. He looked back. Another excubitor had fallen awkwardly away from the red door, its las-lock clattering onto the flagstones.

'Come on!' Gaunt shouted.

Mkoll raced to join him. Landerson was already heading out onto the side street.

'Which way?' Gaunt hissed.

'Down here...' Landerson began. He shut up quickly. They heard the squeaking clatter of vehicle treads, and a half-track swung into view at one end of the street. Dark figures leapt out, long coats flying. Gaunt heard challenges shouted through augmetic voice boxes.

They turned immediately, but three excubitors were emerging from the alley they had just left. Gaunt wrenched out his auto. Mkoll was already firing.

One excubitor keeled over, speaker box blown out in a spurt of acrid sparks and synthesised howls. Gaunt's

auto bucked as he put three muted shots through the
hip and ribs of a second, punching holes in the grey-
scale armour coat and spattering the wall behind with
gore. The third got its long, ornate weapon up to fire but
Mkoll crashed into it, bearing the excubitor down onto
the cobbles under him. The silencer of Mkoll's auto
pressed against the excubitor's sternum and he executed
it with two quick rounds before it could get up.

Then the three of them started to run down the street
away from the half-track and the oncoming patrol. Landerson led the way, sprinting, his autorifle bumping
against his hip. Gaunt and Mkoll followed him. Gaunt
presumed Landerson had some sort of plan, that he was
working on local knowledge.

Then again, maybe he was just fleeing in blind panic.

He heard a shot. The hyphenated *zzt-foff* of a las-lock
firing. The bolt blew stones and brick chips out of a wall.
Gaunt glanced back. The gang of excubitors was closing
fast. They seemed like figures from a nightmare: their
armour coats billowing out behind them, their
grotesquely long, thin legs carrying them in huge, headlong strides. Gaunt fired a couple of shots in their
direction then pounded on after Mkoll and Landerson.

The street opened out into a wide yard with a pillared
stone colonnade along one side. On the far side of the
yard, the mouth of the adjoining street was blocked by a
battered troop transporter. The excubitors lined up in
front of it swept their weapons to their shoulders.

'Feth!' Gaunt cried. The three men hurled themselves
into the scant cover of the colonnade as the las-locks
started to blast. Bolts smacked off the old pillars, or flew
between them and detonated against the colonnade's
inner wall. Mkoll got his back to a pillar, and Landerson
scrambled on hands and knees for cover. Gaunt threw
himself down behind another stone column. His nostrils burned with cooked stone and burn-dust. The
las-lock fusillade sounded like whipcracks. They were

pinned, and in a second they were going to be out-flanked. For in a second, the foot patrol was going to round the corner, with a clear field of fire down the shadowed colonnade.

Gaunt pressed his back against the pillar, his leather jacket scratching on the rough stone. He pulled out his bolt pistol so he had a weapon in each hand.

'I've got our backs! Take them!' he yelled.

Landerson heard the shout. He was still on his hands and knees, shielding his head from the lock-fire. What the Throne did Gaunt mean by 'take them'? There were just three of them, cornered like rats, and the excubitors were everywhere.

'Use that fething weapon!' Mkoll snapped at him. The scout had holstered his pistol and was swinging the las-rifle off his shoulder. He didn't even bother extending the wire stock. He leaned out from behind the pillar and let off a burst of las-fire, rapid auto. The line of excubitors by the transport on the far side of the yard scattered for cover. Mkoll chuckled at the sight of it, and raked them again, cutting two down in a flurry of sizzling bolts.

'Come on!' he shouted.

Landerson struggled up onto his knees, and started firing his autorifle. The shots coming out of the suppressed muzzle sounded like wet kisses. He saw a row of raw metal holes punch into the side of the transport and raised his aim, knocking an excubitor off the back of the truck.

The patrol ran into view, shouting. Gaunt stepped out of his partial cover behind the pillar and opened fire with both handguns. The first three figures jerked and fell backwards. The clip of his auto out, Gaunt aimed the boltgun steadily and boomed out four more loud reports. Another dark shape folded violently, as if struck by a sledgehammer.

Gaunt ducked back behind the pillar, reloading. Las-lock rounds squealed down the colonnade. Behind him, he heard the furious crackle of Mkoll's las, and the splutter of the resistance fighter's old rifle. Gaunt peered out to the left of the pillar and fired his bolt pistol, then jerked back as las-locks answered him, before popping out to the right to fire his autopistol. The hard rounds smacked an excubitor in the face and forehead and walloped it onto its back. Then he leaned out to the left side again, and fired a bolt shell that pulped the chest of another excubitor who was trying to make a dash down the colonnade.

'Moving,' he heard Mkoll yell. The air around the colonnade was thick with dust and gunsmoke. Gaunt fired a few last bright flashes into the pall and turned to run after his chief scout.

Mkoll and Landerson had emerged from cover, firing their weapons from the hip as they ran across the yard. Their hammer-fire was forcing the second excubitor squad to cower behind walls and ragged heaps of trash and masonry. Gaunt caught up with Landerson. Mkoll had spotted a boarded door in the far wall of the yard. He reached it, kicked it savagely several times until it splintered open and then knelt down to deliver wholesale blasts across the yard with his lasrifle as Landerson and Gaunt charged in through the gaping doorway. As soon as they were inside, he barked off a final burst and plunged after them.

It was some kind of storage shed, unlit apart from the daylight slanting in through holes in the tiled roof. Old furniture was piled up against the walls. Gaunt edged his way in, with Landerson close behind. Mkoll paused in the doorway and pulled a tube-charge from his pack. He wedged it on one side of the splintered door, tied a length of monofilament wire to the det-tape, and then played the almost invisible wire out taut across the doorway at shin height, wrapping it off around a broken hinge on the other side.

Then he hurried after Gaunt.

'Know this place?' Gaunt whispered to Landerson. Outside they could heard guttural shouts and the occasional shot as the relentless patrols regrouped.

'Tillage Street bunkers. They lead into the manufactory district.' Landerson peered around in the gloom. 'Let's go that way. We want to come out on the south side of Rubenda.' Landerson sounded a little frantic, and Gaunt had a feeling it wasn't only the fun and games they'd just experienced.

'Where do we head for–' he began.

'Shut up. Please,' Landerson said. 'This is really bad. Really bad. We're not doing anything right now except finding a place to hide.'

'Of course,' said Gaunt.

'You don't understand,' Landerson said.

'What the feth is that?' Mkoll said behind them. They froze, listening. They could still make out the noises of the excubitors in the yard outside, but there was something else now. Horns were blowing, harsh and strident. And behind them, a rustling, like a gathering wind. A moaning that threatened to become a howl.

'Is it just me, or is that a sound no one wants to hear?' Mkoll whispered.

'Wirewolves,' said Landerson. 'Oh Throne. We've woken the whole place up.'

'What are–' Gaunt started to ask and then stopped. He didn't want to know. 'Your call, Landerson. A place to hide, you said.'

'I'll do my best,' said Landerson.

They found another door on the south side of the store, pulling broken tables aside to clear it. It let out into a dingy alley that was running with sewage from a broken drain. The moaning in the air had become a howl now. A keening.

Mkoll had slung his lasrifle again, and was leading the way with his silenced pistol raised. Behind them, in the store, they heard a dull, reverbarative *crump*, and a good deal of augmetic shrieking. An excubitor's shin had snagged Mkoll's tripwire.

They sloshed away through the muck. On a nearby street, transports rumbled by, their badly maintained engines rattling and coughing. Another booming note echoed from the city horns. More keening howls shrilled in the damp air. Gaunt felt his skin prickle. He could smell the unholy magic loosed on the wind.

Mkoll gestured with his pistol to a dark alley to their left.

'No,' Landerson said, without breaking stride. 'That's a dead end. This way.'

They turned right up a steep cobbled street and then Landerson immediately darted left into a covered alley between two boarded premises. The alley led through into a ramshackle clutch of overgrown walled gardens behind the tenement row. Only then did Landerson slow down.

'How did you know?' Gaunt asked.

Landseron beckoned the Ghosts after him. They followed a weed-infested path behind a row of broken cold frames and cultivator shacks, and into a yard piled with hemp sacks full of nitrate fertiliser.

'How did you know?' Gaunt repeated. 'Back at the red door.'

'They gave the wrong response. The warning response. The excubitors must have had them at gunpoint.'

'They knew you were coming,' said Mkoll.

'They knew someone was coming. That house was a key contact point. We'll have to use another. If there are any left they haven't found.' Landerson slid the bar on the rotting wooden door of a workshop and they went in. It was dirty, and piled with junk and machine parts.

'What's here?' Gaunt said.

'Nothing. It's a way through. We have to keep off the streets.'

Landerson led them to the far end of the workshop and moved some old cans of paint and sheets of fibre-plank so he could pull a section of the flakboard wall aside. The dust he disturbed spilled up into bars of pale light slanting in through the windows and made mote galaxies.

They ducked through and came out into a stone shed that, judging from the promethium stains on the floor, had been used until recently to garage vehicles. Landerson checked the street door.

Outside, the sound of howling had risen a notch. The air was charged. Gaunt felt nauseous. In the corner of the shed, an old engine block rested on a wooden pallet.

'Help me with this,' Landerson said. With Mkoll's aid, Landerson shifted the pallet load and exposed a trap-door. He yanked it open and dropped down into the darkness.

Mkoll and Gaunt followed. Landerson closed the hatch with a rope-pull and they were plunged into darkness. Mkoll lit his lamp pack. By the light of it, they moved on through a series of cellars. The brick walls were mildewed and rotten. Clumps of black fungus sprouted from the mortar. Vermin scuttled from the wavering light beam.

They reached a flight of dank steps, and edged down into a narrow tunnel that was flooded knee-deep with cold, noxious water. Landerson sloshed ahead, and located a set of iron rungs fixed into the tunnel's brick-work. Dripping, they clambered up it into a dry, vaulted cellar where the roof was so low they couldn't stand up straight. By the light of Mkoll's lamp, Gaunt could see there was a pile of old equipment crates and sacks of dried provisions heaped against one wall.

'Where are we?' he asked.

'The undercroft of the Ineuron flour mill. It's one of the bolt-holes the cell uses.'

'Are we safe here?' Gaunt asked.

Landerson laughed. 'Of course not. But it's safer than other places. Safer than out on the streets. Pray to your Emperor that it'll be safe enough.'

'The Emperor protects,' Mkoll whispered.

'He's your Emperor too,' Gaunt said.

'What?'

'Pray to your Emperor, you said. As if he wasn't yours.'

Landerson shrugged. 'This is my world, Colonel-Commissar Gaunt. And I love it dearly. My family line dates back to the original colonist-founders. Landerson. Sons of the First Landers here. I am true to the God-Emperor of Mankind, but honestly... do you think I trust him to protect me any more? Where was he when doom came to Gereon?'

'I can't answer that,' said Gaunt.

'How long must we stay here?' Mkoll asked.

'Until it's safe to show our faces,' said Landerson.

'Which means–'

'Later tonight at the earliest. When things have calmed down.' Landerson leaned his rifle against the undercroft wall and sat down. 'Then, maybe, we can start trying to hook up with the underground again. If we're not found in the meantime.'

THE SUN WAS setting. In the dry, starchy air of the silos outside the town, the rest of the insertion team waited fitfully.

'You hear that?' Bonin asked.

Larkin nodded. He was drooped as if asleep over his long-las. 'Been hearing it now for a good few minutes.'

'What the feth is it?'

Larkin didn't like to say. It was a distant howling sound, murmuring from the town below them. It sounded just like his worst nightmares. It made the noise of his migraines, the chatter of his darkest thoughts.

'I say we try the link,' announced Tona Criid, rising to her feet.

Beltayn shook his head. 'Nothing like range. Not with micro-beads. My set won't pick them up.'

'We wait,' said Rawne, emphatically. 'That was what his orders were.'

'I hear that,' said Feygor.

Varl looked as if he was about to say something then just shook his head.

Mkvenner paced into the silo, just finishing his latest sweep. He stood in the doorway, backlit by the sinking sunlight. 'Something's wrong,' he said.

'We figured that much,' Bonin replied.

'Have you heard the noises?' Mkvenner asked.

'Yes, I have,' said Rawne. 'Worst case scenario, our beloved leader has run into seriously shitty trouble and is either dead or about to be.'

'Right. Best case, major?' Ana Curth asked.

Rawne shrugged. 'Best case? Our beloved leader has run into seriously shitty trouble and is either dead or about to be. Sorry, was that a trick question?'

'Screw you, Rawne,' Curth sneered.

'I look forward to it,' smiled Rawne, and got to his feet. 'Listen up, Ghosts! We wait until tomorrow. Then we do things my way.'

SIX

NIGHT CAME, AND was no safer than the day.

A silence fell. Even the horns went quiet. Spectres haunted the town, snuffling and whining in the dark, and terror stiffened the air. In the deep stone undercroft, the three men waited it out.

At Landerson's instruction, they had turned the lamp off, and made no sound, uttered no word. Gaunt felt the cold through the thick walls. The undercroft was so massively built it would have withstood an artillery bombardment, but in the dark it felt fragile and insubstantial, as if no more than a canvas field tent sheltered them.

And there were things moving in the night.

The chill ebbed and flowed through the stones, as if transmitted by some fluid, tidal motion outside. Sudden cold spots froze the air, and frost foamed on the dank ceiling. Gaunt heard distant moaning, mumbling noises from the streets outside, the slow slide and squeal of metal blades or claws tracing along tiles and outer walls. Once in a while, there came a long scream or a sudden, truncated shriek.

He tried not to imagine what might be outside, what manner of abomination was loose in Ineuron Town. In the biting dark, his mind played wicked tricks. His hand clamped around the grip of his boltgun. He fought to arrest his own anxious breathing.

Every now and then, they heard marching feet in the distance, the rumble of motor engines, the bark and fuss of hounds. Those were dangers too, but somehow they seemed honest and solid. Dangers they could face down and deal with.

The drifting, half-heard sounds of the spectres were something else again.

Then utter silence fell outside. By his chronometer's luminous dial, Gaunt saw it was two hours past middle night.

Landerson lit the lamp pack. The sudden brilliance hurt Gaunt's eyes.

'They've called them off,' Landerson announced, speaking for the first time in over eight hours.

'You're sure?' asked Mkoll. It dismayed Gaunt to see how pale and worried his stoic chief scout looked.

'Sure as I can be,' Landerson replied. 'Once they're summoned, the wirewolves bleed power quickly. They've gone for now.'

'Gone?'

'Folded back to replenish their energies.'

'Folded back where?' Mkoll asked.

'Into the warp, I suppose,' Landerson replied. 'Oddly enough, I've never had the chance to ask.'

He got up on his feet, his head hunched down under the low roof. 'Come on,' he said. 'We've got a window of comparative safety between now and dawn. Let's not waste it.'

He led them back down the iron rungs into the flooded tunnel, and they churned along through the cold water. The tiny, frail bones of rats floated in the channel, forming a brittle skin. Thousands and thousands of rats, rendered down to buoyant bone litter. The lamp pack's beam lit them as an undulating white crust.

They reached steps and clambered up out of the cold flow. The steps were slimy and treacherous. Wet-rot clung to the walls.

As they climbed, the steps became drier and the rot receded. They came up through a wooden storm door onto a narrow back street. The night was still, and feeble stars glimmered in the narrow patch of sky visible between the close-leaning roofs above them. To the west was the ruddy glow of the ahenum furnaces.

Landerson beckoned them on, down to a junction between two quiet streets. At a crossroads up ahead, they could see a barrel fire burning, scattering flame-light and shadows back down the cobbles. Two excubitors stood by the fire, chafing their hands.

The trio slipped to the left, and ran down through the darkness of an adjoining street. Then right, up a shallow hill where the cobbles were worn and buckled, and left again into a silent court where ornamental plants had overgrown and wrapped around the brickwork. At Landerson's direction, they sprinted across the court and made their way along a sloping alley that ran down between a furniture manufactory and a defunct distillery. There was an iron gate at the end of the alley, fletched with moss and weed. Landerson shooed them down into cover.

A patrol rumbled by. Not excubitors, a military unit. Behind the weeds, cowering, Gaunt saw the grinding treads of a light tank, the pacing feet of the enemy. A searchlight flashed their way, breaking its light on the bars of the iron gate.

Then it was gone, and the patrol had passed on too.

'Come on,' Landerson whispered.

* * *

THEY MADE THEIR way down around the skirts of the commercia into the depths of the town. On one of the main avenues, a torch-lit parade was winding past, filling the night with the din of drums and cymbals. A mixture of excubitors and battle-troops formed the vanguard. Many of them held aloft spiked, racemose standards and filthy banners on long poles. The bulk of the procession was citizenry, shackled in long, trudging lines, singing and clapping.

These were proselytes. It saddened Gaunt to see so many. Every day, more and more members of the cowed populace elected to convert to the wretched faiths of the enemy. Some saw it, perhaps, as their only chance to survive. Others regarded it as a way of securing a better life, with greater liberties and consents. For the most part, Gaunt thought darkly, they converted because Chaos had swallowed their bewildered souls.

Ordinals led the parade towards the temple. Landerson had told Gaunt that 'ordinals' was a blanket term for the senior administrators of the enemy power. Some were priests, others scholars, bureaucrats, financiers, merchants. They wore elaborately coloured robes and headdresses, and their be-ringed fingers hefted ornate staves and ceremonial maces. Some were female, some male, others indeterminate, and many displayed horrifying mutation traits. Gaunt couldn't tell – didn't want to tell – what the variations in dress and decoration denoted. They were all enemies. But they intrigued him nevertheless. In his career, he had faced the warriors and the devotees of the Ruinous Powers in many guises, but this was the first time he had properly laid eyes on the dignitaries and officials who ordered their culture and society. These were the fiends who followed the smouldering wake of battle and established rule and control over the territories conquered by their warrior hosts.

Once the parade had passed, the three men hurried on into the low pavements where the town's administratum buildings had once stood. Here, the faces of the broken walls and chipped plasterwork were covered with paint daubs and scribbles that made nonsense words and strange designs. In one large square, lit by fierce bonfires, hundreds of human slaves laboured under the attentive guns of excubitor squads. The slaves, some on makeshift ladders, were painting more designs on the open walls.

'Petitioners,' Landerson whispered. 'Or criminals trying to atone for minor infractions. They labour day and night until they either drop of exhaustion, or make a mark that is deemed true.'

'True?' Mkoll echoed.

'The enemy does not teach its signs and symbols, except to the converted. It is said they believe that those touched with Chaos will know the marks instinctively. So the petitioners make random marks, scribing anything and everything their imagination comes up with. If they make any mark or sign that the ordinals recognise, they are taken away for purification and conversion.'

Amongst the gangs of excubitors, three ordinals lurked, overseeing the insane graffiti. One of them sat astride a mechanical hobbyhorse, a bizarre machine whose body rose above its small wheels on four thin, strut-like legs. The ordinal trundled around on his high perch, shouting orders. He looked like a child with a nursery plaything, as dreamed up in a nightmare. There was nothing childish about the twin stubber pintle-mounted in place of the hobbyhorse's head, though.

Avoiding the square, they darted from cover across an empty street and into the breezeway opposite. This was a narrow rockcrete passage, which smelt of urine. At the far end of it, behind a row of overflowing garbage canisters, was a low hatch.

Landerson glanced at Gaunt. 'Let's pray they haven't found this one too,' he said.

'Let's,' Gaunt said, and looked round at Mkoll. At his commander's nod, Mkoll vanished into the shadows.

Landerson stepped up to the hatch and knocked. After a moment, it opened slightly.

'How is Gereon?' asked an echo from behind the hatch.

'Gereon lives,' Landerson replied.

'Despite their efforts,' the echo responded. The hatch opened.

Landerson and Gaunt stepped into the darkness.

They'd gone no more than five paces into the darkness when rifle snouts poked against their backs.

'On your faces! Down! Now! On your faces!'

'Wait, we–' Landerson began. He grunted as a rifle stock rammed his neck.

'Down! Now! Now!'

They got down. Hands clawed at them, fishing out weapons, forcing shoulders flat. Boots came in and kicked their legs apart.

'Get on your faces, you bastards!' a voice barked.

A lamp pack suddenly flicked on and bathed the chamber in light.

'I so, so wouldn't be doing that if I were you,' Mkoll said from the doorway, his lasrifle aimed.

'MY APOLOGIES, COLONEL-COMMISSAR,' said Major Cirk.

'Not necessary,' Gaunt replied. 'I understand the rigorous nature of your security.'

She shrugged. 'Your man would have had us dead even so.'

They looked across as Mkoll, who was sitting with his back against the chamber wall and his rifle across his lap, observing the scene.

'Yes, he would,' said Gaunt. 'But as far as I know, he's the best there is, so don't beat yourself up.'

The chamber was small, and lit by a single chemical fire in the corner. Six ragged resistance fighters sat in a huddle with Landerson, talking quietly. Another two, armed with homemade charge-guns, watched the door.

'The scare today,' Cirk asked. 'Did you trigger it?'

'I'm afraid so,' Gaunt replied. 'We got into a duel with a couple of patrols. We were trying to make contact.'

She nodded. 'They've closed a lot of our outlets down. After last night.'

'What was last night?' Gaunt asked.

Cirk sighed. She was a tall woman in her early forties, with cropped brunette hair and a face made fabulous by high cheekbones and a full mouth. She might once have been beautiful, voluptuous. Food shortages had thinned her frame, drawing her face and emphasizing her breasts and hips. Her fatigues were ill-fitting. 'Last night,' she said, 'we staged a diversion.'

'A diversion?'

'To get you in, sir.'

Gaunt nodded. The idea stuck painfully.

'The cell deployed, and staged attacks at various key locations to occupy the attention of the archenemy forces. The idea was to draw focus away from the team contacting you. We were successful.'

'Define success.'

'Three tactical targets hit. Forty per cent casualties. The reprisals shut down a lot of our active houses. Four out of nine in Ineuron Town. Another half dozen in the agriburbs.'

'How many dead?'

'Dead? Or captured, sixty-eight.'

'I was supposed to link up with a colonel called Ballerat,' Gaunt said.

'Dead,' she replied. 'Killed last night in the firebomb raid on the Iconoclave. I'm cell leader now.'

There was no emotion in her voice, and nothing on show in her face. Like Landerson, like everyone on Gereon, Cirk had been through too many miseries to register much of anything any more.

'We've actually closed up shop here,' Cirk said. 'Ineuron's too hot now. What's left of the underground here has fled. Except for a few skeleton units like mine.'

Gaunt nodded. 'Waiting for us.'

She nodded back. 'Contacting and aiding you was a vital function. That much was passed down the line to Ballerat and me.'

'From where?' Gaunt asked.

'Not for me to say, sir. The underground only survives by compartmentalising its strengths. No one gets more than they need to know. That way, if anyone is captured…'

She let it hang.

'I understand,' said Gaunt. 'And I'm grateful to you.'

'Don't be,' she said simply.

'All right. But understand that my gratitude comes from a much higher place.'

'That's enough for me,' said Cirk. 'So, what do you need?'

'Immediately? I need to get word to the rest of my outfit. Let them know we're good.'

'Are they voxed?' she asked.

Gaunt nodded.

'All right, we have access to a set. I don't like to use it, but it's better that than trying to get a runner out of the town just now. Can your message be short?'

'Yes. Two words. "Silver" and "standby".'

'Good. Channel?'

'Anything between two-four-four and three-one on the tight high-band.'

Cirk beckoned over one of her team, a thin blonde girl who looked no more than a teenager.

She gave her careful instructions, and the girl slipped out into the night.

'Right,' said Cirk. 'What else?'

Gaunt paused. He thought for a moment about the bitter wranglings he'd already had with Landerson. 'Let

me ask, first of all, what are your thoughts about liberation?'

Cirk stared at him. She was truly beautiful, he realised,
but the mix of lingering pain and beauty was almost too
hard to look at. The stigma mark cut into her cheek both
marred her beauty and reminded Gaunt of the poison
infecting Gereon. 'I understand it's not coming any time
soon, sir,' she said.

'You do?'

'First off, I'm not a fool. Second, Ballerat briefed me.
We didn't share the information with too many of the
cell members. Bad for security and bad for morale. But I
know you're here for an insertion mission, not as the
vanguard of some glorious counter invasion.'

Gaunt sighed. 'I'm relieved. Breaking that to Landerson was hard. I'd have hated to see the same
disappointment on your face.'

'Why?' she asked, interested.

'Not for me to say,' he replied.

She smirked and sat back. 'So what is next?'

'You don't know what we're here for?'

'Compartmentalised, remember? Ballerat and I were
privy to the fact you were an insertion mission, but I
don't think even he knew what that might be.'

'I'm here to kill someone,' Gaunt said quietly.

'Anyone in particular?' she asked. 'From what I've
heard Landerson say, you've been clocking up quite a
body count already.'

'Yes,' said Gaunt. 'Someone very particular. An old
friend.'

Cirk stroked her cheek and grinned. 'There were
inverted commas around that word, if I'm not mistaken.'

'You're not.'

'Who is he?'

'I didn't even say it was a he.'

'Compartmentalising, colonel-commissar?'

'Indeed.'

'Fine. I'd rather not know, actually. This old "friend"…
I imagine you want to find him?'

'I do,' said Gaunt. 'I need the underground to furnish
me and my team with passage into the Lectica heartlands.'

She exhaled heavily. 'Shit! You don't want much, do
you?'

'Is that going to be a problem?'

Cirk leaned forward again. He could smell her stale
sweat and the grease in her cropped hair. 'If you needed
to get into the heartlands, you could have picked a better starting point than Ineuron Town.'

'Because?' asked Gaunt.

'Because you're about three hundred kilometres south
of where you want to be.'

'I know,' Gaunt replied. 'But this is a slow-burn operation. Guard Intelligence was conferring secretly with the
Gereon underground for months before we set off. A safe
drop point was the first priority. The underground advised
that the marshes south of Shedowtonland would be the
safest territory to make a rapid drop from a lander. Anything closer to Lectica would have been too hazardous.'

'True enough,' she said. 'You came in by lander?'

'By grav-chute from a low flyby over the marshes, actually.'

'Holy crap, that can't have been any fun.'

'It wasn't. When the time came, my marksman refused
at the hatch. His name's Larkin. He's not the most
together man in my command.'

'What did you do?' asked Cirk.

'I had Brostin – the biggest man in the team – throw
Larkin out of the lander. He's come to terms since then.'

Cirk laughed. He liked her laugh.

'What were you, Cirk? Before the enemy came, I
mean?'

She hesitated and looked at the flames of the pallid
chemical fire. 'I was a farm-owner, sir. My family held

two thousand hectares west of the town. Canterwheat and soft fruit. The bastards torched my orchards.'

'What's your name?' he asked.

'I'm Major Cirk of the Ineuron undergr–'

'I asked your name. Mine's Ibram.'

'My name is Sabbatine Cirk,' she said.

Gaunt paused, as if he had been slapped.

'What is it?' she asked.

'Named after the Saint, I imagine?'

'Of course,' she said.

'Everywhere I go, she's there to lead me…' Gaunt murmured.

'Sir?'

'Nothing. So, what about Lectica?'

'I'll see what I can do. We have a line of contact with the Edrian cell. They might be able to get you cross country and into Lectica. After that, we'll be relying on their contacts in the field.'

'That's a start,' Gaunt said.

SEVEN

ANOTHER DAY ROSE, languid, above the bastion. The pheguth had been undergoing transcoding for the better part of the morning. Desolane had heard his screams rolling up and down the windy halls.

Desolane went to the day room to review security. Light spilled in through the barred windows. Assisted by a half-dozen warriors in enamelled green armour, three ordinals were sorting the report dockets and adjusting the light-pins on the chart table.

'Anything interesting?' Desolane asked.

One of the ordinals looked up. 'A lively night, lifeward. Insurrectionists torched the temple in Phatima, and an underground cell assassinated two ordinals in Brovisia Town. A firebomb. Excubitor reprisals have been rapid and thorough. A decimation order has been placed on Brovisia Town.'

'Anything else?' Desolane wondered.

'This, from the south provinces,' said another ordinal, holding out a data-slate. Desolane took it and reviewed it. 'Ineuron Town? Where the hell is that?'

'South of here, life-ward, in the marshlands, along the edge of the Untill. A minor farming centre. Last night there was a flurry of insurrectionist attacks. A great deal of damage. It is now contained.'

'You think so?' Desolane asked.

'Life-ward?'

Desolane tapped the slate. 'Did you not study the detail? An excubitor patrol slaughtered in the farm lands. Las-weapons used. And a firefight against unknowns in the town itself that was so furious it woke the wirewolves there.'

'Local governance has control of the situation, life-ward,' said one of the ordinals.

'They don't know what they're dealing with,' Desolane growled. 'Las-weapons? You simple fools! Since when has the underground been using las-weapons?'

The ordinals fell silent. They were powerful beings of great substance, but they quailed in fear before one of the Anarch's own life-wards.

'Inform the office of the Plenipotentiary, but advise him we have the matter in hand.'

The ordinals bowed their heads and covered their mouths with one hand. 'We serve the word of the Anarch, whose word drowns out all others,' they chorused.

'And once you've done that,' said Desolane, 'get me Uexkull.'

DESOLANE WAITED FOR Uexkull in the annexe outside the day room. Two of the bastion's antlered footmen appeared at the far end of the annexe, dragging the pheguth between them from the transcoding chamber. The pheguth was shivering and retching, barely conscious.

'Be careful with him, you idiots!' Desolane shouted. 'Take him to his chamber.'

The footmen nodded, and began heaving the limp human up the marble stairs towards the tower room.

Fifteen minutes passed, and then Desolane heard boots thumping across the inner hall. Desolane rose, expecting Uexkull, but it was Mabbon Etogaur.

Desolane had divided feelings about the etogaur, but was prepared to admire him. Mabbon Etogaur had commanded many signal victories for the Anarch.

'Etogaur, good day,' Desolane said.

'Life-ward, my greeting. Is this fair time to talk with the pheguth?'

'Not the best. He's been in transcoding all morning. He'll be weak.'

'Even so.'

'Go on up. Wait for me, and I will take you in to see him.'

Mabbon nodded. 'Thank you.'

The etogaur had been gone for five minutes when Uexkull arrived. Attended by a coterie of four Chaos Marines, Uexkull clanked down the long hall in his burnished power armour, vapour wisping from the smoke-stacks rising from his back. He towered over Desolane, but still made an effort to bow.

'Life-ward,' he creaked. Uexkull's voice was hard as leather. Dry, stiff, calloused. 'You sent for me?'

'Yes, magir. I'd like you to look at this.' Desolane handed him the data-slate.

Uexkull's massive armoured hand took hold of the device almost daintily. He reviewed it. 'Las-fire,' he creaked.

'Indeed.'

'A patrol annihilated.'

'It speaks volumes, does it not?' Desolane said.

'Ineuron's a backwater.'

'Yes, but someone's there. Probably because it's a backwater.'

'Astartes?'

'No, I don't think so.' Desolane said. The huge warrior looked disappointed. 'But mission specialists. Guard. You know what to do.'

Uexkull nodded. 'Find them. Kill them. Gnaw on their bones.'

'The last part is optional,' Desolane said.

'Consider it done, life-ward,' said Uexkull.

AT DESOLANE'S INSTRUCTION, the footmen had taken the pheguth out onto the terrace. The fresh air and sunlight seemed to rouse him from his sickness a little, but there was still a palsied droop to one side of the pheguth's face that concerned Desolane. Perhaps they were pushing the transcoding too hard. The life-ward would consult a master of fisyk.

The terrace was a machicolated parapet crowning a huge talus at the north end of the bastion. The grey stone of the talus dropped away three hundred metres into the dark and ragged gorge beneath. From the terrace, unaided, it was possible to see nearly a hundred kilometres out across the heartland. The mountains rose, hard and angular, to all sides, and off to the west climbed higher than the perilous bastion itself, forming great, snow-capped summits that framed the distance in veils of icy mist and bright low cloud.

Beyond the rampart mountains, the vast farmlands of the midland bocage covered the land to the horizon with a lush green patchwork.

Desolane brought the pheguth a cloak. It was chilly on the exposed terrace, with a fresh, buffeting wind. The life-ward was sure that the pheguth would do nothing foolish, but instructed the footmen to lock the pheguth's ankle-cuff to an iron ring.

'You think I might end my life, Desolane?' the pheguth asked. 'Hurl myself into the oblivion of the gorge below?'

'I think it unlikely,' said Desolane. 'To have suffered and contended with so much only to submit now would seem... weak. And I do not believe you are a weak man. However, even strong men have moments of weakness, and the transcoding has not been kind.'

'You're right,' said the pheguth. 'Oblivion is quite attractive to me just now.'

'Perhaps conversation will divert your mind. The eto-gaur craves audience.'

The footmen led Mabbon Etogaur out onto the ter-race. One carried a tray of refreshment. Then Desolane withdrew, leaving one footman to watch the entry.

Mabbon Etogaur looked out over the towering scene for a moment, then offered his pale, soft hand to the pheguth as he had done the day before.

'Sit down,' said the pheguth. Mabbon took a place at the other end of the iron bench.

'How is your health, sir?' he asked.

'Not as rude as I would like. I'm sure the psykers are trying to be gentle, but every session leaves me feeling as if I have been adrift in warp space.'

'Transcoding is a necessary evil,' said Mabbon. 'Why do you smile, sir?'

'It surprises me to hear you use the word "evil". I am well aware of its importance. My life depends upon it. If my mind cannot be transcoded, and its secrets unlocked, I am of very little use to you or your masters.'

'I believe you will be useful to me,' said Mabbon.

'Indeed? What shall we talk about then?'

'The one thing we both know,' said Mabbon Etogaur. 'Soldiering.'

ANA CURTH RINSED her mouth with the last water in her flask and spat in the weeds. They'd been confined to the grain silos for a day and a night, and the rancid dusty interiors – which by day became hot, sweltering, rancid dusty interiors – had made her hoarse and plugged her sinuses. She hoped to the God-Emperor that prolonged exposure to yeast mould and other airborne spores had not complicated the agues they would all be suffering from soon.

It was good at least to be outside for a spell. Bonin had found a small stone well at the edge of the ramshackle property from which issued water that, if not exactly potable, could be efficiently refined using the decontam tabs they carried in their packs. Curth, desperate for air, had volunteered to go and fill all the water bottles.

It was nearly midday. The sun was harsh and bright, and she was grateful for the shade along the track. Sickly trees clustered together along the side of the muddy yard, and insects sizzled in the merrymach and the hanging flowers. The yard, the morass, was slowly baking hard in the sunlight and exuding a strong, fecal odour. A stronger scent still came from a plank-covered silage pit halfway down the track.

But her mood was better, and it wasn't just the open air. After a night of waiting, they'd got the message by vox just before dawn. Curth had been beginning to think that they'd never see Gaunt or Mkoll again. The sounds that had been coming from the town during the night…

Even Rawne had seemed alarmed. On another occasion, the news that Gaunt was dead and he was in charge would have been like all his paydays rolled into one. But not here. Not now.

The well was a little stone post over a drain grate, with an iron tap fastened to the post. Curth found it easily enough, clutching the empty water bottles to her body to stop them knocking. She pulled a few strands of weed away and turned the tap. After a moment, brackish water began to spatter out.

She unstoppered the first flask, filled it from the flow, dropped in one of the tabs from her pocket, then rescrewed the top and gave the flask a good shake to mix the contents. That was one. She started on the second.

Just as she was about to start filling the fourth bottle, she heard a sound that made her turn off the faucet and listen in silence. An engine. She was sure she'd heard an engine from the direction of the road. Traffic had come and gone through the morning, and each time they'd laid low.

Nothing went past. Just her imagination then, or the sound of the splashing tap coming back from the leaves.

She picked up the fourth bottle and reached for the tap.

A hand closed over her mouth.

Curth went rigid with fear.

'It's me,' a whisper said into her ear. 'Don't make a sound.'

The hand came away. Curth looked round. Varl stood behind her, his finger to his lips. He saw the question in her eyes and pointed towards the roadway. She couldn't see anything.

Varl edged round the well. His rifle was slung over his back, but he'd drawn his autopistol. He beckoned her after him. She followed, forcing her feet to remember the basic stealth techniques Mkoll had drilled into her before the mission.

They moved into the thicker undergrowth under the trees. The road was a sun-bathed space beyond the black trunks. Varl suddenly went so still she almost bumped into him. He pulled her down until they were kneeling in the weeds.

A figure moved past on the road, little more than a silhouette. The silhouette had hard edges – a pack, a helmet, shoulder guards, a weapon. It was moving slowly in the direction of the silos. In less than minute, a second figure passed the same way.

This time Varl got a better look. Gleaming green combat armour, unit patches of a shouting or singing human mouth on the shoulder guards.

A military outfit.

Varl squirmed forward through the foliage and got a view out down the dusty, sunlit road. About two hundred metres down the rutted trackway, a quad-track troop carrier was parked in the shade of some mature talix trees. A squad of enemy troopers – Varl counted at least a dozen – was fanning out along the road towards the silo.

What was this? A chance patrol? A betrayal? Or had they somehow given their hiding place away? Varl screwed his body back into the undergrowth and thought hard for a moment. Curth was looking at him, rising panic in her eyes. He couldn't risk the vox, even a simple mic-tap. The hostiles had comm-sets and might well be listening.

He beckoned her again, and they slithered back the way they'd come, heading down to the path where the well stood. They'd have to sneak back around through the yard and carry the warning in person.

Curth grabbed his arm. Another hostile had just stepped into view on the overgrown path, near to the well. They'd put part of their force in through the treeline to encircle the silos. There was no way, no fething way in creation, that Varl could get himself back to the agri-plex now without being seen.

He closed his eyes. *Think, man, think…*

Varl cupped one hand around the other in a curious conjunction of grips and raised them to his mouth. Curth stared at him as though he was a lunatic.

He blew.

AT THE REAR of the silos, Brostin stood in the shade of the eaves. He'd told Rawne he was going out to take a leak, but he really just wanted to quell his cravings. He slipped one of the lho-sticks from their waterproof packet and put it between his lips. Ven had been straight as silver about this: no smoking, under any circumstances. What Brostin wouldn't give to light the thing. And not for the draw of smoke. Not so much. Really, what he craved to see was the tiny flame cupped in his gnarled hands. Larkin often called him a pyromaniac. Like it was a bad thing.

'Of course, you weren't going to light that, were you?' Bonin asked quietly. Brostin started. Fething scouts, popping out of nowhere.

'Course not,' he said.

'Course not,' Bonin echoed, leaning against the silo's side in the shade beside him.

'Just reminding myself of the feel of it.'

'That's fine.'

Bonin suddenly straightened up, listening. 'You hear that?' he hissed.

'What?'

'That. Just then.'

'Mmm. Yeah, Just a treecrake. Nesting, probably.'

Bonin drew his pistol. 'Get inside. Tell Rawne.'

'Tell Rawne what?'

'Since when were there Tanith treecrakes here… or anywhere else, for that matter?'

EIGHT

CLOSE TO THE well, the enemy trooper paused and looked round into the undergrowth. He'd heard the odd, warbling call. He raised his weapon to his chest and began to advance.

Varl and Curth lay as flat in the brambles and weeds as they could. Slowly, very slowly, Varl slid his warknife out of its sheath.

The armoured trooper stopped suddenly, glancing down. Curth knew exactly what he'd seen. Ten Guard-issue water bottles on the grass beside the well.

Bending, the trooper reached up to activate his helmet vox.

Varl slammed into him, knocking him off his feet. The silver blade plunged in but glanced sideways off the shoulder armour. The trooper fought back, shoving Varl sideways. Undeterred, Varl punched the knife up under the helmet's chinstrap. The trooper rolled away, clutching his throat. Blood was pouring out more copiously than the water had flowed from the tap. The man got upright, gurgling. Varl grabbed him by the shoulders and slammed him, face-first, against the top of the well post. There was an ugly crunch.

Varl caught the deadweight before it hit the ground and dragged it into the undergrowth. Then he went back for the water bottles, pausing briefly to make the call again.

SILENTLY, SPURRED BY quick hand signals, the troop patrol came up around the silos. Insects ratcheted in the noon heat. The heavy boots of the combat detail made only slight, dull sounds on the dry earth. Some fanned out along the front of the silos, others slipped down the track and came around the rear, panning their weapons. In teams of two, they came up to the flaking doors of the silos.

THE LONG FIELD ended in a line of trees, and was covered down its entire length by rotting propagation frames around which soft fruits had once been trained. A rotten organic mulch festered in the trenches under the frames.

Cirk took a quick bearing and moved the team into cover in the field's hedge. They crouched down with her, two of her own cell members, as well as Gaunt, Mkoll and Landerson.

'We're close,' she said. 'The road's beyond those trees, and the agri-plex is down that way, about a kilometre.'

Mkoll nodded. That agreed with his own mental map, which was seldom wrong. The shifting forests of Tanith bred an unerring sense of direction in its sons.

'We should have range now,' Gaunt said. He adjusted his micro-bead.

'One,' he said. There was a pause.

Then a single word reply. 'Bragg.' Then the vox channels went entirely dead.

'We've got trouble,' Gaunt said to Cirk.

* * *

THE PATROL COMMANDER, who bore the distinguished rank of sirdar, moved down the track from the road, checking his team's disposition. He was sweating in the heat inside his taut combat armour and presently wished a doom upon this stinking world worse than the one his kind had already visited upon it. His unit, along with a dozen like it, had been called up from the Ineuron garrison first thing that morning with orders to sweep the surrounding countryside. A job for excubitor crews, not combat troops, surely? Still, the alerts in the night had been extreme, and word was the martial response had been ordered by a senior ordinal. Another report said that Uexkull himself was en route to take charge, and the last thing the sirdar commander wanted was to be found shirking his duties by that monster.

They'd searched six deserted farmsteads that morning already. This one promised no more than the last, but the sirdar had remained true to his briefing. They'd left their transport back down the road and advanced on foot in a quiet, spread operation.

He reached the yard, and was about to give the signal to enter. The pincer squad had now moved up from the treeline ditches, and the place was pretty much surrounded, although it seemed as if one of the squad was missing. Lost in the woods, probably. The sirdar decided that when the trooper turned up, he'd shoot him himself and save Uexkull the bother.

He raised his hand, then paused. He'd distinctly heard a vox signal, and it wasn't from his squad. Only the resistance had vox-sets…

The sirdar commander felt a prickle of anticipation. They were on to something. He drew his sidearm, and then made three quick hand gestures: contact suspected, lethal force, go.

His troops went in.

* * *

A SILO DOOR splintered open. Two armoured troopers thrust into the gloom, weapons raised. They crunched forward. Just heaps of mouldering grain. One looked up. Rafters, crossbeams. Shadows and cobwebs. The place was empty. They turned to leave.

Bonin and Feygor, knives drawn, rose up out of the spoiled crop heaps behind them, grain streaming off them in hissing rivulets, and seized them by the throats.

THE LATCH ON the storage outhouse parted at a kick. The first trooper in the gloom lit a lamp pack and played it around as his companion covered him with his assault weapon. They advanced into the main shed, which was stacked with old wooden crates. Piles of old hemp sacking covered the floor. The second two troopers went left, into a lean-to area where a rusted threshing machine sat up on blocks. They heard a thump from the main shed and backed up to check it.

The store shed was now empty. There was no sign whatsoever of the duo that had split that way. The troopers edged forward. A shadow seemed to flicker across one of the yellow, dirt-crusted window slits, and they turned rapidly to face it.

But Mkvenner was behind them.

He grabbed one by the edges of his tightly-strapped helmet and wrenched hard, snapping the neck in one twist. The corpse collapsed into the sacking Mkvenner had spread on the floor, its impact muffled. Before it had even landed, Mkvenner had turned, bent low at the waist, and driven the heel of his right foot into the throat of the other hostile. The trooper staggered backwards, unable to breathe, unable to even cry out. He dropped onto his knees, head bowed over, and Mkvenner drove the tip of his fingers down into the man's neck, finishing him off with a click like bone dice knocking together. The man collapsed forward onto his face, and Mkvenner dragged the bodies behind the crate stacks where the first two already lay.

THE END SILO also seemed empty. The two troopers sent in to check it approached the pungent, mildewed grain, searching for somewhere anything bigger than a rat could hide.

The cable shivered down out of the roof space and the noose on the end hooked neatly around the neck of one of them. Before he could exclaim his surprise, it had pulled ferociously tight and he was leaving the ground, feet kicking, hands to his throat.

Criid let gravity do the rest. As she jumped down off the rafter, she dragged the cable after her, and the trooper rose like a counterweight as the cable slid tight over the crossbeam, friction sawing it into the wood. The other trooper turned, astonished, as his companion shot up vertically into the roof, and she pendulumed into him, kicking him backwards onto the grain. Criid let go of the cable. The slicing noose had already finished the first man. Twitching, his body fell hard from the loosed cable.

Criid landed on the other one. She pinned his shoulders and shoved his face down into the polluted grain, her hand clamped around the back of his helmet. After a brief struggle, he went limp.

A trick? Her warknife made sure it wasn't.

THE PATROL'S SIRDAR suddenly realised something wasn't right. There were no signals of contact, no shots, but his men weren't coming back out of the silos and the sheds.

With a violent gesture, he moved the remainder of his unit in across the yard. Those positioned to cover the front now circled in too, down the side of the end silo.

The trooper next to the sirdar commander fell over on his back. Furious, the sirdar turned to reprimand him, then saw the small, bloody hole in the man's glare visor.

On the silo roof, sheltered by a vent hood, Larkin
braced his aim and fired again. Using the silenced
autopistol was no fun, but at least it was a challenge. It
wasn't just a matter of hitting the targets. They were
armoured and would easily shrug off a small cal round,
especially one underpowered by a silencer. The art was
to aim really well and hit them where they were soft.
Visor. Throat. The armpit gap between chest plating and
shoulder guard. Larkin fired off three more shots, and
dropped two more of the hostiles in the caked mud of
the yard.

Coming down the side of the silos from the road, one
of the troopers turned at the sound of a heavy impact
behind him. He saw the man at his heels had been felled
by a devastating blow to the head that had cracked his
helmet. Gleeful, Brostin swung the old threshing flail
he'd found in the shed and smashed the second man
into the clapboard siding of the silo. Wood seams
popped and burst. Rawne rose up out of the undergrowth and cut down the last two before they could take
a pop at Brostin. His silenced gun spat.

Then he and Brostin hurried down to the end of the
path and added their quiet firepower to Larkin's. The
final few troopers crumpled in the yard.

The sirdar had started running, along with his last surviving man. The silent sniper on the roof shot the man
through the neck just short of the outbuildings, but the
sirdar made it into cover, struggling with his helmet vox,
trying to get a clear channel. He had to warn someone.
He had to get a call out to the other units and–

Nothing. The vox was dead. Like it was being jammed.
How was that even possible?

On the straw-littered floor of the shed in front of him,
the sirdar saw an Imperial field-vox set, infantry issue. It
was powered up and active, the dials set to a white noise
broadcast that would wipe vox contact, at least anything
in the locality of the farm.

The sirdar commander took a step towards it.

The silencer of an autopistol pressed into the side of his head.

'Something awry, sir?' Beltayn asked, and pulled the trigger.

NINE

'ONE,' GAUNT SAID softly. They'd been lying low for over fifteen minutes, and this was the third time he'd tried the link. Now at least there was a background fizzle on the channel that suggested the link was finally live again. The sudden, jammed deadness had made his heart race.

'One,' he repeated.

'Silver.'

They moved off quickly, along the drainage ditch on the field side of the road, with Mkoll at the front. A little way down, they sighted the quad-track carrier parked on a dusty verge under the trees.

Mkoll shot a look at Gaunt.

'Occupation troopers,' whispered Cirk.

They pushed on and cautiously crossed the dry road-pan to the silos of the ruined agri-plex. The place lay still and silent in the hot afternoon. Insects buzzed. The hazed, polluted sky had broiled to a toxic ochre laced with sickly clouds.

121

Mkoll suddenly brought his weapon up. Bonin appeared from behind a low fence. He smiled. 'Good to see you,' he called.

They jogged up to join him. Bonin clapped his hand against Mkoll's briefly extended palm in a simple acknowledgement, then led them down the track to the rear of the silos.

Rawne and the others were dragging the enemy corpses into the yard and heaping them up. Feygor and Brostin were busy pilfering pockets and packs for anything useful. Or valuable. Most things they tossed aside: ugly charms, unholy texts printed into tiny chapbooks, inedible or inexplicable rations. Even gold coins lost their lustre to seasoned looters like Feygor when they came stamped with a mark of the Ruinous Powers.

'Been busy, major?' Gaunt asked.

Rawne looked up and shrugged. 'They came looking, so we showed them some Tanith hospitality.'

'Any survivors?' Mkoll asked.

Rawne gave the scout sergeant a withering look. 'Mkvenner's sweeping the area to double-check, but I think we were pretty thorough.'

'And very discreet,' Feygor added.

Cirk looked at the crumpled bodies and raised one eyebrow. 'That's... a whole unit,' she said.

Rawne shrugged. 'They didn't get off a single shot. And we didn't make a sound.' He turned to Gaunt. 'Who's this?' he asked.

'The contact we were after,' said Gaunt. 'Major Rawne, Major Cirk.'

They nodded to each other.

'The others are with her. Acreson and Plower. That's right, isn't it?'

Cirk nodded again. The two cell members who had accompanied her were greeting Purchason and Lefivre. The underground was a close-bonded group.

'As soon as they're listed overdue, the enemy will come looking,' Cirk said, gesturing to the dead.

'We'll be long gone,' Gaunt assured her. 'Rawne. Assemble the team and make ready to move out. Major Cirk's here to direct us to our next point of contact.'

'Good. I'm tired of waiting,' Rawne said.

'Anywhere we can dump these bodies out of sight?' Gaunt asked.

'The silos?' Bonin suggested.

'First place they'll look,' Cirk said.

'There's a silage pit down that way,' Varl said, walking over and wiping his dagger on a handful of straw.

'Let's do that,' Gaunt agreed. Brostin, Varl, Feygor and Bonin began hefting the corpses away down the track.

'What about the transport?' Landerson asked. 'That's not so easy to hide.'

'We could use a transport,' Mkoll said quietly. Gaunt looked at him.

'It's big enough,' Mkoll added. 'And they're less likely to stop a military vehicle.'

Gaunt paused thoughtfully and glanced sidelong at Cirk. She shrugged. 'It's a risk, but then so's everything. It would certainly shave some time off our journey. Edrian Province is a good sixty kilometres away. I was anticipating a couple of days to reach it on foot.'

'We'll take the transport,' Gaunt decided. 'At least for now. We can ditch it if needs be. Varl and Feygor both have some experience handling heavy rides.' He turned and called out down the track towards the men sliding bodies into the pit. 'Varl! Save two sets of armour. Helmet and shoulder guards at least!'

'Sir!' Varl called back. 'Can we wash them first?'

'Do what you have to.'

Gaunt walked across the yard and joined Curth. She was seated on the cross-spar of an abandoned mould-board plough, checking her narthecium. 'Good to have you back,' she said. There was real feeling in her voice.

'Any trouble?' he asked.

'Apart from the obvious?' she said, with a nod to the dead.

'I mean the sort of thing a military surgeon shares with her mission commander.'

'Ague's taking a hold. Beltayn and Criid are both complaining of head colds, like pollen fever. Feygor's running a temperature, though he won't admit it, and he seems to be developing an infection in the flesh around his augmetic voicebox. I've given him another shot, and I'm keeping an eye on it. Larkin says he's fine, but he's sleeping badly. Nightmares. I heard him. He was talking to Bragg in his sleep. Talking to the dead. Can't be a good sign.'

'With Larks, that's borderline normal.'

She smiled at his cruelty. 'Brostin's just edgy. Bad-tempered.'

'Again, borderline normal. That's just withdrawal. Brostin would be chain-smoking lho-sticks under usual circumstances.'

'Ah,' she said. A pause. 'I know the feeling.'

'Anything else?'

'Everyone's tired. More than ordinary fatigue. And everyone's got this.' She pulled back her cuff. Her pale forearm was dotted with a prickle pattern like angry heat rash. 'Allergic reaction. I was wondering if it was the spores in those damn silos.'

Gaunt shook his head. He yanked down his own collar and showed her a comparable rash along the base of his neck and collarbone. 'We've all got it. It's an allergic reaction, all right. To this world. To the taint here. Major Cirk says it afflicted everyone on Gereon in the first few weeks after the invasion. When it fades... that's when I'll worry. Because that's when we're acclimatised.'

'When we've become tainted?' she asked.

He shrugged.

'Major Cirk,' Curth said, squinting across the yard at the resistance officer, who was standing in conference with her men and Landerson. 'She's… a good looking woman, don't you think?'

'Can't say I gave it any thought,' Gaunt replied.

'I'd better check you over,' Curth said, getting up. 'It would appear the taint of Gereon is suppressing your hormones.'

He chuckled. 'Check yourself too, Ana. Gereon may have a contagious strain of jealousy.'

She smacked him on the arm. 'In your dreams, colonel-commissar,' she smirked; and walked away.

Gaunt watched her go. He thought about his dreams. For so long now, they had been haunted by the beati, by Saint Sabbat. It felt as if she'd been in his mind forever, from the aching alpine vistas of Hagia to that small, neglected chapel in the woods on Aexe Cardinal. Guiding him, leading him, confusing him. Sometimes he dreamed of Sanian, and sometimes poor Vamberfeld appeared, bleeding from the nine holy wounds he had taken at the Shrinehold as the Saint's proxy.

Gaunt's life and his destiny was tied to the Saint now, he knew that. It had been ordained by some higher power, and he hoped with all his soul that power sat upon a golden throne.

Herodor, bloody Herodor, just a year gone by now, had been a watershed. Gaunt had presumed that a face to face encounter with the Saint Incarnate might have exorcised his dreams. But, if anything, the dreams had grown worse in the time since then. His sleep was visited by the Saint in her glory, so beautiful it made him weep and awake with tears streaking his face. Figures attended her, half-seen in the mists of his swirling visions, people he missed dearly. Old Slaydo sometimes, hunched and pale. Bragg, dear Try Again Bragg, looking around himself in wonder at the enfolding darkness. Sometimes, very occasionally, Colm Corbec, laughing and calling to Gaunt to join him. Behind Corbec, every time he came, a proud honour guard of ghosts waited, rifles shouldered… Baffels, Adare, Lerod, Blane, Doyl, Cocoer, Cluggan, Gutes, Muril…

Gaunt shook the memory away. Despite the stifling heat in the silo yard, he felt cold sweat leak down his spine. Ghosts. Ghosts he had made, and then made ghosts.

Most chilling of all, he remembered, was the screaming. The dream where there was only darkness and a man's voice screaming piteously through it. Who was that? Who *was* that? He seemed to recognise the voice, but…

It seemed so helpless and so far away.

And not once, not once since Herodor, had he dreamed of the one face he missed more than any other, more even than Colm. Brin Milo had never featured in any of his dreams.

There was one final fact that nagged at his mind. From the moment he had set foot on Gereon, he had not dreamed at all. Months of dreams and faces and hauntings, and now not one, as if the watchful spirits could no longer reach him on this poisoned planet.

That was why he had responded so strongly to Cirk. To Sabbatine Cirk.

It had been the first clue he'd had since his arrival that the Saint had not forgotten him.

'Do we really have to go through this again today?' the pheguth sighed.

'We do,' said Desolane, walking him down the stone hallway. 'You do, pheguth.'

'I'm tired,' the pheguth said.

'I know,' Desolane replied. There was something close to compassion in the life-ward's musical voice. 'But demands are being made. Plenipotentiary Isidor is under pressure from host-command. It is said that the Anarch himself, whose word we serve and whose word drowns out all others, is frustrated at the lack of progress. As a resource, you promise much, pheguth, but you have yet to deliver. Great Sek may yet regard you as a waste of energy and have you executed if you don't yield up your secrets.'

The pheguth considered this, a slight smile creasing his face. His conversation with Mabbon Etogaur had revealed much about Magister Sek's plans. Too much, perhaps. It was clear to the pheguth now that Magister Anakwanar Sek, lord of hosts, Anarch, chosen warlord of the Archon Urlock Gaur himself, had ideas above his station. Sek wanted power. Control. Command. And the bastard considered the traitor general a key instrument in obtaining that power.

The pheguth remembered some of the briefings he had sat through as a high commander of the Imperial Guard. At Balhaut, the Crusade had destroyed Nadzybar, who had been the Archon of the Chaos host. Broken in retreat, the archenemy forces had been riven by a succession struggle as Chaos factions warred to elect a new Archon. Many of the notorious magister-warlords had been in contention – Nokad the Blighted, Sholen Skara, Qux of the Eyeless, Heritor Asphodel, Enok Innokenti. Rumour had it that more of the archenemy numbers were killed in that internecine war of succession than had been lost to the Crusade armada at that time.

Of all the contenders, Nokad had the charisma, Asphodel the temperament, and Qux the sheer weight of loyal servants. But Sek, Anakwanar Sek (whose word we serve, the pheguth reminded himself, and whose word drowns out all others) was the obvious choice. No other magister was quite so brilliant a battlefield technician. Sek's command of tactics and leadership was peerless, better than Slaydo, better than Macaroth himself.

Damn the Warmaster's life and name.

But Gaur, an obscure warlord from the fringes of the Sabbat Worlds, had become Archon. Why? Because he possessed the one thing that all the other magisters lacked. Even the great and blasphemous Sek.

What Urlock Gaur brought to the table was a refined, trained and disciplined military force. All the other magisters commanded vast legions of zealot cultists and insane worshippers. Hideous forces, but utterly without focus, and vulnerable to the rigid drive of the Imperial Guard.

Urlock Gaur's host was known as the Blood Pact. They were sworn to him, utterly loyal, their bodies ritually scarred by the serrated edges of Gaur's own armour. They had discipline, armour, tactical ability and great combat skill. They were, in fact, an army, not a host.

The pheguth had never encountered the Blood Pact in action, but he knew of them from intelligence reports. They were mankind's worst fear, a force of the Ruinous Powers guided and orchestrated on military models. They could meet with and defeat the Imperial Guard on its own terms, out-fighting them.

For the simple reason that the Blood Pact was modelled directly on the structure of the Imperial Guard.

They borrowed their weapons and armour, they stole their uniforms, they seduced Guardsmen into their ranks and made them traitors, stealing their skills. They were a force the Imperium must reckon with, and they had secured Gaur the rank of Archon.

Throne take them, they might even have the skill to drive Macaroth's Crusade back out of these stars.

And that, very simply, is what Sek wanted. He reviled Gaur for his success. Sek wanted, yearned, longed, to be named Archon. He was biding his time, playing the part of a loyal magister to the most high Archon. But he prized that rank as his own. He felt he deserved it. He was, by any measure, a finer leader than Gaur.

And the first step along the way was to build a Blood Pact of his own. A fully and finely trained military force as good as, if not better than, the Blood Pact.

This was the delicate matter Mabbon Etogaur had spoken to him about. Mabbon – and how very much the pheguth had warmed to the fellow – was a traitor in his own right. Etogaur was a Blood Pact rank. Mabbon had, by means the pheguth could not imagine, been tempted away from Gaur's service and employed by Sek to use his knowledge of the Blood Pact's workings to forge a similar force.

Gereon was the base for this work. The pheguth, with his intimate knowledge of the Imperial Guard, an invaluable tool. Alongside Mabbon, the pheguth was to use his skills, training and abilities to build the Sek's force.

Mabbon had given it a name during their conversation on the windy terrace: the Sons of Sek. A force of warriors that would eclipse the Blood Pact and defeat, without quarter, the vaunted Imperial Guard.

'Pheguth?' Desolane said. The hatch stood open.

'Are they ready for me?' the pheguth asked.

Desolane nodded.

'Desolane... please understand, I do so want them to learn my secrets,' the pheguth said. 'It's just this...'

'Mindlock,' answered Desolane. The life-ward tapped one finger against its own bronze mask as if to indicate the skull beneath. The taps sounded alarmingly hollow, as if the bronze mask was empty.

The pheguth stepped through the hatch and walked into the small stone chamber. He sat down in his seat. It had been scrubbed and sterilised since his last visit. He settled. The electric cuffs snapped down over his wrists and ankles. The chair rotated backwards until he was staring at the arched roof.

'Pheguth,' a voice whispered.

'Hello,' he replied.

'Again, we begin.'

The pheguth could not see the alien psykers, but he could hear them shuffling close. The chamber went cold.

Icicles formed above him. He braced himself, and his augmetic hand clenched hard against the steel restraints. The psykers edged closer.

Scabby hands reached up and plucked the little rubber plugs from the pre-drilled holes in his skull.

'Gods, how I hate this...' the pheguth murmured.

There was a mechanical whine of servos, and a high pitched shrill. The delicate psi-probe needles, mounted on a bio-mechanical armature, approached his shaved skull and slipped into the holes.

The pheguth convulsed. His mouth opened wide.

'Let us start again at the beginning,' the psi-voice commanded.

'Gaaaah!' the pheguth responded.

'Your rank?'

'Ngghh! General! Lord general!'

'Your name?'

'Nghhh! I can't... I can't remember! I- aghhh!'

'Unlock! You must unlock! Unlock!' the voices called.

'Nyaaaaa! I can't! I can't! I can't!'

Desolane listened for a while, then when the screaming became too much for even the life-ward to bear, it closed the hatch on the transcoding chamber and walked away.

TEN

FOLLOWING CIRK'S GUIDANCE, they drove north, avoiding Ineuron Town and its outlying agri-habs, and joined a major arterial route that ran in a long, straight line across a flat immensity of pasture land. Varl drove, quickly becoming accustomed to the quad-track's spare, functional controls.

There was little traffic. They passed a couple of slow convoys of vittaler wagons plodding towards Ineuron, and a few battered trucks running errands for the occupation with consented locals at their wheels. Once in a while, they sighted figures on the dusty road ahead – refugees and vagabonds – but these ragged souls fled into hiding in the overgrown pastures at the sight of a military transport.

They'd been going for about an hour when Larkin, sharp-eyed as ever, warned them that a vehicle was coming up behind them. Gaunt told Varl to maintain speed and took a look. It was an armoured car, a STeG 4,

lighter and faster than the quad-track. The Ghosts immediately checked their weapons.

Thundering along on its four, big wheels, the STeG
came up behind them and sounded its horn.

'Feth!' Varl said. 'Do they want me to pull over?'

He dropped his speed slightly and edged over towards
the gutter. The armoured car immediately accelerated
and went round them, blasting its horn again. Two
armoured troopers stood in the top of the SteG's cabin
well and waved salutes to their 'comrades' in the quad as
they overtook. Standing up in the quad-track, Bonin
waved back. He was wearing the borrowed helmet and
shoulderguards. His lasrifle was just out of sight behind
the handrail.

The armoured car quickly shot past and pulled away,
leaving pink dust in its wake.

THE PASTURE FLASHING by on either hand was, like so
much of the fecund agri-world's premium land, sadly
neglected. The grasses had grown out, springing tall
and lank, and had dried to straw. The pastures
appeared bleached, like silver wire. Profusions of weed
flowers had flourished: hot red emberlies like spatters
of blood, and millions of white grox-eye daisies.
Gaunt stared at the passing view. The archenemy had
broken Gereon, and tainted it, but even in its undoing
there was accidental beauty like this. A transient glory,
seen by very few, had been produced by miserable
neglect. Not for the first time, Gaunt reflected that
whatever the actions of mankind and the foes of
mankind, the cosmos asserted its own nature in the
strangest ways.

The afternoon began to fade. The seared sky became
a darker, acid green, and then dark clouds began to
heap in the west. Thunderstorms fizzled into life, and
mumbled in the distance. The air became heavy and
charged.

They drove on for another half hour, until Varl was forced to switch on the transport's running lights. The sky had now bruised a dark, unhealthy brown. There was rain in the wind. They drove through several burned-out villages, and then the land became more hilly and they reached the fringes of a belt of forest.

'We're just crossing into Edrian Province,' Cirk said. 'A little further, and we should stop for the night.'

During the invasion, fighting had been fierce along the province's borders. The roadway had been repaired in many places. Stretches of forest had been bombed or burned flat and the road wound through scorched wildernesses where only the splintered, black trunks of trees poked from the ash. They saw the wreckage of abandoned war machines, most of them PDF armour, and dry, shrivelled heaps that had once been bodies. Elsewhere, the forest had been mutilated by acid rain. The team aboard the quad had been chatting amiably on the open road, but now they fell silent, their faces solemn.

They had just reached another village on the woodland road when the rains began. Beltayn and Criid raised the tarp roof over the transport crew compartment, and they heard the caustic rain sizzling as it ate at the treated canvas.

Drum fires had been lit along the roadway. Ahead, beside a grim ouslite customs house, a roadblock had been set up. A small queue of vehicles was drawn up to it, headlamps on and engines running as the guards checked consent papers and imagos.

Varl slowed down. 'What now?' he asked.

'Just a routine inspection post,' said Landerson. Cirk nodded agreement.

'Go round,' she said. 'Follow my lead.' She picked up the helmet and shoulderguards Bonin had used. Varl downshifted the transmission, and rolled the quad-track round the tail-end of the queue. Peering out, Gaunt could see a lot of hostiles on the ground under the awnings of the checkpoint. Excubitors and occupation troops. Several officers. He wondered if they had dogs, or worse. By the roadside just ahead, the rotting corpses of executed law-breakers hung on display from a wooden scaffold.

Varl overtook the line of waiting trucks and came up to the barrier. A trooper in a rainslicker poncho approached, holding up one mailed hand.

'Voi shet! Ecchr Anark setriketan!' he shouted above the drumming downpour.

Cirk stood up, disguise in place. 'Hyeth, voi Magir!' she called, pitching her voice low. 'Elketa sirdar shokol Edrianef guhun borosakel.'

'Anvie, Magir!' the trooper replied, and waved them through at once. The checkpoint barrier lifted smartly, and Varl gunned the quad forward.

'What did you tell him?' Gaunt asked Cirk as she sat down next to him and pulled the helmet off.

'That my commanding officer was late for a meeting in Edrian thanks to the damn rain, and was in the mood to shoot the next idiot who delayed him.'

Gaunt nodded and then thought for a moment. 'Major?'

'Yes?'

'*How* did you tell him that?'

'I used their language, colonel-commissar. You pick it up. It's essential for underground work.'

'Right,' said Gaunt. He leaned back, not at all reassured. Rawne sat across the compartment from him, facing him. Gaunt knew the look in his number two's eyes. 'Vouchsafe?' Rawne mouthed.

Gaunt shook his head.

Plower, one of Cirk's people, got up and took a look out ahead into the dismal night. 'Next turning left leads to the Baksberg ornithons. We can find shelter and a good place to lie low.'

Cirk agreed. 'Give Mr Varl instructions,' she said, then turned to look at Gaunt. 'If that's all right with you.'

'Carry on,' said Gaunt.

THE TRACK TURNING led them off the main arterial into the festering darkness of the woodlands. The heavy rain had turned the track into a mire, but the quad's big tread sections coped well. White smoke drifted from the acid-bitten trees around them, and there was a pungent stink of halides and sulphur.

The headlamps picked out a cluster of buildings up ahead. The ornithon, typical of the poultry farms common in that woodland region, comprised a low-gabled main house, stores, feed bins and the long, mesh-walled hutches of the batteries. The place was ruined. A loading tractor, stripped to its bare metal by months of corrosive rain, slumped in the main yard on decomposing tyres.

The main house had lost its roof, but the batteries were still intact and relatively dry. They reeked of birdlime and decay. The mission team and its allies dismounted and dashed into the shelter. While the scouts checked the area for security, Larkin, Criid and Feygor cleared some floor space of the foul-smelling straw, and Brostin set up a few lamps. Beltayn went to work preparing food. Landerson and Plower volunteered to help him, setting up the portable stove, and fetching water from the outside pump for purification. Cirk sat down in a corner, in deep conversation with Purchason and Acreson. Lefivre settled alone in the shadows, lost in his own thoughts.

'Check everyone,' Gaunt told Curth. She nodded. 'Including our associates,' he added.

'What do I tell them?' she asked.

'Tell them I'm concerned for the health of everyone in my team.'

Curth began to prepare her kit.

Varl came in from the rain, having parked and shut down the quad-track. He was heading for the stove to warm his hands, but Gaunt caught him by the sleeve as he went by.

'Sir?'

'Find a good reason to lurk in earshot of Cirk. I want to know what they're talking about.'

'You got it,' Varl said.

Gaunt turned to Rawne. 'Arrange a watch. But make sure everyone gets a decent rest.'

'Right,' said Rawne. He paused.

'Something else on your mind?'

Rawne shrugged. 'I was just thinking,' he whispered. 'If we didn't need their help so badly, I'd kill them all.'

'But we do need their help.'

'Maybe,' Rawne said. 'Keep your eye on that one, though,' he said quietly, indicating Lefivre with a roll of his eyes. 'I mean, Landerson seems all right, and Cirk knows what she's about, it would seem. But that one…'

'Strung out?'

'And then some.'

'I noticed. Landerson seems to be carrying him, as if he's close to losing his nerve.'

'One word, that's all it takes. One word from you.'

'I know,' said Gaunt. 'For what it's worth, major, I'm inclined to agree. If we didn't need their help so badly, I think I'd kill them too.'

'WHO'S IN CHARGE here?' Uexkull growled as he burst into the room. The light from the hovering glow-globes shone off his ribbed copper armour. Chief Sirdar Daresh rose quickly to his feet, scraping back his chair. He put his fork down next to his half-finished supper and hurried to swallow the mouthful he was chewing.

'I am, lord,' he said. The dining hall of Occupation Headquarters, Ineuron, fell silent, and the other officers sprang to their feet from the long table in a terrified hush. Rain beat against the shutters. Uexkull was so massive he'd had to turn his shoulders sideways to pass through the doorway.

'You are an incompetent weakling,' Uexkull said, and shot Daresh through the head with his bolt pistol. The single shot made a deafening boom in the close confines of the chamber. Daresh's almost headless corpse cannoned backwards from the end of the table, knocking over his chair. A blizzard of blood and tissue spattered the officers standing to attention at the table. They winced, but none of them dared move, not even to wipe clots of brain matter from their faces.

Uexkull walked down the length of the table, his armour's hydraulics clicking and whirring. The wooden floor creaked under his great weight. Two of his warriors took up positions at the doorway.

Uexkull reached the head of the table. He rolled Daresh's limp body out of the way with his foot, and set the chair upright. Then he sat down on it. The chair groaned under the monster's bulk.

Uexkull put his engraved bolt pistol on the table beside the place setting. Pale wisps of smoke still fluted from the muzzle.

'Who is,' Uexkull asked, his voice like the slither of dry scales, 'second in command? Say, for instance, if the garrison commander is suddenly deprived of brain activity?'

There was a nervous silence. Uexkull picked up Daresh's fork, speared a piece of fatty meat off the half-finished plate, and popped it into his mouth, oblivious to the speckles of fresh blood that dotted the food, the fork, the plate and the table.

He chewed. Swallowed. 'Do I look like I have all night?' he creaked.

'I... I am, lord,' said the officer standing to his left.

'Are you? Name?'

'Erod, vice sirdar.'

Uexkull nodded, toying with his fork. Then he swung round and impaled Erod through the throat with it. Erod staggered backwards, hands to his neck, face contorted, and collapsed backwards, writhing and vomiting blood.

'Lesson number one,' Uexkull said over the sounds of a man drowning in his own body fluids. 'When I ask a question, I expect an immediate answer. Vice Sirdar Erod would not be in that pretty fix now if he'd just spoken up when asked. I am not, by nature, a dangerous man…'

The warriors at the door sniggered.

'Oh, all right. I am. I really am. I am bred, trained and equipped for one purpose. To kill the enemy. I understand that I lack subtlety. Subtlety was not part of my training. I am not a governor, an ordinal, an arbiter of laws, a calculator of tariffs. The Plenipotentiary keeps me here as part of the Occupation force for a single reason. To kill the enemies of the Anarch.'

There was a long pause.

'Who is third in command?' Uexkull asked.

'I am, lord,' said the officer to his right, an older trooper whose face was heavily spotted with Daresh's blood.

'Good,' Uexkull nodded. 'Quick. Obedient. And your name is?'

'Second Vice Sirdar Eekuin, lord.'

'You answered promptly, Eekuin. You have learned. I will not kill you. Unless you are an enemy of the Anarch. Are you, perhaps, an enemy of the Anarch, Eekuin?'

'I am not, lord. I am true to the Anarch, whose word we serve–'

'And whose word drowns out all others,' Uexkull finished, raising one hand to cover his mouth. 'Eekuin, you're now in charge. Command of the Ineuron Town occupation is in your hands. Your first task will be to explain to me why the enemy insurgents have not been located and destroyed.'

'Lord, we have searched the town. During the night, the wirewolves were roused and they found nothing either. Checks have been doubled, house to house–'

Uexkull raised his hand. 'I have been in the town now for three hours. I have seen the patrols, the search sweeps. I know what's being done. What concerns me is what is *not* being done.'

'Yes, lord.'

Uexkull slid a data-slate out of his belt pouch and speed read the display. 'An excubitor patrol slaughtered at the Shedowtonland Crossroads. A terrorist campaign. Bombings. A firefight in the midtown areas yesterday that left the better part of two more excubitor squads dead. Las weapons used. This is not the work of the resistance cells.'

'No, lord. I did not suppose it was.'

'So… something more dangerous than a resistance cell has been active in this backwater. Call me old-fashioned, but wouldn't that make it a priority for the senior staff here to find the interlopers and obliterate them?'

'I believe it would, lord,' Eekuin replied.

'Yet… and yet, you're sitting down to dinner.'

Eekuin risked lifting his right hand to wipe away blood that was beginning to trickle into his eye. 'I request permission, lord, to rectify that at once and organise the senior staff into a hunting pattern.'

'That would be good,' said Uexkull. 'Permission granted.'

Eekuin stepped back from the table, saluted, and turned to issue an order to the frozen officers around him. Uexkull picked up his bolt pistol.

'Eekuin?'

The man halted, shaking.

Uexkull expertly swung the pistol over in his hand so that the grip was pointing at Eekuin. 'Before you start with that, shut Erod up, will you? He's making a bloody awful noise down there.'

Eekuin took the bolt pistol, cleared his throat, and walked round the table. Erod, his face blue, thrashed on the floor in a pool of blood. He clawed at Eekuin's ankles. Trying to look dismissive, Eekuin shot him between the eyes. The shot's impact punched the impaling fork up into the air.

It landed with a clatter. The ghastly gurgling fell silent.

Eekuin handed the weapon back to Uexkull.

'Find me something,' Uexkull told him. 'Find me something in the next fifteen minutes, or I'll be asking after the next in line.'

THE GHOSTS WERE settling down to sleep, weary and fed well enough from the stew Beltayn had concocted. Acid rain still belted against the ornithon's low roof. Curth came over to Gaunt, nursing a cup of caffeine.

'Anything?' he asked.

'Not here,' she said, and drew him away towards the back of the long hutch. Brostin and Feygor chuckled as they observed the game of regicide Criid was playing with Varl. Everyone else was dozing.

'What?' Gaunt asked.

'I checked them all out,' Curth said. 'Your lady friend, and her man Acreson… they have parasites embedded in their forearms.'

'You sure?'

'Ibram, they made no effort to conceal them. Throne, they're filthy, awful things. Bedded deep. Landerson and the others had theirs cut out.'

'Right,' Gaunt said. 'Go find Mkoll for me.'

EEKUIN STRODE INTO the control room and saluted Uexkull. Around them, by lamplight, the ordinals and servitors manned the clanking codifiers and instruments of the command annexe.

'What do you have for me, chief sirdar?' Uexkull asked.

Eekuin held out a data-slate.

'A military patrol has not reported in, lord. It went out this morning, searching farms along the Shedowtonland road. Garrison lists it as missing.'

Uexkull studied the chart. 'A full unit? How is that possible? And where's their damned vehicle gone?'

'Vox log records the unit's last check was just before midday. They were dismounting to search Parcelson's agri-plex.'

'Where the Eye is that?'

'Just out of town on the foreroad. I've sent another unit to check it out.'

'There's something else, isn't there, Eekuin?'

'Lord?'

'You look pleased with yourself.'

Eekuin produced another data-slate. 'The unit was using a quad-track, pool serial II/V. A vehicle bearing that mark was passed by the border checkpoint at Baksberg earlier tonight.'

'Baksberg? Location?'

'On the Edrian provincial border, lord.'

Uexkull smiled. The sight of his teeth made Eekuin feel unwell. 'Contact Edrian Occupation. Tell them I want a vox-link to their area commander. Tell them about the mood I'm in, Eekuin. Tell them how I murdered your senior officers without compunction. Tell them I'm inbound. Have the link relayed to my ship. I want a full battalion mobilised and ready at Baksberg by the time I arrive.'

'Yes, lord,' Eekuin replied. As Uexkull marched out of the room, Eekuin sagged a little. He was still alive.

'Get me Edrian Command,' he snapped.

'COLONEL-COMMISSAR?'

Cirk stepped into the feed store under the low doorway. A single lamp burned. The rain fell outside.

'Hello, Cirk,' Gaunt said, appearing from the shadows.

'What is this?' she asked, her attractive face tilted inquisitively. 'I need to sleep. We've a long day ahead of us.'

He stepped closer. 'The day can wait,' he said. 'Sabbatine… may I call you that? Sabbatine, there's something about you. Something that utterly intrigues me.'

She smiled. 'Well, I have felt it too. But this isn't the time or the place…'

'Why not?' he asked. He was in her face now. Tall, thick-set. Warm. His nose almost touched hers. His hands went around her waist.

'Sabbatine…'

'Really, I… I don't think this is…'

His strong hand gripped her arm. Twisted. She yelped. 'Gaunt, what?'

'What indeed. What the Throne is this, Cirk? Answer me that?'

He had pulled up her sleeve. The imago, in its dark blister, throbbed against her pale skin.

'You bastard!' she said.

'Oh, please,' he snapped, pulling her arm around so the lamplight caught it. 'Why don't you explain–'

Her punch caught him by surprise. Base of the neck. Nerve point. As he folded, he cursed himself for being so stupid. His knees hit the straw. Wrenching free, she kicked him for good measure, right in the ear.

'Feth!' he snarled, hurt.

'And that's about all I'll let you get away with,' said Mkvenner, sliding out of the shadows.

She whipped round to face him. He was holding a two-metre length of slender-gauge fence post, a ready-made quarter-staff. One end smacked round and knocked the autopistol away even as she drew it. The other end winded her and, as she doubled over, the staff dropped down over her shoulders and pinned her arms.

'Thanks, Ven,' Gaunt said, getting back on his feet.' Obviously, in future, I won't want you to constrain my dates like this.'

Ven laughed.

'You have an imago,' Gaunt said to Cirk. She spat at him, wrestled tight by Mkvenner's horizontal staff.

'You bastard! I thought we had a degree of trust!'

'We did. We have. But I want that explained.'

'This?' she said, looking down at the grub in her arm.

'Yes, Cirk,' Gaunt replied, pulling one of his bolt pistols out of its chest holster and cocking it. 'I'm a commissar, first and foremost. The next words you speak had better be fething good.'

'This imago is consented for day and night, you idiot. I'd have been a fool to let it be removed. How the hell do you think the resistance remains active? We need to use everything we have to beat their glyfs and their scanners. You think I like having this thing eating into my arm? You bastard! I can't get you into Edrian without this. I can't get you anywhere! It's all about consent! Some of us have them removed if they're restrictive, but Acreson and me, we have full clearance.'

She stopped. 'Acreson. What have you done to him?'

'Nothing, yet,' Gaunt said.

She looked at him. 'We have to work their system, Gaunt. Please believe me. That's the only reason I haven't had this thing taken out of me. It's too useful. Ibram... please.'

Gaunt reholstered his weapon.

'Let her go, Ven,' he said.

JUDDERING THROUGH THE torrential rain, the pair of deathships swung in towards Baksberg. In the lead ship, Uexkull readied his weapons. Seated with him, his four warriors did likewise. They'd been through the fires of many war-theatres with him. He knew them, trusted them.

Uexkull latched his autocannon against his shoulder plate and connected the servo feeds.

'Baksberg, coming up now. Four minutes,' the pilot voxed.

Uexkull slammed a sickle mag home in his bolt pistol.

'Prep for exit,' he hissed.

The vox beeped. 'Lord, this is Eekuin.'

'Go ahead.'

'The search unit has reported back. They found the entire patrol in a silage pit. All dead. A variety of wounds.'

'Commando tactics, Eekuin?'

'Most certainly, lord.'

'Understood. Uexkull out.' The monster turned to his warriors. 'Imperial Guard. Specialists. Damn good at what they do, it would appear. But still, just men. This will be over quickly.'

His warriors growled their agreement.

'Do we have a location yet?' Uexkull barked.

The pilot came back smartly. 'Baksberg checkpoint directs us on a likely target zone, lord. There are a number of abandoned ornithons in the backwoods off the main road here, and activity has been reported at one.'

'Poultry farms?' Uexkull questioned.

'Yes, lord,' the pilot said.

Uexkull smiled. 'Consider them plucked.'

ELEVEN

THERE WAS NO quarter. The first of the deathships, its thrusters whining, dropped low until its hull was brushing through the wood's wet canopy, and then opened fire with its forward gunpods. The rainy night suddenly lit up with strobing flashes of bright yellow radiance that captured rapid snapshots of the slanting rain like stop-frame playback. Clouds of steam billowed off the gunpod vents as they heated. The hail of heavy fire disintegrated the walls of the main house and threw tiles and broken stone high into the air.

The deathship steadied, and swung around on a low hover above the ornithon's yard. Its gun pods started up again, pulverising a row of store sheds.

The other ship dropped in low on the approach track and opened its hatches. Uexkull was first out, splashing along the muddy lane in the dark. Augmetic sensors embedded in his collar-plate and the side of his cranium automatically selected low light scoping. Nictating filters

145

slid over his eyes. The world resolved into a ruddy blur, the crimson wash of cold areas graduating to the palest pink tells of heat sources. The muzzle flash cones of the hovering deathship up ahead read as searing white blinks that overlapped as their after-images gently faded.

Uexkull reached the edge of the yard, his squad at his heels. He heard the first hand-weapon discharge: bolter rounds whipping like small comets through the night to his left as Czelgur began firing on the rear of the main dwelling. Uexkull's enhanced aural sensors heard the bat-squeak pain of a human voice behind the furious noise of the guns and the lifter jets. Guttural vox inter-play chattered back and forth between the monstrous Chaos Space Marines.

'Main dwelling secure,' Gurgoy voxed. 'Three kills.'

'Stores cleared. Another two dead here,' Virag reported.

A grenade detonated, filling the edge of Uexkull's vision with a bolus of light. More bat-squeaks, and a single, lingering wail of agony. The downwash of the hovering deathship spattered liquid mud across him, and he felt the delicious sizzle of the acid rain on his flesh. He smashed through the loose plank wall of the nearest hatching battery. Something scrambled in the shadows to his right, but he saw only heat and cold. His cannon slammed into life, licking out a sizzling flash, the recoil smacking it back against the locking harness in his upper body armour. Something made of meat and bone atomised. Another heat spot, right ahead, moved against the cold-streaming fuzz of the rainwater driz-zling in through the roof. Uexkull fired his bolt pistol and saw a human-shaped pink outline crash over onto the floor. He strode forward, smelling blood now over the birdlime, the acid and the driven smoke.

Nezera burst into view to his left, shredding chain-link mesh aside with his powered claw, his bolt weapon barking into the depths of the battery as he broke his way inside.

'Go left!' Uexkull grunted. He took another few steps and then paused as a burst of small-arms fire – small calibre solid rounds – was stopped harmlessly by his carapace armour. Tracking round, he unloaded his cannon again, ripping down part of the hutch roof. He saw the shooter's shape on his optics briefly, spinning away, torn, just before the roof collapsed on it.

More pathetic gunfire came his way. Resistance at last, though hardly the sport he'd been looking forward to.

BONIN POINTED. THERE wasn't much to see – just a distant flashing that delineated trees against the encompassing night. But the sounds were enough, carried through the rain. The dull thwack of heavy cannons. The whistle of lift-jets.

'Feth,' Gaunt murmured. 'How far?'

'No more than two kilometres,' the scout replied.

Gaunt hurried back into the battery. 'Up now! Everyone! We're moving now!'

The party began to stir from sleep, cold and numb.

'Come on! By the Emperor! Now!'

The Ghosts needed no further urging. Cirk also leapt to her feet and shook her fighters into shape. Lefivre woke up screaming, and Cirk clamped her hand over his mouth, trying to get him to remember where he was.

'The quad?' Varl asked Gaunt as he ran up.

'No, we can't risk starting it. On foot, out the back. Mkoll! Get those lamps off! Ven! Find us an exit path. Consult Cirk!'

Mkoll and Beltayn gathered up the lamps and killed their glow.

'Sound off!' snapped Rawne, shouldering his pack.

He got a curt reply from everyone except Larkin.

'Lead them out,' Gaunt said to Rawne. 'Double-time it. I'll find him.'

Larkin was curled up in a straw-filled roosting pen. He'd slept on through the fuss. Gaunt shook him.

'Larks! Come on!'

Larkin's face was a pale, thin shape in the gloom.

'Is it time, Try?' he whispered.

'Come on, Larkin!'

'What's it like being dead?'

Gaunt slapped the sniper across the face. 'Larkin! Wake up! We're in trouble.'

Larkin roused with a start and moaned quietly as he realised his surroundings.

'Get your kit. Don't leave anything. Come on, Larks, I need you to be sharp.'

'Feth this,' Larkin whimpered. 'I was dreaming I was dead and now I wake up and find things are much worse.'

RAWNE AND MKVENNER led the group out through the back yard of the ornithon towards the trees. It was pitch black, and they'd wrapped their camo-capes around themselves against the burning rain. The wet air was caustic and caught at their throats. Criid came close behind, urging Cirk's men along.

Last out of the ramshackle farm were Gaunt and Larkin. In the distance, the gunfire had stopped.

CZELGUR RAISED A spitting flare in his left paw and by the light of it Uexkull crouched and turned over the nearest body. Bolter fire had mangled it, but not so much that Uexkull couldn't see the rag clothing and the emaciated, malnourished build. The others were the same.

'Fugitives. Unconsented,' Uexkull muttered, his voice stiff and dry like caked mud cracking. One of the bodies clutched an old vermin-gun, a rusting small calibre weapon. There was no sign of any lasguns.

'Unless standards have dropped, these are not soldiers of the False Emperor,' Uexkull said. Czelgur snorted at his leader's ironic scorn. 'We've wasted the night tracking unconsented outlaws.'

Static warbled on the vox-link.

'Go,' said Uexkull, rising to his feet.

'Auspex is showing a large metallic contact in the woods two point three-one kilometres east of us, lord.'

'Let's move!' Uexkull shouted.

THEY WERE A good way into the acid-bitten woods when they heard the sound of the deathships behind them. The machines circled over the ornithon, playing their stablights over the ruined outbuildings.

'They'll find the transport,' Varl said.

'No helping that,' Rawne replied.

'Let's just keep going,' said Gaunt. His skin itched from the rain, and the vapour drifting up from the dissolving leaf mould under their feet was making them all short of breath.

According to Cirk, deeper forest lay to their west, and then something she called the Untill, which didn't seem to be an option. She directed them north. They were, she insisted, about ten kilometres short of one of the main arterial routes through Edrian Province, and once they hit that they would be close to the outer townships. In one of those, she hoped, they could make contact with the local cell.

'But handling your team north through the province isn't going to be easy now,' she said. 'The enemy is likely to be fully alerted. The garrisons will be mobilised. But we'll have to risk it.'

'Is there an alternative?' asked Mkoll.

'We could go wide to the east, maybe up through hills. But that's a long detour. On foot, a month. And that's without trouble. The search zones will widen if they don't find us around Edrian.'

Gaunt said nothing. He'd expected trouble from the outset, but this was bad luck. The occupation was tighter than he'd hoped and he doubted the enemy would take long figuring out what they were doing on Gereon.

Unless, he thought, they could manage a little misdirection. But putting that notion into effect would take a little time. They had more immediate problems to deal with.

'THAT'S THE MISSING transport,' Gurgoy said. Uexkull nodded. Clutching an overhead handgrip, he leaned a little further out of the hovering deathship's open hatch and peered down. The shifting stablights flickered through the rain below, lighting up the abandoned ornithon.

'Life signs?'

'Nothing human, lord,' the pilot voxed.

'Move us north,' Uexkull ordered. 'Slow and low.'

'Yes, lord.'

The two gunships began to prowl forward above the woodlands. Uexkull knew there was no point trying to track the insurgents on the ground. The acid rain would have obliterated any traces or spores already. He activated his heat vision again, gazing down at the canopy, hoping to pick up some pale flicker of bodywarmth in the wood. He got nothing but a vague pink fuzz. The acid decomposition had raised the background temperature of the leaves and the woodland floor as it digested the organics. Nothing was reading back. A human could be standing in plain view down there and be invisible against the ambient radiation.

'Where's the local battalion now?' he asked.

'At the Baksberg checkpoint as per your orders, lord,' the pilot responded. 'Another brigade strength force is in transit along the Edrian road.'

'Transmit my orders. The battalion moves into the woods and fans out. Search pattern, northward sweep. The brigade forms a picket along the road way and holds for anything the sweep flushes out.'

'Yes, lord.'

'This will be done in the name of the Anarch, whose word drowns out all others,' Uexkull said. He felt a hint of failure. That was something he did not enjoy, and seldom experienced.

By dawn, perhaps he would have made that feeling go away.

DARK SHAPES AGAINST a darker sky, the two deathships passed overhead, the long white beams of their searching lights penetrating the rotting tree cover. Their downwash made the branches stir and rustle.

Once they had gone by, the Ghosts stirred out of hiding. They'd covered themselves with their camo-capes, huddling down with the resistance fighters so they could share the concealment.

'Thank you,' said Landerson. He'd sheltered under Criid's camo-cape.

She shrugged. 'They find you, they find me,' she said.

'No chatter,' said Rawne. 'Let's get moving again.'

At the back of the file, Mkoll paused, his head slightly cocked, listening.

Behind them, to the south, fetch-hounds had begun to bay.

TWELVE

WHEN THE PHEGUTH woke up, he noticed three strange things.

The bastion seemed very quiet, that was the first thing. It was early still (he guessed, he had no chronograph), and his tower chamber remote, but even so, there was no sound at all.

The second thing was that the door to his chamber stood ajar.

That was truly odd. The life-ward would never do something so careless. One of the bastion footmen, maybe? If so, the moron would not enjoy Desolane's reprimand.

Still, for whatever reason, the door was open. The pheguth could feel a draft blowing through it, cool air against his skin. An open door…

The pheguth sat up on the steel frame that served him as a bed. As soon as he was upright – rather too suddenly – the lingering, cumulative pain of the transcoding sessions ambushed him. It felt as if the back of his skull was being used as a regimental dinner gong. Pain gusted against the back of his eyes and he felt a pounding in his ears. Naked, he half-stepped, half-fell off the frame and threw up violently into the steel pot that served him as a toilet. His retches were violent, and by the time they had subsided, blood was running from his nostrils.

Shaking, his head still churning, he got to his feet. And that was when he realised the third strange thing.

He was not shackled to the frame.

He stood, puzzled, for a long moment. Then he hobbled over to the chair in the corner and pulled on the tunic and trousers lying folded on the seat.

Very slowly, he approached the door.

'Desolane?' he said quietly, his throat hoarse from the retching. No one answered. He reached out and touched the door, and, when it didn't simply slam shut, he pulled it open warily.

'Desolane?'

The anteroom beyond was empty. Strong, cold sunlight lanced down through the high window slits. On the far side of the anteroom, the reinforced shutter into the hallway was also open.

The pheguth took one more step forward.

'Desolane?' he called.

FORTY-FIVE MINUTES LATER, Desolane found the pheguth. He was in his chamber, seated on the wooden chair, facing the open door.

'Good morning, pheguth,' Desolane said.

'The doors were all open. I was unshackled.'

'Indeed?' The life-ward said. 'Someone has been remiss.'

'I didn't know what to do. I called out for you, but you did not answer. So I sat down here.'

'The doors were open and you were unshackled, pheguth. Did you not think to make your escape from this prison?'

The pheguth looked appalled at the suggestion. 'No. Of course not. Where would I go? I know I'm only in here for my own protection.' He paused and looked up at the life-ward. 'Was this…' he began, 'was this another trick? A test?'

'You may care to call it that, pheguth,' Desolane admitted, summoning the footman with the tray of breakfast. 'Last night, I spoke with the psykers. They reported that yesterday, for the first time, the transcoding bore fruit. Outer mnemonic barriers were erased. An entire layer of engrammatic suppression was removed.'

'What… what did they learn?' the pheguth asked.

'Nothing. Nothing yet. But they have removed the, if you will, casing of your mindlock at last, and can see its inner workings. They estimate that within a week, precision transcoding will have unlocked your memory entirely.'

The pheguth thought about this. 'Then why this test today?' he asked.

'It was considered prudent. The psykers conjectured that, as your mindlock was loosened, your personality might reassert some measure of free will. They wondered how this might affect your loyalty, and your decision to side with us.'

'So you left the door open?'

'Yes, pheguth.'

'To see if I suddenly became loyal to the Golden Throne again?'

Desolane winced. 'Yes, pheguth. Please, try not to use that phrase.'

The pheguth smiled. It was a curious, bleak expression. He held up his augmetic hand. The prosthetic implant was over five sidereal years old, but time had not softened the ridges of scar tissue where it was married to the wrist stump. 'You see this?' he said.

'Yes,' said Desolane.

'For this, and for so much else, I can never go back. Do not test me again. It's beneath us both.'

BY FIRST LIGHT, the Ghosts had reached the northern boundary of the woods. What lay beyond – rolling arable land, apparently – was obscured in a thick blanket of fog. The rain had stopped before dawn, but the air remained wet and ripe with acidic rot.

In the middle distance, like a row of behemoth sentries lining the borders of Edrian Province, gigantic air-mills rose up out of the fog, their great sails motionless in the still air. Dormant since the invasion, the mills no longer ground flour. Vast, lank banners hung from some sets of sails, adorned with the mad emblems of the Ruinous Powers.

They took a brief rest at the edge of the treeline. From the sound of it, the hunting parties that had been scouring the woods at their heels all night were less than half an hour behind them.

The arterial road ran along the bottom of the vale below the trees, some half a kilometre away. For most of its visible length, it was set on a raised causeway. Though partly obscured by the fog, vehicles and figures could be seen along this causeway. Hostile troopers. Transports. They had the road hemmed close. This was the other edge of the pincer, the trap that the hunting parties were driving them towards.

'We've got no choice but to go forward,' Gaunt said.

'Have you seen the numbers down there?' Landerson replied. Cirk just shook her head.

'Correction,' Gaunt said. 'We have two other choices: we stay here and die, or we turn back into the woods and die. We have to cross that road, get beyond the trap. And I'm not asking for your approval. I'm telling you what's going to happen.'

He looked at Cirk. 'Once we're over that highway, which way is our ideal heading?'

She deferred to Plower, who seemed to have a better knowledge of the district. He pointed to the north-east. 'Edrian Town is about ten kilometres that way. If I had a choice, I'd head in that direction. There's a greater chance of contacting the local cell there.'

'But that's the way they'll expect us to be going,' said Cirk. 'More chance of capture.'

Plower pointed north-west. 'Two smaller settlements over that way. Millvale and Wheathead. We might find a contact there, I suppose. No promises. Last time I came this way, the excubitors had tightened up on the smaller communities.'

'We go that way, then,' said Gaunt. He gestured to the waiting Ghosts. 'Close up, listen good. We're going to try and run the picket. Get beyond that road. Now's the time, while the fog's still with us. Everyone see that airmill?'

He pointed to one of the nearest structures to their left, three kilometres away. It looked like a cathedral spire breaking the white mist. A scarlet banner was draped across its sails.

'The one with the red banner on it,' Gaunt said. 'That's our rendezvous point. We'll cross the road directly below this point, so we're in the open for the shortest possible time. And we'll be covering Major Cirk's people. That means sharing capes. Criid, look after Landerson. Beltayn, take Acreson. Varl, you'll have Purchason. Feygor, Plower. Rawne, you'll cover the major. I'll take Lefivre with me.'

'I think I should–' Rawne began.

'It's settled,' Gaunt interrupted. 'Now, we need a diversion. Mkoll?'

The scout-sergeant scratched his upper lip. 'I'll take Ven and Bonin east. We'll think of something.'

'Sir?' It was Larkin. He'd been scanning the road with the scope of his long-las. They turned to see what he'd spotted.

Some way over to their right, a truck was approaching along the causeway. A fuel bowser. It stopped every now and then to replenish the tanks of the picket vehicles.

Mkoll looked at Gaunt and raised an eyebrow.

'All right then,' Gaunt said. 'The Emperor provides. Take Brostin with you. Leave me Bonin.'

Mkoll nodded.

'See you at the mill,' Gaunt said.

BEFORE THE FOG could dwindle any further, they slid out of the treeline and down the slope through the long, wet grass towards the causeway road. It seemed a short distance, but the effort was great. They moved on their hands and knees with their camo-capes tied over them. Bonin led the way, followed by the teamed pairs awkwardly sharing cloaks. Curth followed, under her own cape, with Larkin crawling along at the rear.

It was hot under the camouflage and they began to sweat. Before long it became an effort not to pant, an effort to keep their advance unhurried and smooth. Huddled up with Purchason, Varl was finding it particularly onerous. He was carrying Brostin's heavy weapon lashed to his belly and chest. They'd swapped so that Brostin could move more lightly. The ammo hoppers were draped around Purchason's shoulders. He'd volunteered to carry them. In the half-light under the camo-cape, Varl wiped perspiration from his brow and grinned at the resistance fighter. Purchason just closed his eyes and edged on, droplets of sweat dripping off the end of his nose.

They closed on the roadway, one gentle hand-set at a time. By now, they could hear the low conversations of the troopers up on the causeway. An occasional crunch of footsteps. A vehicle door slamming. Curth swore she could smell a lho-stick.

Gaunt felt Lefivre beginning to tense up beside him. The man's breathing became more shallow, and he kept pausing to fidget at his face. Gaunt had to keep checking his crawl. If Lefivre stopped suddenly, Gaunt risked dragging the cloak off him and exposing him.

Somewhere above them, an officer called out to his men. The voice was loud, harsh. Lefivre froze. Gaunt could feel him trembling. The man stank of sour sweat under the cape. His jaw ground, and his mouth moved, forming noiseless words.

Gaunt took hold of the man's shoulder and pulled Lefivre's face round to look at him. Gently, Gaunt shook his head.

The officer called out again. Gaunt saw the panic attack vicing on Lefivre and rolled the man over into the grass, his left hand pressed to Lefivre's mouth.

'Breathe,' he whispered, 'nice and slow. Breathe. Fill your lungs. A sound now, and we're all dead, so breathe, for the Emperor's sake.'

Lefivre's breathing wasn't slowing. His eyes were wild, drawn white in the gloom beneath the cape.

He began to shake.

MKOLL, MKVENNER AND Brostin hurried through the thickets of the treeline, keeping an eye on the fuel truck. The scouts disturbed nothing, but Brostin, big and clumsy, kept snapping twigs and swishing wet fronds with his shins.

Mkoll glanced back at the trooper, his expression disapproving.

'Do better,' he hissed.

Brostin shrugged.

'You're a fething Ghost. Use your skills!'

'I'm trying!' Brostin whispered back. 'Fething scouts,' he mumbled to himself.

Mkvenner turned and placed his open hand against Brostin's neck. Brostin swallowed hard. He was a brute of a man, packed with muscle, and the pressure was light, but there was no mistake at all. One twitch of the wrist, and Mkvenner would snap his spine.

'Do as the sergeant says,' Mkvenner mouthed. 'We need you for this, but not that badly.'

Brostin nodded. Mkvenner withdrew his hand. They crept on.

BROSTIN CUDDLED VARL'S lasrifle up under his armpit and stared at Mkvenner's back. The scout had a rep, a real rep, and all the regiment respected him. One of Gaunt's chosen, one of the favoured, like all the fething scouts. Brostin, whose loyalties lay with Rawne, despised every one of them. One more trick like that, Brostin thought, and someone's going to get unlucky in the confusion of the next firefight.

Mkoll came to a halt and made a signal. They pulled their capes up over their shoulders and began to belly down the slope towards the road.

DIRECTLY BELOW THE causeway embankment, the sloping pasture of the woods rolled down into a waterlogged culvert. Bonin reached it first and, wading gingerly into the cold pool, got to his feet. He pulled back his cape. The shadow of the bank fell across him, and the mist was streaming. Gradually, the others reached him: Rawne and Cirk, Criid and Landerson, Beltayn and Acreson. Then Curth, then Feygor with Plower. Then Varl and Purchason, struggling with the heavy weapon in its canvas boot.

Bonin fanned them out behind him with a gesture, and made a swift signal for them to prep weapons. They leant in the ooze, their backs to the bank. Larkin appeared out of the grass, and scuttled in beside Bonin, his boots making the merest ripple in the standing water.

Bonin nodded to him.

Where's the boss? Larkin signed.

Bonin felt his heart skip and looked round. Twenty metres up the slope, he could just see a huddled shape covered by a camo-cape in the long grass. It wasn't moving.

'CONTROL IT! CONTROL your fear!' Gaunt hissed. 'Feth it, Lefivre, don't lose it now!'

Lefivre's eyes rolled back. Choking, suffocating on Gaunt's hand, Lefivre began to convulse.

THERE WAS A RICH stink of promethium in the air. Voices gabbled. They could hear the sound of a chattering pump running off the tanker's idling engine.

Mkoll, Mkvenner and Brostin slunk along the culvert with the shadow of the causeway over them. The sun was rising hard now, casting the roadway shadow out across the grassy slope. They could see the elongated shapes of the vehicles above them, the huddled figures, stretched like giants.

Mkoll and Mkvenner slung their lasrifles across their backs and took out their silenced handguns. Mkoll looked at Brostin.

Ready? he signalled.

Brostin breathed in the fuel stink again and smiled. He nodded.

BONIN STARED AT the huddled shape in the grass. It was still in the causeway shadow, but at the rate the sun was climbing, it wouldn't remain so for much longer. The cape was twitching, quivering. What the feth…?

'Lefivre's lost it,' Rawne whispered.

'I'm going back–' Bonin began.

Rawne shook his head. 'You'll blow us all. Stay here.'

Bonin glared at him. 'But–'

'You heard me.'

Above them, on the roadway, the voices came again.

'Voi alt reser manchin?'

'Eyt Voi? Ecya ndeh, magir.'

What? What had they seen? Rawne glanced at Cirk. She shook her head and made the signal 'stay put'.

Rawne drew his warknife all the same.

GAUNT HAD NO choice. With his free hand, he tugged out one of his bolt pistols and smacked Lefivre across the temple with the butt. The cell fighter slumped unconscious.

And still. At last.

THERE WERE TWO half-tracks on the stretch of roadway, the bowser truck, and a cluster of troopers. They were starkly lit by the sunlight. Around them, below the lip of the causeway, the white fog drifted like smoke.

Mkoll rolled up over the causeway edge, and scurried into cover behind the nearest track. He could smell the fuel, hear the thump of the cycling pump. He slid under the half-track's chassis, into the greasy shadow, as two troopers crunched past.

He smelled smoke.

'Akyeda voi smeklunt!' a voice shouted.

'Magir, magir, aloost moi!' another voice protested. The figures moved past the other way. Two troopers, smoking lho-sticks while they waited, rebuked by their sirdar to stand clear of the bowser. They wandered over to the edge of the causeway and looked out at the woods.

Under the track, Mkoll heard a rattle. The pump had stopped, and the feed line was being withdrawn. He heard more voices, and a cab door open.

The fuelling was done. The tanker was leaving.

He looked back at the edge of the roadway.

Mkvenner rose behind the smoking, chatting troopers, tall and lean, like a spectre from the mist. He caught one in a choke hold, and knifed the other in the small of the back. As the stabbed trooper fell backwards off the roadway silently, Mkvenner twisted his grip and snapped the other's neck. He lowered the corpse to the ground gently and raised his silenced pistol.

Brostin clambered into view behind him, getting up on the roadway. Somehow, he had caught one of the half-smoked lho-sticks the men had dropped. Upright, nonchalant, as if he were taking a morning constitutional, Brostin leaned back, and put the smoke to his lips.

He drew deeply, inhaled, exhaled, and smiled in satisfaction.

Two occupation troopers came around the rear of the half-track and saw them.

'Voi shet–' one began to cry.

Mkvenner was already down on one knee, his pistol raised in a two-handed grip. The weapon popped rapidly and both men tumbled over with a clatter.

'Doess scara, magir?' a voice called.

Mkvenner ran forward until he was snuggled in behind the rear fender of the half-track. He winced as a salvo of las-fire ripped the air behind him.

Mkvenner looked round. Three more troopers had appeared behind him. Lasrifle cradled in one meaty arm, Brostin had cut them down, the lho-stick pressed to his mouth with the finger and thumb of his other hand.

The roadway went mad. Troopers appeared from all around, alerted by the sound of gunfire. Alien voices bellowed and screamed.

Brostin leant into the recoil and fired another burst, one-handed, that sent two more archenemy troopers over onto the road. Las-shots chopped his way.

Mkvenner holstered his pistol and swung his lasrifle out, firing as the muzzle came up. He kept it on single-shot. He seldom wasted ammo on blurts of auto.

The gun up to his shoulder, he ran forward, aiming and slaying. Each bolt was a perfect kill-shot. Men dropped.

Mkoll was still under the half-track. He had crawled forward until he was under the front fender. His pistol spat. The officer who had, until recently, been chatting beside the bowser went down. Then so did his adjutant. Another trooper ran for cover and dropped on his face.

'Brostin!' Mkoll yelled.

BONIN LOOKED UP. Gunfire echoed down the causeway. Fierce gunfire. The figures above them began to break and run. Engines started. Trucks rolled away.

'Diversion,' he said to Rawne.

'Let's take them over,' Rawne said.

'Do it yourself,' Bonin snapped, and began to run up out of the culvert towards the figure in the weeds.

'Let's go!' Rawne called, and the main force began to scramble up the embankment onto the road.

Bonin reached Gaunt.

'Come on, sir!' he yelled.

'Help me with him,' Gaunt protested, trying to drag Lefivre's dead weight.

'There's no time, sir!' Bonin exclaimed.

'Now, Bonin! The Emperor Protects!'

With a curse, Bonin grabbed a limp arm.

MKOLL GOT UP from under the track and started firing his lasrifle. Mkvenner was covering his back. Serious fire was coming from both directions along the causeway. Squads were closing on foot, and trucks were approaching too.

'Brostin!' Mkoll yelled. 'Brostin, now or never!'

He looked round. Rifle under his arm, Brostin stood beside the fuel bowser. The driver hung, limp and shot, from the cab. Brostin had unhooked the hose and started the pump again. Promethium flooded out over the road, gushing across the hardpan, trickling down the embankments, pooling under the halftracks and the crumpled bodies.

Brostin was still smoking the lho-stick. It was down to the stub almost.

Mkoll skidded to a halt.

Brostin smiled at him. 'All right, sarge. I got it from here. This is my thing.'

Mkoll gaped. 'But–'

'Seriously, take a fething hike. You and Ven. *Now*, you got me?'

Firing off the last of their clips, Mkoll and Mkvenner threw themselves off the causeway into the deep grass on the mill side of the road.

The stink of promethium in the air was now unbearably strong.

The occupation troopers closed from both sides, stumbling to a halt as their boots splashed into the edges of the widening lake of liquid fuel ebbing out over the roadway. Hurriedly, they stopped firing and began to back away.

They all saw the man. The big-built, hairy man, standing beside the fuel bowser with the flooding pump in one hand and lho-stick in the other. He glistened from head to toe, as if he had dowsed himself in fuel as well.

'That's it,' Brostin grinned. 'Guess what's cooking.'

He took one last, long drag on the lho-stick, exhaled a sigh, then flicked the butt away.

It circled twice in the air.

Then two hundred metres of causeway went up in a wall of fire.

THIRTEEN

RISING, DAZED, MKOLL and Mkvenner toiled up through the long grass away from the road, the furnace-heat of the fire on their backs. Patches of the field around them were ablaze, and sparks and burning cinders fluttered down out of the sky. Glancing back when they dared, shielding their eyes against the blazing light, they saw the ruin of the causeway stretch away. An inferno, in which the vague outlines of consumed vehicles could just be made out. The blast had been so intense it had conjured up a swirling doughnut of flame that mushroomed into the sky and even now was spilling out in a wider and wider halo.

On the road, they could see the picket line disintegrating as men rushed to aid their comrades and then were beaten back by the unquenchable heat.

'Holy Throne,' Mkoll muttered.

'Let's get to the mill,' Mkvenner said. His voice was cold. Nothing ever seemed to ruffle the stoic scout, not even a spectacle of this magnitude.

Then he paused. At long last, something penetrated his reserve and produced a response.

'Feth me...' he said.

Mkoll looked. A figure, trailing flame, was staggering through the grass below the causeway. It fell, and rolled, trying to stifle its own burning clothes. Then it got up again and began to limp towards them.

It was Brostin. His clothes were scorched, his hair and eyebrows singed, his skin blackened and blistered.

But he was alive. And smiling.

They hurried down the slope to him and helped him along.

'I'm fine,' he said, his voice hoarse and wheezing.

'How the feth... how the feth are you not dead?' Mkoll asked him.

Brostin hesitated before replying. There had been a drum of detergent gel on the back of the bowser, retardant material carried in case of spills. Just like the stuff Brostin had used back in his days on the fire watch in Tanith Magna. He'd poured it over himself just before his trick with the lho-stick. It wouldn't stop him burning, not in an inferno like that, but it would protect him long enough to get clear. Brostin considered explaining this to Mkoll and Mkvenner, but he realised that, for the first time, he had shown skills and secrets that impressed the unimpressable scouts. He wasn't about to waste that moment of superiority with a mundane explanation.

He said: 'I know fire. Been waging war with it for years. It wouldn't dare harm me, not after all we've been through together.'

The scouts looked at him, suspecting they were being hoodwinked, but lost for an answer. Brostin clambered on up the slope.

'Come on,' he said. 'We haven't got all day.'

'THANK YOU, SIR,' Landerson said.

Gaunt turned to look at him. 'For what?'

'For Lefivre. You could have left him. By rights, you should have killed him. He nearly blew it for everyone.'

'He was scared. I can't blame him for that.'

'We're all scared,' Landerson said. 'We all deal with it. Lefivre's nerves are shot and he's a liability–'

Gaunt held up a hand. 'Listen, Landerson. You and Lefivre and the other cell members have risked everything to help my team. I can't repay you the way you'd like me to. I can't save your world. But I'll damn well save any of you if it's in my power to do so. If we don't look out for each other, we might as well quit now.'

'You're not at all what I expected,' Landerson said.

'I know.'

'No, I mean… you're a Guard commissar. I've heard stories. Stories of ruthlessness. Brutality. Iron rule and unflinching punishment.'

'I'm all of those things,' said Gaunt. 'When I have to be. But I have a soul too. I serve the beloved Emperor, and I serve mankind. I believe that service extends to the weak and the frightened. If I'd executed your friend or left him to die, what kind of servant of mankind would that make me?'

Throughout Gaunt's career, the ability to turn out an inspirational phrase had served him well. A key part of any commissar's job was to inspire and uplift, to make a man forget the privations he suffered or the horrors he faced. He was good at it. Right now, with some distaste, he realised he was playing on that skill, saying what Landerson needed to hear. The truth was he hadn't wanted to leave Lefivre's body behind, nor any other clue the archenemy could exploit. If he was going to pull Lefivre out, it might as well have been alive.

But Gaunt wanted to keep Landerson on his side. The Ghosts needed the resistance now, more than ever. Without their cooperation, the mission was doomed. Gaunt had serious misgivings about Cirk, and by extension her associates Plower and Acreson. But Landerson seemed the soundest of them. Solid, dependable, driven. And loyal. Gaunt didn't want to breed any resentment between the mission team and the cell fighters by treating them as expendable.

So he did what commissars had been doing since the inauguration of the Officio Commissariat. He put a positive spin on things. He inspired and kindled trust.

They had been at the air-mill now for twenty minutes. Ruined and derelict, the structure rose above the thinning mist at the top of the fields. There was a decent view down across the three kilometres to the causeway. Gaunt could see the shimmering light of the huge fire, and with his scope he could pick out the commotion along the enemy line.

So far there was no sign of the diversion team. Cirk was pressing to move on. 'They'll be scouring the area before the hour's out,' she'd told Gaunt. Gaunt decided to give Mkoll's team another ten minutes.

He prayed they were alive. The fireball had been vast. Had it been the promised diversion, or an accident?

'Go check on Lefivre,' Gaunt said to Landerson. 'Tell him… tell him we're fine. Him and me, I mean. No hard feelings.'

Landerson turned and went back inside the mill, leaving Gaunt in the stone doorway. Gaunt looked up at the winch window twenty metres above him in the tower's side.

'Anything?' he called.

Larkin's head appeared and shook.

'Keep watching, Larks.'

Gaunt wandered around the mill's vast base and entered the loading yard. Feygor stood watch on the gate, and nodded to his commander. Criid had found a rusting water tank and was purifying water to refill their flasks.

'Any sign of the sarge?' she asked Gaunt. Criid was a sergeant herself, a platoon leader, the first female sergeant in the Tanith First. But everyone called Mkoll 'the sarge'.

'Not yet, Tona.'

She shrugged. 'I had a dream last night,' she went on. 'Saw Caff and the kids. They were fine.'

'Good,' he smiled. They were all suffering from vivid, sometimes delusional dreams. Tona Criid had been a gang-girl on Verghast, hard-forged by that tough and uncompromising life, but she still displayed a wonderful naïveté. The florid dreams Gereon was fermenting in their minds were not illusions to her. She reported her dream as a matter of fact, as if she'd had a pict message from home. Gaunt wasn't about to contradict her. Criid was one of the most dependable and four-square people in his team, up there with Ven and Mkoll.

'How light are we getting?' he asked. Criid and Beltayn shared responsibility for supervising the team's supplies of food and ammunition.

'Down to two days on rations,' she said. 'Four if we switch to emergency conservation. I don't recommend that. Doc Curth agrees. We'll get slow and tired. Time to start foraging.'

Gaunt nodded. There had been no way they'd have been able to bring enough rations for the entire mission. Foraging was a necessary evil, and he'd been putting it off. Once they started eating the native resources, it would likely accelerate the effect of Chaos in their systems.

Time was running out.

'Ammo?' he asked.

'Plenty for the heavy, and almost a full set of charges. Las down by a third. Hard rounds is a different story. Pretty short. We've been into a gak of a lot more fire-fights than we were expecting at this stage.'

Gaunt pursed his lips. They certainly had. The stand-off in Ineuron Town alone had almost cleaned him out of bolt and slug clips.

'Sir?'

'Yes, Tona?'

'Do you know someone called Wilder?'

'Wilder? No, I don't think so.'

'A Colonel Wilder. He has dark hair, and is a good looking man.'

'No, sergeant. I don't believe I do. Why?'

She smiled, screwing the lid onto one of the flasks. 'He was in my dream too. Caff kept calling him "sir".'

'I'm afraid I don't know what that's all about, Criid,' Gaunt said.

'Oh well,' she said. 'I'm sure Caff will tell me.'

Feygor called out from the gate. Out of the mists, Mkoll, Mkvenner and Brostin had just come into view.

A WRETCHEDLY THICK pall of smoke hung over the causeway. Uexkull swung down out of the deathship hatch and walked along through the jumble of transports until he reached the point where the road surface became black and blistered. Behind him, the occupation troopers cowered on their knees.

Before him lay a stretch of destruction. Buckled rockcrete, charred heaps, the torched, molten residue of vehicles.

'A fuelling accident?' he asked.

At his side, Virag cleared his augmented throat. 'Lord, we think not. There was a report of gunfire just before the ignition. A firefight.'

Uexkull turned slowly to look up-country at the airmills now slowly being revealed as the fog breathed away. 'Then they died here. Or they used the confusion to slip past the picket.'

'They have shown themselves to be devious and resourceful thus far,' Virag said. 'I think we have to presume they are beyond the road. Some of them, at least.'

'Agreed,' said Uexkull. 'Start a point by point search of the region. Begin with the mills and the nearby villages.

I have a nasty feeling they have played me for a fool, and that is not a sensation I wish to prolong. Find them, Virag. Find them, or at least point me at them. I want to kill them myself.'

'Yes, lord.'

'One last thing,' Uexkull said. 'Summon all the sirdars and other seniors in charge of the picket line. Have them come to me in the next five minutes.'

Virag nodded. Uexkull drew his bolter and checked the clip load.

'The next five minutes, you hear me? I wish to discipline the morons who let this happen.'

IDRESHA CLUWGE HAD been belching at him for three hours now. True, her skeletal hand-maids had been translating her guttural questions, but the pheguth felt like he'd been burped at for long enough.

'I'm tired,' he said.

The Anarch's chief ethnologue leaned back in her grav-chair and steepled her massive fingers across her domed chest.

'We have barely begun, pheguth,' she said, via one of her life-wards.

The pheguth shrugged. The ethnologue bemused him. Not as a person – she was a grotesque monster, and that was bafflement enough. No, it was her purpose. It was her 'duty to learn in all detail about the life and culture of the enemy'. That's what she'd told him on the dam. She asked him curious questions like:

'How does a man make the sign of the aquila, and what does it represent?'

or

'Eggs, when fried, are popular amongst men of the Imperium, are they not?'

or

'How old must an Imperial child be before he or she is considered fit for military service?'

or

'Explain simply the financial mechanisms of the Munitorum.'

THEY KNEW NOTHING. Nothing! It made the pheguth laugh. For all its might, for all its frightening power, the archenemy of mankind understood virtually nothing about the day-to-day workings of the Imperium.

The ethnologue was, in his opinion, the archenemy's most formidable weapon. The forces of the Ruinous Powers might lay waste to worlds, conquer planets, and burn fleets out of the void, but they did not even begin to understand the mechanisms of their sworn enemy.

Cluwge was an instrument in that subtle war. She asked the questions that were unanswerable during the heat of combat. She asked about the little details, the small particulars of Imperial life. The hosts of the Archon might crush the warriors of the Imperium, might drive them to rout, but Cluwge's understanding offered them true mastery. Defeating the enemy was one thing. Comprehending the workings of its society so that it might be controlled and suppressed – that was quite another.

Idresha Cluwge was a tool of domination. What she learned informed the higher powers and armed them for rule.

The pheguth had answered his best.

'I want to go now,' he said. The nagging pain of transcoding soaked his brain. 'Tomorrow, or the day after, we can take this up again.'

Cluwge shrugged.

The pheguth rose. 'A pleasure,' he said and walked out of the room.

He had expected to find his antlered handlers in the anteroom, but there was no sign of them. The door stood open and bright sunlight beckoned from the gallery beyond.

The pheguth walked through the door and out onto the gallery. Daylight spilled in through the windows. The gallery was empty right down its length. At the far end, the next door was also open.

'Desolane, Desolane,' the pheguth tutted as he scurried down the gallery in his slippers. 'When will you stop these tests of my loyalty?'

A figure stepped in through the doorway at the end of the hall. It was not Desolane. The pheguth had never seen this person before. He came to a halt, eyes narrowed in curiosity.

'Who–?' he began.

The man was tall and clad in dark khaki fatigues. He was sweating, as if he was scared.

'Are you the pheguth?' he asked in a curiously accented voice.

The pheguth began to step backwards. 'That is what they call me...' he replied, his voice tailing off.

The man in khaki produced a laspistol from his tunic and aimed it at the pheguth's head.

'In the name of the Pact and the Archon!' he said.

And fired.

FOURTEEN

THE PHEGUTH STOOD where he was and blinked. There was an odd, stinging pain in the left side of his face, and a warmth on his left shoulder. The man in khaki continued to point the pistol at him, his hand shaking, his eyes wide.

The pheguth glanced down slowly. Blood was soaking his left shoulder and the front of his tunic. *His* blood. He raised his hand and gently prodded the fused mess of his left ear. His fingertips came away bloody. The man in khaki had been so scared, so worked up that he'd botched the point-blank headshot.

The pheguth was simply stunned. He blurted, 'God-Emperor of Mankind!'

The words saved his life. The would-be assassin, already hyped up on adrenaline, flinched at the sound of the heretical phrase and took a step back, raising his hands to his ears. In that moment, the pheguth felt his own adrenaline surge. He swung his fist and broke the man's nose with an audible crack.

The assassin fell to one knee, snorting blood. The pheguth turned and ran.

'Murder!' he shouted. 'Murder!' There was a door to his left. He threw it open and ran through as the first lasbolts spat after him. The assassin was on his feet again, running after him, firing his pistol and spitting blood.

The room was a well-appointed retiring chamber, dressed with many pieces of antique furniture and elegant floor-length wall-tapestries. There was an open door on the far side of the room, but the pheguth knew he'd never reach it and clear it before he came into the firing line again. Instead, he threw himself down and crawled behind a chaise on his hands and knees.

The assassin ran into the room making an ugly gurgling, panting noise through his split nose. He crossed to the far door and peered through. The pheguth could see his feet from under the chaise.

The assassin turned back from the door and began to search the chamber. From his hiding place, the pheguth watched the man's feet as he pulled back chairs and peered behind tapestries. In another few moments, he'd turn his attention to the other side of the room.

A second set of feet entered the chamber, booted like the first.

'Did you kill him?'

'He ran in here,' the first man replied, agitated.

'You fired. Did you kill him?'

'He ran in here!' the first man repeated. 'I wounded him…'

The newcomer cursed. His feet disappeared from view. The pheguth heard a heavy sideboard scrape on the floor as it was pulled out.

'You mean he's hiding?'

'Yes! Help me look for him!'

The second man mumbled something else. A chair moved. 'Look. Look! Is this your blood? Here, on the rug?'

'No.'

'He's behind that chaise,' the second man said.

The pheguth dropped flat on the floor and pulled his arms around his head. Two laspistols fired, and multiple shots perforated the back of the chaise, punching through the fabric into the tapestry and the wall behind, puffing out blossoms of kapok stuffing. One shot, low, kissed across the pheguth's left hip and made him squeal in pain. He writhed forward, scurrying from the cover of the chaise until he was behind a hand-painted spinet.

But one of them at least had spotted him moving. Now the shots renewed, tearing into the instrument. Strings burst and broke in weird jangling discords; box panels splintered, and pieces of the keyboard flew into the air.

A weird howl filled the room and the rain of las-shots stopped abruptly. A man cried out. Then there was a bright shriek of pain. Something was switching the air like a whip. The pheguth raised his head, hearing solid impacts and muffled weights striking the floor. Liquid spattered across the tattered spinet, as if shaken from a loaded sponge.

A final las-shot. A final scream. A final wet impact.

Shaking, the pheguth looked out from under the spinet's stand. He saw a pair of hooves. He rose, and peered out over the top of the broken instrument.

Desolane faced him. The life-ward's arms were extended. Blood dripped from the fighting knives brandished in each hand. The smoke-cloak wreathed about Desolane's torso like a swarm of insects. A few tiny dots of blood glinted on the bronze mask.

Through the mask slits, the life-ward's watery blue eyes fixed on the pheguth. 'You can come out now,' Desolane said.

The pheguth blinked. He got to his feet. To say that the two assassins were dead was as much of an understatement as saying that a supernova is the end of a star's life. It conveyed nothing of the catastrophic violence involved.

The room was wet with great quantities of blood that had been spilled with explosive force. It soaked the tapestries and the soft furnishings, ran down woodwork and pooled on the floor. The rug was drenched crimson. The two killers had been dismembered with such sharp frenzy that not even their skulls remained intact. The pheguth had seen his share of horror, but even so he decided not to look at the surgically split and severed remains. He focused instead on a bloody laspistol that had been cut cleanly in two.

Desolane sheathed the twin ketra blades. 'Pheguth, my humble apologies,' the life-ward said.

THEY REACHED THE village Plower called 'Wheathead' in the early part of the afternoon. It was dark and cold, with a constant threat of rain from the east. The sky churned in sulphurous, lightless patterns. Cirk led them down through a sparse copse of trees towards the hedge-line that flanked the main road into the place. To either side lay raw fields of decaying vegetable crop and rows of collapsed incubation cloches.

From the trees, Gaunt used his scope to study the village. 'I see two troop trucks,' he said.

'A search will be underway already,' Cirk replied.

'There, by the granary. What are those masts?'

Cirk took a look. 'The local excubitor house. The vox links belong to them.'

'I have a plan in mind,' Gaunt said. 'I've been discussing the practicalities with my adjutant, Beltayn. We'll need your help to make it work.'

'What sort of plan?' Cirk asked.

'You won't like it. Not at all. We need a diversion.'

Cirk snorted without much humour. 'I've seen what you and your kind do as a diversion, colonel-commissar.

Set half the world alight. No wonder you think I won't like it.'

Gaunt shook his head. 'I mean a real diversion. One to put the enemy off the scent. Otherwise, it's not going to be long before they figure out why we're here.'

'Go on,' she said, dubiously.

'In a moment.' Gaunt adjusted the scope's focus. 'There, to the north of the village. That space there. What is it?'

He had pinpointed a wide acreage of freshly-turned earth surrounded by a long chain-link fence. Clusters of hooded figures moved slowly about the broken ground.

'A boneyard,' Plower said. 'There's one in almost every settlement. Thousands died during the invasion. Many were left to rot on the battlefields, but in towns and villages, the enemy heaped the dead in mass graves.'

'Those people look like mourners,' Gaunt said.

'That's right, sir,' Plower replied. 'The archenemy understands that certain allowances must be made to placate a conquered population and keep it in check. They permit the consented to visit the boneyards, provided they do not break any laws governing religious worship. Of course, no one knows who exactly is interred in any given pit, but it helps some people to be able to pay their respects at a graveside.'

Gaunt closed his eyes briefly. Once again, the abominable foe had surprised him. It was almost an act of humanity to allow public mourning at the mass burials. Or was it merely another way of reminding the people of Gereon how little their lives were worth?

'Let me get this straight,' Rawne said quietly. 'The fething enemy forces allow people to come here and visit the grave?'

'Yes,' said Cirk.

'That's our way in,' said Rawne. 'Posing as mourners, I mean.'

'I thought that,' Gaunt replied.

'Our first priority is to try and establish contact with the resistance here,' Cirk said.

'Agreed,' said Gaunt. 'My other plan can wait.'

AN INFLUX OF mourners had gathered around the head-road into the village. Most were dressed in filthy travelling robes. A few rang hand bells, or rattled wooden beads. Lost in their own little worlds of misery, they paid little attention to the clutch of shrouded mourners who joined them from a side path.

Cirk and Acreson – with their damnable consented imagos – led the group. Rawne followed with Bonin, Criid, Feygor and Lefivre.

There had been what Colm Corbec had once called 'robust discussion' about who should make up the team. Gaunt insisted on being part of it – this was his show, after all, and every Ghost knew it. But Rawne had been sidelined at Ineuron, and didn't want to be left waiting again. He and Gaunt had argued fiercely.

'One leader goes, one stays!' Gaunt had said. 'We must maintain the viability of the mission. If both of us die–'

'Then Mkoll takes over! You treat him like a fething senior as it is, and we both know he can do the job. I want to be part of this! I want to know what's going on!'

Gaunt had looked at Rawne coldly. Maybe it had been a mistake bringing him in the first place.

'With respect to Mkoll, that's not an option. We do this by the book.'

Rawne just nodded. 'In that case, sir, it's my turn.'

Rawne had picked Feygor and, on Cirk's advice that women were less frequently checked than men, Criid.

They'd been all set to go when Lefivre asked to join them. Gaunt and Rawne had both said no at first, but Lefivre, looking stronger and more determined, had insisted. It seemed to Gaunt that the cell fighter desperately wanted to prove himself to the Guardsmen after his foul-up at the causeway.

'There is another thing,' Lefivre had said quietly. 'I come from this region originally. There's every chance my mother, father and both my brothers are buried in that boneyard.'

Not even Rawne could argue with that.

FROM THE TREES, Gaunt watched their slow advance through his scope.

'You can trust Rawne, you know,' Mkoll said quietly.

Gaunt looked round. 'I know. I just wish he could trust me.'

Mkoll smiled. 'He does, sir. In his way.'

'Sir?' Larkin's call was no more than a whisper. He was laying the sight of his long-las across the low roofs of the dismal village. 'What the hell are they?'

Gaunt adjusted his own scope. Near the central cross-roads of the village, there rose several talix trees, shorn of their branches, transformed into gibbets. A pair of broken, puppet-forms dangled from them, swaying in the breeze.

'Landerson?' Gaunt handed the cell fighter his scope and pointed.

'What are those?' he said.

'WIREWOLVES,' SAID CIRK. 'Don't look at them.'

Rawne turned his gaze towards the muddy track. He had a lasting memory of puppets, two life-size mannequins loosely made of metal parts, strung together on wires.

'They're dormant now, but don't look at them,' Acreson whispered. 'It provokes them.'

Fine by me, Rawne thought.

They moved on. A glance told Rawne that Bonin and Criid were doing fine, heads bowed under their hoods. Feygor too, if he'd only relax his fething shoulders. He was the most damn upright and rigid mourner in the history of grief.

Rawne looked at Lefivre. He inwardly cursed Gaunt for his decision to allow the man into this play. Gaunt had even had the brass balls, before they left, to draw Rawne aside and tell him 'vouchsafe' was not an option as far as Lefivre was concerned.

'You want this lead, Rawne, all right. I'm giving it to you. But Lefivre comes back alive if any of you do. Got me? I owe them this much.'

The mourners with them moaned and rang their bells.

You and me both, Rawne thought.

Wheathead was a miserable place. They passed what had once been an inn before an artillery shell had closed it down. Only the sign still swung.

Loose, in the wind, like the wirewolves.

The procession of mourners drew to a halt. Up ahead, excubitors were checking the line. Rawne reached in under his cloak and took hold of his mk III.

He heard the rank voices of the grim excubitors. They barked and cursed in their foul language, not even bothering to let their voice boxes translate.

He saw them check Cirk's imago with a funny, paddle-like device.

'You are a long way from home, consented,' one excubitor said, suddenly translating in a delayed crackle.

'I am come to visit my dead, magir. I have walked a long way, and paid the tariffs,' he heard Cirk reply.

The excubitors waved the rest of them by. Rawne could smell the excubitors. Sweat, grease, and some other odour too rank to describe. The mourners trudged on up the hill towards the boneyard.

Cirk dawdled until she was alongside Rawne. 'There is a house off to our left. I think we can contact the cell there.'

He nodded.

They slipped away, leaving the road and the plodding mourners. Behind them, the excubitors at the checkpoint showed no sign of noticing. Hugging the shadows, the mission team hurried along the side street and stopped at a stone porch. Acreson reached up and turned one of the loose stones in the gate post around.

'We'll go to the boneyard now,' said Cirk. 'If the resistance is active here, there'll be a feather under that stone by the time we come back.'

'All right,' Rawne nodded.

They began to climb the hill towards the boneyard. Rawne kept looking back. He could see the parked troop transports, and the Occupation troopers going from house to house.

And then he saw something else.

'What the feth is that?' he asked.

Cirk turned. She uttered a low gasp. 'It's a glyf,' she murmured. 'Look away. For the God-Emperor's sake, look away!'

'I've LOST SIGHT of Rawne's group,' Gaunt said. 'I think they went down that street there, left of the main road. But the buildings are blocking my view.'

'Be patient,' said Mkoll.

'Is that a lantern? What is that?' Larkin murmured.

'Where?'

Larkin suddenly jerked back, as if he'd been stung. He pulled the sniper scope down from his eye. Larkin was deathly pale and his eyes were wide with fear. 'Emperor protect me! Feth! What did I just see?'

Gaunt panned round. He saw the light, a glowing mass, bright as neon, the size of a trooper's backpack, drifting along at the height of the eaves. It made no sense. But it seemed to have some kind of glowing structure. He–

The scope went black.

Gaunt looked up. Landerson had clamped his hand around the end of Gaunt's scope, blocking his view.

'What the feth are you doing?'

'It's a glyf,' said Landerson. 'Believe me, the last thing you want is a good, magnified view of it.'

'What the feth is–' Rawne began.

'Shut up, Rawne!' Cirk hissed. 'Keep walking. No one look at it!'

'But–'

'No talking!'

Rawne did as he was told. He turned back to make sure everyone was following, struggling to keep his eyes off the strange, curling light that lingered over the street behind them.

Everyone had obeyed Cirk's order. Everyone except Feygor.

Murtan Feygor stood transfixed, gazing at the illuminated symbols that coiled and chittered against the sullen sky. So bright, like words written in lightning, and such words! He did not understand them, but they made his flesh crawl.

In his head, the sound of scuttling insects grew louder and louder.

'Murt!' Rawne called as loud as he dared. There was an edgy pitch to his voice. Everyone turned.

'Oh shit!' Cirk gasped as she saw how the Guardsman was transfixed.

Rawne reached Feygor's side and pulled at his arm. Feygor was frozen like a statue. His eyes were wide and almost glazed. His mouth lolled open and drool hung from his slack lips.

Rawne dragged harder. He was panicking. The worst part of it was he wanted to look too. He wanted to tilt his head and understand what his old friend was staring at. There was a buzzing sound in the air, like the burr of the swarms they'd found in the Shedowtonland fields.

Bonin appeared, his eyes also deliberately turned towards the ground. He grabbed Feygor too, and together they heaved at the rigid man. Feygor refused to budge. Without thinking, Bonin slapped his hand across Feygor's eyes.

Feygor let out a strangled moan as his view was blocked. He staggered backwards into their arms and there was a sharp stink as his bladder let go. He began to struggle, shake, like an obscura addict in the throes of withdrawal.

'Come on!' Cirk called. 'Carry him if you have to!' She had a hand raised to blot out the glyf as if she was shielding her eyes from bright sunlight. The team began to move again.

But now Lefivre had looked at the glyf too.

'EXPLAIN TO ME what it is,' Gaunt said to Landerson bluntly. Landerson shrugged.

'I can't… I mean, I'm no magister, no sorcerer. I don't understand the workings of Chaos.'

'Try!' Gaunt snapped.

'It's an expression of the warp,' Plower said. 'That's what I was told. The archenemy has branded our world in every way, even the atmosphere. A glyf is the way Chaos makes its mark on the very air. A glyf is a thought, a concept, an idea… an utterance of the Ruinous Powers somehow conjured into solid form. Some say they're sentient. I don't believe that. Glyfs are Chaos runes, sigils, symbols, whatever you want to call them. The ordinals summon them into being and release them to watch over the populace. They drift, they patrol, they lurk…'

'Great,' cut in Curth sourly. 'But what do they *do*?'

Plower looked at her. 'I suppose you could describe them as tripwires. Sensors. Alarms. They react to human activity. I've no idea how. Certainly, they respond to imagos. If they detect anything unconsented, they… they react. They summon.'

* * *

THE FIRST SIGIL was hooked like a crescent moon, but also coiled somehow. The second was like the pattern a spider's steps might make in dust. The third, like the valves of a human heart. Bright. So bright. So cold. There was no order to the sigils, no arrangement, because they constantly switched places or transformed. There were more than three. Less than one. A thousand, twisted into a single light.

Lefivre knew he should be doing something other than looking at this wonder. He tasted acid reflux in his mouth. The sore wound on his forearm where the imago had once been buried ached and throbbed.

The memory of his previous encounter with a glyf came back to him. He remembered biting Landerson's palm. He remembered fear.

He wasn't frightened now. Not now. Because now he understood the symbols that crackled in the air before him. He understood what they meant. He couldn't think of a human word that meant the same thing, but that didn't matter.

He understood.

Acreson was closest to Lefivre. As Bonin and Rawne dragged the thrashing Feygor back down the muddy street, Acreson ran forward, waving at Cirk to get the others clear.

Acreson's own imago jerked and tightened. He felt it fidget in the flesh of his arm. He loathed the grub with every atom of his body, but now he counted on it, and counted on his decision not to have it removed. It consented him for night and day. Maybe it would appease the glyf and distract it from poor, unconsented Lefivre.

Acreson slammed into Lefivre, knocking him to the ground. Averting his eyes from the trembling light-form, Acreson raised his arm and exposed his imago.

The sight of it seemed to still the glyf's crackling noises for a second. Was it backing off? Had he diverted it?

There was a hard sound, like a stick breaking. Acreson gasped. Time seemed to slow down. He felt a hot pain in his belly, as if a white-hot skewer had been rammed through it. Then he felt his feet leave the ground. He was flying…

Flying backwards. Impact recoil snapped through his body like a whip-crack. For one long, silent moment, Acreson saw glittering drops of blood drift lazily up into the air before him.

His own blood.

Acreson hit the ground hard in a concussive blur of pain and sudden real-time. The las-lock bolt had blown clean through his belly and thrown him three metres backwards. Down the narrow street, summoned by the glyf, a pack of excubitors was running forward, weapons raised. Several more bolts stung down the street. Prone, rigid with pain, Acreson watched them flash over him.

'Oh. God. Emperor,' he sighed.

Its work done, the glyf was already drifting away across the low rooftops, as if bored with the game. Calling the alarm, the excubitors ran on. A carnyx horn blasted, echoing across the dismal streets of Wheathead.

The mission team was already running. Cirk and Criid led the way, with Bonin and Rawne close behind, struggling with Feygor. Lock-bolts ripped around them.

Thirty metres behind them, Lefivre got to his feet, puzzled and dazed. He felt as if he were waking from a deep sleep. What the hell was going on? He couldn't remember.

Nearby, Acreson lay on his back, twitching. The man's belly was a crater of gore. Darts of light crisped through the air.

Lefivre turned. He saw the excubitors charging towards him. By some freak of fate, they had not yet managed to hit him.

Instinct took over. PDF ranger programme training. Lefivre calmly pulled the shoddy old autorifle out from under his ragged clothing and opened fire.

His jury-rigged silencer snorted like a pressure cooker valve. Lefivre's first shots killed the two excubitors leading the charge stone dead, blowing them over onto their backs. He winged a third and then hit another in the forehead as he raked his cone of fire across the street.

The excubitors dived for cover. A las-lock bolt took off Lefivre's right earlobe and another dug a searing gouge through his left shoulder. Lefivre emptied the last of his magazine and dropped two more of the skeletal foe face-down in the mud.

Change clip. He had to change clip. His hands fumbled, dropping the empty, reaching into his belt back. A passing bolt lased off his left shin and burst the meat of his calf.

Swaying, Lefivre found a fresh magazine and rammed it home.

Autofire licked down the street. At first, Lefivre thought it must be him, but then he saw Acreson. The man had sat up, his legs crooked under him, and he was blasting with his assault weapon. The man's hands, belly and lap were soaked with blood. Ghastly black and purple spools of entrail were pushing out of Acreson's exploded stomach.

'For the God-Emperor of Mankind!' Lefivre screamed. 'For Gereon! For Gereon!' He opened fire again. The two resistance fighters hailed their fire down the narrow street. Several more excubitors toppled and died. The rest were driven back, trying to reload their slow, single-shot light muskets.

Lefivre ran to Acreson.

'Come on!'

Acreson looked up at him. Blood leaked from the corners of his mouth. 'I'm not going anywhere,' he said.

'Yes, you are. Yes, you are!'

Acreson looked up at Lefivre strangely. 'You don't remember, do you?'

'Remember what? Shut up and let me help you!'

'The glyf,' said Acreson. 'You triggered the glyf.'

Lefivre hesitated. He remembered something, a light, a word. But not...

'I didn't mean to do anything,' he said.

'I know,' said Acreson, blood bubbling around his lips. 'Run.'

'But—'

'Run, Lefivre. Save yourself.'

The excubitors had suddenly stopped shooting. A clammy chill fell across the street. In the lingering quiet, the wind rose, and the carnyx horn started to boom again.

Down at the talix tree gibbet, ball lightning seethed into being, curling and licking around the axl-beam. The wired mannequins began to tremble and quiver.

'Dear God-Emperor who protects us all...' Acreson murmured. 'We've woken them up.'

FIFTEEN

THE EXCUBITORS SCATTERED, wailing. Townsfolk and mourners fled for cover in a blind panic. Even the arch-enemy troopers, who had been mustering at the sudden alarm, now began to run. Some dropped their weapons.

There was a taste of ozone in the air. A dry, bald scent, like a heated wire. The clouds closed in over Wheathead, blooming fast like ink in water. Thunder boomed.

On the stark gibbet, the ball lightning frothed and bubbled, brighter than any sun. Warp-light shone out of it. The lightning mass sputtered and then began to drip down from the cross-beam like lava, like molten, white-hot rock, pouring down into the hollow metal puppets, filling them with light.

The wired puppets twitched as they filled. Metal segments ground against each other. Wires hummed like charged cables. The air temperature in Wheathead plunged. Frost powdered the roof tiles and the muddy streets became stiff with ice.

The wirewolves woke.

The glyf had summoned them. Arcane practices had made the space above the gibbet thin so that the immaterium could finger its way through the aether when the correct command came. Now the crude metal puppets, engineered to contain the energies of the warp and coalesce them, vibrated into life.

There were two of them. They took the form of men simply because the puppets had been fashioned to bottle them in that shape. Jerking spastically from their wires, they looked like ancient knights in full plate armour, illuminated from within by the brightest lanterns ever lit. The suspending wires shivered and sang, taut with power.

The puppet hosts had not been fashioned well. Just crude metal shoes, shin-guards, thigh plates, hauberks. Hungry radiance speared out through the gaps and chinks of joints and seams. The arm sections jerked. Light speared out through the helmet eyeslits as bright as a Land Raider's stablights.

The arms of the puppets were unfinished. Shoulder plates, metal sections for upper and lower arms. They had no gloves or hands. The supporting wires suspended loose bouquets of razor-sharp steel blades from the forearm cuffs that tinkled together as the rising wind stirred them. Extending, controlled by governing magicks scratched into the armour, the baleful light sprouted from the wrists and made long, crackling claw shapes of solid light into which those blades became embedded like fingernails.

'Run!' gasped Acreson.

Lefivre took a step or two backwards on the suddenly brittle mud. His heels cracked panes of ice. He could not believe what he was seeing. He felt his bowels turn to water.

'Run, Lefivre! Run, for Throne's sake!' Acreson pleaded.

The gibbet wires, whining frantically like live tele-graph lines, trembled and then snapped.

The wirewolves dropped from the gibbet.

Shedding ghastly light from every joint, they landed hard, then stood upright. Slowly. Very, very slowly.

The first one took a step. There was a sound like a tank's tracks as it moved. The second one followed.

Grating metal noises, blistering power.

Their bright eyes, lancing like target beams, swept across the scene ahead of them. They began to snuffle, then whine.

Then they began to howl.

'Oh my God-Emperor...' Lefivre began.

The wirewolves started forward, moving faster than any man. A deathly chill surrounded them. Their blade fingers scraped and squealed against the stone walls as they slithered along, feeling their way down the village streets with lascivious caresses.

'Please... run,' Acreson repeated.

The howling was growing so much louder.

An excubitor, caught in the open, fell to its knees before the oncoming wirewolves. One of them slashed at it with its claws of light and steel. The excubitor fell in a haze of violet light and came apart, torn into pieces. Smoke wafted from its sliced remains.

Lefivre started to run.

'WHAT THE FETH is that noise?' Rawne cried.

'Ignore it. Ignore it!' Cirk jabbered. 'We have to find cover and we have to find it now!'

Feygor had fallen again. Now Criid joined the effort to lift him.

'For Throne's sake, come on!' Cirk yelled.

They were at the edge of the village now, the sky black above them. Hideous light shone from the narrow street they had just left.

'Head for the treeline!' Cirk ordered and they began to race across a bare field that sloped away from Wheathead's western edge.

'WHAT THE HELL are you doing?' Landerson cried. 'We have to get out of here!'

'I have people down there,' Gaunt replied, shaking off the cell fighter's grip.

'Not any more,' said Landerson. 'Trust me, sir. The wirewolves are loose now. If we run, we might make it out of here with our lives.'

Gaunt looked Landerson in the eye. He knew the man wasn't lying. He had no idea what he was getting himself into. The mission was too important, too vital. Every one of his team was expendable. That's what Van Voytz had stressed. All that mattered was getting to the prize.

Gaunt had believed that was acceptable at the time. But now, as his faith was put to the test, he realised it wasn't. Rawne was down there. Feygor. Criid. Bonin.

Bonin. 'Lucky' Bonin, who'd offered his life to take Heritor Asphodel on Verghast and survived to earn his nickname. One of Mkoll's finest.

Criid, dear Tona, the punk-girl ganger, who'd come out of Vervunhive and become not only a Ghost but the First's first female officer. She had Caffran's heart. And then there were the children, of course…

Feygor. Gaunt owed nothing to Feygor except that he'd always been there and always fought like a brazen bastard.

And Rawne. His nemesis. His shadow. The man who would, Gaunt was sure, one day kill him more certainly than the forces of the archenemy.

But Rawne was Rawne. Without him, there would be no Tanith First. And now Corbec was dead and buried on distant Herodor, Rawne was the last remaining strand of that founding spirit that had been born years ago on Tanith.

Gaunt wasn't going to lose that. He wasn't going to lose any of them.

Feth take the mission.

'Mkoll!' he shouted. 'Get the team up and moving. Get them clear. If I don't come back, you know what we've come to this world to do and I trust you to get it done.'

Mkoll nodded. 'I'll do my job, sir. For what it's worth, I don't think you should be leaving us, sir.'

'Neither do I,' said Gaunt, 'But I must. Rawne's down there.'

'The man who you said never trusted you?'

Gaunt nodded. 'Consider this my way of proving him wrong.'

Mkoll smiled. Then he raised his voice. 'Varl! Brostin! Get the group moving! Turn south into the woods. No noise, you understand?'

Mkoll paused. 'Mkvenner... go with the commander.'

'I don't need–' Gaunt began.

'Ven's going with you, sir. My instructions.'

Gaunt nodded. He'd already drawn his bolt pistols and was hurrying down the bank out of the trees.

'Bring him back, Ven,' Mkoll said.

Mkvenner nodded and turned to run after the Tanith's colonel-commissar.

Mkoll hurried into the trees. 'Move it! Move it now, you bastards! Come on!'

LEFIVRE HAD GONE. Acreson, close to passing out from blood loss, maintained his sitting position and aimed his weapon down the street.

The wirewolves slithered and bounded towards him, keening. Acreson retched involuntarily at the sight of them. Wiping bile from his mouth, he opened fire.

The frantic bullets spanked off the armour of the nearest wolf, and where they hit solid light at the junction of limb armour, they melted into steam.

Acreson fired again, and again, until his clip was out.
'Oh Emperor Emperor Emperor…' he began.

The first wirewolf was on him. It sliced around with its
savage claws. Acreson's head flopped sideways, his neck
almost severed. The claws bit deep and lightning
seethed. A violet glow suffused the body of the cell
fighter. In a second, Acreson was reduced to a skeleton,
coated in blue-white ash, his exposed bones smoking.

RAWNE'S PARTY FLED Wheathead through the edges of the
field, the sky swirling with dark clouds overhead.

'Run!' Rawne ordered. Cirk was already sprinting
through the coarse grass. Criid and Bonin were struggling with Feygor.

Rawne took a tube-charge out of his jacket and
plucked the det-tape upright between finger and thumb.

The howling was getting closer now. The sky looked
like blood.

They were all going to die. Fact.

How well they did it was up to Rawne.

SCREAMING AND FIRING his weapon, Lefivre reached the
end of the street. Over the fence behind him, the lifeless
fields rolled away to the woodline.

The first wirewolf lunged at him and he opened fire,
emptying his clip into its chest. The kinetic force of the
bullets drove it back.

But the second one had slithered up at Lefivre's right
hand. It didn't strike. It reached out with its claws and
the smoking blades sank into Lefivre's shoulder.

He shuddered. His mouth opened in pain. A violet
aura lit up around his body.

Then his flesh evaporated in a drizzle of blue dust and
his blackened, cooked bones clattered onto the pathway.

SIXTEEN

LANDERSON WAS RUNNING through the gloomy trees. He was close to panic. Purchason and Plower were ahead of him, sprinting headlong. The Ghosts were–

Landerson skidded to a halt and fell over into the loam. He looked back. The Ghosts had stopped. They had stopped and they were arguing.

In the name of the Throne! Death is at our heels! What are you doing?

'You let him go? Alone?' Curth was yelling.

'I sent Ven with him…' Mkoll said.

'This isn't right. We shouldn't be running,' Beltayn announced.

'Thanks for sharing, trooper,' Mkoll growled. 'Now move it.'

'You heard the sarge,' Brostin said. 'Let's go!'

'No,' said Larkin.

'Well then, feth you, Larks!' Brostin said, and began to run on anyway.

Mkoll looked at Varl, Curth, Larkin and Beltayn. 'I've given you an order. Gaunt's own order. Don't do this. Not now.'

'My dear sir,' Curth hissed. 'If not now, when?'

She turned, and started hurrying back through the undergrowth towards the village.

'Stop it! Stop it, woman! Ana!' Mkoll cried. No one had ever seen the master of scouts display such open emotion. It didn't stop Varl, Beltayn and Larkin from following her.

'Sorry, sir,' Beltayn called back over his shoulder. 'He needs us. Something's awry.'

'Stop where you are!' Mkoll shouted. He almost raised his weapon to aim at them, then he thought how ridiculous that would be. 'Please!' he called. 'Gaunt told us to go!'

The four Ghosts stopped and looked back at him. Beltayn stared at the forest floor, unwilling to catch Mkoll's fierce gaze. Curth shrugged. Larkin kept looking back towards the village, listening to the howling that rang up the fields towards them.

Varl just smiled. 'Sarge... since when did Ibram Gaunt go into a fight and not expect the Ghosts to be right behind him?'

'We have a mission here,' Mkoll began. 'We have a duty. It's important. We can't just...'

His voice tailed away. 'Feth, I'm not even convincing myself.'

He turned and looked at the departing form of Trooper Brostin heading away through the trees. 'Brostin! Get back here! Now! For Tanith and for the Emperor, we're going back! Move it, trooper!'

They turned, raised their weapons, and began to run back towards Wheathead.

'WE'RE WHAT?' BROSTIN said. Panting, he set down his heavy cannon and looked back through the trees. 'You've got to be fething kidding me...'

'You need a hand with that?' Landerson said, slipping through the undergrowth behind him.

'What?'

'The cannon. It's awful heavy if we're going back all that way.'

'Feth! You too? Has everyone gone fething mad?'

Landerson was sure they hadn't. Once in a lifetime, an officer came along who was worth following. Call it love, call it respect, call it duty, it was something about the man that made you want to push yourself, right to the limit, even in the face of horror. Ballerat had been that sort of man, Throne rest him. And Gaunt was that kind too. Landerson had seen the look in the faces of Varl and Curth, Beltayn and Larkin. That was all he had needed to know.

He looked over his shoulder. Plower and Purchason were long gone. Brostin looked like he might just follow them.

'Coming?' Landerson asked. 'If you're not, let me take the heavy. They're going to need it.'

Brostin glared at him. 'Feth you. Feth you, you stupid gak. Are you all fething crazy?'

STREAMING RIBBONS OF light in their wake, the wirewolves leapt the perimeter walls of Wheathead and swept down into the fields. Rawne turned again and saw them coming.

'Move! Move!' he yelled at Bonin and Criid as they stumbled with Feygor. The treeline was so far away. They'd never make it. Rawne swivelled the tube-charge in his hand like a baton and decided that this was the moment to stand his ground. The field's dry grasses swished around his legs.

The wirewolves came for him, wailing.

CIRK WAS STRUGGLING up the rise towards the treeline when she saw Gaunt and Mkvenner leap past her, dashing the other way.

'Where are you going?' she cried. 'In the name of Terra, run, you idiots!'

They ignored her.

Fools, Cirk decided, and ran on. She tripped over a root and fell hard. Getting up again, she looked back down the field and saw Rawne, isolated amid the dry grasses, facing down the warp monsters that were bounding towards him.

RAWNE COULD SMELL their fury. Taste their evil. The wire-wolves thrashed through the spent corn to meet him, daemons bottled in clanking suits of metal.

Rawne pulled out the det-tape, raised the charge, and threw it.

The blast knocked him off his feet. His timing had been perfect. The tube had gone off right under the leading wire-wolf. It disappeared in a volcano of fire and exploded earth.

The dust cleared. The wirewolf came on. He hadn't even slowed it down. Not even sightly.

Rawne's fingers slid into his jacket and grabbed his last tube-charge.

The wirewolf pounced at him, its claws slicing the air.

No time. No time. No–

Bolt rounds hit the monster in mid-leap and blew it back into the grass. It got up again immediately, and then was felled a second time by sustained bolter fire that thumped off its chest plating like hailstones off a tin roof.

Rawne looked up. Gaunt ran past him up the field, firing a bolt pistol in each hand. Every round slammed home, twisting the daemon back again and again, buckling its armour sleeve.

But it refused to die.

And the second one was right on them. It reared up, its claws unfurled.

Rapid las-fire knocked it over into the grass. Mkvenner arrived, right on Gaunt's heels, blasting at the thing with relentless rifle shots.

The second wirewolf shrugged, rising again. Where it had fallen, it had burned a patch of dry grass black and scorched the earth. It flew at Mkvenner.

His mag was spent. He spun the lasrifle like a staff and hit the attacking daemon in the face plate with the butt-end of his weapon, jerking it back. Then he ducked and jumped sideways as the claws cut for him. Another jab with the butt-stock into the crackling breastplate and the wirewolf recoiled again.

Darting back, legs wide and braced, Mkvenner drew his warknife and fixed it to his rifle's muzzle. As Rawne looked on, awe-struck, Mkvenner spun the weapon a second time, the straight silver gleaming in the dull light, and speared it at the wirewolf's renewed attack. Lunge, stab, block, sweep, another blow with the stock.

It had been rumoured that Mkvenner had somehow received training in the ancient art of *cwlwhl*, the martial art of the long-vanished Tanith wood-warriors, the Nalsheen. In the old days, it was said, the Nalsheen had banded together in the oblique forests of Tanith and, armed only with fighting staves tipped with silver knives, had overthrown the corrupt Huhlhwch Dynasty, ushering in the age of modern, free Tanith.

A lot of old balls, Rawne had thought. All part of some mythic and patriotic legend from Tanith's past. There were no Nalsheen any more, no wood-warriors. It was all a load of old crap and Mkvenner played it for all he was worth to boost his rep as the mysterious, quiet type.

Rawne rapidly revised his opinion. He watched in quiet wonder as a lone man, armed only with an exhausted rifle, fought hand to hand with a daemon from the warp, blocking, striking, sweeping, stabbing. Mkvenner's movements were like some violent ballet. He was matching the thing's every blow, every slice, fending it off, driving it back, avoiding every lethal hook it swung at him with sheer agility and grace.

Until his luck ran out.

The wirewolf ripped, and Mkvenner tumbled over, legs pinioning, his lasrifle staff shorn in two by the murderous claws.

The wirewolf leapt at the sprawling scout.

Rawne reached for his last tube-charge, knowing he would be too late.

A hotshot round hit the monster in the jaw plating and blew it sideways violently. It rolled and writhed, burning the ground.

Up at the treeline, Larkin reloaded and re-aimed.

'Wanna go again?' he breathed, and fired his second shot. Beside him, Mkoll and Beltayn opened up too.

THE OTHER WIREWOLF had launched itself at Gaunt again, howling fit to break the sky apart. His bolters spent, Gaunt holstered them and unslung the weapon he had asked Beltayn to care for during his mission into Ineuron Town.

The power sword of Hieronymo Sondar.

He triggered the ignition stud. It lit up like a firebrand in his hands. Gaunt swung it at the wirewolf and sent the creature staggering away, a deep gouge hacked into its chest plate.

But that was nothing like enough to kill it. It came back at him with renewed fury.

Gaunt knew he wasn't going to get his sword up to block in time.

'MY MASTER,' VIRAG said, and handed the printout wafer to Uexkull. The warrior read it.

'Is this correct?' he asked, his voice creaking like a dry tree in a slow wind.

'Yes, lord,' said Virag. 'Intelligence reports that the wirewolves have woken at Wheathead.'

'That's what… ten kilometres from here?'

'A dozen at most.'

Uexkull hurried towards the waiting deathships. 'We have them now. I just hope something's still alive by the time we get there.'

THE WIREWOLF'S ARM swept round, its luminous claws whistling towards Gaunt's throat. But the blow didn't land.

A bright stream of heavy cannonfire ripped into the wirewolf, hurling it backwards a good three metres. Some of the hammerblow shots broke the metal threads articulating the daemon's arm, and its claws and wrist-guard ripped away. Blinding energy began to spit and bleed out of the broken limb.

In the treeline, close to Larkin, Beltayn and Mkoll, Landerson squeezed the autocannon's stirrup trigger again and hit the stricken wirewolf for a second time.

It juddered backwards, weeping warp-power out of its stump in a flurry like welding sparks.

'You'll probably need these,' a voice said.

Landerson looked up. Brostin hunkered down beside him, pulling feeder belts out of his ammunition hoppers.

'Load me,' said Landerson.

HEAVY FIRE WAS streaking out of the trees, along with las-blasts and devastating shots from a long-las. But the wirewolves weren't beaten. Shuddering from the impact of incoming fire, shrugging off hard rounds and las-bolts alike, they drove themselves forward to get at Rawne, Gaunt and Mkvenner.

Gaunt had seen what the cannon shots had done to the arm of one of them. Already, the wirewolf seemed to be moving more sluggishly, its inner light dimmer. Gaunt remembered Landerson saying, back in Ineuron Town, that the things used up their power quickly. The precious sword held in a two-handed grip, Gaunt swung at the damaged wirewolf. The powered blade slashed into the metal threads of the thing's neck.

The taut wires snapped. Its containment armour now entirely broken open, the wirewolf released its channelled energy.

It ignited, blasting ferocious white flame out in a wide shockwave that smashed Gaunt, Rawne and Mkvenner to the ground.

Struggling up from the detonation, Gaunt shook his head. His ears were ringing. The grass around them was burned and scorched, and littered with pieces of the daemon's metal suit. The flesh of Gaunt's face tingled. It felt like sunburn.

He shook his head again and his hearing began to return.

That was when he heard a rumbling sound.

SEVENTEEN

A MILITARY TRUCK was thundering across the field towards them. It was an Occupation force troop transport, painted matt green, churning up the rough surface of the field with its six big tyres. It had come from the outskirts of the village, and demolished at least one low wall in its urgent effort to reach them.

Great. Now they had troops closing on them too.

Gaunt tried to get Rawne and Mkvenner up. Both were badly dazed, concussed, and had red heat burns on their faces.

'Come on!' Gaunt urged. He was none too steady on his feet himself.

The second wirewolf was still intact. As the smoke from the blast drifted around it, it halted for a second, as if trying to work out what had happened to its twin. Then it lifted its iron-cased head, its eyeslits blazing pits of light, and began to stride towards the stumbling Ghosts. Its pace increased. In a moment, it was bounding along, closing fast.

Rawne still had hold of his last tube-charge. He threw it behind them, and the charging wirewolf vanished in a veil of grit and flame.

Rawne, Gaunt and Mkvenner ran towards the trees. Back on its feet, the wirewolf leapt through the thick black smoke from Rawne's munition and gave chase.

The truck slammed through the smoke behind it and drove straight into the wirewolf, mashing it down. It vanished under the bellowing transport. Gaunt heard metal screech and grind.

The truck swung round and came to a halt. There was a figure standing in the open back. It was Curth.

'Get on!' she yelled.

They ran towards her. She helped Rawne and Mkvenner clamber up into the back. Gaunt struggled into the cab to find Varl behind the wheel.

'What the feth are you doing?' Gaunt said.

'Improvising,' Varl replied, and threw the vehicle in gear. 'It was the doc's idea, actually. The others were giving you cover-fire, and she had no weapon, so she said, Varl, she said–'

'Spare me the details,' Gaunt said.

Varl slammed the heavy machine forward. Criid and Bonin were ahead, approaching the treeline with Feygor slumped between them.

'Pick them up first. Then we have to g–'

There was a rending noise, metal on metal, and the truck lurched as a savage shudder ran through it.

'What the feth–' Varl began.

Electric discharge lit up the cab, crackling across the metal dash in lambent blue, jellyfish patterns.

The wirewolf wrenched its way up over the tailgate, its talons gouging the bodywork, and landed in the back. Its armour was buckled and dented, and power spurted out of the cracks. It swung its claws at Rawne. Mkvenner threw himself forward and tackled the major out of its way. But the force of the desperate bodyslam carried them over the side of the still-moving truck, and they hung there, scrabbling for handholds. Rawne slipped. Mkvenner had one leg and one arm hooked over the truck's sideboarding and managed to grab Rawne's wrist. If he let go, the Tanith officer would disappear under the rear wheels.

Curth stumbled back away from the advancing wire-wolf. 'Feth you!' she yelled and hurled her narthecium case at it. The daemon-thing swatted it aside, and the case bounced across the cargo space, its contents spilling. The truck lurched violently again, and even the wirewolf staggered. Curth fell, knocked her shoulder, and reached for something – anything – to use as a weapon.

Her hand closed over something small and hard. A flask of inhibitor suspension from her case. She hurled it.

It smashed against the wirewolf's dented chest plate. The inhibitor solution contained a number of compounds manufactured by the Departmento Medicae to counteract the effects of warp-contact on the human metabolism. The fluid they were suspended in was blessed water from the Balneary Shrine of Herodor.

The wirewolf screamed. It staggered backwards, clawing at its face and chest, wounding itself with its own claws. The inhibitor solution ate into the thing's armour where it had sprayed, gnawing like molecular acid.

Eyes wide, Curth looked round, found another flask, and threw that too.

The wirewolf screamed again.

Curth saw her dermo-needle gun. It had fallen out of the spilled narthecium. She grabbed it and loaded a third flask into the gun's dose reservoir.

Fuelled by a stubborn courage that surprised even herself, Curth lunged forward and jammed the dermo-needle tip into the wirewolf's left eyeslit. Her finger squeezed the activator.

The wirewolf shook, as if it were suffering from a grand mal seizure. Liquid energy, terribly bright and sickeningly viscous, bubbled and frothed out of its eye-slits. Its face plate began to fester and melt like paper in the rain.

It staggered backwards, limbs twitching, and fell back over the tailgate.

Then it exploded.

The blast threw Curth back down the length of the cargo space. The truck itself was almost thrown over. It skidded to a halt, spraying up soil.

Silence. Smoke billowed.

Still half-hanging over the sidewall of the transport, Mkvenner gasped and let go of Rawne's wrist. The major dropped down onto his feet and looked back up at Mkvenner.

'Thanks,' he said.

THE GHOSTS IN the treeline were running down towards them. Cirk and Landerson were with them. Gaunt climbed up into the back of the truck and helped Curth to her feet.

'You all right?'

She nodded. She was still holding the dermo-needle. It was broken and smoking.

'What did you do?' he asked.

'I… I think I used up our entire medical supply in about thirty seconds,' she said ruefully.

'Right now, I don't think that matters,' he replied.

Varl got the truck restarted and the mission team hauled themselves aboard. There was no sign of Plower or Purchason.

'Do you want us to wait?' Gaunt asked Cirk. 'To look for them?'

She shook her head. From across the field, the horns of Wheathead were blowing, and troopers were emerging, fanning out into the grass.

'We have to get out of here now,' she decided.

Varl drove the battered truck up the slope and into the trees, zigzagging them through brambles and brushcover until they reached a narrow trackway.

East or west? There was no choice now. The enemy forces were closing from the east. In the distance, they could hear the drone of deathship engines. West was the only way now.

Varl put his foot down and they rattled away along the track.

Sitting in the cab beside Varl, Gaunt turned round and opened the small window through to the cargo bay.

'Cirk?' he called.

She made her way over, and leaned close to the other side of the window.

'We'll use this ride as far as we can, to put some distance between us and that place. Earlier, you told me west wasn't an option. Something called the Untill. What is that?'

'Marshland,' she said. 'We're heading into the deep forests now, and that marks the boundary. Beyond it lie the marshes themselves. Vast areas, un-navigable. The word "Untill" comes from the earliest maps of Gereon, the colonists' maps. Gereon was found to be a fecund, fertile place, hence its reputation as one of the chief agri-worlds in the cluster. But some regions, like the marshes, were unfarmable. "Untillable". That's what the name means.'

'So there's no way through?'

Cirk shook her head. She seemed tired and edgy, and the stigma on her cheek more raw than ever. It pained Gaunt to see her beauty so irretrievably spoiled.

'I'm afraid, sir,' she said, 'that your mission is now over. There's no way to achieve it. Not for a long time, at least. We might be able to hide in the Untill, I suppose. Right now, it's as good a place as any. Even the forces of the Occupation avoid the Untill. A few months lying

low, maybe, and we might risk coming out. Once the
fuss has died down. Maybe start trying to hook up with
a resistance cell.'

'A few months,' Gaunt echoed. He knew they had
nothing like that. The mission was desperately time-sen-
sitive. And besides, a few months and they would all
have succumbed to Gereon's taint. Especially now
Curth's medicines had gone.

'We'll see,' he said.

'We won't,' she replied. 'You asked me to face up to
hard truths when you enlisted my help, sir. I did that.
Now face up to hard truths yourself. Your mission has
failed. There is no chance now we can accomplish it.'

'We'll see,' Gaunt repeated.

SLEEK AND UNLOVELY, like carrion birds, the two
deathships circled Wheathead. Wan smoke drifted from
the dry fields under the trees where patches of grass were
burning. Uexkull used a scope to scan. Below, squads of
troopers and excubitors were extending out in a wide
search pattern into the forests. They had packs of fetch-
hounds, and some rode in half-tracks. On Uexkull's
orders, a full brigade strength was moving in on the village to bolster the units.

He turned back to the report Gurgoy had given him.
The Wheathead wirewolves had been woken, but they
had not returned to their gibbet when their power was
spent. That made no sense. They always returned to
sleep again, unless they were destroyed.

And nothing could destroy a wirewolf, surely?

Uexkull felt uneasy, as if the nature of the cosmos was
out of balance. He hated impossibilities.

Was it plausible that the False Emperor had sent warriors to this world who were actually capable of
destroying the merciless implements of Chaos?

'My lord?' said Virag suddenly. His face was alarmed.
He was staring at Uexkull.

'What?'

'Are you unwell, lord? Have you ingested poison?'

Uexkull blinked. 'Of course not! Why do you ask me that?'

'Your face, great lord. It was twisted into a rictus, a grimace, as if toxins infected you. And you were gurgling and choking, like you were dying of some foul–'

'I was laughing,' said Uexkull.

'Oh,' the warrior said. He paused. 'Why, lord?'

'Because we have prayed for a test, have we not?' The warrior pack all grunted *yes*.

'We have yearned to face down the bright Astartes in war, but our beloved Anarch, whose word drowns out all others, decided in his wisdom such glory was not for us. He did not send us to the frontline. Instead, he honoured us with the task of overseeing this wretched occupation. Now it seems we might have worthy prey here after all. Rivals in war. Soldiers who can destroy wirewolves and make the common troopers and the excubitors chase their own tails.'

Uexkull looked at his men. 'We have grown lazy. Now there is a true challenge. I will enjoy killing them.'

The warriors began to beat their steel-clad fists against their chest plates and bark out approval. Above the din, Uexkull heard the link chime.

'Report?'

'My lord,' the pilot's voice crackled over the intercom. 'The auspex has detected a metal object twenty-four kilometres west of this position, moving into the forests. A vehicle, lord.'

'Lock on,' Uexkull said. 'Hunt speed. Take us to it.'

THE LONG DAY was drawing to a close, and they were running out of road fast. A dark, sludgy brown light filled the sky, and the forests were growing increasingly dark and forbidding. The trees were closing around the track, which had now dwindled to an overgrown rut, and branches swished and flapped against the truck's sides. Varl had dropped his speed.

Beside him in the cab, Gaunt was talking to Mkoll. Like Cirk had done before, Mkoll was leaning to speak through the cab's little rear window. He could only see Gaunt's mouth through the slit. Both of them realised it was unpleasantly like a confessional booth. Mkoll knew he was owning up to his sins as surely as in any Imperial templum.

'I gave you an order,' Gaunt said.

'Yes, sir. I know you did.'

'Get the team away.'

'Yes, sir. I take full responsibility. We should have gone like you said.'

'But you came back, all of you. You abandoned the mission and you came back.'

'Yes, sir. We did that. Like I said, I take full responsibility. The others were just doing what I told them to.'

'Like feth!' Curth called out.

'Shut up,' Mkoll snapped. He looked back through the slit at Gaunt. 'My fault, sir. I'll gladly remove my rank pins. Mkvenner can take scout-command and–'

Glimpsed through the window slit as the truck bounced and jarred, Gaunt's mouth was smiling.

'I can pretty much guess what happened,' he said softly. 'We wouldn't be here now but for you.'

'Sir,' said Mkoll. 'Sir,' he added.

'Cirk says we're doomed, Mkoll,' Gaunt went on. 'She says we're heading into a marsh waste and that there's no hope of finding our way through. Feel like proving those rank pins to me?'

'I do, sir. Me, Ven and Bonin. We'll get us through.'

'I'm counting on it.'

'Sir?' It was Beltayn. He shuffled forward along the rattling cargo bay and Mkoll slid aside so he could reach the window slit. Beltayn had his vox-set's phones around his neck, and dragged the set behind him.

'What have you got, Bel?' Gaunt asked.

'Monitoring enemy traffic, sir.' He paused to blow his nose. His eyes were swollen and red. 'They're spread out in force behind us, closing out the woods. I'm picking up chatter from at least two airbornes. Three maybe. They're tracking in fast. I can't get a triangulation, but I think they're close.'

'The boy's right,' said Mkoll. 'I can hear jetwash. East of us, low and fast.'

In the cab, Gaunt turned to look at Varl. 'We won't get much further, will we?'

'Does the God-Emperor sit much?'

'Pull us over, Varl. Let's ditch the truck.'

THE TEAM JUMPED down the moment Varl brought the truck to a halt. There was no real trackway any more. The truck's wheel arches were throttled with torn strands of bramble and choke-weed.

'Make sure we've got everything,' Gaunt told Rawne.

'Everything?' Rawne replied sarcastically. 'Gee, what will everybody else carry?'

He was right. They were in poor shape. Ammo was perilously low. Gaunt had only a clip or two left for his bolt pistols, and everyone else was down to their last few las cells. The cannon had fired off so many rounds at the wirewolves Brostin had barely half a hopper left. Mkvenner didn't even have a rifle. The wolves had destroyed it. He had his autopistol, and he'd salvaged his warknife. Rawne had no tube-charges left. Varl still carried the team's last six in a satchel. They were low on food, and down to half on drinking water. Except for a few basics, Curth's narthecium was empty.

And that was the worst part, really. The ague was gripping them all now. Rashes, ulcers, headaches. Everyone seemed to have a head cold, especially Beltayn and Criid, who were sniffling. Feygor was still so dazed from exposure to the glyf that he had to be helped to walk.

Curth told Gaunt quietly that the infection around Fey-gor's voice box implant seemed to be getting a great deal worse, and spreading.

'Whatever you've got, give it to him,' Gaunt said.

And that was just the start. Brostin had weeping burn blisters from his pyrotechnics on the causeway. Rawne, Mkvenner and Gaunt himself had a bad case of what seemed like sunburn from the wirewolf immolation. Curth nursed her badly bruised shoulder. Rawne's wrist was sprained from Mkvenner's life-saving grip. A hundred other knocks and cuts and–

Gaunt sighed. *It won't be easy.* That's what he'd said. It won't be easy. He could picture himself saying it. Standing to attention in a sunlit hall on Ancreon Sextus, with the windflowers nodding in the breeze outside the mansion walls. Biota had just finished his briefing, and Van Voytz had risen to his feet.

'I know it won't, Ibram,' Van Voytz had said. 'But do you think you can do it?'

Gaunt had glanced sideways to his waiting officers. Rawne, Daur, Mkoll, Kolea and Hark. Rawne had just folded his arms. Mkoll had nodded. One tiny nod.

'Yes, general. The Ghosts can do this,' Gaunt had said.

'There's a fast picket already prepped to leave high anchor,' Van Voytz remarked. 'What's it called, Biota?'

'The Fortitude, lord.'

'Ah, yes. That's an appropriate word, don't you think, Gaunt?'

'Yes, general.'

'Tac suggest you should choose a team of no more than twelve. The groundwork's been laid. Intelligence has made contact with the local underground to welcome you. Ballerat. Ballerat, right?'

'Yes, sir,' Biota replied.

'He's the man to find. So... any first thoughts about who you'll take?'

Both Kolea and Daur had raised their hands, interrupting each other.

'I'd be anxious to–'

'If I could offer my–'

'Thanks,' Gaunt said, looking at them. 'I'll pick the team tonight.'

'Just as you say, Ibram… this won't be easy.' Van Voytz had turned to stare out of one of the hall's deep windows. The sunlight fell across his face. It betrayed nothing. 'There's a good chance you won't come back.'

'I realise that, general sir. I'll make sure a strong command structure for the Tanith First remains in my absence.'

'Of course. Just so. Look, Ibram…' Van Voytz turned to face him. 'This is a messy business. But crucial. I won't order you to do it. If you want to back out, say so right now and we'll forget this meeting ever took place.'

'No, general. I won't. I feel this is down to me, sir. But for my decision, this situation would never have occurred. I'd like the chance to clean it up.'

'I thought you might. Because it's him?'

'Yes, general. Because it's him.'

'Sir?'

Gaunt blinked and came out of his thoughts. Night was closing in. The team was ready to move out.

'I'm coming, Criid,' he said. She nodded, and moved up to the head of the file.

'Let's go!' Gaunt called. They started to march away into the dense, dark forest.

Cirk was beside him. 'Gaunt, there's one other thing I think you should know.'

'Really? More bad news?'

'Yes,' she said. 'The Untill. It's not safe. Not at all safe.'

'Because?'

'Apart from the predators and the toxic plants… there are the partisans.'

'The what?'

'Partisans, sir.'

'Oh great,' he replied.

EIGHTEEN

DESOLANE DREW ONE of the vicious ketra blades from under the drifting smoke-cloak and set it down on the table beside the pheguth.

The pheguth turned slowly to look at it. His ear and hip were wrapped in surgical wadding. He had been given pain-killers for the first time, on the advice of the doctors of fisyk. They hadn't helped with the headache.

'What's this for?' he asked.

Desolane spread one hand on the table, fingers splayed.

'For punishment. Punish me, pheguth.'

'What?'

'I failed to protect you. You were injured. You are now permitted to exact punishment.'

'I'm sorry?' The pheguth looked up into the pale blue eyes behind the bronze mask.

'For failure. For my failure of charge as a life-ward. You are allowed to exact punishment.'

'What sort of punishment? Am I supposed to kill you?

Desolane shrugged. 'If that is what you desire. For this type of failure, a master would ordinarily sever one of his life-ward's digits.'

The pheguth sat up sharply. 'Let me get this straight. You're suggesting I should hack off one of your fingers?'

'Yes, pheguth.'

'Because I was attacked?'

'Yes, pheguth.'

'Don't be so silly, Desolane. It wasn't your fault.' The pheguth settled back against his pillows. They made a fine change to his usual sleeping conditions. He was quite enjoying the luxury.

'I was absent, and you were left vulnerable,' Desolane said. 'I don't think you understand. I am a life-ward. I am bred to protect my charges. You are my charge. Please punish me.'

'I'm not about to chop off one of your–'

'Please!'

The pheguth looked up at Desolane again. 'You seem very anxious to be maimed, life-ward.'

'The Plenipotentiary is outraged by today's attack. He is insisting that I am not fit to guard you.'

'Well, I don't believe that's true. I believe you're very fit. You saved me from those gunmen.'

Desolane shrugged slightly. The life-ward's hand remained splayed on the table. 'Please,' Desolane said again.

'No,' said the pheguth, turning away. 'This is just stupid.'

'Pheguth... understand me. If you don't punish me, the Plenipotentiary will decide I am not fit to guard you. He will replace me. You hate me, pheguth. You fear me. But you will hate and fear the ones who might replace me even more.'

'What do you mean?'

'The other life-wards available for assignment. They would not... treat you as well as I do. They would make your life harder. Don't let them. I have grown to like you, pheguth. I would hate to see you… discomforted.'

The pheguth sat up and swung his legs over the side of the bed. 'So, unless I maim you, I will subject myself to greater cruelties?'

Desolane nodded.

'Great Throne!' the pheguth murmured. Desolane flinched. The pheguth picked up the blade and balanced it in his palm for a moment. 'You want me to do this?'

'For your own sake, pheguth.'

The pheguth raised the ketra blade and–

Put it down again.

'I can't. The truth is, I have grown to like you too. You look after me, Desolane. You understand me. I couldn't begin to hurt you.'

'But… please, pheguth…?'

'If it's so important to you, take off your own digit. I couldn't possibly do something that coarse.'

Desolane sighed. The life-ward reached out and took the ketra blade, and very quickly lopped off the smallest finger of its right hand. Blood, bright blue-red, spurted out of the stump. Desolane quickly closed a surgical clamp around the wound.

The pheguth stared in astonishment.

'Thank you, pheguth,' Desolane said. The life-ward picked up the severed finger and sheathed the blade.

The pheguth rolled away so he was facing the far wall. Unseen by Desolane, there was a smile on his face.

Now that, he thought to himself, that's real power.

'Desolane,' he said quietly. 'How did two Imperial agents get so close to me? I mean, on a world like this.'

'They didn't,' Desolane replied. 'The two assassins were not Imperial agents.'

'What are you talking about?' the pheguth asked, looking round sharply.

'The matter is closed,' said Desolane, and strode out of the chamber.

THEY SPENT AN uneasy night in the cold blindness of the forest, and then started west just before daybreak.

To the west, the land shelved away in a deep gorge of black earth and broken rock. They descended into the cave-like gloom, screened from the sky by the towering forest. The trees were ancient, twisted things, massive forms that clung to the steep slope with gnarled clusters of thick roots. A furry grey lichen coated most surfaces, and where it didn't, treebark and boulders were caked with foul black moss. Strange fungal forms sprouted from the soil, some fleshy and pink-lipped, some rough and hard like stale bread or shoe leather. The largest of them were several metres wide.

There was no birdsong and no breeze, but the still upper spaces of the sinister forest rang with woodtaps, buzzes, clicks and odd purring clacks. The only sign of animal life was the occasional long-legged fly that hummed past like an intricate clockwork toy set running and slowly winding down.

And the moths. They were everywhere. Some were tiny, and speckled the air like floating wheatchaff. Some were as big as birds. When they flew by, their dusty wings made a sound like the pages of a book being flicked. When they landed, they vanished, their wings perfectly camouflaging them against lichen and crinkled bark. Brostin misstepped and disturbed a fallen log, and hundreds of them took flight into the air, lazy and sluggish, like a flock of birds startled up in slow motion.

It made Brostin jump in surprise, and that amused the scouts. But Curth became jittery.

'I've got a thing about moths,' she confided to Gaunt.

'What do you mean, a thing?'

'They give me the creeps.'

'Ana, yesterday you faced down a wirewolf.'

She grimaced. 'Uh huh. But it wasn't all furry and dusty, was it? I'm just squeamish about them, that's all.'

'You? Squeamish? Feth, woman! You're a surgeon. You regularly deal with stuff that makes even my stomach turn, and–'

'Yeah, yeah, it's all very funny and ironic. Duhh!' She flapped her hands as an albino-white moth beat past her face. 'We've all got something, and mine is moths. All right? And on the subject, isn't it your job as mission leader and, oh – I don't know, *commissar?* – to say something reassuring at this point to keep up the spirits of a valued team member like me? Something along the lines of "everything's fine, they can't hurt you, Ana, they're just moths and I swear by the Throne of Terra to personally swat any that come near you"?'

'Everything's fine, they can't hurt you, Ana, they're just–'

'Ha ha. Too late. I'm creeped out.'

Gaunt looked at her. 'Everything is fine. Ana, if the worst thing I have to do on Gereon is keep you moth-free, I'll be happy. Be thankful your "thing" is moths and not, let me think… Chaos.'

She grinned. 'You'll do,' she said.

Ahead of them, down the steep, black slope, Cirk paused and looked back up the group. 'I forgot to say,' she called. 'The moths are poisonous. Don't touch them or let them touch you.'

Curth glared at Cirk, then at Gaunt. 'She was listening. She's got it in for me.'

'She wasn't and she hasn't.'

'Yes, she has.'

'Well, you killed a wirewolf. It's probably an alpha-female assertion thing.'

'You think?'

He nodded.

'Yeah,' Curth said, almost to herself. 'You're probably right. She's probably making it up to mess with me.'

Without even looking back, Cirk called, 'I'm not making it up.'

THE DEEPER THEY went, the darker and hotter it got. The gorge seemed to drop away into the belly of the earth. It was humid, and an increasing odour of putrefaction filled the close air. Their faces began to bead with sweat. The thick foliage of the trees around and above them was glossy black and moisture dripped from it. Parasitic vines and veiny epiphytes knitted about the trees. The weird sounds grew louder and more frequent.

By the time the steep slope began to level out, most of the team had stripped down to their vests and undershirts. Their arms shone with sweat and their throat-hollows gleamed wet. Feygor was still fully clothed.

'You feeling all right, Murt?' Rawne asked him quietly. Feygor was walking unaided now, but the trauma of the previous day had not left him yet. There was an unblinking, unfocused look in his eyes, and his face was pale.

'I'm cold,' he said. 'This place is so cold and wet.'

Rawne, sponging perspiration out of his eyes with the corner of his cape, just nodded.

Feygor was shivering. The flesh around his throat implant was swollen and angry, and when he spoke the augmetic tone sounded like it was drowning in phlegm. Casualties of war, Rawne thought. There were always some. It was the price of combat, and this time it was going to be Murt.

Beltayn and Criid kept stopping to catch their breath. The humid air combined with their streaming head colds made breathing a real effort. Both were hyper-fit, but now both seemed to have the endurance of the aged or the frail.

The ground underfoot had become spongy and waterlogged. The ancient trees populating the forest and the gorge slope were giving way to an infestation of spider-rooted mangroves and bulbous cycads. But these tree forms were just as abundant, and still screened out the sky with their meaty leaves and groping tendrils. Down here, the moths were fat and dark-coloured.

'This is the Untill?' Gaunt asked Landerson.

'Not quite. We're in the fringes of the marshland. Another few kilometres, and we'll reach them proper.'

'Tell me what you know about these partisans.'

Landerson shrugged. 'Been here as long as anyone can remember. They call themselves the Sleepwalkers.'

'Sleepwalkers?'

'Don't ask me. Apparently their name for themselves is something like noctambulists. Sleepwalkers. Anyway, they're outlaws, essentially, that's what I understand. They believe in an independent Gereon. They want no part of the Imperium.'

'They deny the Emperor?' Gaunt asked.

'Yes,' said Landerson. 'They're descendants of religious radicals who came here on the colony ships. There was a war, early on, in the first histories. The partisans lost and were driven out into the Untill. Into any places that were agriculturally worthless. They've been out here ever since. Sometimes they used to raid, or mount terrorist attacks. We used to worry about them terribly, you know? Inquisitors came here to purge them, but got lost in the marshes and never returned. They were always Gereon's embarrassing secret. A fine, upstanding Imperial world that harboured a secret population of secessionists.'

Landerson glanced at Gaunt. 'I used to hate them. They were an insult to my family name and my birthright. And like I said, they were an ongoing problem. The bogeymen out in the swamps. And then the real enemy came.'

He looked away and took a deep breath. Gaunt knew the man was trying not to let emotion overtake him.

'The real enemy. And suddenly worrying about a few deranged backwoodsmen in the marshes seemed like a luxury. Throne take me, I long for the days when the partisans were our biggest problem.'

Three black moths fluttered across the gloomy path ahead of them, as dark and heavy as Imperial hymnals.

'If they're anti-Throne, have they sided with the archenemy?' Gaunt asked.

'No idea. Maybe. The Untill is so impenetrable, even the Occupation forces leave it alone. Far as I know, the partisans are still out there. They may not even know the world outside has changed.'

'MY LORD, HE'S here,' said Czelgur.

Uexkull climbed down from the parked deathship and walked through the misty dawn out across the woodland clearing. The shuttle descended out of the rosy sky, lights blinking, vector jets shuddering. Uexkull's warriors came out to meet it, standing alongside their master.

In a final flurry of downwash, the craft landed. After a long pause, the side hatch opened pneumatically and a hydraulic ramp unfolded. Climate-controlled cabin air billowed out into the cold morning as steam. Two excubitors ran down the ramp and took up position to either side of it, their las-locks shouldered.

Ordinal Sthenelus had to duck his head to emerge from the hatch. He was old, wizened, and his shrunken body had long since atrophied. One emaciated arm still appeared to function. His withered head lolled back against a neck rest. He walked towards them over the wet grass on six long, stilt-like limbs.

Sthenelus sat in a braced seat, secured by a harness, surrounded by intricate brass devices that he manipulated with his one good arm. Sighing gyros balanced the seat on a small augmetic unit from which the elongated limbs extended. Perched on top of the slender legs, he towered over the huge Chaos Space Marines, almost four metres tall. He seemed frail to Uexkull. One sweep of his hand would demolish Sthenelus and his delicate walking carriage.

But Sthenelus was a senior ordinal, one of the Plenipotentiary's chief advisors. Respect and deference were in order.

'Nine point three metres from ramp base to this place. An incline of two per cent. Terrain soft. One hundred and eighty metres above local sea level. Sixteen hundred cubic metres of forest and–'

'My ordinal,' Uexkull said.

'Hush! I am recording.' Sthenelus adjusted some of his complex instruments. His voice was a dry whisper. 'Subject one, Lord Uexkull, masses five hundred and thirty-three–'

'My ordinal!' Uexkull said. 'I have not called you here to chart and record.'

Sthenelus's creased face frowned. 'But that is what I do. In the name of the Anarch, whose word drowns out all others. I am his planetary assessor. I make precision maps, and assay every measurable detail of the conquered worlds. I was busy in Therion Province when your call came through, busy measuring hectares of arable land for plantation seeding. The topography there is very interesting, you know. No more than eight per cent variation–'

'Ordinal, I have summoned you for a special purpose.'

'One, Lord Uexkull, that I trust involves codification. That is my duty. That is how I serve the Anarch, whose word drowns out all others. It had better be important. Plenipotentiary Isidor requires a full survey of Therion by the end of the fortnight. Show me this urgent and special purpose. Do you require me to count the trees in this region? To label their forms and species? Do you perhaps wish me to survey and sound a lake or other body of water? I smell water. Humidity of eleven over five, with a rising gradient–'

'My ordinal, no. I require you to track and locate someone for me.'

Sthenelus was so astounded that he blinked. As his parchment lids closed and opened, tiny augmetic wires whirred forward from his temples and puffed lubricating moisture into his dry eyeballs to stop the lids from sticking.

'There has been some mistake,' Sthenelus said. 'I do not track. I am no common bloodhound. This is a regrettable waste of effort. In the time it has taken to travel here from Therion, I calculate that I could have charted fifteen point seven hectares of–'

'This is the Anarch's work, ordinal,' Uexkull said. 'This is a matter of world security. Nothing – not even your scrupulous labour of measurement – has more priority. Check with the Plenipotentiary, if you must, but he will surely reprimand you for wasting time on such an urgent concern.'

'Indeed, lord.' Sthenelus paused. 'Explain this matter to me.'

'Insurgents, ordinal. Dangerous men, agents of the False Emperor. They are loose on Gereon, and they have murdered many brave servants of the Anarch. They must be found and they must be stopped before they achieve the purpose for which they have been sent here.'

'Which is, lord?'

Uexkull hesitated. 'Which is something we will discover as we torture the last of them to death. They have fled into the Untill beyond. We must find them.'

'Ah, yes. The Untill. A marsh and/or swamp region covering nine hundred thousand square kilometres of land from–'

'Ordinal.'

'I was told the Untill was to be left unmapped for now. Because of the difficulties involved. It is not tenable land. Compared to the crop production of, say, the Lectica bocage, which runs at an annual average of eight billion bushels per–'

'Ordinal!'

'Though I must say, I was itching to map the Untill, Lord Uexkull. A search, you say? It sounds rather vigorous.'

'My warriors and I will supply the vigour.'

Sthenelus licked his thin lips with a pallid, slug-like tongue. 'I have no doubt. But why would you request me, lord? I am no soldier.'

'At the feast to celebrate the first month of Intercession, the Plenipotentiary chatted with me. He told me of your talents and your matchless instruments. Designed for mapping and measuring, of course, but they have a side benefit, do they not? Nothing escapes your scrutiny. Not one bent blade of grass, not one broken twig. You have tracked fugitives before, he said. On Baldren. On Scipio Focal. Located men who believed themselves lost. Picked out the veritable needle in the wheat.'

'I admit I have. As a diversion.'

Uexkull nodded. 'The Untill is a trackless waste, and it is said that no one can chart it. Except, I would think, you. Find these enemies for me, ordinal. Lead me to them, and the Anarch himself will thank you.'

THE MARSHES SPREAD out before them, vast and mysterious. Yellow mist fumed beneath the tortured, spidery trees. Moths and flies flickered in the scant shafts of etiolated sunlight that speared down through the dense canopy. Everything smelled of rot.

They were wading now. The land had vanished, and only pools of stagnant water remained. Mkoll and Bonin led the way, probing the liquid with long poles, like the steersmen of punts. Every few minutes, the party had to turn onto a new course as a stabbing pole revealed no detectable bottom to the water ahead.

The mangroves lowered over the thick water on their crusted rafts of roots. Algae coated the water's surface, and bubbles of gas flopped up from the rot. It felt like

they were wading on through a flooded cave, except that
no cave would be so swelteringly hot. There was only a
vague suggestion of daylight.

Leeches wriggled in the fermenting water. Curth had
to remove several from bare arms. They were fat and
black, and fought against her pliers. Things moved
under the surface, darting and sliding. Varl got a glimpse
of something half-fish, half-eel that was so ugly he
nearly shot it. Long-limbed insects dappled the surface
tension as they ran upon the water top.

Larkin raised his long-las suddenly.

'What?' Gaunt hissed.

'Movement,' the sniper replied. Something emerged
out of the dark. It was a wading insect, the sized of a
small dog, stalking the swamp water on long, stilt legs,
its bladed mouthparts tilted downwards, ready to duck
and stab any submerged prey. There were several more
behind it. When they became aware of the human
intruders, they took flight, opening wing cases and soar-
ing into the hot air, trailing metre-long legs beneath
them.

Larkin lowered his weapon. 'Feth that,' he said.

Criid had to stop again. She could barely breathe.
Curth used the last of her inhibitor shots to relieve the
trooper's discomfort.

Mkvenner had cut a long stave like Bonin and Mkoll.
He'd fixed his silver warknife to one end, like a spear,
and was using it to slash down overhanging plants.
Some vines writhed back like snakes from his blade.

No one saw whatever it was that attacked Cirk. She
suddenly fell, pulled down into the water, thrashing. She
vanished. The Ghosts splashed through the water
towards her last position and she abruptly surfaced several metres away, fighting and wailing.

Something had her. She went under again. Cursing,
Gaunt stabbed into the water with his sword and
Mkvenner jabbed with his spear. Cirk came up again in

a rush, coughing and gagging, covered with weed and algae, and Landerson grabbed her. Something long, sinuous and dark rippled the water as it swam away.

Cirk's left calf was ripped and bloody. A tooth had been left in one bitemark. Five centimetres long, thin, transparent.

'Can you walk?' Gaunt asked her.

'Yes!'

'Sabbatine…'

'I'm fine. Let's get on.' She tried to wipe the sticky algae out of her hair.

'Curth can bind your wounds and–'

'Let's get on,' she snapped. 'Tell your lady friend to save her bandages.'

'My what? Ana's not my lady friend. She's a–'

'A what, Gaunt?'

'A valued team member.'

'Yeah?' Sitting on a root bole, Cirk reached down and pulled another, smaller tooth out of her leg. Her fingers were running with diluted blood. She tossed the tooth into the undergrowth. 'I've seen the way she looks at you. I've seen the way you treat her.'

'Cirk–' Gaunt began, then stopped and looked away. 'I don't have time for this. It's redundant. If you can walk, fine. We have to get on and–'

A piercing scream echoed across the dank water.

'That's your lady friend,' Cirk said.

Gaunt was already moving, churning up septic water as he ran. The others were closing in too, weapons raised.

Curth hadn't meant to scream. She really hadn't. But what she'd seen, in the shadows of the undergrowth. What she'd seen…

She'd sunk to her knees. The water was up around her chest.

'Ana!' Gaunt cried as he reached her, one bolt pistol drawn. 'What is it?'

She pointed with a shaking hand. 'There. In there. I saw it.'

'What?'

'A m-moth.'

Gaunt holstered his gun and made to wave the others back. 'For feth's sake, Curth, I told you–'

'You don't understand, it was big, Ibram.'

'Yes, but.'

'I mean big! Big, you bastard! The size of a man!'

'What?'

He turned and pulled the pistol out again.

'It was crouched there, looking at me. Those fething eyes…'

'Get up. Curth, get up. Beltayn, move her back. Help her.'

Beltayn waded forward.

'Come on, doc. Up we go,' he said, getting her arm around his neck.

Gaunt took another step forward. There was something in the dim undergrowth ahead all right. A grey shape.

Bonin arrived at Gaunt's side, his lasrifle aimed.

'What did she see?' he whispered.

'Something. In there. I can make out–'

Gaunt's voice trailed off. The shape stirred. He saw glinting multi-facet eyes and furry grey wings. They unfolded. A moth. A moth man.

Who was aiming a las-lock right at him.

'Feth me,' said Bonin. 'I think we've found those partisans.'

'Actually,' said Landerson, raising his hands and barely daring to move. 'I think they've found us.'

NINETEEN

'NOBODY,' MURMURED GAUNT, 'make any sudden moves.'

'Should we drop our weapons, sir?' Beltayn whispered.

'No. But nobody aim anything. If your guns are on straps, let them hang.'

'What are we doing?' Rawne hissed, the outrage in his voice barely contained. 'Are we surrendering? Feth that! Feth all of–'

'Shut up, major,' Gaunt told him through gritted teeth. 'Can't you feel it? They're all around us.'

Rawne fell silent and slowly turned his head. The members of the mission team were spread out across the pool. Grey shapes seemed to lurk and stir within every root ball and behind every tree surrounding them.

'Dammit!' he spat, and let his weapon swing on its strap.

His weapons sheathed, Gaunt kept his eyes on the figure facing him, and slowly raised his hands to show his

233

open palms. The figure stiffened slightly, the grip on its own aimed weapon tightening.

'Pax Imperialis,' Gaunt said. 'We intend no fight with you.'

The figure kept its las-lock raised. It said something, but Gaunt couldn't make it out.

'I'm not your enemy,' Gaunt said, hands still open. Landerson shot him a look. From what the cell-fighter had told him earlier, that wasn't exactly true. But the partisans – if that's what these beings were – had them trapped and pinned down more completely than anything the forces of the archenemy had managed since they'd arrived on Gereon. Talking was the only way out of this. Any attempt to fight would lead to two things and only two things: their deaths, and the end of their mission.

'Pax Imperialis,' Gaunt repeated. 'We are not your enemy. My name is Gaunt.' He tapped his own chest. 'Gaunt.'

The thing in the shadows still did not lower its aim. But it spoke again, more clearly now. 'Hhaunt.'

'Gaunt. Ibram Gaunt.'

'Kh-haunt.' The voice was glottal and wet, thick with a strange accent.

'They say,' Landerson whispered, slowly and very carefully, 'that the Sleepwalkers still use the old tongue. Old Gothic. Or a dialect form of it.'

Gaunt's mind raced. The principal language of the Imperium was Low Gothic, with a few regional variations, and the stylised High Gothic was used by the Church, and other bodies such as the Inquisition, for formal records, proclamations and devotions. All strands had their roots in a proto-Gothic that had been the language of mankind in the early Ages of Expansion. Like most well-educated men, Gaunt had been required to study Old Gothic as part of his schooling. At the scholam progenium on Ignatius Cardinal, High Master

Boniface had taken an almost sadistic pleasure in testing his young pupils on such Old Gothic epic poems as *The Voidfarer* and *The Dream of the Eagle*. So many things had filled Gaunt's head since then, so many things, forcing the old learning out.

Think! Remember something!

'Histye,' Gaunt began. 'Ayeam… ah… ayeam yclept Gaunt, of… er… Tanith His Worlde.'

'What the feth?' Bonin muttered, glancing at his commander.

Gaunt's brow creased as he concentrated. He could almost see old Boniface now, smell the musty scholam room, Vaynom Blenner at the desk beside Gaunt, doodling cross-eyed eldar on the cover of his slate.

'No looking at your vocab primer now, Scholar Gaunt,' Boniface called. 'Parse the verb form now, young man! Begin! "Ayeam yclept… Heyth yclept…" Come on, now! Blenner? What's that you're drawing, boy? Show the class!'

'Histye, soule,' Gaunt said, more deliberately now. 'Ayeam yclept Gaunt of Tanith His Worlde. Preyathee, hwat yclepted esthow?'

'Cynulff ayeam yclept,' the partisan replied. 'Of Geryun His Worlde.' His voice dripped like glue in the sweaty air.

'Histye, Cynulff,' said Gaunt. 'Biddye hallow, andso of sed hallow yitt meanye goode rest.'

'Are you off your fething nut?' Rawne whispered.

'Shut up, Rawne,' Curth spat. 'Can't you see he's getting somewhere?'

Gaunt dared another step forward. The marsh water slopped and bubbled around his boots. 'Biddye hallow,' he repeated. 'Biddye hallow andso of sed hallow yitt meanye good rest.'

The partisan gradually lowered his las-lock and took a step forward himself. He emerged from the mangrove shadows. Gaunt heard Curth gasp.

The partisan was not, as Gaunt had begun to fear, some mutant hybrid of human and moth. At first sight at least, he appeared to be essentially human.

That made him no less frightening. He was tall, a head taller than either Gaunt or Mkvenner, the tallest members of the party. He would have towered over even Colm Corbec or Bragg, Throne rest the both of them. But as much as he was tall, he was thin. Big boned and powerful, but starvation-lean, his long shanks encased in tight, fat-less muscle. What Gaunt had at first mistaken as the bulging multi-facet eyes of an insect were revealed to be oval arrangements of glittering scales, fixed like a mosaic around his kohl-edged eyes and spreading up across his shaved skull. The eyes themselves were tiny, glittering slits. His wings were a segmented cloak that appeared to have been fletched with masses of grey feathers. The cloak hung from a harness around the man's throat and shoulders. His clothes were wound rags, and both these shreds and his skin itself were caked with some clay-like material that glowed a sheened, iridescent grey colour. Silver pendants were strung about his neck, and silver bands decorated his fingers and his long, slender arms. He had a long, lank moustache, also stiffened and slathered in grey woad, which resembled an insect's mandibles and added to the impression that he was a moth in human form. His long, trinket-dangling weapon was not, as Gaunt saw it clearly, a las-lock. It was an actual musket of archaic design, as long as the partisan was tall. A wound-back hammer mechanism with a lump of flint in the claw served as a firing lock. The muzzle-end of the long, thin rifle had a dirty, serrated blade built into it.

Holding the weapon steady in one hand, the partisan raised his other and opened his grey palm to Gaunt.

'Cynulff ayeam yclept, of Geryun His Wolde, ap Niht. Biddye hallow Kh-haunt and otheren kinde, andso of sed hallow yitt meanye goode mett wherall.'

'I...' Gaunt began. 'That is to say... I mean... I am... I mean, ayeam...' He struggled, panicking, trying to think. High Master Boniface had, many times, told his students that 'a lack of good learning will kill a man more surely than a thousand guns.'

I hope you're happy now, you old coot, Gaunt thought, because you're about to be proved right.

'Ayeam yclept Gaunt...' he began again. No, already done that. Think. Think!

The partisan stiffened, wary, and his open hand returned to its grip on the preposterously long musket.

Feth, I've blown it, Gaunt thought.

'Histye, Cynulff ap Niht,' a voice suddenly called out behind him, 'and so beyit akinn. Sed hallow seythee, yitt be wellcomen into thissen our brestas owne us, and of fulsave yitt be hered. Well mettye, Frater, wherall so withe yeall!'

Gaunt looked to his side. Mkvenner had walked up to flank him, his long, makeshift spear trailing in the mire, his left hand held palm-up. The partisan nodded to him.

'Ven?' Gaunt breathed.

'A moment, sir.' MKvenner paused and then said, 'Histye, soule, so beyit pace twine us eitheren kinde. Brandes setye aparte, withe rest alse, as yitt meanye goode mett wherall. Council yitt shall sey akinn, preyathee.'

The partisan seemed to notice the Tanith warknife fixed to Mkvenner's spear.

'Preyathee, seolfor beyit?'

'Yclept beyit so,' Mkvenner nodded.

The partisan lowered his rifle and splashed into the pool until he came face to face with Mkvenner. He studied the blade with great interest, and Mkvenner calmly allowed him to take the spear in his hand. They exchanged words, too fast and too complex for Gaunt to keep up.

'I don't like this at all,' Bonin whispered to Gaunt. 'What the feth is this about?'

'At the moment, it's about us not getting mown down in a hail of musket balls. Wait, just wait,' Gaunt urged. He looked around. Rawne and Brostin were close to snapping, and ready to reach for their weapons. Cirk too, damn her. The others just seemed alarmed or confused. All except Feygor. He had sat down with his back to a treebole, up to his waist in the swamp, his head leaning forward.

'Ven?' Gaunt called.

Mkvenner looked at him, and saw his gesture at Feygor. The tall scout exchanged some further words with the towering partisan and the fellow nodded.

'Curth can look to him,' Mkvenner called.

'Thank you,' Gaunt replied. 'And thank him for me. Ana?'

Curth slopped through the marsh water to reach Feygor and began to examine him. Beltayn went with her.

Gaunt turned his attention back to Mkvenner and the partisan. They were still talking, fast and unfathomably.

'Seolfor beyit!' Mkvenner suddenly called out. 'Show him your knives,' he added. 'Quickly!'

The Ghosts quickly brandished their warknives. Some of them had to unfix them from the bayonet lugs of their rifles. Gaunt held his own up.

The partisan – Cynulff – nodded, as if pleased.

'Sheathe them now,' Mkvenner ordered. He bowed his head to the partisan and splashed across the pool to Gaunt.

'He's agreed to a parley. You and his leader. It seems they are impressed with our silver.'

'How safe is this?' Gaunt asked.

Mkvenner shrugged. 'Not safe at all, sir. They'll kill us in a second if we make the wrong move. We may even be walking into a trap. But I think it's the best chance we've got.'

Gaunt nodded.

Cynulff made a sign, and almost forty partisans, clad just like him and just as tall, emerged from the smoky shadows. Grey and sinister, winged with articulated capes, they were armed with muskets and curious, cross-bow-like weapons.

'Aversye wherall!' the partisan cried, gesturing with his rifle.

'He wants us to move,' Mkvenner said.

'Thanks,' said Gaunt. 'I actually got that one.'

THE PHEGUTH SUBMITTED to the next transcoding session that morning, but when Desolane informed him that during the afternoon, instead of resting, he was expected to make a visit to Mabbon Etogaur, the pheguth refused.

Desolane stared at him for a moment. 'This is not for discussion, pheguth.'

'I'm tired, and my head feels like it's about to split, Desolane,' the pheguth replied. He sat on the simple chair in his tower cell, trying to staunch a heavy nosebleed with some surgical dressing the life-ward had given him. 'I want to cooperate, of course I do. But the transcoding is wretched enough as it is. You force me to take meetings, undergo interviews that are little short of interrogations. I think you should cut me some slack.'

'Cut you some slack?' The life-ward repeated the words as if they were unclean.

The pheguth nodded. This was a dangerous game, and he knew it. He had a certain pull over Desolane now, but the life-ward was still quite the most dangerous being he had ever encountered. The pheguth had to test his new-won power, but not too far. There was a line even Desolane would not cross.

'What use will I be to you if I'm exhausted, Desolane? Burned out? I am already weary to my bones. I feel sure the transcoding is taking longer because of my fatigue.'

'That is possible, I suppose,' Desolane said uncertainly.

'Have I not been obliging in every way possible?' the pheguth asked.

'You have, pheguth.'

'And I'm only thinking of the grand scheme of things. I know my potential value to you and your Anarch. Believe me, I'm looking forward to the day when I can offer my full help. But I have to consider my own health.'

The pheguth let the words hang. He had deliberately not mentioned the attempt on his life, or made any reference to Desolane's oversight in allowing the killers to get so close. But the implication was clear by its very omission. *You owe me, life-ward. Because you failed me and I didn't even punish you. Don't push me.*

Desolane was still for a few seconds, and then nodded. 'I'll see what can be arranged,' it said, and left the cell.

THE PHEGUTH WAS allowed his afternoon of rest. Food was brought. In truth, despite the nosebleeds and a lingering headache, and despite the wounds the assassins had inflicted, the pheguth felt better than he had done in months. Clear-headed, calm, purposeful.

The transcoding was finally unlocking the shackles that the psykers of the Imperial Commisariate had placed on his oh-so-valuable mind. The pheguth had known how much of his memory had been repressed by the mindlock, and very little of that had been recovered yet, but he hadn't realised how much of his own self had been repressed too.

That was what was returning to him now, with each passing day. His character. His personality. He felt like a man of distinction again. He felt like a leader, a commander, a lord general. He remembered what it was like to be respected and feared. He could taste the addictive flavour of power again.

He relished it. It had been a long, long time. Years. He had been an officer of great import, a master of the Imperium. Hosts of men had charged into battle at his merest word. And then that bastard, that jumped-up bastard, had taken it all away from him and reduced him to this enfeebled misery.

That bastard's name had been the one thing he'd never forgotten. Even the mindlock had failed to dim its echo in his brain.

Ibram Gaunt.

The pheguth relaxed, and sipped some more tea. Fortune was turning to favour him again. He would rise once more, and become a master of armies. Different armies, perhaps, but power was power. Already Desolane was his willing pawn, and Mabbon, the pheguth fancied, his ally. He had a great destiny again, when for so long he had presumed his life over.

Desolane returned near nightfall. 'Pheguth. Once I appraised the etogaur of your weary state, and postponed your visit to him, he insisted he would visit you.'

'That's kind of him,' the pheguth replied. 'But I think I might sleep now. Give the etogaur my apologies. Like you, I'm sure, he knows how much Great Sek values my well-being.'

Desolane took a step forward. Its cloven foot rang hard on the stone floor of the chamber.

'Pheguth, there are some words I cannot allow you to speak with your heathen lips and tongue. The name of the Anarch, whose words drown out all others, is chief amongst them.'

The pheguth sat up sharply. He realised immediately he'd gone too far. The life-ward was in his thrall only so much.

'I apologise,' the pheguth said quickly. 'Please, show the etogaur through.'

Appease the creature, win it back…

'I will. Thank you, pheguth. I will warn him not to stay too long and tire you.'

Mabbon Etogaur entered the chamber a few moments later. He shook the pheguth by the hand very formally, and then sat down on a second chair that had been provided by the footmen.

'Your life-ward tells me you are indisposed, sir,' he said, settling the tails of his brown leather coat.

'A fatigue, no more. Thank you for your concern. I apologise for missing our appointment this afternoon. Was it something important?'

'It can wait,' Mabbon replied. 'I had drawn up the first trainee regiment to parade for you. I thought you might like to look them over.'

'By trainee regiment, you mean... the Sons of Sek?'

'The Anarch, whose word drowns out all others, has charged me to establish the first training camp here on Gereon. It lies in the heartland bocage, about thirty kilometres from here. The men are doing well. They keenly anticipate your arrival to oversee training.'

'I look forward to my first review.'

The etogaur opened a despatch case and took out a sheaf of high resolution picts. He passed one to the pheguth.

'Here you can see them in file order, sir.'

The pheguth looked at the pict. He was impressed. It was a remote-view shot of some three hundred men in rank, to attention. They were all big brutes, shaven-headed but for a cock's comb of hair across their skulls. They were wearing fatigues that were unmistakably Guard issue, but dyed ochre.

'They seem a fine body of men, etogaur,' the pheguth said.

'They are. Hand-picked.'

'By you?'

'Naturally, sir.'

Mabbon arranged some more shots and passed them to the pheguth. 'When you called off your visit this afternoon, I decided to run an exercise instead. The men were armed, and given an objective. As you can see, they accomplished the task well.'

The pheguth slowly turned through the pictures. His hands began to quiver slightly.

'What–' he began. 'What objective did you give them, etogaur?'

'A village in the bocage. It's called Nahren Town. Population sixteen thousand. That's consented, of course. Nahren is a known centre for the resistance and the unconsented.'

'They… they really took the place apart, didn't they?'

Mabbon nodded. 'Expertly so. In this shot, and in this, you'll see the firefight that began when the resistance showed themselves. I think those poor fools were actually trying to stop the civilian slaughter.'

'I suppose so…'

'Bad tactics, in my opinion,' the etogaur said lightly. 'The resistance here has prospered by keeping its head down and remaining covert at all costs. The raid on Nehren brought them out like rats. An elementary combat mistake. Better to flee and retain your secrecy. They were outmatched. You see? Here… and here too.'

'You killed them all.'

'All of them. Fifty-nine resistance cell fighters. With no losses on our end.'

'No, I mean… you killed everyone.'

'Oh, yes, sir. The entire population was accounted for. A fine showing, do you not think?'

The pheguth stared for a moment more, then shuffled the picts back into a block and handed them to Mabbon. 'Excellent. Excellent work. Simply excellent.'

Mabbon smiled. 'The men will be so pleased when I inform them of your pleasure, sir.'

'Sixteen thousand…?'

'Yes sir, and the bodies are burning now. The Sons made a pyre of them. Dedicated it to our beloved Anarch.'

'Whose word drowns out all others…' the pheguth said.

'Indeed so. Pheguth? Are you all right?'

'Just… just a little weary. Don't mind me, etogaur. That's quite a… quite a display your men put on today. Very… ruthless.' The pheguth looked up and met Mabbon's eyes. 'I'm very impressed,' he said.

Mabbon seemed pleased. 'I'm ordering another exercise for the day after tomorrow. A town called Furgesh. Population forty thousand. Does that meet with your requirements?'

'That would be perfect,' the pheguth sighed.

Mabbon slid the picts back into his case and got to his feet. 'I thank you for your time, sir. I know you're tired. I… I was told about the attack. Are your wounds troubling you?'

'Not at all,' the pheguth replied.

The etogaur nodded, and turned to go.

'Mabbon?' the pheguth called out. The warrior paused and turned back.

'Sir?'

'My life-ward told me that the assassins were not Imperial agents. Why would that be?'

'Sir, I'm not at liberty to–'

'Tell me, Mabbon.'

Mabbon walked back and resumed his seat. His voice was low. 'The assassins were men from the Occupation force, sir. Men whose loyalty to the Archon exceeds their loyalty to his lieutenant, Great Sek. You are considered by some to be a heresy and a monster of the enemy that should not be entertained in any wise. In short, sir, you are still an Imperial general to them, and that makes you a target.'

'I have renounced the Imperium of Man. I am a traitor general.'

'I know that, sir. But many believe… what's bred in the bone. Some individuals loyal to the Archon fear you'll betray him by aiding the Great Sek. Others simply cannot understand why a man who has made a career out of fighting us can now be watered and fed as a friend.'

'But you understand, don't you, Mabbon?'

Mabbon nodded. 'Yes, sir. I understand, because I am a traitor myself.'

THE SLEEPWALKERS' ENCAMPMENT covered over an acre of marshland, but very few parts of it touched the ground. It had been built in a glade of particularly old and massive mangrove trees, and was essentially a series of wooden platforms suspended like stages between the trunks. The lowest were supported on root balls, or wedged onto islets of land that rose from the stewing bog, often with a tree or two projecting from their tops. Others, the larger stages, had been constructed between the tree boles, some two metres above the surface of the mire. They were supported by a mix of stilt-beams sunk into the ooze and heavy wooden brackets dovetailed into the living tree trunks. Higher up, smaller platforms depended from the heavy branches on frames of rope. Plank walkways connected the lower stages, and woven ladders ran up to the higher platforms. Their dwellings dotted the stages, domed tents woven from some pale fabric and articulated like the partisans' cloaks.

The encampment had an eerie glow to it. Braziers were burning to light the place, and the glow reflected back off the water and the foliage gave the place a grey-green cast.

Brostin smiled when he saw the brazier flames. He sniffed the air. 'Promethium...' he said.

The nearest Sleepwalker glared at him to be quiet. Brostin shrugged.

It had taken more than three hours to reach the encampment, and they had trudged in forced silence. Gaunt was dying to speak with Mkvenner, but the partisans made it clear they would tolerate no talking, so he kept his mouth shut. He didn't want to antagonise them now.

Besides, they were outnumbered almost four to one. The Sleepwalkers had allowed them to keep their

weapons, but there was no mistaking who was in control. And Gaunt was certain that the partisans' weapons,
however primitive, would be quite lethal. He was particularly interested in the crossbows which, on closer sight
turned out not to be crossbows at all. In structure, they
bore a superficial resemblance to machine bows, but
they were not strung in any way. Each one was hand-
made and individual, though they all followed the same
basic pattern: a long, hollow tube of metal or hardwood
with a trigger grip set behind it, and a shoulder-stock
behind that. As far as Gaunt could tell, there seemed to
be a power cell built into the shoulder stock. The arms
of the bow coiled back sharply on either side of the
tubular barrel, more sharply than any crossbow's, even
under tension, and were made of metal, with metal
weights on the end of each arm. The weapons were a
puzzle. A lack of visible hammer or lock suggested they
were not firearms, not bows either. Some form of ener-
gised launcher, perhaps. The Sleepwalkers who bore
them were also slung with what looked to Gaunt like
satchel quivers.

Beltayn and Varl were half-carrying Feygor, who
seemed to be lolling in and out of consciousness fever-
ishly. Cirk was limping badly, and kept shooting Gaunt
evil looks as if the particular situation was somehow all
his fault.

Gaunt ignored her. The 'sunburn' on his face was
becoming raw and painful, and seemed to attract the
local bugs. He was sure it was the same for Rawne and
Mkvenner.

He wondered what lay in store for them now. The mission to Gereon had seemed an overwhelming challenge
right from the outset, but for a while there, they had
seemed to be getting somewhere. Now he seemed to
have lost sight of the mission entirely. Bad luck had driven them further and further away from their goals, and
now they had fallen into this surreal world. It was like a

dream. En route to Gereon, he'd imagined many fates that might befall them there. This was so unlike any of them it almost made him laugh.

The partisans brought them through the pools to the encampment. Many more Sleepwalkers, silent and pale, watched them approach from the platforms. The watchers were mostly male, but Gaunt saw womenfolk and children too. All of them were tall, slender and grey-skinned.

Cynulff ap Niht, or whatever his name was, led them up the walkboards onto the lower stages, and they trudged up into the camp, the silent figures gazing at them. He took them to where a heavy wooden chest sat bolted to the platform and lifted the lid.

'Setye brandes herein,' he ordered in his strange, thick voice.

'Weapons,' Mkvenner said. 'He wants us to put them here in the coffer.'

'Is that an order?' Gaunt asked. Mkvenner asked Cynulff and listened to the reply.

'It's their law,' he told Gaunt. 'Guests are not permitted to carry firearms in the camp. We must leave them here, where they will be safe. We can keep our blades, apparently, and he doesn't seem bothered by your sword.'

'Do it,' Gaunt told the team. Lasrifles and pistols went into the chest, along with Brostin's cannon and the autorifles Cirk and Landerson carried. Larkin sighed and kissed his long-las before he put it in.

Cynulff closed the lid and then beckoned them again. They followed him up onto a larger platform, and he pointed up a woven ladder that dangled from a much smaller hanging stage suspended from the canopy.

'He wants us to wait up there while he consults his leader,' Mkvenner said.

One by one, they climbed the ladder. It took a few minutes to get Feygor up onto the platform. Once he was there, he laid down and fell asleep on the mossy boards almost at once. The others sat down and rested wherever there was space. The platform swayed slightly under their moving weight.

Gaunt stayed by the top of the ladder and looked down into the camp. Cynulff and the other partisans who had brought them in were moving away towards the dome-tents on the main platform. No guard had been set on the Ghosts, but Gaunt knew they were absolutely expected to stay on the small stage until Cynulff returned.

Mkoll crouched down beside Gaunt. 'Well, this is all pretty odd,' he said.

'It could be worse,' Gaunt began.

'We could be dead,' Mkoll finished. They both smiled.

'If you like, I can slip away. Up that tree there, maybe. Take a look around. Get some weapons back.'

Gaunt shook his head. 'We're up here in trust, I think. Throne knows, Mkoll, we could turn this to our advantage. If we could get them to help us...'

'They don't look to me much like the helping kind, sir,' Mkoll replied.

'What do they look like?'

'The freaky dangerous kind who just happen not to have killed us yet.'

'Uh huh. That's my reading too. But let's give them the benefit. It's clear to me that if they wanted us dead, we wouldn't even have known about it until it happened. I think we intrigue them. They're curious. Speaking of curious, get Ven over here.'

Mkvenner came across to them at Mkoll's signal.

'Sir?'

'Ven, I believe we're only alive now because you possess a previously undisclosed facility with proto-Gothic.'

Mkvenner shrugged.

'A shrug isn't going to cut it, Ven. I need to know.'

'It's a personal matter, sir. Private. I'd prefer not to speak of it.'

'I'd prefer not to have to ask you, but I'm asking. The needs of this mission supercede any private issues any of us might have. That's the way it is.'

Mkvenner took a deep breath.

'I'll be over there, checking on Feygor,' Mkoll said, and got up quickly to leave them alone.

'So,' said Gaunt. 'Even the sarge doesn't know the secrets of his best scout?'

'He knows some. More than anybody else. But not everything.'

'You can speak the old tongue.'

'Yes, sir.'

'Because…?'

'I learned it as a child on Tanith, sir.'

'I learned it as a child too, in a classroom on Ignatius Cardinal. But you speak it like a native, Ven.'

'Maybe.'

Gaunt took off his cap and ran his fingers though his lank hair. 'I'm not a dentist, you know, Mkvenner.'

'A… what, sir?'

'This is like pulling teeth. We haven't got much time. Talk to me, for feth's sake. Is this to do with the Nalsheen?'

Mkvenner seemed wary suddenly. 'It is, sir. Who's been talking?'

'Ven, there have been rumours about you since the day of the First Founding. There's not a man in the regiment who hasn't heard them. And not a single man who's seen you fight hand to hand that doubts them. Your skills are like no one else's.'

'Sir.'

'The Nalsheen are supposed to be extinct, Ven. A memory from the feudal days of Tanith. As I heard it, the Nalsheen were wood-warriors, a fighting brotherhood who dwelt in the nalwoods and who overthrew the old tyrants. Some think them a myth. Some think they never existed at all. But they did, didn't they, Ven?'

'Yes, sir.'

'Come on, man. I'd like to think that you can trust me.'

Mkvenner sat down next to Gaunt. Their feet hung over the edge of the platform. 'The Nalsheen existed, sir. Right up until the day Tanith died. They continued their traditions in the remote woods, passing on the lore of *cwlwhl* from father to son. There were very few of them, but they had sworn to keep the brotherhood alive in case tyranny ever rose again on Tanith. My family line has been Nalsheen as far back as records go.'

Gaunt nodded, and waited for Mkvenner to continue.

'I was trained from an early age, three or four, I think. I was taken to the old master in the nalwoods by my father, and the lore was passed to me. The fighting skills, the woodcraft, the faith itself. And the language. The Nalsheen had always used the old form of Gothic as their private tongue. The same language the first woodsmen spoke when they settled Tanith in the Early Times.'

'Just the same as here,' Gaunt said.

'Yes, sir. When I heard the partisan speak, it chilled my blood. It was like hearing the voice of my father again.'

Mkvenner stared silently out across the marshland trees for a long moment, lost in his own memories.

'That'll do, Ven. You've answered my questions. Not all that I'd like to ask, but enough.'

'Thank you, sir. But you should ask the rest of them, I think. You deserve to know. I don't believe I should have secrets from my commander.'

'Right. Are you Nalsheen, Mkvenner?'

'No, sir. I have many of their skills and craft, but I never finished my training. My father wanted me to, and so did the old master. But I was a headstrong youth. I… thought I knew better. I wanted to serve the Emperor, you see. I joined the militia of the nearest city and, when the Founding was called, signed up to the Guard. The last of the Nalsheen… men like my father and the other wood masters in the remote places… died when Chaos burned our world.'

Gaunt nodded. 'Ven,' he said, 'if you hadn't been that headstrong youth, if you hadn't quit the woods and joined the Guard, you'd also have died with Tanith. And if that had been the case, two men would have been very sorry.'

'Sir? Who?'

'Me, for one, because without you so many of the Ghosts' battles would have been lost. How many times have you saved me? Just yesterday, on that field, against the wirewolves. I owe you. The Ghosts owe you. I know Corbec owed you to his dying day.'

'Is Colm the other man, then, sir?' Mkvenner asked.

'No, Ven. The other man is your father. If you had stayed in the nalwoods, and died with him as Tanith died, there wouldn't have been a Nalsheen to guide the last men of Tanith today.'

BROSTIN SAT ON the far side of the hanging stage, looking out over the swamp and mock-smoking one of his precious lho-sticks. He didn't care who saw him.

'Can I bum one of those?' Curth asked, sitting down beside him.

Brostin grinned. He was a massive brute, but his smile was infectious. He hooked the pack out of his tunic pocket and let Curth take one.

They sat for a while, pretending to smoke.

'Mmmm... tastes good,' she murmured.

'Finest rolled Imperial grade,' he agreed, playing along with the charade.

'Of course,' she said, 'as a Guard medicae, I ought to warn you of the health risks. Smoking lho-sticks is very, very bad.'

'Oh, I know, doc. Really, I do. Filthy things.'

'Exactly. Smoking lho is, frankly, stupid. Only stupid people do it. Really, really stupid people.'

'You know,' Brostin said, hooking the heel of his right boot up on the edge of the stage and making another, laborious fake draw on the smoke. 'You know what's really stupid though?'

'Tell me, trooper.'

'It's people pretending to smoke.'

She laughed. 'I hear that, Bros. What I wouldn't do for a light.'

He glanced at her and raised his thick eyebrows suggestively. She laughed again.

He chuckled too, then pointed out across the camp. 'There's a light,' he said.

He was pointing to one of the camp braziers, throbbing with flame.

'Too far away,' she said.

'Its burning promethium,' he said. 'Crude prom, not refined stuff. They use it here for fuel. In fact, that's why their camp is here.'

'What do you mean?' Curth asked, momentarily forgetting to keep up her pantomime of smoking.

'Over yonder,' Brostin replied, nodding towards the swamp pools west of the stage-camp. The water there was murky and brown, and bubbled lazily. The Sleepwalkers had planted several marker poles in the centre of the pools.

'A natural well,' Brostin said. 'Gushing up from the silt. Raw, mind you, not synthesised. My guess is the mothfreaks built this camp at a place where they could dredge up fuel for burning.'

'Are you sure?' she asked.

'I can smell it, doc,' he said, tapping the side of his fleshy nose with a dirty finger. 'Besides, just look at the oil patterns on the water there. Like a rainbow, they are. That's crude prom, coming up from the deposits. Sure as I'm not a petite blonde lass called Ana.'

She looked at him. 'I'm guessing, but you have an overwhelming desire to set fire to it right now, don't you?'

'Doc,' he replied, 'many call it arson. Many call me a pyromaniac. I just think of it as fun with matches. But I tell you this: I'd toss my whole pack of lhos into the marsh for a chance to light that baby up. Fire, y'see. It's what I do.'

Curth pretended to flick ash from her lho-stick. 'Let's just keep pretending, shall we?' she said.

THERE WAS ACTIVITY down on the lower platforms suddenly. Cynulff ap Niht reappeared with a gang of armed Sleepwalkers, and gestured for Gaunt to descend.

'Ven, with me,' he said, getting up. 'Rawne, you're in charge.'

For the life of him, Gaunt had wanted to give Mkoll command of the group he was leaving, but Rawne had rank.

'Just don't do anything stupid,' Gaunt told Rawne.

'As if.'

'You, or anyone else.'

Gaunt climbed down the rope ladder onto the lower stage, Mkvenner behind him. They followed Cynulff's men towards the main platform.

'So, they call themselves sleepwalkers?' Gaunt whispered to Mkvenner.

'No, sir. They call themselves *nihtgane*, which means "those who go about in the night". Simply put, they are *nightwalkers.*'

Gaunt nodded. How easily the locals had translated that word into *noctambulists* and therefore *sleepwalkers.* They'd missed the point entirely.

'The niht is the darkness of these marshes,' Mkvenner said. 'That's all they know.'

THE MAIN TENT, articulated like a giant umbrella, was lit from within by a single large promethium burner, hanging from a chain. The partisans had packed in, surrounding the chieftain, who looked more like a gigantic moth than any of them. His cloak was long and thick, and trailed out across the platform around him.

His eyes glinted from within the mosaic ovals. His woaded moustache was so long it was plaited.

His name was Cynhed ap Niht. He was 'of the night', that was a thing he insisted on making clear through Mkvenner's translation. He introduced his sons: Eszekel, Eszebe, Eszrah and almost a dozen others. Gaunt lost track. In their grey skin paint and capes, they all looked alike.

When his turn came, Gaunt tried to explain his identity and his purpose. It was slow work. Mkvenner did his best to translate, but the chieftain kept asking questions and interrupting.

'Gereon has changed,' Gaunt found himself repeating. 'The world outside the niht has changed. The Imperium is no longer your enemy. Chaos has come.'

'Khh-aous?' the chieftain repeated. 'Hwat yitt meanye thissen werde?'

'The archenemy of us all,' Gaunt tried to explain. 'My team, my men, we are here on an important mission. It is vital to the Imperium. Many will die if we don't–' he looked at Mkvenner, who was still translating.

'This is getting us nowhere, isn't it?'

'Keep going, sir,' Mkvenner said.

'Tell him… tell him I want the help of the partisans. The nihtgane. I want guides to lead us through the Untill so we can reach Lectica and the heartlands. Tell him many lives–'

'Many lives will be saved, Yes sir. I've told him that. Twice. He seems fixated on the notion of another enemy.'

'Another enemy?'

'Chaos, sir.'

'Preyathee,' the chieftain said, leaning forward. 'Hwat beyit thissen khh-aous, soule?'

'Ven, tell him that the archenemy is a murderous beast, one that seeks to murder him and his kind as much as it wants to kill us. We are here to fight it. In the name of the God-Emperor.'

Mkvenner translated again. The chieftain listened with interest.

'Tell him—'

Cynhed ap Niht interrupted, holding up a grey hand. 'Histye, lissenye we haf. Council beyit takken, preyathee. Goye from heer, withe rest alse, as yitt meanye goode mett wherall. On yitt we shalle maken minde.'

The Sleepwalkers led them out of the tent.

'Well?' Gaunt said.

'Now, we wait,' said Mkvenner. 'They're going to consider what we've said and decide what to do about it.'

ONE OF THE ordinal's excubitors had accidentally inhaled a moth. It writhed in the thick water, splashing and vomiting itself to death.

Uexkull looked down at it. It wasn't worth a bolt round to put it out of its misery. The ordinal had five more. Hell knew why he'd brought them in the first place. Sthenelus had an escort of five warrior Marines. What did he need with excubitors?

The ordinal stalked his way over to the dying excubitor. The choking wretch clawed at Sthenelus's slim metal limbs with slippery hands, hoping for benediction and relief. The ordinal simply extended a thin sampling hook and took a swab of the excubitor's bloody froth.

'Toxin levels at eight point one on the Fabius scale. Air humidity now nine parts to level. Land is pooled to a half metre, and shelves away at two degrees. Flora sampling now follows.'

The ordinal's pict-coders began to click as they recorded the surrounding tree mass. The excubitor convulsed one final time and expired.

Around them, in the gloom, Sthenelus's remote mapping psyber skulls hovered and recorded.

The ordinal continued his non-stop vocal cataloguing, engaging the flimsy brass sensors of his walker frame to chart. The articulated rods reached out in all directions.

'Thick-husked berry fruit with red exocarp, toxic, but with potential commercial value for seed oils. Small pendule fruit with brownish pith, approximately–'

'My ordinal,' Uexkull said. 'Please concentrate. The enemy. Where is the enemy?'

One of Sthenelus's long brass samplers lifted from the ooze, sucking.

'One moment, lord Uexkull. Hmmm… one part in ten million, but human blood nevertheless. Someone was bitten here. I detect an odd concentration of moth venom too. Curious. An artificial compound.'

'Which way?' Uexkull demanded.

Sthenelus pointed.

ON THE HIGH, suspended platform, the members of the mission team waited. Minutes swelled into hours. Time seemed to pass at the most laborious rate. Around them, the quiet camp and the slow, swirling fogs of the vaguely illuminated marsh seemed to match the crawl of time.

'This is worthless!' Rawne announced.

'Sit down,' said Gaunt.

'This is a waste of–'

'Rawne, sit the feth down. I won't tell you again.'

'For feth's sake, we should get our scouts out at least. Mkoll's boys could cover the area, secure weapons. They–'

'No, Rawne.'

'But–'

'I said no and I believe I meant it.' Gaunt looked up at his flustered second. 'We wait, Elim. We wait and see what they have for us. If it's nothing, so be it. But if it's something, I'll not be ruining our chances with hasty measures.'

'I agree with Rawne,' Cirk said.

'Gee, no surprises,' Curth muttered. Varl sniggered.

'Shut up, female,' Cirk said, looking at Curth.

Curth got to her feet and faced the cell leader. 'Maybe I was imagining it, but I think I was part of this mission team long before you came along. I have rank–'

Cirk shrugged disparagingly. 'Really? We all know the reason you're here, female.' She jerked her head in Gaunt's direction.

'The pack leader only keeps his mind on the job if he's happy and serviced on a regular–'

'Whoa, lady!' said Curth, coming forward. 'Your mouth just doesn't know when to stop, does it?'

Cirk drew to her full height. She was significantly taller than the Ghosts' medic. She smiled. 'Touch a nerve, did I?'

'I can locate and trigger more nerves than you've ever dreamed of, you b–'

'That's enough. Both of you,' Gaunt said.

'Mamzel Curth… Doctor Curth… is here because of her medical training,' Landerson said, getting to his feet. He got in between them and stared Cirk in the eyes. 'To suggest anything else would be unbecoming of a Gereon soldier.'

Cirk glared. 'Landerson, you're a sycophantic piece of sh–'

There was a dull crack. Curth had landed her small, tight fist right on Cirk's mouth. The cell leader reeled back, and only the urgent hands of Beltayn and Criid stopped her from toppling off the platform.

'You little witch!' she snorted.

'Want some more?' Curth laughed.

'Shut up! Shut up!' Larkin spat. 'Shut them up, for feth's sake! They're coming back!'

Below, Cynulff and several other Sleepwalkers were striding towards the ladder.

'You'll keep,' Cirk simmered.

'Uh huh. Bite me,' Curth whipped back.

'Shut up,' Gaunt said.

'Well now, the ladies are fighting over you…' Rawne clucked.

'You can shut up too.'

'Oh, how I relish these moments,' Rawne said.

Cynulff pointed up at Mkvenner and gestured.

'He wants you,' Gaunt said.

Mkvenner nodded and jumped down onto the lower platform to join the partisans. He looked back at Gaunt briefly as he was led away. Gaunt splayed his hands across his chest and made the sign of the aquila.

'I'M SORRY,' CURTH said quietly. 'I apologise.'

'Right. Think you could apologise to her?' Gaunt asked, nodding across at Cirk, who sat on a corner of the platform, her faced turned to the marsh beyond.

'If you ask me nicely,' Curth replied.

'I shouldn't have to. Cirk's a superior officer. Other commissars would have shot a soldier for striking a superior, without question.'

Curth stared at him. 'You're kidding me.'

'It's true. I've seen it happen.'

'You'd shoot me?' Curth whispered. Her eyes were very wide.

'Not in a million years,' Gaunt said. 'So go and make nice.'

'I don't think that's going to be very easy,' Curth said. She opened her battered narthecium and rooted around in the remains of its contents. 'I ran a test. Using the last of my kit. It's not definite. I haven't got the equipment left for it to be definite. But I trust the result.'

'Which is?' Gaunt asked.

'The mood swings. The intolerance. It's all part of the Chaos taint here. It's infecting us. Changing us. Rawne's at your throat. Cirk is completely off her chuff.'

'Who did you test?' Gaunt asked.

'Me,' she replied. Tears welled in her eyes. 'I hit her because… because it's in me now. It's making me… different… It's making me violent. It's affecting our hormones. Altering them, boosting some of the repressed aggressional–'

'Ana. Shush.' Gaunt hugged her to his chest. Curth started to cry. 'If what you say is true, it's too late for us all. But I think we can overcome it. I think we can be strong. You stood up for me because you cared and because you hated to hear her slurs. We'll make it.'

She said something, but it was muffled by his chest. He pulled back. 'What?'

'I said, you're doing that commissar thing, aren't you? Saying the right things, the way you were trained.'

Gaunt smiled. 'If I say no, you'll think that's just part of the training too, won't you?'

'Maybe.'

He sat down beside her. 'Then I'm damned if I do and damned if I don't. Ana, we'll be fine. If the taint is affecting us, then it's slow. We've only been here a short while.'

'Cirk hasn't. She's been here from the start.'

Gaunt thought about that. 'Yes, she has,' he said. 'Yes, she has.'

'WE GAVE YOU everything,' Sabbatine Cirk said, as Gaunt crouched beside her. 'We'd lost our world, and you brought no word of liberation with you, and still we gave you everything we had. The entire cell was destroyed getting you in. Ballerat. So many others. For what? This nonsense. This madness.'

'I'm sorry,' Gaunt said. 'If it's any help, most of what I do… most of what my Ghosts do… appears to be madness in the doing of it. I have a mission and a goal still. We will get there, I firmly believe that.'

'You're a liar.'

'And so many other things besides. Stick with me, Sabbatine. I need you.'

Beltayn called out.

Mkvenner was coming back.

'THEY SAID NO,' Mkvenner announced as he climbed up onto the platform.

'No?' asked Brostin. 'No what?'

'They're not going to give us guides. They're not going to help us find our way out of the marshes. We're the old enemy. They've fought us for so long they're not going to aid us now.'

'Feth,' moaned Rawne.

'Ven,' said Varl. 'Where's your fething cap-badge gone?'

'I don't know. I must have dropped it.'

'They really said no?' Curth asked.

'Bel,' Mkvenner said, ignoring her and gesturing to the team's vox man. 'Tune your set to my channel.'

'What?' Beltayn asked.

'I dropped my earplug and transmitter out of sight in the chieftain's lodge. Tune it in.'

'I'll do my best.'

Mkvenner looked at Gaunt. 'They're up to something. They're not going to help us but I got the impression they don't want us to leave either.'

'Getting nothing... just fuzz...' Beltayn said, the phones clamped to his head.

'The bastards are going to sell us out,' Rawne said.

UEXKULL CAME TO a halt. His lowlight vision was scoping nothing in this miasmal world. Heat on heat. But he trusted his eyes.

Figures were emerging out of the pools and root balls ahead of him. Tall, dusty-grey figures, flimsy as ghosts.

'Hold fire,' Uexkull ordered his men.

The spectres approached.

'How fascinating,' Sthenelus announced. 'Locals, indigens...'

'Quiet!' Uexkull barked.

The lead figure approached, wading through the stagnant pool. He was draped with a cloak of moth fur, and carried some sort of crossbow.

Peasant, Uexkull thought.

But he raised his massive gauntlet in greeting.

'Hail to you,' he called out.

'Preyathee,' the lead figure replied. 'Beitye Khhaous, soule?'

'What is he saying?' Uexkull snapped over his shoulder.

'Extraordinary,' replied Sthenelus. 'The being appears to have no concept of what we are. Indeed, he appears inquisitive.'

'Khhaous? Beitye Khhaous? Preyathee?' the partisan repeated. He held out one grey, long-fingered hand and showed them the glinting skull-crest Tanith cap-badge he had stolen.

'They have contact with the insurgents,' Uexkull cried as soon as he saw it. 'Ordinal, can you track these beings to point of origin?'

'Of course, lord. Pheromonally, and also by the wake of concentrated moth toxin they leave behind them.'

'Excellent,' Uexkull said, racking his storm bolter. 'These grey souls have come looking for... what was it again? "Khhaous"? Was that it?'

The lead partisan nodded eagerly and held the cap badge out again.

'Let us show them what "khhaous" means,' Uexkull cried.

The five Chaos Marines opened fire. Their shots mowed down the first rank of the partisans, exploding them backwards in wretched drizzles of crimson. Some ran, and were cut down. A mist of blood fumed the air.

The Tanith crest cap-badge tumbled out of a dead hand and sank quickly into the churning silt.

TWENTY

'THERE,' SAID BELTAYN, concentrating as he made minute adjustments to the dial of his vox set. 'I'm picking up voices. Very faint…'

He handed the headphones to Mkvenner, who pressed them against his ears and craned to hear.

'The bastards are going to sell us out,' Rawne repeated.

'Shhh!' Mkvenner said. 'I can barely… Bel, can you boost the signal at all?'

'Trying,' Beltayn replied. 'Better?'

'A little.' Mkvenner listened hard. 'Hnh. Yeah. There's talking. I hear the chieftain. Couple of other voices. Talking about waiting. Waiting to learn something. Hang on.'

Everyone except the still-sleeping Feygor grouped around Mkvenner in silence, even Cirk. It seemed to take an age for Mkvenner to hear enough. Finally, the scout looked up at Gaunt.

'It's not good,' he said. 'The partisans have located another group moving into this area. Other outsiders.'

'Searching for us?' Gaunt asked.

Mkvenner shrugged. 'That's a good bet. The chieftain has sent a group of his warriors to make contact and find out more about them.'

'I told you!' Rawne snapped. 'Sell us out! They're going to sell us out!'

'The sort of monsters who are looking for us won't be interested in doing deals,' Gaunt said.

'Whatever,' said Cirk. 'The partisans will lead them right to us, whether they mean to or not.'

'Right,' said Gaunt. 'This is a bust. We tried, and it didn't come off. Time to cut our losses. Let's retrieve the weapons and get mobile. If the partisans don't like it, tough. Be ready to–'

Mkoll was suddenly ignoring him. The scout leader turned and looked out off the platform into the foggy darkness. 'Gunfire,' he said.

UEXKULL AND HIS warriors came in out of the swirling marsh mists, wading through the soupy water and firing indiscriminately. Their weapons' flash lit up the gloom. Bolter and cannon shot lashed from Uexkull, Nezera and Virag, plasma shots lanced from Czelgur and roaring cones of fire belched from Gurgoy's flamer. Ordinal Sthenelus followed them, fanning out his excubitors to lend support.

The western end of the encampment withered under the remorseless assault. Tree trunks splintered, foliage shredded, platforms shook as they were punctured, tents burst into flames.

Sleepwalkers died. Many of the grey-skinned people watched in a mystified daze as the attack came on, baffled by the massive warriors invading them. Uexkull's warriors cut them down: men, women, children. Others began to run. Czelgur raised his plasma weapon and speared bright, purple beams of energy at the encampment site. An entire platform section collapsed into the water, sending dozens of partisans tumbling into the swamp. Thrashing and struggling, they were mown down in the next hail of fire.

Uexkull strode up one of the walkways, which groaned under his weight. He fired his cannon and ripped down three fleeing partisans. Burning scads of grey feathers drifted like ash from their torn segmented cloaks.

'Fan out,' he ordered. 'Kill everyone. Find the Imperials and bring their bodies to me.'

'MOVE!' GAUNT YELLED. He could see the flashes and hear the ugly roar of the assault breaking across the far end of the encampment. 'Rawne! Brostin! Larkin! Recover the weapons! Beltayn and Landerson... pick Feygor up! Move!'

'We have to run!' Cirk yelled.

'They're massacring these people!' Gaunt replied.

'Oh, for feth's sake,' Rawne shouted, already halfway down the ladder. 'These people were going to sell us out, and they're not even Imperial citizens anyway!'

'Follow my orders!' Gaunt shouted back. 'We need our weapons! No more damn running! We face them here!'

Ignoring the protests behind him, Gaunt leapt off the platform and landed on the lower staging with feline grace, rising from his bended knees and drawing the power sword. 'The Emperor protects!' he yelled, and ran towards the attack.

Partisans fled past him, running the other way. Gaunt realised that one crucial thing was missing from this terrible scene. There was no screaming, no cries of horror. Even the Sleepwalker children were silent.

The guns weren't. He heard plasma fire, a flamer's crackling hiss and spit, and bolter weapons. Heavy stuff...

Pushing ahead, he got his first sight of the attackers as they strode forward through the camp, firing wholesale.

And he realised he had made a bad call. A very bad call. Maybe Curth had been right. Maybe the taint was so deep in them now they were acting rashly and irresponsibly. They should have run. Just run. Forgotten the weapons. Just fething run for their lives.

The attackers were giants, clad in the whirring power armour of Space Marines. Gaunt glimpsed ceramite plates as polished and luminous as mother of pearl, gold laced with filigrees of rust, adorned with abominable badges.

Chaos Space Marines. The most grotesque, most powerful warriors in the archenemy's host. Imperial Guard didn't fight Space Marines. They left that job to the superhuman Astartes, for the simple reason that there was precious little a Guardsman could do that would even annoy a Chaos Marine. On the battlefield, brigades of well-armed Guardsmen regularly fell back in rout when even a few Chaos Marines appeared.

Gaunt had about a dozen Guardsmen in his team. They were unarmed, their weapons shut up in a coffer somewhere. Outclassed didn't even begin to cover it.

Bad call. Bad, bad call.

BELTAYN, LANDERSON AND Curth were struggling to get Feygor down off the platform. Criid and Varl jumped down past them. The others had already taken off in the direction of the coffer.

'He's gone in alone,' Criid was insisting. 'Gaunt's gone in alone and it's Marines.'

'You're kidding me,' Varl said.

'Look for yourself.'

'Holy feth. We are dead. We have to get our guns…'

'Why?' snapped Criid. 'So we can fluster them a little?'

'Tona–' Varl warned.

'Give me your satchel. Now, Varl. Right now!'

Without thinking, Varl tossed her the satchel containing the last six tube-charges. She caught it and started to run after Gaunt.

'Tona! Don't be a total gak!' Varl shouted. But she was already gone.

Varl started to run in the direction of the weapons chest, then came to a halt. 'Feth!' he cussed, and turned back to chase after Tona Criid.

GREY BODIES LAY everywhere amongst the burning tents and damaged trees. Some hung from the edges of the platforms, draping dead limbs into the green water, their segmented cloaks broken and disarrayed like the wings of dead birds, or swatted moths. Nezera, nearly two and a half metres tall in his hulking carapace armour, thumped up the walkboard bridgeway onto a higher level, and turned his cannon on a group of partisans who were trying to cower behind the remnants of a buckled tent dome.

Gaunt came out from behind the thick tree that provided central support for the platform's weight. He put all his strength into the two-handed sword blow. One chance.

Nezera had just enough time to realise a figure had appeared to his right. Then the scalding power sword of Heironymo Sondar sliced round and through him. Ceramite armour could withstand just about anything… lasfire, bolt rounds, even cannon shot. But it was like paper to the powered blade. Gaunt's lacerating blow cut through Nezera's chest plating, through the torso inside, and out through the spine in a fog of gore. His body half-severed at mid-rib height, Nezera stumbled, amazed, his system trying to manage the pain and repair the traumatic damage.

It was far too grievous. Blood poured out of the huge fissure in the plating like water over the edge of a wide cascade, jetting wildly in places. The cut edges of the armour plate glowed and crackled.

Nezera fell, heavy and dead, face down on the platform. The impact was so great that the platform shuddered and wobbled.

Gaunt looked at the cowering partisans. Their mosaic-edged eyes were wide in awe.

'Get up!' he yelled, not even trying to use their language any more. 'Get up and fight back, or they'll kill us all!'

SOMETHING'S CHANGED, UEXKULL thought, raking bolt fire through a cluster of tents and bursting open more grey flesh in bright splashes of blood. He could feel it. Like the change in the air before a thunderstorm. He–

The first shots came at him. Metal quarrels, hissing in the air like angry hornets. They pinged off his carapace armour, stopped dead by the bonded ceramite casing.

So, the peasants are fighting back, he smiled.

Then an iron quarrel smacked through the flesh of his left cheek.

There was some pain, but his bio-motors countered it. Uexkull closed his jaw and plucked the metal arrow out in a spurt of blood. Immediately, he felt his body glanding antivenin at a furious rate, the product sluicing through his system. The arrows were poisoned. An extremely lethal compound, no doubt derived from the local moths. An ordinary man would have been stone-dead in a second or two.

Uexkull was not an ordinary man. Not even slightly. His body-system rejected the formidable poison. He savoured the burning rush of the antidote. Shrugging off the rain of quarrels that spattered against his armour, he moved forward.

And continued to kill.

INSPIRED BY THE example of sheer, thoughtless bravado Gaunt had displayed taking down the Chaos Marine, the Sleepwalkers began to rally. Many continued to flee, guiding the womenfolk and children into the waters to get clear of the doomed encampment. But others took up their weapons and turned back against the attackers.

Muskets fired, their loads glancing off the Marines' power armour. The crossbows fired too.

Moving forward through the smoking devastation that the enemy had wrought on the camp, Gaunt witnessed the crossbows in use. Drawing a poisoned iron quarrel from his quiver satchel, each partisan dropped the projectile down the snout of his bow's barrel and then shouldered the weapon to fire. The bows made no sound, just a whistle of release as they launched the iron darts with huge force.

Magnetics, Gaunt realised. The heavy lobes on the end of each bent-back bow arm were powerful magnets. They sucked the quarrels down into the weapon and, at a flick of the trigger, the charged polarity reversed and spat them out. Simple, perfect.

But utterly useless against Chaos Marines in full armour, Marines who could gland against toxins if they took a scratch.

If this battle were to be won – and Gaunt doubted there was a tactician in the whole cosmos who would predict that outcome in his favour – it had to come another way.

Unarmed Guardsmen and locals packing primitive weapons would not, could not stop a pack of Space Marines. But Gaunt had slain one, thanks to the sword. And he'd do it again.

Even if that meant facing them one by one.

STALKING FORWARD ON his high seat, Sthenelus blinked as two of his excubitors fell face down into the stinking water and did not get up. Metal quarrels hissed around him, and two plinked off the base of his walker.

He used his articulated probe limbs to retrieve one from the water.

'Crudely-fashioned projectile, perhaps deserving the name "quarrel", fifteen centimetres in length, smelted from poor-quality iron ore. Latent polarisation indicates magnetic delivery, tip reveals evidence of a resin compound manufactured from the toxic wing scales of the local moth-forms.'

The excubitor beside him walloped over into the thick water with a splash as a musket load burst its skull. The two remaining excubitors fired their las-locks and then began to reload.

Before they had even half-finished the job, they had been felled by quarrels too.

Sthenelus glanced down at the bodies of the excubitors floating lank and limp in the filthy water around him.

'Said toxin has a rapid effect on humaniform biosystems, suggesting–'

He stopped. He looked down. A passing quarrel had torn through the fabric covering his malformed belly. There was a single long scratch in the flesh from which blood welled in ruby beads.

'Lord Uexkull?' he said. 'Lord Uexkull!'

Ordinal Sthenelus tried to call the name a third time, but his mouth had filled with clogging foam by then. The tiny measure of poison killed him an instant later, turning his blood to sludge. His little body spasmed violently, and then fell still. A moment later, two more quarrels smacked into his torso, but they did nothing more than knock his walker carriage over. The misshapen man on the tall machine toppled backwards into the bog, and the stinking water rolled in to cover his face.

SHE SAW THE partisans were fighting back now, but knew it wasn't going to be enough. The four remaining Chaos Marines were reducing the camp to blazing wood pulp. Criid clambered higher into the boughs of one of the main trees, her hands tearing on the damp bark. The satchel of tube-charges swung about her slender body on its strap.

Below her, she saw one of the monsters, the ⌐
the plasma weapon. He was storming forward, ⌐
ging off the rain of quarrels and musket ⌐
vapourising everything in his path.

Don't look up. Don't look up, Criid willed.

RAWNE KICKED OPEN the chest's lid and started throwing
weapons out. Mkoll, Mkvenner and Bonin caught their
lasrifles and took off towards the mayhem. Brostin
pulled out the heavy cannon and started to feed in the
last rounds in his hopper.

'Long-las!' Rawne yelled. Larkin caught it neatly and
smacked home a hotshot pack. If anything could dent a
Chaos Marine's armour, it was a high-yield hotshot.
Larkin knew he'd have to place it right. Between the
plate joints. That's the one chance he had.

Brostin was suddenly firing. The cannon was kicking
out a huge, vibrating sound. One of the enemy monsters
was right on them.

Not even fazed by Brostin's cannonfire, the Chaos
Marine thundered forward. His swinging power fist
crumpled the autocannon like tinfoil and sent Brostin
flying. Limp and spinning over in the air, Brostin
splashed into the swamp water off the platform.

'Larks!' Rawne yelled.

Larkin raised his long-las. The Chaos Marine brought
his flamer to bear. The world vanished in a blaze of
white flames.

UEXKULL PAUSED IN his onslaught, and knelt down,
smoke wreathing from the muzzles of his overheated
weapons.

He had come upon a body. One of his own.

Nezera was dead, his corpse split open. Dead? How
was that possible? Uexkull reached out with his steel fingers and touched the steaming innards that had spilled
out of his warrior's sliced armour.

challenge. That's what Uexkull had said. That's
ne'd boasted of to his warrior band. That, it
ned, was just what Nezera had found. By the laugh-
g gods, what waited for them here?

Uexkull's inhumanly sharp senses suddenly warned
him he was about to find out.

Gaunt launched himself out of the shadows and
swung the power sword at Uexkull. Jerking back at the
last moment, Uexkull raised one gauntlet to deflect the
blow. The sword clanged off in a flurry of sparks, the savage rebound stinging Gaunt's forearms. He tried to
reprise, but Uexkull was up on his feet again now. The
scything blade cut the end off Uexkull's bolter. The severed edges of the metal sizzled.

With a deep roar, Uexkull lunged forward, dropping
the mutilated weapon and reaching for Gaunt.

Gaunt threw himself flat and rolled away.

'You little bastard!' Uexkull creaked, smashing his fist
at his human prey. Stage planking split and cracked.
Gaunt was already up again, clambering up a rope ladder onto the next platform.

'You can't escape me!' Uexkull roared, and opened fire
with his shoulder cannon. The furious salvo punched
upward through the stage, and shredded the wet canopy
overhead. Gaunt rolled sideways, wincing as huge holes
exploded in the wood beside him.

Uexkull fired again, raking the upper stage, and decap-
itating several of the supporting trees. With a terrible
shriek of wrenching timber, the entire stage platform
buckled and collapsed. Gaunt flew into the air, falling
with it.

HER BREATHING SHORT and panicky, Criid balanced herself between two branches, legs splayed, and looked
down. The Marine was almost directly beneath her, firing on anything that moved. Criid plucked the satchel
off her shoulder, weighed it in her hands as a test, and

then pulled out one of the tube-charges. She knotted the satchel strap around the charge as a counterweight, then pulled off the twist of det-tape and threw the bag down.

It spun in the air. Her aim was dead on. The loop of the satchel landed around the Marine's neck.

The tube detonated. A millisecond later, the other five in the bag went off too.

The Marine vanished in the blinding flash.

Criid had a brief moment to enjoy her success. Then the rushing, rising fireball rippled upwards through the trees and engulfed her.

Screaming, she fell into the expanding flames.

LARKIN WAS DOWN, felled in the concussive rush of the Marine's flamer-surge. Dead? Unconscious? There was no time to check. There was fething little time for anything at all.

Not even a prayer.

Rawne grabbed the fallen long-las. Smoke and wood fibres swirled in the air. The Chaos Marine turned, saw him through the haze, and began to raise his weapon.

One chance. One shot. Rawne was no marksman, not like Larkin. He wasn't even practiced with the long-las. But it had a hotshot loaded and Rawne knew he had to make it count. He wouldn't get another.

The Chaos Marine's flamer came up to roar again.

Rawne relaxed into the butt stock and fired.

Range was almost point-blank. The searing round took the Chaos Marine's head clean off.

CANNON FIRE CHEWED the swamp water behind him. Clutching his sword, Gaunt surfaced with a splutter, and fought his way up onto a walk-board. He ran, dripping, across the next platform, trying to stick to the shadows.

But Uexkull saw him and followed, wading into the mire, his cannon barking out tongues of muzzle-flash. Gaunt frantically got a heavy tree bole between him and the line of fire. He heard shots slam into the body of the ancient cycad. Leaves, insects and droplets of water rained down from the shaken canopy above. He started to run again, up a walk-bridge onto the next stage.

Uexkull's weight quaked the staging behind him as he got up out of the ooze onto the boards. Filthy water streamed off the lower half of his ceramite armour. Gaunt heard a distinctive clatter as the enemy's suit-loaders automatically engaged a fresh ammo supply to the smoking cannon. He looked for cover, moved, slipped and fell hard. Cannon shots zipping over his head.

Gaunt rolled violently, shots chewing into the old wood, and ducked down behind one of the anchor posts from which several of the platform's supporting ropes ran. The ropes were old and hand-wound, and had been treated with some kind of lacquer to harden them. He sliced his blade through the central knot. The platform trembled, creaked, and fell, one end first.

Uexkull toppled back into the water as his end of the stage dropped down violently. His wild cannon shots ripped up into the canopy as he fell, and churned up a showering downpour of leaf-mulch.

Gaunt slithered down the shelving slope of the stricken platform. He got a purchase, and began hauling himself up onto the next stage section. Making deadly, almost feral sounds now, Uexkull dragged himself out of the marsh water, thrashing up from the stagnant liquid like some rising swamp-beast. Festooned with weed and algae, he seemed to be a hideous, primeval daemon of the marshes, submerged for eons, and woken to anger now by the tumult of war.

Uexkull ascended the slumped stage after Gaunt.

CRIID LANDED BADLY on the splintered platform. The impact drove the breath right out of her. Limp, winded, she rolled over. The boards beneath her were hot and smouldering. Right next to her, the steaming Chaos Marine lay crumpled and dead. The combined satchel charge had burst it open, its armour fractured like an egg shell, the bloody interior oozing out like yolk.

Criid tried to get up. She was dazed and close to grey-out. She couldn't breathe. Gasping, trying to refill her lungs, she writhed, her vision dim and starred with lights. Little circling lights, like moths in the night.

A partisan, grey-faced and silent, was pulling at her to move. A second partisan, armed with a crossbow, stood over them, uttering something urgent in their guttural language.

Criid began to roll to her feet.

'All right,' she choked. 'All right…'

The partisan pulling at her smiled. Then he vanished from the chest up in a boiling cloud of blood and tissue. His ruined corpse fell over to one side. He was still holding her hand.

A second Chaos Marine came roaring out of the smoke, bolter still firing. Criid felt the scorching heat of shells zipping past her head.

The second partisan fired his bow weapon and died a moment later as one of the bolt rounds struck his chest and detonated. But the partisan's quarrel had punched through the radiator vanes of the Chaos Marine's helmet. He staggered backwards, dropping his bolter with a heavy thud. Blood was gushing from under the snout of his helmet where the quarrel had stuck, transfixed. He clawed at his snout with both hands, making monstrous, squealing noises that were amplified by his suit's vox-system.

As Criid tried to crawl away, she heard a twang of snapping, parting metal. The Chaos Marine had pulled the arrow out. He came forward, unsteady, reaching his huge paws at Criid as she flinched back. The Marine's armoured gauntlets were immense, each one big enough to enclose her head, and strong enough to crush it like a berry.

'Feth you!' she shouted.

One steel hand grabbed her around the lower leg and began to pull. She kicked back, pointlessly.

Varl appeared from somewhere. He grabbed the Marine's fallen bolter and raised it, grunting under the weight of the thing. Varl jammed the fat muzzle up under the lip of the warrior Marine's helmet.

And fired.

Varl kept his finger depressed. The huge, antique weapon shook as it emptied its clip, threatening to knock him down with its gigantic recoil. He braced against it, his augmetic shoulder locking in place.

On the fifth shot, the Marine's helmet began to deform and buckle from within.

On the seventh, the helmet burst. Varl, Criid and the now headless Marine were saturated in the glistening material that sprayed out. Small shards of helmet metal tinkled down around them.

The Marine's mighty form swayed for a second, and then fell backwards.

UEXKULL HESITATED, LOOKING around. The platform area was dark and hot and his enhanced vision was useless. He listened instead, hearing moisture drops rolling down leaves, the thrum and tick of insects, the creak of the support ropes, the nearby hum of his cannon's auto-coolers as they steamed and hissed.

Close, close.

A good fight, better than he had expected. A true challenge. But over now. The power sword, that had been a dangerous surprise, but the man who had carried it...

Just a man. A lump of flesh and bones. An eminently destroyable thing.

Uexkull took another step. He deliberately started glanding an adrenaline-based stimm, feeling the killing lust rise in his biosystem. This would be a precious kill, one to celebrate. One to compose songs about. The murder-mist began to cloud his vision, the hunger for blood engorging his soul.

His senses became acute. He smelled sweat dripping from a man's raw knuckles, smelled the tang of an ignited blade, heard the drumming of a frantic heartbeat and racing breath that could not stifle or disguise itself.

'Who are you?' he called. Insects chirruped. Flames crackled. Water rippled.

'Who are you, warrior?' he called again, prowling forward. 'I am Uexkull. You have fought well. Beyond the measure I had expected of you. For that, I make you a promise.'

Bird calls. Insects. Slapping water. A heartskip, somewhere close now.

'Did you hear me? A promise. A mark of respect. Surrender now, and tell me who you are, and I will kill you quickly, without lingering pain. That is my promise, one warrior to another.'

Insects shrilled. Branches creaked. Leaves fluttered down. Each leaf impact sounded like a gunshot to Uexkull. The smell of human sweat was strong now. So close. He could hear the fizzling power of the accursed sword now. He could actually taste meat, wet boot-leather, silver.

Lure the enemy out, make him show himself...

Leering, still moving forward, Uexkull clapped his steel palms together slowly. 'Bravo, warrior. Bravo, I say. Guardsman, are you? Bravo! Quite a dance you have led me. It ends now, of course, and I swear to make that end brief.'

Right there. Behind that tree to his right. The rank salt-wet of a man, the quick-tempo thump of his heart. Right there...

'But I tell you, I have not met so fine a warrior in all the ranks of the enemy Guard that I have killed.'

'You should get out more,' Gaunt snarled, and came out around the other side of the tree. His sword raked in and sliced the cannon off its shoulder mount in a crackling discharge of severed cables.

Uexkull roared as he came about. His furious cry shook the platform and shuddered water and leaves, like heavy rain, from the canopy above. His fist swung at Gaunt.

Gaunt ducked, rolled, and came up again to plant a killing stroke through the Marine's armoured torso.

But Uexkull was much, much faster.

His fist hit Gaunt and sent him flying across the platform, blood spattering from a torn cheek. Gaunt landed awkwardly, and the power sword of Heironymo Sondar skittered out of his hand and slipped away across the wet boards.

Gaunt tried to rise, his head swimming. His knees refused to lock and his legs shot out from under him, dropping him onto his belly. He clawed with his hands, feeling the platform jump as Uexkull stormed towards him.

Covering his head, he rolled away instinctively. Uexkull's armoured fist mashed a hole in the boarding. The giant warrior cursed, turned and rose to his full height to smash both hands, fingers interlaced, down onto his prone foe.

With an ugly thwack, an iron quarrel suddenly impaled his nose. Uexkull staggered backwards, mewling with pain. A moment later, and the undergrowth began to hiss. Three more quarrels clattered off his shoulder plating. Another speared his cheek like a darning needle. Another smacked through his chin.

Then yet another lanced itself in his left eyebrow.

His face streaming with blood, Uexkull cried out and tried to move forward. The iron quarrels were smacking into him like rain now, bouncing off his plates or burying themselves between the segments. An arrow popped his left eye and remained there, rigid and embedded.

Uexkull began to scream. The sound was deafening, abhuman. It tore through the clearing. It made the Untill marshes shake to their waterlogged depths.

Another quarrel embedded itself in his cheekbone. Uexkull stumbled forward, his continuing scream unbroken. His mouth was wide open in a raw, carnassial rictus.

Gaunt was on his feet. He had retrieved the power sword, but there was no need for it any more.

The partisans were emerging from the shadows all around, swathed in their grey cloaks, firing and reloading their mag-bows, then firing again. They were aiming for the bare, exposed head.

Uexkull stopped screaming because he couldn't any more. His head was a head no longer. It was a distorted mass of meat and broken bone so thickly stuck with iron barbs that many of the bow-shots ricocheted back off the close-packed metal stalks.

Blood ran down his chest plate and shoulder guards. Lord Uexkull, his skull just a malformed pincushion, sank down onto the decking and died.

TWENTY-ONE

'WHAT THE FETH did you do to my las?' Larkin muttered.

'Saved your life, so shut the feth up,' Rawne replied.

'Only asking...' Larkin said, nursing and tweaking the long-las, and shushing at it like it was a girlfriend of his who'd been goosed while his back was turned.

'Well, don't,' said Rawne. 'Feth, I don't even know if this is over.'

'It's over,' Mkoll said, emerging from the thick smoke that billowed from the burning tents upwind. That much was evident from the quiet that had settled over the shattered camp. The gunfire had stopped.

The Ghosts regrouped, numbed by the ferocity of the savage fight, and quietly dazed at the simple magnitude of what they had accomplished. Between them, they had taken out five enemy Chaos Marines, and with no losses of their own. Criid and Larkin were both bruised, but the closest they had come to losing a man was Brostin, who had nearly drowned. In the midst of the mayhem,

Landerson had dived in after him and dragged his
unconscious form to safety.

'Five,' breathed Rawne. 'Five of the bastards. How the
feth did we manage that?'

'Luck?' Bonin suggested.

LUCK DIDN'T SEEM to have favoured the partisans. The
archenemy warriors had slaughtered over forty of them,
including women and children. Their platformed
encampment was devastated. Gaunt ordered his team to
help them in any way they could, and the Ghosts spread
out, running triage under Curth's direction. She collected up the remaining supplies in her kit and all the
field dressing sets in their own packs to treat any man-
ageable wounds. But some injuries were too extreme
even for her abilities.

'There'll be another five or six dead in a few hours,' she
told Gaunt.

He nodded. His own cheek was a bloody mess where
Uexkull's armoured fist had torn it, but he refused a
dressing. 'I'm all right. Others need it more.'

The partisans seemed not to understand the Ghosts'
intentions at first, but Mkvenner did his best to explain,
and they reluctantly permitted their wounded to be
taken to Curth. Brostin, still belching up swamp water
occasionally, supervised the extinguishing of those parts
of the camp set ablaze in the attack. His knack with fire
was as impressive when it came to quelling flames as it
was when making them thrive.

Landerson assisted the Ghosts as best he could. Only
Cirk refused to involve herself with the partisans. She sat
on one of the lower stages, keeping watch over Feygor's
supine form.

The surviving partisans, silent and sombre in their segmented cloaks, seemed to be gathering up the
salvageable items from their campsite. The cleverly constructed dome tents – those that had not been shredded

or burned – were collapsed into portable spindles of tight-wrapped fabric. Sewn-leather packs were filled with possessions, and gourd flasks brimming with crude prom sealed so they could be carried on shoulder yokes.

'They're leaving,' Gaunt observed.

Mkoll nodded. 'As far as Ven can make out, they're nomadic anyway. There are many platform camps like this dotted all through the Untill. All of them built an age ago. They move from one to the next, stay a few weeks, move on again. Apparently, they're not likely to return to this one again. It's been… polluted, I suppose is the word. Polluted by what just happened here.'

'We brought this doom on them,' Gaunt said.

'No, sir, we didn't. They brought it on themselves. Rawne doesn't even think we should be helping them now.'

'Funny thing, Mkoll,' said Rawne, appearing from the shadows behind them. 'I have a rank.'

'My apologies, major,' sniffed Mkoll.

'That true, Rawne?' asked Gaunt.

'Yes, sir. You made me major yourself.'

'I meant the other thing. And you know it. Don't feth around right now, Rawne. I'm not in the mood.'

'Sir.'

'You honestly can't understand why we're helping them?' Gaunt asked.

Rawne shrugged. 'They refused to help us. They tried to sell us out. I don't understand why we fought to defend them. I don't understand why we're wasting the last of our field dressings treating their wounded.'

'Because the Emperor protects, Rawne,' Gaunt said.

'Even those who don't recognise his majesty?'

'Especially those, I should think,' Gaunt said.

Rawne huffed and walked away. 'This place is getting to you,' he muttered.

Is it, Gaunt wondered? That was perfectly likely now. They'd won the battle – somehow – but it had been a mistake to fight it in the first place. Was his leadership now suspect? Was he making irresponsible decisions? Was the taint of Gereon now so deep in him that he was thinking wrong?

He tried to put the nagging fear aside. His mind felt clear and true. He felt fine. But wasn't that how it always started? Men weren't drawn to the madness of Chaos because it seemed like a viable lifestyle change. The clammy influence of the Ruinous Powers wormed inside a man, changed him slowly and subtly without him ever realising it, making the insanity of the warp-darkness seem like the most natural thing in the cosmos.

All his life, as a commissar, Gaunt had understood that. That was why a commissar had to be so vigilant. And so harsh. Right to the end, on Herodor, Agun Soric had seemed like the most reasonable, loyal man. Gaunt had trusted him, loved his spirit, adored his simple courage.

But the man had gone over. The mark of the psyker had been in him. There had been no choice but to send him to the black ships.

Gaunt had dutifully read all the scholarly texts as a young man, and still reread many. Some of them, like the poetic philosophy of his favourite, Ravenor, writing nearly half a century earlier, had implanted this understanding in his mind. Especially where Ravenor wrote so eloquently, so heartbreakingly, about the fall of his master, Eisenhorn. Gregor Eisenhorn's ultimate, terrible fate was an object lesson in the seductive power of the warp.

But Gaunt tried to focus on one memory, a lesson taught to him what seemed a lifetime ago by his own mentor, Delane Oktar. It had been Oktar's deepest belief that a man should simply strive to do what seemed right. Gaunt remembered the thawing snow-fields of Darendara, just after the liberation, the best part of thirty years before. They had been fighting seces-sionists, not Chaos, and there was great debate as to the appropriate punishment of the prisoners taken. Several commissars urged a thorough purge and a programme of execution. Commissar-General Oktar had argued for a different way. More lenient.

'Let us be firm, but let us re-educate. Blood is not always the answer.'

Three of the senior commissars opposing Oktar's view had leaned on Cadet Gaunt, hoping to get the young man to use his pull to influence Oktar's decision. Gaunt had taken supper with his master in one of the lamp-lit rooms of the Winter Palace, and during dinner, he had brought the matter up.

Oktar had smiled patiently. 'My boy,' he said at length – he had always referred to Gaunt as 'Boy'. 'My boy, if we execute everyone who disagrees with us, the galaxy will quickly become an empty place.'

'Yes, but–' the Boy had started to say.

'The Emperor protects, Ibram. He watches us all, no matter what dark corner we lurk in. It should be our sworn duty to convey that message to others, to the lost and the disenfranchised, to the ignorant and the troubled. We should be finding ways to help them learn, to help them come to terms, and benefit from the God-Emperor's goodness, just as we do. There are plenty of things in this thrice-accursed galaxy that we have no choice but to fight and kill, without turning on ourselves too. Think of this... if we do no more than what we feel is the right thing, then the Emperor is watching, and he will see it. And if he approves, he will protect us and let us know he is pleased with our service.'

'You know, sir, some would say–'

'Say what, boy?'

'Some would say that's heresy, sir,'

Throne, had he really said that? Gaunt winced as he remembered uttering those idiot words to his mentor. A few short years after the Darendara Liberation, the new governing council – many of them politicos spared thanks to Oktar's mercy – had formed a new allegiance and renewed their vows to the Imperium. Darendara was now one of the most staunchly loyal worlds in its subsector. Oktar's views had been vindicated.

Gaunt wandered alone along the smouldering platforms, and lingered for a while on the highest stage still intact. He gazed out over the marshes of the Untill.

'The Emperor protects,' he murmured to himself. 'The Emperor protects…'

Judge thyself first, then judge others. That was the first law of the Commissariate. Gaunt took out one of his bolt pistols. He had very few rounds left for either. As long as he still had one shot, he could yet make the most important judgement of all.

THE FOLLOWING DAWN, he was vindicated.

They had all slept badly on the hard platforms. The night had been humid, and the swamp air especially close. Curth had stayed awake until after midnight, tending two partisans who died despite her efforts. Brostin, his cannon destroyed, had been busy all night fiddling with the flamer that one of the Chaos Marines had been carrying. It was a crude thing and, in truth, rather too large and bulky to be carried by anyone without the support of power armour. But he persevered, stripping it of all but the basics, and chiselling away the more offensive Chaos symbols and badges. Finally, he fashioned a shoulder harness from some of the severed lengths of platform cable to distribute its weight. He practised lugging it around, and quickly decided he could only manage one of the three fuel canisters the Marine had carried. More adjustments. Just before first light, he had waded out from the platforms and filled the canister from the natural well.

'Will it work?' Varl asked him.

'You fething betcha!' Brostin snorted, and test-clacked the trigger spoon. A coughing, faltering gust – part flame and mostly steam – exhaled weakly.

'Right,' Brostin said, scratching his head. 'Right. A few adjustments, and you'll see.'

When the Ghosts woke, unsteady and weary, they found the partisans about to leave. All their camp belongings were packed and shouldered. The wounded had been lifted up on makeshift stretchers. The dead were laid out on the broken stages, with swamp flowers on their faces.

Cynhed ap Niht, the chieftain, came to speak with Mkvenner, and brought several of his warriors with him. They talked for a long time. Finally, Mkvenner wandered back to the waiting Ghosts, with one of the warriors at his side.

'What's going on?' Gaunt asked.

'They're leaving now. But the chieftain has had a change of mind. He's decided to help us, after all. After what happened here. It seems we impressed them with our efforts to defend them.'

'Great. What does that mean, Ven?'

'He's given us one of his sons.'

'What?'

Mkvenner gestured to the tall partisan at his side. The grey man seemed like a statue, so silent and still.

'This is his son. Eszrah ap Niht. He's going to act as our guide and lead us through the marshes to the heartlands.'

Gaunt looked up at the towering, thin man. 'Really?'

'Yes, sir.'

And if he approves, he will protect us and let us know he is pleased with our service.

'Then let's get moving,' Gaunt said.

He looked round, and saw that the partisans had already started to leave. They were vanishing slowly into the mist. Eszrah ap Niht didn't even look round to see them go.

Some few, last figures, like phantoms in their segmented cloaks, waited to perform the last rite of

leave-taking. Brostin saw them, dumped his heavy
pack with the not-yet-working flamer, and jumped
off the stage into the water, splashing across to join
them.

'Can I?' he asked. 'Can I do this?'

Not really understanding his words, but understanding his urgent intent and his bright eyes, one of the
partisans handed the flaming torch to Brostin.

'Quethy?' the partisan said.

'You've no idea,' Brostin replied. The partisans murmured several ritual prayers, heads bowed.

'Are we done? Are we all done? Can I do this?' Brostin
asked eagerly.

One of them nodded.

With a swing of his thick, tattooed arm, Brostin threw
the torch. It landed near the centre of the natural well in
the mire. The well lit up with a fizzling suck followed by
a solid bang. In a moment, lambent yellow flames were
boiling out and ripping into the ruined wooden camp.
The glade burned. The dead were consumed and sent to
whatever god or gods they had worshipped since the
dawn of the colony.

Brostin waded back to rejoin the group, who were
already backing away from the fierce heat.

'That's the stuff,' he chuckled.

'Move out!' Rawne cried.

Gaunt looked back one last time. It was hard to see
against the glare of the inferno, but there was no sign of
the partisans now. The Sleepwalkers had vanished into
the Untill.

Eszrah ap Niht still did not look back. He said nothing. He raised one dove-grey hand, and gestured.

So they followed him.

'How DID HE tempt you to his cause, etogaur?' the
pheguth asked as they walked down the field from the
roadway where the transports were parked.

'What do you mean, sir?' Mabbon replied. Desolane was walking ahead of them, and the pheguth was certain the life-ward could hear their conversation, but he didn't care.

'The Great Anarch, whose word drowns out all others,' the pheguth said, raising his hand to mask his mouth in a coy imitation of the archenemy ritual. 'You were a lord of the Blood Pact.'

'I cannot really say, sir,' Mabbon replied.

The pheguth nodded. 'I understand, if it's a private thing…'

'No, it's not like that. I mean I really can't say where my dissatisfaction began. I was a sworn lord, as you say, and I had made the Pact, blooding myself on the sharp edges of the Gaur's own armour. It was a privilege. The Blood Pact is a superb fighting force. To be a commander in their ranks, to be an etogaur, it was all the honour a man might hope for.'

They walked on a little further. The day was sunny but cheerless. Cloudbanks loomed against the sky like blotches of mould on stale white bread. The field was broad, and contained nothing except grit and short, wiry stubble.

Desolane was taking no chances since the attempt on the pheguth's life. The life-ward had insisted on careful security for the day's outing. Twelve soldiers of the occupation force walked with them, surrounding them in a wide, loose circle, weapons ready. Others guarded the road approach, and the line of the hedge. Two deathships hovered, watching, over a nearby field. The pheguth could hear the lazy rush of their lift-jets.

'I suppose,' Mabbon said at length, 'it all changed when I met the Anarch. The Pact division I was commanding was sent into the Khan Group to assist Great Sek. He impressed me at once. He has great personal charm, you see. A ferocious intelligence. The insight to see what needs to be done and the ability to accomplish it. Archon Gaur is a matchless leader in so many ways, but what he achieves, he achieves by brute force. He is a killer of worlds, a dominator, a feral thing. Not once in all the years that I served him as etogaur did he listen to my thoughts or even solicit my opinions. He takes no advice. On many occasions, officer-commanders of the Blood Pact, myself included, were ordered to engage in rash and costly actions at his whim. I've lost many men that way, been forced to send units to their deaths, even when I could plainly see a better way of defeating the forces of the False Emperor. When Archon Gaur gives an order, there is no opportunity for discussion.'

'I see,' said the pheguth. He was only half-listening. The constant, post-transcoding headache simmered within his skull. The fresh air seemed to help a little, but not much.

'Great Sek is different,' Mabbon continued, 'He possesses subtlety, and actively looks to his commanders for suggestions and ideas that he can incorporate into his strategy.'

'I've heard he has brilliance in that regard.'

'You will enjoy meeting him, when the time comes,' Mabbon said.

'I'm sure I will,' replied the pheguth.

'Serving under the Anarch, I won three worlds in quick succession. Each victory was due, in great part, to the active cooperation between Great Sek and the field commanders. It opened my eyes to possibilities.'

'Such as?'

'Such as... that the successful prosecution of this war against the Imperium depends on more than raw strength and fury. Our victory in these Sabbat Worlds will require guile and cleverness. Your Warmaster is a clever man.'

'Macaroth? Why, I suppose he is. A gambler, though. A risk-taker.'

'Audacious,' said Mabbon. There was surprising admiration in his voice. 'That is his strength. To fight as much with daring and intelligence as with iron and muscle. Great Sek has a good deal of respect for your Macaroth.'

The pheguth smiled. 'Not my Macaroth, Mabbon. Not now.'

'Forgive me, sir,' the etogaur said. 'But the Anarch certainly watches Macaroth's moves closely. He has told me that he relishes the prospect of matching his prowess against Macaroth's directly, when the time is right.'

'You make it sound like a game of regicide!' the pheguth laughed.

Mabbon looked at him. 'A bigger board, a billion more pieces, and those pieces alive, but...' The etogaur smiled.

They were approaching the brake of sickly trees that screened the end of the field from the valley beyond. The pheguth glimpsed the hedgerow outlines of the field system covering the heartland bocage all around them.

'So,' the pheguth wondered, 'you felt you might be backing the wrong horse?'

'I beg your pardon?'

'My idiom, I'm sorry. I meant... you made your choice because you felt the Archon might not be the best Archon for the job?'

'Wait here,' Mabbon told the troop detail and they came to a halt. 'You may wait too, life-ward,' Mabbon added.

Desolane glared at the etogaur.

'I will guard him, Desolane. You have my word.'

Reluctantly, Desolane halted too. Mabbon led the pheguth down into the trees. Some form of lice or blight had afflicted them. Their leaves were withered and sere, and their trunks wet with black decay. There was a powerful stench of decomposition.

'We must watch our words,' Mabbon said to the pheguth as they wandered in through the dead stand.

'Desolane vets your guards carefully, but as you have already found, there are some amongst the host who might consider our opinions heresy. The Archon is still the Archon. He is master of us all, even Anarch Sek.'

'But you seek to change that balance of power?'

Mabbon Etogaur paused. He raised his hand and idly touched the deep, old scars that decorated his face and bald head. It was as if he was considering the best way of replying. That, or remembering some past pain and the promise it had contained. 'Many believe that if Gaur remains in command of our forces, he will squander our strengths with his fury, wear our host down with relentless assaults against Macaroth, and ultimately lead us to nothing but defeat and annihilation. Many believe that Sek should have been Nadzybar's successor after Balhaut. Many believe that particular mistake must be corrected, and soon, before we lose the Sabbat Worlds forever.'

'And the first step?' asked the pheguth. 'To give Sek a martial order to rival the Blood Pact?'

Mabbon nodded. 'You know that much already, sir.'

'Yes, I know. But I think it's just really sinking in now. The… the scale of this. The audacity.'

Mabbon chuckled. 'That concept again. I told you, Sek admires the quality.'

'But the Archon could have us all killed. This is tantamount to insurrection. Gaur was my enemy for a long time, and now I've come over, I don't relish the irony of it happening again.'

'As far as the Archon is concerned,' said Mabbon, 'we are helping Magister Sek to improve his forces, and thus the quality of his service to the Gaur. We are not the simple brutes you Imperials seem to think, sir. We are not beyond politicking and intrigue. We will disguise and misdirect, and behind those lies, build our forces. The rest, the dangerous part, can wait. It may be years until Sek is ready to make his move. We have years. This war is old, and it isn't going anywhere.'

'So that's why you turned pheguth too?'

The etogaur laughed out loud. 'Traitor, eh? Traitor to the Archon. Yes, that's why. I believe in the future. And the future is not Urlock Gaur.'

'You renounced the Pact?'

'I did,' said Mabbon. 'My heart and mind were easy to change. My ritual scars were not.' He held up those pale, soft, unblemished hands of his. 'The meat foundries gave me new hands to erase the marks of my pledge.'

The pheguth found himself looking down at his own, augmetic hand. 'It's strange, don't you think, Mabbon? That we both celebrate our treasons, the break of long-held loyalties, in our hands?'

'You must tell me your story sometime, sir,' Mabbon said.

'My dear Mabbon, I will. As soon as I remember it.'

THEY CAME OUT through the trees into the lower field and the pheguth saw what he had been brought there to witness. It was an impressive sight.

Some three hundred men, stripped down to ochre combat trousers and brown boots, were training in paired teams down the length of the field. They were sparring with dummy rifles, roughly-shaped wooden blanks, refining bayonet work. The air was filled with grunts and gasps and the crack of wood on wood. Every man wore a distinctive amulet on a chain around his neck. The badge of the Anarch.

These were the Sons of Sek.

Mabbon led the pheguth down towards the clattering rows. The practice weapons were toys, but there was nothing playful about the practice itself. Dummy rifles splintered under the repeated blows, sweat glistened on the huge backs and thick arms of the trainees. Broken wood drew blood. Scratches bled freely down chests and bellies. Some men were down, fysik attendants treating deep gashes and gouges. Two men were actually unconscious.

Discipline masters – Mabbon called them scourgers – walked the lines with whips and whistles, punishing any half-hearted efforts. The scourgers were brutish men dressed in blue chainmail and iron sallet helms.

'The Gaur based the Blood Pact formation on the structure principles of the Imperial Guard,' Mabbon explained. 'But he did not duplicate all aspects. The Blood Pact has no equivalent of the... what is the word?'

'Commissars?'

'Exactly. This is something my magister seeks to correct in the Sons. The scourgers have been selected from veteran units, and are trained separately from the Sons, along with my officer cadre. The scourgers' duties are discipline, education and morale.'

'The Magister is perspicacious,' said the pheguth. 'Without the Commissariate, the Guard is nothing.' The pheguth watched as one burly scourger lashed a man's back with his whip for slacking, and then turned and gently advised another on technique. Just like the bloody commissars, he thought, one hand teaching, one hand striking.

'You approve, sir?' Mabbon asked.

The pheguth nodded. The martial excellence on display was undeniable. The sheer savagery. But his headache was growing worse. Pain flared and ebbed behind his eyes. Perhaps it was the sunlight. He'd been out of it so much recently. He wondered if he should have asked Desolane for a hat.

They strolled down the lines, admiring the display. The noise all around was hard and brutal: clacking weapon-dummies, snorts of breath, whip cracks.

'How many?' the pheguth asked, rubbing his aching brow.

'Sir?'

'In the first year, how many men do you think you'll raise?'

'This is the trial unit, pheguth. My officers intend to establish two more camps of similar size here in the heartland in the next few weeks. But I plan to have a force of at least six thousand come winter, here, and in camps on two nearby worlds. Subject to your advice and assistance, obviously.'

'Obviously.'

The pheguth winced as the fighting pair next to them ended their latest bout with one man on his back, his nose mashed by a well-placed stock.

'Fysik here!' a scourger called, blowing his whistle for emphasis.

'We'll begin the exhibition this afternoon, sir,' Mabbon said. 'Furgesh Town is just over the hill. Before then, I was hoping you'd address the men. Say a few words.'

'I'd be happy to.' The pheguth massaged his pulsing head again. Colours seemed very bright suddenly, sounds far too stark.

'I'd also appreciate it if you'd talk with the senior scourgers. Maybe a little insight into the workings of the Commissariate?'

'No problem,' the pheguth replied. Damn the pain. Right behind his eyes. Like hot needles. Nearby, one of the sparring Sons lost a chunk of meat from his shoulder as his partner sliced in with a dummy bayonet. The man cried out as his wound squirted into the warm air.

The pheguth shivered. The cry felt so loud, like a physical slap, and it seemed to echo in his head, over and around.

'Are you all right, sir?' Mabbon asked.

'Fine. I'm fine,' the pheguth said, realising he was sweating profusely. 'Fine. Just the effects of transcoding. All this talk of commissars, I think. Touched a nerve, Mabbon. I have a thing about...'

...about

about

about

a thing about

about…

A rushing sound, like water down a drain. A humming. No light. Darkness. No light. A taste of blood.

And then Gaunt. Ibram Gaunt, in the full, brocaded uniform of a commissar, his eyes like slits, that damned superior expression he so loved to inflict on others. Gaunt was holding something. A bolt pistol. Holding it out, butt-first.

'Final request granted,' Gaunt said. Damn him, damn him, who did he think he was? Who did he think he was…

…he was

was

was

he was…

He wasn't.

It wasn't Gaunt at all. It was Desolane. The pistol was a flask of water. The light came up, as if lamps had been lit. Sound returned. So did the dry smell of the bocage field. Distantly, the pheguth could hear Mabbon ordering the men back.

'Into groups! Groups, now! Scourgers, get them back in line!'

'Pheguth?' Desolane said.

'Nhhn.'

'You fell, pheguth. You passed out.'

'time a lord–'

'What? Pheguth, what did you say?'

'I said… the only time a Lord General passes out is on his graduation review.'

'Are you all right?'

The pheguth sat up. His head swam. But the ache had gone. He breathed deeply and looked around. Silent, staring, the Sons of Sek stood all about him, their dummy weapons lowered. Desolane knelt down and offered up the flask to the pheguth's lips.

The water was deliciously cold.

'You fell–' Desolane began again.

'So help me up,' the pheguth said. His head was amazingly clear suddenly. Clearer than it had been in a long, long time.

Desolane lifted him to his feet. 'Your nose is bleeding,' the life-ward whispered.

The pheguth wiped his nose and smeared blood across his cheek. He looked at the rows of warriors. There was suspicion and disgust in their perspiring faces. Now that just wouldn't do.

'I'm sorry you had to see that,' he said, his voice suddenly strong, and carrying the way it had once done over the Phantine parade grounds. 'Weakness in an officer is not a thing for soldiers to see. And you are most certainly soldiers of the highest quality. You are the Sons of Sek.'

A murmur ran through the assembly.

'That was not weakness,' he cried. It was all returning now, the manner, the effortless rhetoric, the art of voice-pitch, the confidence of command. He'd forgotten how wonderful it felt. He'd forgotten how good he was at it. 'Not weakness, no. That was an ugly aftershock of a process known as mindlock. Can I trust you, soldiers? Can I trust you, friends, with the truth?'

The Sons hesitated, then they began to snarl out a wild assent.

He smiled, acknowledging them, playing them. He raised a hand, his real hand, for quiet. A hush immediately fell. 'You see,' he said, 'your enemy decided my brain was too valuable, my secrets so awesome, that you should never know them. Psykers placed a cage around my mind, a cage that months of careful work is now, finally, undoing. My mind is almost free again. My secrets are almost yours. Yours, and our beloved Anarch's!'

The men roared their approval. Wooden rifle blanks clattered together furiously.

'Pheguth?' Desolane whispered above the rapturous tumult.

Dabbing at his bloody nose, the traitor general turned towards the life-ward. 'Don't call me that. Not ever again. My memory is returning fast now. Like a rock-slide. I have remembered things, Desolane. Even my own name. And that's how you'll address me in future.'

'H-how…?' Desolane asked.

Lord Militant General Noches Sturm didn't bother to reply. He turned to face the uproar coming from the ranks of the Sons of Sek. This time, he raised his augmetic hand, clenched in a fist. 'For the future!' he bellowed.

They began to cheer. Like animals. Like daemons.

Like conquerors.

TWENTY-TWO

NIGHT AND DAY had no particular delineation beneath the dank canopy of the Untill.

They walked, waded, and clambered, moving on through a permanent gloom fraught by warm fogs and miasmas of marsh gas. The sluggish green pools pulsed and bubbled, and unimaginable things snaked through the slick water, betrayed only by their rippling wakes. Other life clicked and fretted in the lowering black canopy above. What little light there was seemed as hard and unyielding as green marble.

This was not a place for men, for men had no mastery of it. They hadn't had it when they first arrived on the planet and named it Gereon, and they didn't have it now. Not even the Sleepwalkers, seasoned to the Untill's murky dangers. Though they had dwelt here for generations, they were only tenants, tolerated by the true rulers of the marshland.

For this was the domain of the insects. They were everywhere. They were lice in the hair, parasites on the

skin, formations of tiny waders, a billion strong, hurrying upon the surface tension of the water. They were
crawlers on tree bark, marching in formation, burrowers
in mud, gnawers into wood. They criss-crossed the
humid air on dank, trembling wings.

And in the swelter of the Untill, they had not been
told when to stop growing. Moths swooped amidst the
upper canopy like hawks, taking flying beetles as air-
prey. Dragonflies thrummed across the glades,
primordial gliders the size of vultures. Stalking grazers,
bloated like balloons, stilted their way through the
waterbeds, gorging on silt-dwelling creatures that they
raked up with their mouthparts and then sucked dry.

Treading onwards, the Ghosts saw skaters the size of
small deer, travelling over the water surface on hundreds
of long, paired legs. They saw grubs like fat, pallid, glistening fingers, waving as they extruded from rotten trees.
They saw mantis-spiders as big as hunting dogs dancing
slow, jerky tangos with wasp-worms.

The wet air stank of gossamer. Gossamer, wood-rot,
steam and stagnation.

The three scouts moved on ahead, trailing Eszrah ap
Niht, who seemed to know where he was going. To
Mkvenner's quiet disgust, Larkin had decided that the
partisan's name was 'Ezra Night'. The nomenclature
would undoubtedly stick. Larkin had a knack for coin-
ing simple names. They had become 'Gaunt's Ghosts'
because of him, after all.

The tail end of the party was lagging. Feygor had not
recovered consciousness, and Beltayn, Curth, Landerson,
and sometimes Gaunt himself, took turns carrying him.

Rawne was tense. Gaunt had ordered him to keep the
group together, but the slower the back-end got, the further the scouts led away.

He slopped to a halt in a glade where engorged, fist-
sized aphids suckled in their hundreds around the
albino taproots of a fallen mangrove. The forward party

was now out of sight, and the only sign of the rest of them was some distant splashing behind him.

'Feth this,' he said.

'Agreed.' Cirk appeared, her weapon over her shoulder. Her skin was glowing with sweat, and dark half-circles stained the armpits of her jacket. Rawne didn't like her at all, but he found himself admiring her. And not for the first time. She was a damned attractive woman. Fully loaded, that would have been Murt Feygor's description. Her jacket was unbuttoned and loose, and her damp, clinging undervest accentuated her bosom as she strode towards him.

Cirk came right up to him, face to face. He swallowed hard. He could smell her musky perspiration. Her generous mouth curled in a slight smile. She tilted her chin down slightly and coyly widened her eyes.

'Uh, seen something?' she inquired.

Rawne realised he was staring at her. This was wrong. He knew it. She couldn't be trusted. That mark on her cheek. That... brand of Chaos. He forced himself to look at it. He tried to curb his libido by thinking about that sickening thing inside Cirk's arm. That did the trick. The fething imago. Rawne was at a loss to know why Gaunt hadn't just executed her. She was dangerous. For a while now, Rawne knew Cirk had been playing him off against Gaunt. She'd picked up on their old enmities, and since then she'd been siding with Rawne on every call, every argument. The woman was trying to build an alliance that Rawne wanted no part of. Ibram Gaunt would never, ever be Elim Rawne's friend, but for the good of the mission, there was no way he'd let this–

'Rawne? What's the matter?'

He glanced up and their eyes locked. Her gaze was full of simmering heat, hotter than the damn marsh itself. A promise of something illicit and taboo. Rawne tried to tear his eyes away to the cheek-brand. But now even that wretched mark on her cheek seemed to be just part of her allure. He wondered what it would feel like to touch the scars of the stigma. He–

Shocked by his own desires, he looked away. He was a soldier of the God-Emperor, feth it! Not the purest, he'd be the first to admit that. But he was an officer of the Guard. And he had a woman of his own. Since Aexe Cardinal, he'd enjoyed a liaison with Jessi Banda, the Verghast girl serving as a sniper in three platoon. Their affair was secret, but it meant something to him. For Throne's sake, Rawne had a lock of Banda's hair in a spent cartridge case around his neck!

'They're falling behind, major,' Cirk said.

'I know, major,' he replied.

What was wrong with him? According to Curth, the taint of this world was now so deep inside them, it was affecting their hormonal balance, their emotions, their self-control. Was that it? Were they all beginning to lose it, him included?

'Time to cut the poor man loose,' she said, wiping the sweat from her forehead on her jacket cuff. Her raised arm accented her full breasts.

'What?' he said.

'I said time to cut the poor man loose. What's the matter with you?'

Rawne hesitated. 'Nothing. Nothing. Not a thing. I just thought I saw a bug. There. On your… throat.'

'Is it gone?'

'Your throat?'

'No, idiot!'

'Yeah, it's gone.'

Rawne tore his eyes away from her considerable appeal. He thought of the mark. The brand on her cheek. He tried to remember Banda's face.

'You mean Feygor?'

'That's right. He's… lost.'

'We're not leaving Feygor behind,' Rawne replied, looking at the trees behind her. That was no better. The arrangement of the coiled branches seemed to mimic the shape of the mark on Cirk's cheek.

'Really? Why not?'

'Because we look after our own.'

Cirk laughed darkly. 'Tell that to Acreson. To Lefivre.'

'Give me a break, Cirk. Gaunt stuck his neck out to get them clear. So did I. They died well.'

'No such thing, major.'

'Whatever.'

Cirk shrugged. Throne, she was really beautiful, Rawne thought. Luminous. And the swirling mist behind her... for a second, the wafting vapour made shapes, pictures. Figures entwined. A man and a woman.

'Anyway, what I think hardly matters,' Cirk said. 'Your commander is about to ditch Feygor.'

'What?'

'I heard him say it.'

That, finally, snapped him out. He felt a new emotion, as primal as lust. Rawne started to move. 'Stay here. No, go get the scouts. Get them back.'

He ran back the way they'd come.

BELTAYN AND LANDERSON laid Feygor's body on a bulging root-mass, and tried to make him comfortable. Beltayn was trying to shoo the blood-flies away from Feygor's face.

'We can't carry him,' Gaunt said.

'We can, sir,' Beltayn said. 'All the way.'

'No, Bel,' said Gaunt. 'I mean we can't afford to carry him. It's slowing us down badly. Exhausting all of us.' He looked over at Curth, who had sat down on a muddy tussock and was cleaning the leeches off her calves. He'd never seen her look so tired. She was like a faded pict of herself, drained and bleached out.

'He's not dead yet,' she said, without looking up.

'I know, Ana–'

Curth got to her feet and sloshed over to them. She pushed Landerson and Beltayn aside and ran another check on Feygor's vitals.

'Murt's a feth-hard son of a bitch,' she said. 'It's gonna take a lot to kill him.'

Gaunt peered over her shoulder. Feygor's skin was abnormally pale and waxy. His eyes – closed – had sunken back into deep, dark pits and the flesh of his face was slack. Brown liver spots freckled his shoulders and arms, and Gaunt was rather afraid to ask Curth what they were. He suspected some kind of mould. A sweet, corrupted scent came out of the dying man with every shallow, ragged breath, and the flies seemed drawn in by it. Worst of all was Feygor's throat. The flesh around his implanted larynx augmetic was swollen and sore, and it was beginning to fester. It looked like the soft, expanding rind of a rotting ploin, about to burst with its own putrescence. Stinking yellow mucus threaded out of Feygor's chapped lips. Every weary breath rattled phlegm in the man's throat.

'He's going to die soon, isn't he Ana?' Gaunt asked.

'Shut up,' she snapped, sponging Feygor's infected neck.

'Ana, for my sake, and for Feygor's, tell me the truth.'

Curth looked around. There were tears in her eyes again. 'Shut up, Gaunt!'

'Just tell me one thing, ' Gaunt said. 'Is there anything else you can do for him?'

'I can–' She trailed off.

'Ana? Is there really anything else? Anything?'

Curth turned and punched at Gaunt. The blow struck his shoulder. She threw another punch, another, and then began pummelling against Gaunt's chest, hammering with the balls of her clenched hands. She was too weary to do any damage. He put his arms around her and pulled her close, pinning her thumping fists. She started to weep into his chest.

'There's nothing else, is there?'

'I've got... I've got nothing... nothing left... no drugs... no stuff... oh Throne...'

'All right,' he said, embracing her tightly. 'It's all right. This is just the way it goes sometimes.'

'Sir?' It was Landerson.

Gaunt slowly let go of Curth and allowed Beltayn to lead her over to a root-clump where she could sit and recover.

'Yes, Landerson?'

'I'd like to volunteer to carry Feygor, sir.'

'Noted, but–'

Landerson shook his head. 'I understand this, sir. I understand you need to ditch Feygor because he's slowing the team down. I understand the importance of your mission. But I'm not one of your team. If I fall behind, so be it. I'd just like to try, to give that man a chance.'

Gaunt looked Landerson in the eyes. He was amazed to feel tears of his own welling up. The man was offering such a sacrifice, and after all that–

'Landerson,' Gaunt began, sniffing hard and fighting to stay in control of himself. 'You'd be dooming yourself and I won't have that.'

Landerson was about to answer when Gaunt heard a snarl behind him. Rawne appeared out of nowhere and crashed into Gaunt, smashing him down into the water.

'Holy feth!' Beltayn cried.

Struggling, thrashing, the two figures surfaced. Rawne had Gaunt by the throat and was forcing him back down into the swamp. 'Feth you! Leave him to die? Feth you!' Rawne was screaming, water spraying from his face. 'You'd leave us all to die! Like you left Tanith to die!'

Blowing bubbles, Gaunt went under again.

'Holy feth!' Beltayn yelled again, and splashed forward to break up the fight. Landerson was with him.

'Let him go, sir!' Beltayn yelled, pulling on Rawne's arms.

'Feth you too!' Rawne shouted back.

'Major Rawne, stop it now!' Landerson cried. He grabbed Rawne by the collar and yanked hard. Rawne twisted backwards and Gaunt surfaced again, spluttering for air.

'Get off me!' Rawne bawled, and chopped Landerson across the windpipe so hard, he buckled and fell over, gasping.

Curth rose to her feet. 'What, now?' she said. 'Now? Right now? Are you fething kidding me, Elim?'

Rawne was too busy drowning Gaunt and fighting off Beltayn. Curth ran over to the floundering Landerson and propped him up out of the marsh water.

'Stop it! Stop it!' Beltayn yelled, yanking as hard as he could. Rawne swung round and smacked a fist into Beltayn's face. The adjutant blundered backwards.

Rawne locked both his hands around Gaunt's neck and dunked him yet again into the thick, green water.

'I don't fething believe this,' Curth barked. 'This is it, is it? The moment you finally decide to settle your score? Rawne, you're fething unbelievable! How many years have you waited and you choose now? Thanks a fething lot, you stupid bastard!'

'What?' Rawne said.

'Your feud with Gaunt! You decide to settle it now?'

Rawne swayed and blinked. 'What?' he repeated. He let go of Gaunt's neck. 'This isn't about him and me, this is about Feygor–'

Released, Gaunt came up out of the water and punched Rawne across the clearing.

Rawne slammed into a tree-bole, scraped his face on the bark, and then turned back.

Gaunt had the point of his warknife aimed at Rawne's throat. Straight silver.

'Are we really going to do this, Rawne?' Gaunt asked.

'I won't let you just leave him,' Rawne said, wiping his mouth.

Gaunt slowly put his blade away. 'I'm going to make allowances, Rawne. This place is making us crazy. We all knew that would be a risk when we signed up for this. I don't think any of us is really thinking straight any more. Gereon is screwing us up. Do you understand?'

Rawne nodded.

'But we have to try and hold this together. We have to try and keep our minds on the mission. Have you forgotten the mission, Rawne?'

'No, sir.'

'Have you forgotten the mission's classification?'

'No.'

'And you remember what that means? The mission is paramount. Everything else, everyone else, is expendable. We all understood that at the start. We all knew that a bad business like this might come along and we'd have to deal with it. Feth knows, we may yet face choices even harder than this one. But this is how it has to be.'

Rawne sighed. 'Yes. I know. Fine.'

Gaunt nodded. He looked at the others. 'Let's break here for thirty minutes. Rest and collect our wits.' To Rawne, he said 'Thirty minutes. Then I'll make the final decision on Feygor.'

'Don't just… leave him here to die,' Rawne said.

'I won't. I wasn't going to,' replied Gaunt. 'If the Emperor can't protect, then he can at least show mercy.'

The scout party appeared, brought back by Cirk. Brostin, Varl, Criid and Larkin were with them. Sensing that something had happened, Mkoll looked at Gaunt.

'We'll take a short rest here,' Gaunt said. Mkoll shrugged, and the scouts found places on the roots to sit.

'I'm sorry,' Curth said quietly to Gaunt. 'That's twice now I've lost it completely. I'm crying all the time, I don't know what's wrong with me–'

'Yes, you do,' Gaunt said. 'It's not you. So we'll forget about it.'

'All right, b–' Curth broke off. 'Hey, what's he doing?'

Gaunt looked round. Eszrah ap Niht was standing beside Feygor's body, studying him curiously.

Gaunt and Curth waded across to him, and Gaunt signalled Mkvenner to join them.

'Preyathee?' Gaunt asked.

Eszrah regarded the colonel-commissar with his dark, unreadable, mosaic-edged eyes and muttered something as he gestured to Feygor. It was too complicated for Gaunt to follow.

'Slow down,' Gaunt urged.

The Sleepwalker began to repeat himself, but it was still too complex. Mkvenner asked a question in proto-Gothic, and they exchanged a few words.

'He says his people have seen several cases of infections like this in the last few months,' Mkvenner said.

'Since Chaos came,' said Gaunt.

'Exactly,' Mkvenner nodded. 'The partisans had a way of treating it that sometimes worked. He's offering to try that, if you permit him.'

Gaunt glanced at Curth.

'Look,' she said, making a helpless gesture with her hands, 'I'm standing on the edge of Imperial medical science, gazing into the dark. At this point, anything's worth a try.'

'Right,' said Gaunt. He nodded to Eszrah. 'Do it.'

The Sleepwalker drew back the folds of his segmented cloak, and revealed a number of small gourd flasks suspended from his waist-belt. He selected one, opened the stopper, and wiped two fingers around the inside rim. When his fingers withdrew, they were smeared with a grey paste, the same colour as the pale dye that covered every centimetre of his skin. He leaned forward, and gently smudged the paste around Feygor's swollen throat. Feygor stirred slightly, but did not wake.

'What is that stuff?' Curth asked.

'Hwat beyit, soule?' Mkvenner asked and listened to the reply. He looked back at Gaunt and the doctor. 'It's… um… it's essentially moth venom.'

'What?' Curth spluttered. 'Moth venom?'

'Basically,' said Mkvenner.

'Fantastic,' said Curth. 'Maybe we could help Feygor by stabbing him as well.'

'Look,' said Mkvenner. 'As I understand it, the stuff works. The only way the partisans have survived over the centuries in an environment this toxic is to understand it. Their skin dye, that's for camouflage, and for ritual show, but it's made from ground-up scales from moth wings. It's built up an immunity in them. There are very few venoms in the Untill that can actually affect them now. They use a more concentrated version to tip their quarrels. That paste stuff has enough in it to purge taint infections.'

Curth exhaled as she considered this. 'There might be some sense in it,' she admitted. 'But what works for them may not work for us. Feygor's got no immunity.'

'Feygor's got no other chance, either.'

Eszrah finished his treatment and restoppered the flask. Then he crouched down beside Feygor, folded his arms, and waited.

THE REST PERIOD Gaunt had set was over. He'd let it overrun a little, in the hope that they might see some change in Feygor's condition. Forty minutes, forty-five. He was about to get up and call them all to order when he heard a strange, chilling moan.

Feygor was suffering some kind of violent fit. His body convulsed and his back arched. The noises coming out of him were made all the more distressing by the flat tone generated by his implant.

'Feth!' Curth cried. Everyone was already getting up and coming close. The partisan was gently trying to restrain Feygor.

Abruptly, Rawne's adjutant writhed to his feet, slithering down off the root ball. His flailing hands lashed out and knocked the Sleepwalker off him. His head was tilted back and his howling mouth was flecked with foam. Feygor's eyes had rolled back into their sockets.

'Grab him!' Gaunt yelled. 'Hold him down!'

Bonin was nearest, but the lunatic strength in Feygor's arms took the tough scout by surprise. Feygor threw Bonin back into the water.

And began to run.

Wailing, arms waving like a man on fire, he ran blindly, crashing into trees, tearing through undergrowth. Clouds of moths burst up into the air like confetti, disturbed by his frantic progress.

Gaunt and Rawne ran after him. Rawne shot a threatening, malevolent look at the Sleepwalker as he ran past him. 'Hold the team here!' Gaunt yelled over his shoulder to Mkoll.

They ran out into the marsh, ducking under fibrous branches and shawls of lank moss, their boots churning up the muck. Already, Feygor was out of sight in the gloom, but they could still hear him, and still see his footprints in the water.

Dark brown blooms of disturbed sediment stained the green pool in a long, twisting line.

'Well, that's it then,' Rawne spat as they ran on.

'I was trying to help him,' muttered Gaunt.

'Good work,' said Rawne.

'Wasn't anything better than nothing?'

'I suppose.'

'The toxin must have been too much.'

The miserable screaming came from off to their left now.

'He's doubled back,' said Rawne. 'Feth, he sounds like he's in agony.'

'There he is!' Gaunt cried.

Feygor's pale, ragged figure had stumbled to a halt in the next clearing. His awful moans had subsided and he had slumped forward against the trunk of a leaning cycad. His scabbed hands clawed and dug weakly at the bark.

Gaunt and Rawne slowed down as they approached. Gaunt glanced at Rawne and took out his silenced autopistol.

'He won't know a thing,' Gaunt said. 'Better it's quick, than a drawn-out death by poison.'

Rawne blocked Gaunt with a raised hand. There was a terrible look of fatalism in his eyes.

'Better it's me,' he said.

Gaunt hesitated.

'For this sort of kindness, it should be a friend.'

Gaunt nodded, and handed the pistol to Rawne.

Rawne waded across the pool, clutching the pistol to his chest. 'Golden Throne of Earth, forgive me...' he whispered. Feygor had slumped down in a heap, his face against the tree, his trailing arms, curled around it.

Rawne racked the gun and aimed it at Feygor's head.

At the sound of the slide, Feygor suddenly looked round. He stared at the gun Rawne had levelled at him.

'What the feth is that for?' he asked.

TWENTY-THREE

'Is THIS GOING to take much longer?' Sturm asked. Desolane looked at the hunch-backed master of fysik and the man quickly shook his head.

'Not much longer now, pheguth,' Desolane said.

'Desolane...?' There was a warning note in Sturm's voice.

'My apologies, ph– My apologies, sir. I am having trouble getting used to the new name.'

'Old name, Desolane. My old name.'

The master of fysik completed his battery of tests. He lifted the articulated chrome scanner hood away from Sturm's head and removed the needles from his scalp.

'You may sit up,' the master of fysik said.

Sturm sat, small motors whirring the examination couch back upright to support him. The traitor general gazed with some distaste across the hall of fysik. Ornate medical apparatus was arranged all around: sensoriums, transfusers, servo-surgery tables, wound baths, blood drains and metal frames for laser scalpel assemblies. Steel surgical tools were laid out on bright red silk. Bottles and flasks containing fibrous organic specimens in urine-coloured fluid lined the shelves, and on the walls were charts and parchments, maps of nerve distribution, blooding points, trepanning techniques and other anatomies described in brown ink. Articulated skeletons, some human, some sub-human, hung from metal frames, their bones and joints labelled with parchment tags.

The master of fysik pulled open Sturm's right eye and peered in, reading the capillaries of the retina through a lensed scope. 'Your headache?'

'Barely there.'

'And the anomia is passing?'

'I remember my own name. The names of others who were just blank figures in the fog that clouded my memory until this morning.'

'There is considerable improvement in brain activity,' the master said to Desolane. 'But I can detect very little physiological trauma. I recommend the psykers see him as soon as possible.'

'More transcoding?' snapped Sturm, getting to his feet.

'We must make sure the collapsing mindlock has left no nasty surprises,' Desolane said. 'This is the most critical time.'

Sturm was naked, but he did not cower. The change in him was quite startling. Even his posture had altered. There was a marked difference in his bearing and even the tone of his voice. Confidence, and a regal arrogance that had straightened his back and squared his shoulders.

Desolane held out his tunic.

'No,' said Sturm. 'Not those rags. I can't abide them. Find me something suitable to wear, or I'll go naked.'

Desolane turned and barked orders to the footmen at the door of the hall. They vanished in a hurry.

'I take it the Plenipotentiary has been informed,' Sturm asked, idly inspecting some of the bladed chrome tools laid out on a nearby trolley.

'He has. He is making arrangements to come here as soon as possible. Command echelon leaders, strategists and other key ordinals have also been summoned. After the transcoding, you will need to rest well. The next few days will be demanding.'

Sturm nodded. 'I want a better room. With a proper bed in it. And no more shackles.'

'Sir, I–' Desolane began.

'I want a better room, a proper bed and no more shackles. Is that clear?'

'Yes,' said Desolane.

THE FOOTMEN RETURNED with a uniform. It was the dress garb of a sirdar of the Occupation force, though all rank pins and badges had been removed. Black boots and shirt, green breeches and a long green jacket. Sturm dressed quietly and then admired his reflection in a looking glass hanging on the wall of the fysik hall.

He stared at his image for some time. He'd seen his own face in mirrors several times since entering custody, indeed the transcoders had often shown him his reflection in the hope that it might aid the loosening of his memory. That had been frightening. The face he'd seen had been unknown to him, an alien thing.

Now it was like an old friend. Every line and fold and crease had a comfortable familiarity. He scratched at his stubbled chin.

'I want to shave,' he told the life-ward. 'This is unacceptable.'

'Yes, sir,' said Desolane. 'But first, the psykers.'

THEY WALKED TOGETHER along the echoing halls and galleries of the bastion, passing hurrying servants, patient soldiers, lean excubitors and chattering gangs of ordinals. Desolane noticed that the pheguth no longer shuffled. He marched, back straight.

An impish little creature was waiting for them at the door of the loathsome transcoding chamber. He was little more than a metre tall, his bent, simian frame shrouded in a red velvet robe with gold-thread decoration. The hem of the robe spread out over the flagstones. He wore a mechanical harness around his torso, the front of which formed a lectern that was braced against his chest. Fastened to this was a black metal printing machine, with rows of wiry letter levers and a thick roll of parchment wound into the spindle-lock. The little man had the lever section hinged up as they approached, and was carefully applying ink to the back of the letter press using a suede paddle. He looked up. His eyes were beady and he had nothing in the way of a nose, but his mouth was a lipless grimace of exposed gums and discoloured, spade-like teeth. In place of ears, he had augmetic microphones sutured into his flesh, and a wire armature from each secured flared brass ear trumpets to either side of his head.

His name was Humiliti, and Desolane had summoned him.

'What for?' Sturm asked.

'He is a lexigrapher. He will accompany you at all times, and record your comments so that nothing can be lost.'

Humiliti closed his machine's lever section with a sharp metallic clatter, put the suede paddle back in a pouch at his side, and flexed his long bony fingers for a moment. Then he began to type on the keys, a jangling sound, and the parchment roll began to turn.

Desolane opened the door, and Sturm entered. The little lexigrapher waddled after him. Sturm sat down on the seat and the electric cuffs immediately closed over his wrists and ankles.

'They will not be necessary,' he said, and heard the lexigrapher record the words. After a moment's pause, the cuffs disengaged. The chair tilted back until he was look-ing at the arched roof.

'Pheguth,' a voice whispered.

'Not this time,' he replied.

'Again, we begin.'

Sturm heard the shuffling, and felt the chamber go chill. Foetid fingers picked the rubber plugs from the holes in his skull. Then, making their distinctive high pitched squeal, the psi-probe needles swung in and slipped into the holes.

Sturm grunted slightly in discomfort.

'Let us start again at the beginning,' the psi-voice com-manded.' Your rank?'

'Lord militant general.'

'Your name?'

'Noches Sturm.'

'How do you come to be here?'

Sturm cleared his throat. Over the murmuring acoustics of the warp filling his head, he could hear the damned lexigrapher jabbing away at his machine. 'As I understand it,' he replied, 'I was a prisoner aboard a military transport ship that was caught in an ambush near Tarnagua. When the attackers realised they had captured a senior branch officer of the Imperial Guard, I was taken directly to a safe world for interrogation. That was where the mindlock was discovered. I was then sent here to Gereon, away from the front line, so that the mindlock could be undone.'

'What do you understand of the mindlock, Noches?' another psi-voice asked. This one sounded distressingly like a small child.

'It is a standard provision. In cases where a subject knows sensitive information. The guild can blank a man's mind entirely, but that does not allow for any future recovery of his memory.'

'Your mind is full of secrets, Noches,' the male voice said. 'Intelligence of the highest level of confidentiality. Why would they not have just blanked you?'

'I've no idea,' Sturm said. *Chatter chatter* went the lexi-graph machine.

'That is not true,' an old, female voice asked. 'Is it? Think about it. This is a memory you can reach.'

Sturm closed his eyes. He realised he could remember now. It felt amazing. 'I was being prepared for trial. Court martial. The Commissariate did not want my mind wiped, because I would not be able to face their cross-examination. But until the trial date, it was considered too risky to leave me... accessible. The Guild Astropathicus placed the mindlock on me, securing my secrets. They intended to remove it at the time of the trial.'

'You didn't like that much, did you, Noches?' the child-voice asked.

'I hated it. I implored them not to do it. But they did it anyway. It was monstrous. Numbing. Afterwards, I had no idea what they'd done. Just the nagging memory that something barbaric had been accomplished in my mind. It took everything away. I'm only now just under-standing quite how much was stolen.'

'Your memories are returning rapidly.'

'Yes, but I'm not just talking about facts and figures, names and dates. I'm not talking about the empirical data they shut away. I had forgotten myself. My charac-ter. My nature. My soul. They had taken my personality. The man you have been transcoding these last few months was just a shell. He was not Noches Sturm. I'd forgotten even how to be myself.'

There was a pause. The acoustic murmur circled around him.

'Hello?' Sturm called.

'Why were you in custody, Noches?' asked the male voice. 'Why were you facing trial?'

'It was a mistake. I was betrayed.'

'Explain.'

'I was serving in the defence of Vervunhive, on the planet Verghast. It was a bitter fight, and for a while it seemed we would be overrun. But my worst enemy was a commissar in the Guard. Our paths had crossed before, and there was some animosity between us. I was prepared to let it go – we had a war to win, no time for petty squabbles. But he manipulated the situation and accused me of forsaking my post. Trumped up charges. But he was a commissar, and enjoyed some popularity in that dark time. He made the charges stick, and, with the backing of his superiors in the Commissariate, kept me incarcerated and forced me to trial.'

'Doesn't the Commissariate ordinarily perform summary executions?' the child-voice asked.

'On low-lifes and dog-troops. Not on lord militant generals. My family has powerful connections to the High Lords. There would have been uproar if he'd taken my life.'

'What was his name?'

Sturm smiled. The one thing that the mindlock had never closed off was that name. 'Ibram Gaunt. May he burn in hell.'

The voices swooped and whispered around him.

'Are we done?' Sturm asked.

'We are pleased with the state of your mind, Noches. Your memory has almost entirely returned. The last tatters of the mindlock are falling away from your psyche. Our work is all but finished.'

'And I thank you for it,' said Sturm. 'Even on the days you made me scream. I'm glad to have myself back.'

'There is one last question,' the female voice asked.

'Ask it.'

They asked it together, all three voices as one chorus. 'When you first came to us, you swore allegiance to the Anarch. You promised that once we had unlocked your mind, you would renounce the cause of the False Emperor and fight with us against his forces.'

'I did.'

'But today you have admitted that you are a different person now. You have told us that the pitiful wretch who

swore that oath was not Noches Sturm. So, we ask you...
have you changed your mind?'

'You have changed my mind,' Sturm said. 'If I'm lying,
you'll read this in my head. So listen well. I served the
Imperium loyally, and devoted my life to the Throne.
But the Imperium turned on me, and kicked me down
like a dog. There is no going back. The Imperium has
made me its enemy, and it will live to wish it hadn't.'

Behind the chair, Humiliti's type-levers were clattering
almost frantically.

'I swear allegiance to the Anarch, whose word drowns
out all others,' said Sturm. 'Does that answer your question?'

THE SLEEPWALKER LED them up through the great basin
of the Untill, through the steaming glades of the Niht.
They skirted vast thickets of crimson thorn, so dense
that there was no way through. They waded through
green water, through stinking amber bogs. When the
water level finally began to drop, where the land
shelved up and away, the world became a mire of thick,
grey mud. White globe fungus clustered on the black
bark of the gnawed trees. Some of it was photolumi-
nous, and created clearings of frosty blue-white
radiance that the moths flocked to in their millions.
Blizzards of them swirled through the air. There was still
no sunlight. The canopy above was an impenetrable
black roof.

The team pushed on. It had taken them two full days'
march from the partisan camp to reach these upland
marshes. The temperature had dropped by several
degrees, and the humidity was less. Consequently, they
felt chilled. Their clothes, soaked from hours in the
thigh-deep water, clung to them. They were hungry and
they were exhausted. They had regular rest-breaks, but it
was almost impossible to find a place to sleep in the liquid mud.

However, some spirit had returned to them. Feygor was alive. His health was still poor, and he was by far the weakest member of the team. But he was conscious, lucid and walking. The infection in his throat was less angry. Eszrah ap Niht's poison paste may have nearly killed him, but it had saved his life too. Neither Rawne nor Gaunt spoke of how close they'd come to the mercy killing.

Their route led on through the thick grey sludge and the rank trees. These higher marshes were the haunt of lizards: bright tree scurriers, and balloon-eyed amphibians that lurked under stones and fallen logs and took moths out of the air with whipping, adhesive tongues. A bladdery, burping chorus of amphibian voices bubbled and popped all around them as they walked.

Their rations were all gone, and hunger would have long since killed them all, leaving their picked bones forgotten in an Untill glade. But Eszrah provided. He showed the scouts some basic tricks for finding game, and taught them what was edible and what should be shunned. The Sleepwalker made most kills himself, using his mag-bow. He allowed each scout in turn to try his hand with it. Mkvenner took to it best.

Curth used the remnants of her medical kit to analyse the partisan's poison pastes, and also scrutinise the prey that was brought in. Some things, she ruled, only Eszrah's immunity could deal with. But there were certain types of mud-eel, and a rat-like tree lizard that they could all ingest, provided they were carefully roasted or boiled. Brostin's flamer, still misfiring, at last had a use as a cooking tool. Gaunt had considered ordering Brostin to ditch the weapon. It was a Chaos thing. But in the circumstances, given the taint inside them all, it had seemed ridiculous to worry. He was glad now he hadn't. Without it, they would not have eaten.

On one occasion, Gaunt sat with Eszrah as they finished a meal. The partisan allowed him to examine his weapon.

'Preyathee, soule,' Gaunt asked, tapping the bow. 'Hwat yclept beyit?'

'Reynbow, beyit,' Eszrah replied. He was delicately picking meat from a spindly frog-bone with his small, white teeth.

'Reyn-bow, seythee?' Gaunt repeated.

Eszrah nodded. 'Thissen brande sowithe yitt we shalle reyn yron dartes thereon the heddes of otheren kinde, who gan harm makeyit on us.'

A rain-bow, to rain quarrels on the heads of the enemy. Gaunt smiled. He'd seen that. Emperor bless the nightwalkers.

THE TRAIL LOOPED north-west now, following the lip of another deep miasmal basin. They kept to the upper ground, the piled mud, slithering along the edges of the frog territory, their legs caked with clay. They passed another forest of crimson thorns, this one the largest they had yet seen, and then wandered the fringes of an eerily silent woodland, crisp with leaf mulch, where the trees were straight and tall and thin, like spears planted into the ground. Beyond that, reed beds furred a quagmire where flies billowed, then rose onto a crusty black slope of forest that stretched for several kilometres.

The trees here were ancient and gnarled, twisted into grotesque shapes and leprous deformations. There was a constant creaking sound, and Gaunt realised it was the canopy in motion. The trees were moving in the wind. He was painfully tired, but this roused him. That was a good sign, surely?

A little further on, Eszrah hushed them down into cover. Higher up the slope from them, something wandered past in the gloom. No one saw it clearly, but they all felt its footfalls shake the ground and heard its snorting breath. The drier uplands of the Untill were evidently the hunting grounds of the marshland's most massive predators.

Three hours later, Bonin was the first of them to see the light. He was scouting ahead through the mossy groves, and at first he thought it was a strange, white-barked tree, perfectly straight and branchless. Then he realised it was a single shaft of daylight spearing down through the interminable dark canopy.

He walked under it, and turned his face upwards, circling slowly, smiling, as the precious light flooded into his eyes.

'This way!' he called. The others quickly joined him, several cheering the sight. They gathered around it for a short while, some of them just daring to reach their fingertips out into the beam, others doing what Bonin had done and basking under it. Even Cirk touched the beam, as if for luck.

Only Eszrah ap Niht kept well away.

UPLIFTED, THEY PRESSED on, making better time. They found other shafts of light, then they became commonplace as the tree cover finally began to thin. The Niht reduced to a pale twilight. The ground became firmer.

Surely, we've begun to reach the far edge of the Untill now, Gaunt thought. Many of the Ghosts were laughing and joking about their trek being at an end.

'Ask him,' Gaunt said to Mkvenner. 'Ask him how much further before we reach the end of this place.'

Mkvenner nodded, and phrased the question to Eszrah. He frowned at the answer.

'Well?' asked Gaunt.

'He doesn't know, sir,' said Mkvenner. 'He's never been this far before.'

TWENTY-FOUR

DAY WAS BREAKING over the Lectica heartlands, revealing the misty patchwork of the endless bocage in soft russets, greens and yellows. This vast territory was the breadbasket of Gereon, the most productive of all its agricultural provinces. In the distance, like a blue mark against the horizon, lay the heartland massif, an upthrust of mountains crowned with cloud. So far away and yet, at last, in sight.

The early sky was glassy, and threaded with ropes of jumbled clouds like twists of cotton. Rawne lay in the long grass and watched them. Every damn one had a discernable shape. There, a woman on a horse. There, a larisel. That one was a bird, or maybe a pair of narrowed eyes. That one, a hand holding a knife.

He was going mad. He knew that now. He rolled over onto his back and closed his eyes, not wishing to see any more. The frail sunlight fell on his dirty face. It felt hot after their days in the sunless Niht.

They were all sick. All of them. Some, like Feygor,
physically infected. Some, like Curth, emotionally disturbed. They'd been warned about it, by the medicae
and the priests, before they'd embarked, but a warning is
only ever a warning. There was no way they could have
prepared for the reality.

Rawne was seeing symbols everywhere he looked. He
knew it was the taint doing it to his mind, but that didn't
make it any easier. He saw images in clouds, in leaf-pat-
terns, in shadows, in the grass, in the shape of stones.
Every one was specific and could be given a name. Every
one had a specific meaning.

Even now, with his eyelids closed, he could see symbols made by the spots and shapes drifting against the
red. An eel, a ploin, a full-breasted woman. A stigma.

He opened his eyes.

Everywhere, he saw the obscene mark Cirk wore on her
cheek. There it was again, in that clump of grass. There,
in the dried grey clay adhering to his toecap. There, in the
lines of his palm, the whorls of his fingerpads.

'Rawne!'

He looked up. 'What?'

Gaunt was calling. Rawne got to his feet and went over
to the others. The way they were grouped around Gaunt
made the shape of the mark too. Except one part was
missing. And by stepping up to join with them, he
would make the shape complete.

It HAD TAKEN another full day's march to travel between
that first shaft of light Bonin had found to this, the edge
of the heartland proper. The way had led through miserable woodland and deep gulches of caked earth where
weeds grew in thickets, waist-deep. They had been
drawn on to the light, to the promise of actual day
behind the thinning trees.

Then had come the ascent up the shoulder of the
Untill's deep bowl, through blasted uplands thick with

scrub and loose stone. The trees here were bare and dead, thorny antlers of desiccated wood breaking from the steep ground. They saw emaciated grox and other livestock turned feral that had clearly run free from the adjacent heartlands and were now foraging in the flinty heath. One made a good supper, the best they'd yet had on Gereon.

Beyond the heath land, the ground became grassy and they entered the boundary forest of old woodland that fringed the western edge of the Untill. Gaunt could see how unnerved Eszrah ap Niht had become. He kept stopping to sniff the strange new air, and sometimes lingered behind, blinking up at the sky.

'He's never seen it before,' Mkvenner advised Gaunt.

'I realised that.'

'He's crying all the time,' Mkvenner added.

'It's just the light,' Curth said. 'He's not used to the light. His eyes are watering.'

Varl raked through his battered pack, and produced his prized sunshades. He liked to wear them to look cool off duty. Throne alone knew why he'd brought them.

He gave them to Eszrah.

'There you go, Ezra Night,' he said. 'Take them. They're yours, mate.'

The partisan was puzzled, and kept trying to give them back, until Mkvenner slowly explained their purpose. Eszrah put them on. An odd smile flickered across his face. More than ever, with the dark, gleaming lenses masking his eyes, he looked like a human moth.

'Ven, tell him he can go back now. He can go back and rejoin his kind. Thank him for me, carefully. He's done more for us than I could ever have expected.'

Mkvenner came back a few minutes later. 'He won't go, sir,' he said.

'Why not?' Gaunt asked.

Mkvenner cleared his throat. 'Because he's yours, sir.'

'What?'

'He's your property, sir.'

Gaunt went over and talked to Eszrah himself. Mkvenner had to join them to help out. The Sleepwalker was quite definite about it. In return for the efforts made by Gaunt and his team in defending the partisan camp, Cynhed ap Niht had given them one of his sons. It appeared that the partisans were terribly literal people. When Gaunt had originally asked them for a guide to lead them through the Untill, Cynhed had understood him to be requesting permanent ownership of a Sleepwalker. No little wonder he had refused.

But Eszrah's father had felt duty bound after the battle with Uexkull's murderers. He'd given them the guide they had been asking for. Literally given Gaunt one of his sons. Forever. As a gesture of thanks.

'You go back now,' Gaunt told Eszrah. 'You've done all I asked of you. Go back to your father.'

Mkvenner translated. Eszrah frowned and queried again.

'Please, go back,' Gaunt said.

Eszrah made to take off the sunshades.

'He can keep those,' Varl said.

They left Eszrah ap Niht standing alone in the skirts of the forest.

BUT HE FOLLOWED them, at a distance.

'He's not going away,' Mkoll said.

'Ven, go talk to him again,' Gaunt said. 'Make him understand.'

When Mkvenner came back, Ezra Night was with him, wearing his sunshades like a trophy.

'He won't be told, sir,' Mkvenner said. 'I think it's a cultural thing. A matter of honour. His father told him to come with you and guide you, and that's what he's going to do. Quite possibly forever. Don't ask him to go back again. He's never been this far before, and he's not entirely sure of the way. Besides, asking him to go back is the same as asking him to disobey his father's strict instructions. He loves his father, sir. He's made a vow. I don't think you should expect him to break it.'

Gaunt nodded. He turned to Eszrah and held out his hand. Eszrah ap Niht took it gently.

'You're one of us now,' Gaunt said. Eszrah seemed to understand. He smiled.

It was a strange moment of union that Gaunt would remember for the rest of his life.

SO, AT DAWN, under the hem of the woodland, Gaunt gathered his battered team around him. Beyond, the bocage beckoned, tranquil. He knew that the tranquility was an illusion. Briefings had reported the heartland to be the most securely held territory on Gereon.

And also, the location of their target.

'We need good rest, food and resupply,' Gaunt began.

'There's a village about three kilometres north-west of here,' Mkoll said. 'It appears to be deserted.'

'We'll start there. More importantly, we need to find out where we are exactly. Cirk?'

She shrugged. 'Lectica, the eastern fringe. Beyond that, I have no idea.'

'Mr Landerson?' Gaunt asked.

'That town in the distance could be Hedgerton. But then again, it could be half a dozen heartland communities. I'm sorry.'

'Let's head for the village,' Gaunt said.

THE PLACE WAS no more than a clutch of abandoned farmhouses, a farrier's shed, a grain store and a small templum. All of it was overgrown, the windows shattered, weeds festering around the doorposts.

They approached cautiously in the warm sunlight. Insects buzzed. The scouts spread wide, circling the place. There was no sign of life. The village had been vacated months before, probably at the time of the invasion, and no one had visited it since.

They split up and searched a few of the dwellings, recovering some dried goods, salted meats and jars of preserves from the pantries. Beltayn found an old shotgun and some kerosene lanterns. In one upstairs room, Curth discovered a doll in an empty cot. It made her cry again. She swore and raged against the weakness that the taint had bred into her. Criid found her and tried to calm her down. Then she saw the empty cot and began to cry too. It was a blessing for Curth. She forced her emotions into check so she could comfort her friend.

Feygor and Varl searched another house. As soon as they were inside, Feygor saw an old bed with a ratty straw mattress. He laid himself down on it.

When Varl came back to find him, Feygor was fast asleep. Varl sat down on the end of the bed and watched over him.

Rawne pushed his way into the next farmhouse and found a table set for dinner. Six places, cutlery, plates. A charcoal mass sat in the pot on the cold stove. Dinner had been abandoned in a hurry.

Rawne sat down at the head of the table and gazed at the settings. They made the shape of an oared boat. Here was the shape of a rising sun. Rawne reached out and rearranged some of the cutlery, and pushed plates into new positions.

That was better. Now they made the mark of the stigma.

IN THE FARRIER's shed, Larkin and Bonin found a half-empty tank of promethium that had been used to fuel the smithy furnace.

'Go get Brostin,' Bonin said.

The big man appeared a few moments later and, with a delighted chuckle, began to replenish his canister tanks.

The micro-bead pipped.

'One,' Gaunt acknowledged.

'Mkoll. Come to the templum, sir. Bring Landerson.'

GAUNT AND LANDERSON walked into the gloom of the village templum. Like all the buildings in this remote farm community, it was little more than a wooden shack. Sunlight pierced in through holes in the wallboards and lit up the dust the visitors were disturbing. Rough wooden chairs were arranged in rows, facing down the nave to the brass aquila suspended over the altar. Gaunt walked forward and knelt before it. He made the sign of the eagle, and began to utter the *Renunciation of Ruin*.

There was a good chance this was the last undesecrated Imperial shrine on the planet.

Gaunt closed his eyes. In the last few nights, he had started to dream again, for the first time since his arrival on Gereon. These recent dreams had been so vivid; they played back now across his mind. Sabbat, always beckoning him, although sometimes she looked like Cirk. That was fine. As long as the beati was with him, it didn't matter what guise she took.

But there were noticeable absences in these renewed dreams. Some of his long-lost friends were no longer coming to him during slumber. Slaydo was still there, though faint and transparent. Gaunt had seen Zweil too, and the wizened priest had been laughing. But there had been no sign of Bragg. No Vamberfeld either. And Gaunt couldn't remember the last time he'd seen Colm Corbec's face.

Worst of all, Brin Milo still hadn't appeared to him. Gaunt still hadn't seen Milo in his dreams since leaving Herodor. But, and this made him uneasy, there was always the screaming. The man screaming in the void. Who the hell was that? He was quite certain he knew the voice...

Ibram Gaunt took dreams seriously. He believed they were the only conduit through which the God-Emperor could make his purpose understood to the common man. Gaunt hadn't always thought that way, but the visions that had led him and the Ghosts to Herodor had been so real, he now regarded every single dream as a message.

He was glad they had come back at last, no matter how disquieting they seemed.

'Sir?'

Mkoll called him over to a massive book he was leafing through.

'What is this?'

'Parish records, sir,' Mkoll replied. 'Look here.' He opened a dusty page and tracked a dirty finger down the copperplate entries. 'Births and deaths. Marriages.'

'This is what you wanted me to see?'

Mkoll folded shut the heavy, brass-cornered volume and then reopened it on its title page.

'See?'

'Parish registry of Thawly Village,' Gaunt read. 'Landerson?'

Landerson hurried over to them.

'Thawly? Know it?'

Landerson shook his head. 'Sorry, sir. I don't. I could ask Cirk...'

'Never mind that,' said Mkoll. 'There's more.'

He unfolded the page and spread it out. It was a flaking chart of the parish boundaries. It showed Thawly and the nearby bocage towns.

'Great Throne...' Gaunt said. 'We've got a map.'

THEY GATHERED IN the porch of the templum, and Gaunt showed them the old chart. 'Mr Landerson was right. The town over there is Hedgerton. And that's Leafering. Take a look. We're located now.'

'So, where's the target?' Rawne asked.

'Just off the map this way, beyond Furgesh, here. You see?'

Rawne saw all too well. He saw the way their shadows made the shape of a mantis on the porch floor.

And he saw the mark on Gaunt's cheek, the one Uexkull's knuckles had gouged, and which Gaunt had refused to allow to be bandaged. It was scabbing over now, but the shape was unmistakable. The witchmark of Chaos. The stigma. Just like the one that daemon-beauty Cirk wore so proudly.

Gaunt had been branded.

'Isn't it about time you let us in on your mission, sir?' Cirk was asking.

'Soon, major. Very soon,' Gaunt replied. 'Look at the map, tell me what you know.'

Landerson bent forward. 'Hedgerton is a small place. All we're likely to find there are glyfs and excubitors. Leafering is more important. Its a large community, and last I knew there was a cell faction active there. Major Cirk?'

'Landerson's right.' said Cirk. 'There's a good chance of making a connection in Leafering. But it's garrisoned. A well-maintained hab, with a vox base and lots of Occupation troopers. Not to mention wirewolves.'

'I can do wirewolves,' Curth retorted. 'They don't scare me.'

Gaunt decided not to mention the fact that the reason Curth had beaten the wirewolf was long gone.

'A vox base? Are you sure, Cirk?'

She shrugged. 'Last time I checked.'

Gaunt smiled. To Rawne, that twisted the witchmark into even more obscene shapes.

'Leafering's the one,' Gaunt announced. 'Definitely.' He paused. 'Varl, where's Feygor?'

'I left him sleeping, sir,' Varl said.

'Good advice,' Gaunt said. 'Let's all get some decent sleep and move in the morning.'

* * *

Night fell over the hamlet, cool and black. In the various dwellings, the Ghosts had found beds and were sleeping deeper than they had since planetfall. Nobody cared about the musty smell of the cot sheets, the dampness. Compared with the grey ooze of the Untill, it was luxury.

Eszrah ap Niht didn't sleep. He took off his sunshades and hooked them carefully over his belt. It was night now, something he understood.

He saw movement in the hamlet's narrow street and followed it. It was the man called Rawne. He was slipping between the houses, a silver knife in his hand.

Eszrah slid an iron quarrel into the mouth of his reynbow.

Gaunt had chosen a bed in the upper floor of a cottage. The sheets were rank and mildewed, so he lay down on top of them and slept in his clothes.

He was vaguely aware of the chamber door opening. He looked up, into the dark, and saw a woman framed against the starlight from the window.

'Ana?'

She took off her jacket and dropped it onto the floor. Then she sat down on the end of the bed and yanked off her boots. The rest of her clothes quickly followed.

'Ibram,' she whispered. He took her in his arms and they kissed. They both laughed as she struggled to pull off his clothing.

'Ana...' he whispered.

'Shhh...' she said.

His straight silver in his hand, Rawne edged up the cottage stairs in the dark. From above him came faint noises. He trod up the next few steps. Now he could hear orgasmic cries through the thin lathe walls of the cottage.

Then silence.

Rawne went up the last few stairs, quiet as a shadow, and carefully opened the chamber door.

He looked in.

Naked, sleeping, Gaunt and Cirk lay wrapped in each other, their limbs entwined. Just like the symbol Rawne had seen in the Untill mists.

He shut the door and went downstairs again. The business end of Eszrah ap Niht's mag-bow suddenly loomed in his face.

Rawne sheathed his warblade.

'Go to sleep,' he told the partisan. 'Just go to sleep,'

GAUNT WOKE WITH a start. It was early, dark still. He had been dreaming that he was sharing his bed. Confused memories flooded back. He reached his hand out and found the mouldering sheets were still warm to the touch.

Someone had been there with him. He had vivid recall now of soft skin. Of urgency. Of heat.

'Ana?' he called out. 'Ana?'

THEY LEFT THAWLY as the sun rose, hazy and red, above the fields. Decent rest and the chance to wash out clothes and kit at the village pump had lifted their mood. Even Feygor seemed a little better, with some colour back in his face.

Mkoll set a brisk pace. They followed the village track until it joined a lane between fields, which in turn linked to a country road. For the first two hours of the day, they saw no one, but as the sun climbed higher, a few transports came up and down the road, so they left it and cut out across the fields, making a direct line for Leafering.

The heartland fields were in a much better state of repair than the farmlands around Ineuron had been. The invaders had maintained horticulture, and there was evidence of extensive planting programs and the use of pesticides. The bocage was a resource the archenemy intended to use to keep its Occupation force fed, perhaps even generate food supplies that would be shipped off-world to help feed their front-line hosts.

As they got closer to Leafering, they saw signs of more disturbing land use. Huge field zones, some created by the systematic clearance of the old hedgerows to join smaller fields together, had been turned into industrial plantations. The air stank of fertilisers, and the fields were coated with a thick crust of pinky nitrates. Out of this grew row after row of thick, black, fleshy stalks on which millions of bulbous mauve fruits were developing.

'These aren't local production measures,' Cirk said.

'Nor a local crop, I'll bet,' Gaunt replied. Over the years, he'd read many reports of the archenemy mass-planting xeno-crops on captured agri-worlds like Gereon. Highly resistant to disease and climate, perhaps hybridised for accelerated growth, these plantations rapidly tripled or quadrupled the planet's crop yield, but at huge cost to the planet's eco-sphere. After a few decades of xenoculture, the planet would be left barren and infertile, all the organics stripped from the topsoil. He wondered if Cirk had any idea what these plantations would mean for the future of her world.

'If you ever get the chance,' he said, 'advise the resistance to target these plantations. You don't want them here, even more than you don't want the archenemy.'

She regarded him with a strange expression. There'd been an odd look in her eyes all morning, come to that. Gaunt was about to ask her about it when Bonin raised a warning and they all sought cover in the thick hedges that ran along the length of the plantation. A machine was approaching down the field. It looked a little like a stalk-tank, its central body-sections propelled on eight arachnoid limbs. But these limbs were more than twenty metres tall, so that the vehicle towered over the ground, as if on stilts. It straddled the plantation rows, a set of feet on either side of the planting line, so its body hung above the crop. As it walked, it exhaled noxious clouds of pesticide from ducts in its belly.

The Ghosts slipped away through the hedge, along the quiet roadway, and crossed the next plantation field instead.

THEY MADE THEIR way through at least ten kilometres of plantation land. Gaunt wondered just how many thousand square kilometres of the heartland had been infested with the alien crop. The team avoided the other stilted sprayers, and what seemed to be mechanical cropper machines at work in the distance.

Leafering was less than half an hour away now. It looked like a big place with old, grand stone buildings. Once they were close enough, the scouts would conduct a quick appraisal and they'd decide how to move in.

The roads were now quite busy with traffic, mostly transports and tracks, so they kept to the hedge paths, crossing in the open only when they had to. During a rest stop under a copse of talix trees, when the sun was high and hot, Gaunt sat down next to Curth.

'How are you doing?'

'Today? Better. Not feeling quite so overwrought.'

'Me too, I think,' Gaunt said. He took a drink from his water bottle. 'You left.'

'I left what?' she asked.

'You left. This morning.'

'What the feth are you talking about?' she asked. 'Have you been out in the sun without your cap on again?'

'Never mind,' Gaunt said. He decided there was no point pushing it when Curth was quite so vulnerable and prone to mood swings. He got to his feet.

'Let's go,' he called. 'Let's get this done.'

TWENTY-FIVE

THREE EXCUBITORS WANDERED down the yard, the long
barrels of their slantwise las-locks swinging. They
exchanged a few words, then turned right through the
gate arch and disappeared up the flagged street towards
the commercia.

Bonin waited until they were well clear, then slipped
out of the shadows, ran the length of the yard and
ducked down behind a tall stack of paper bundles. Some
of the loose papers were sticking out, and Bonin pulled
one free and read it. It was a crudely printed leaflet
encouraging 'citizens of the Intercession' to become
proselytes and convert. Bonin stuffed it back where he'd
found it.

It was early evening in Leafering, and the street lighting
was beginning to flicker on, though the streets themselves were still quite busy. Another hour and the curfew
would sound, ordering all those consented only for day
to their habs. From his vantage point behind the stacked

propaganda leaflets, Bonin had a good view along the rear of the yard. The large ouslite building to his left was being used as a station house by the Occupation forces. Around the front, there was a lot of troop activity, and a line of half-tracks was parked in the thoroughfare.

But this small yard area, enclosed by a high stone wall, ran around to the rear of the building. There were several smaller annexes out here, one of which had a roof festooned with vox masts and aerials.

No one in sight. And no sign of any nasty glyf-like surprises either. They'd had to shrink past wirewolf gibbets in the outskirts to get into the town, and at least once had seen the shimmer of a glyf behind a nearby row of buildings. The sight had made Feygor shake.

But this little yard was clean enough.

Bonin made the signal.

Mkoll and Mkvenner came in over the wall, dropped down and crossed to the far side of the yard until they had overlapped Bonin. All three had their suppressed pistols drawn.

As Bonin backed up the yard, his weapon hunting left and right, Mkoll and Mkvenner reached the annexe with the masted roof. Mkvenner covered Mkoll as he ducked inside.

Thirty-five seconds later, he came out and gave the all clear.

Bonin nodded, and keyed his micro-bead.

'Silver,' he said.

A door in the back of the main building suddenly opened onto the yard. Mkoll and Mkvenner had slipped inside the annexe doorway, and Bonin threw himself back into the shadows along the outer wall. A uniformed sirdar, accompanied by a junior officer and four excubitors, emerged and began to walk down the yard.

'Bragg! Bragg!' Bonin hissed.

* * *

IN THE SHADOWS of an alleyway on the far side of the yard wall, Gaunt listened hard to his earpiece.

'Bonin? Bragg or silver? Which is it?'

A long pause.

'Bonin?'

'Bragg,' the whisper came back.

Rawne and Beltayn were all set to go over the wall.

'Hold it,' Gaunt said. 'It's not clear.'

'I heard Bo call "silver",' Rawne said.

'Well, he's changed his mind,' Gaunt said.

'I'm going anyway,' Rawne said, gesturing for Varl to cup his hands and boost him over the wall. 'We'll be here all night otherwise.'

'Can't you control your people?' Cirk hissed.

'There's been no evidence of it so far,' Gaunt replied.

'Silver. Silver!' Bonin called.

'Right, go,' Gaunt said.

THE SIRDAR AND his escort had gone out through the gate. Bonin signalled again, and Rawne and Beltayn appeared over the wall and slithered down into the yard. They ran towards Bonin, who ushered them up to the annexe, where Mkvenner was waiting at the door.

The annexe was the vox office for the station house. Inside, in a dingy room lit by yellowed glow-globes, sat a large, non-portable voxcaster unit. Coils of trunking and sheaves of cable sprouted up through the roof to connect it to the mast array. It was part of the Occupation's principal communications network, tuned to the archenemy's main command channels and data relays. Most important of all, it was equipped with a cipher module that decrypted the network's confidence codes. Two operators had been staffing the annexe. Mkoll had left their bodies in the corner of the room.

Beltayn hurried in, and swung his vox-set off his shoulder. He pulled the cover off, and unlatched the door of the cable port in its side.

'Fast as you can,' Rawne urged.

'Don't fuss me when I'm working,' Beltayn answered without looking up. He'd unbuttoned a pouch of tools, and was playing out a connector cable. Then he turned his attention to the enemy machine.

'Sonegraph 160. Really, really old, and clearly modified. I haven't messed with one of these in a long time.'

'Fascinate me further, why don't you,' Rawne growled. He glanced at the outer door where Bonin and Mkvenner were watching for interruptions.

Beltayn test flicked a few of the switches on the big caster, and studied the wavelength display. Then he used a watchmaker's screwdriver to remove the pins holding an inspection plate in place. The plate came away, exposing loops of wire and small plug-in valve shunts. Using small pliers and a voltmeter from his kit, Beltayn tested and then exchanged several of the wire connectors and took out one of the valves. Then he attached one end of the connector cable to his set and the other to an output socket on the caster.

'Hurry up,' Rawne said. He was getting jumpy. The cluster of wires Beltayn had exposed precisely formed the shape of the stigma. He looked at something else.

Beltayn switched on his set's power pack, made an adjustment to its dials, then crossed back to the big machine. He tentatively pressed several keys on the main console and, as gauges glowed amber and needles quivered, he started to scroll down through a column of data presented in trembling graphic form on a small subscreen.

'Got it,' Beltayn said. 'Yep, I've got it. The transmission log. How much do you want?'

'How much is there?' asked Rawne.

Beltayn scrolled down some more, peering. 'Mmm... about eight months at least. It'll take a while to get all that.'

'How long are we talking?'

Beltayn shrugged. 'Probably five, ten minutes per week.'

'Feth!' said Rawne.

'Take the last week,' Mkoll said. 'We don't have time for more. Let's just pray there's something usable in it.'

Beltayn looked at Rawne.

'Do as he says,' Rawne agreed. Beltayn set the device, pressed activation keys on both the main caster and his own portable, and information began to stream down the connector into the set's recording buffer.

'Quiet!' Mkvenner called from the doorway.

Outside, two Occupation troopers had wandered out into the yard and were loitering, smoking lho-sticks. They were making idle conversation.

'Come on,' whispered Bonin. 'Smoke up and get lost.'

Beltayn got up and crept over to his set, studying the small display.

'Something's awry,' he whispered.

Rawne felt his heart go cold. 'What do you mean?'

Beltayn reset his vox and hurried back to the main caster to do the same.

'It's transferring, but the data's encrypted. I'll have to start over. What I've got so far is useless.'

'Feth it!' Rawne hissed.

The troopers in the yard were still smoking and chatting.

'Think, think…' Beltayn said to himself. He located the cipher module and examined it. 'Why aren't you working? Why the feth aren't you working?'

He turned to Rawne and Mkoll. 'It's got a security lockout. The cipher needs a key to start it running.'

'A code?'

'No, an actual key. Goes in here.'

Mkoll went over to the bodies of the operators. He searched their pockets and finally found a small steel key on a thin chain around the neck of one of the dead men.

'This it?'

Beltayn tried it. As the key turned, the cipher module began to hum. Two monitor lights came on.

'We're back in business,' he said, and set the transfer going again.

Bonin was pretty sure the two troopers were close to leaving. Then the yard door opened again, and a uniformed junior ran out with a sheet of paper in his hand. He was heading for the annexe. A runner, bringing an urgent message for the operators to send.

'Someone's coming,' Mkvenner said.

'Here?' asked Rawne.

'Right here,' Bonin replied.

Mkoll came towards the door. 'Let him in,' he said. 'Let him right in and then take him. No noise.'

The runner came up to the annexe door. Then he did the one thing they weren't expecting. He knocked.

The Ghosts looked at each other blankly.

The runner knocked again. Waiting at the door, bouncing eagerly on his toes, the runner turned and grinned at the two troopers. One of them called out something. The runner replied and laughed. Then he knocked again.

'Voi sahn, magir?' he called out.

Everyone was looking at Rawne. 'I don't know!' he mouthed indignantly. How the feth did you say 'Come in'? All Rawne could think of was that Cirk would have known.

In desperation, he called out some made-up sounds, deliberately strangling them into an unintelligible bark.

It did the trick. The runner opened the door and stepped inside. His smile melted. He saw three enemy troopers in filthy black fatigues grouped around the main caster. He didn't see the other two either side of the door behind him. Bonin closed the door. Mkvenner's left hand clamped around the runner's mouth before he could utter a word and his warknife punched. He held the wide-eyed runner tightly as he twitched and shook. When the twitching had stopped, he lowered the body soundlessly to the floor with Mkoll's help.

Bonin gently reopened the door a crack and peered out. The troopers were leaving.

Mkoll looked down at the runner. 'He was in a hurry. He may have been expecting to take back a quick reply. I'd lay money he's going to be missed within the next fifteen minutes.'

Rawne looked at Beltayn. 'How long?' he asked.

Beltayn was watching the set display. 'It's slow. Ten, maybe twelve minutes more.'

Those minutes tracked by painfully slowly. Bonin and Mkvenner crouched by the door. Mkoll sat, perfectly still, in one of the operator chairs. Rawne paced, drumming the fingers of his right hand against the knuckles of his left. He became aware that Mkoll was staring at him, his eyes narrowed. Rawne's fidgeting was really getting to the calm, quiet chief scout.

Rawne glared at Mkoll. 'I'm a major,' he snapped. 'I can do what I fething like.'

'And therein, so often, lies our problem,' Mkoll replied coldly. Everyone looked round. With the possible exception of Mkvenner, Mkoll was the most collected, reserved man in the Ghosts. No one had ever heard him rise to the bait and throw out a jibe like that.

'You say something?' Rawne said, taking a step forward. Mkoll's chair scraped back and he got to his feet. Rawne was a good deal taller than Mkoll, but their eyes locked murderously.

'Do you honestly want some, you asshole?' Mkoll breathed.

Mkvenner and Bonin had both risen, flanking Rawne from behind. Surrounded by three of the most dangerous men in the Tanith First, Rawne seemed utterly unfazed. His eyes never leaving Mkoll's, he said, 'You know, feth-face, I believe I do.'

'Oh for feth's sake!' Beltayn cried, so loudly it made them all start. 'What's the matter with you, major? Is it your plan to pick a fight with everyone on the mission team before we're done?'

All four men looked at him sharply. Beltayn shrank back, raising his hands. 'Or I could just carry on minding my own business.'

His expression made Bonin snigger.

Rawne's shoulders relaxed slightly. 'Boy's right. Feth's sake,' he murmured. 'What am I doing?'

Mkoll backed off too, staring at the floor, his fingers to his temples. 'Holy Throne,' he said. 'That was me, wasn't it? That was me.' He looked up at Rawne. 'I'm sorry, sir,' he said. 'I don't know where that came from.'

Rawne bit his lip and shook his head sadly. 'It's all of us,' he said. 'It's all of us.'

'Transfer's complete,' Beltayn called. He started to uncouple his equipment and stow his kit.

'Let's go,' Rawne said.

'To quote my friend the vox-man,' Bonin said. 'Something's awry.'

A truck, painted in the livery of the Occupation forces, had pulled up in the yard while they had been idiotically facing off. Four men had jumped down and, under the supervision of a fifth, an obese, older man in a sirdar's uniform, they were loading the bundles of propaganda pamphlets onto the flatbed from the pile.

'This we didn't need,' Bonin remarked.

Rawne took a look. 'Emperor kiss my arse,' he sighed. 'It's going to take them ages to get that crap loaded. We're stuck here until they've finished.'

'Or until someone comes looking for the messenger,' Mkoll said.

'Or until we go out there and kill them,' suggested Beltayn. 'Not me, obviously. You guys are the mean, tough types who do that sort of thing.'

'Last thing we want now is a fight that could escalate,' Mkoll said.

TWILIGHT WAS SLIDING into night now. The curfew had sounded, and the streets were clearing. Mkoll's team was taking far too long.

Gaunt had withdrawn the rest of them from the alley, where they were too exposed, and they'd holed up in the back parlour of a derelict tailor's store a few doors down. Larkin was covering the front, Varl the back, and Criid was lookout on the side door of the premises. Gaunt waited with Cirk, Landerson, Feygor, Curth and Brostin in a room full of headless fitting dummies, dusty cloth samples and crinkled paper patterns. Eszrah ap Niht lurked in one corner, slowly leafing through a heavy catalogue book, his grey fingers tracing in wonder across the pictures of fine gentlemen and ladies modelling the styles of the latest season.

'What did you mean, I left?' Curth said suddenly.

'Not now, Ana,' Gaunt said.

'No. What did you mean?'

Gaunt got up quickly and walked away. He went into the back hall. 'Anything?' he called down to Criid.

She shook her head.

'Dammit,' he said and turned back. Cirk had followed him out. She was blocking the doorway.

'What is it?' he asked.

'Your woman didn't leave,' she said quietly.

'What?'

'I left, Ibram.'

Gaunt stared at her. He was about to reply, when his micro-bead blipped. Rawne had been told only to use the link in an emergency.

'One?'

'This is two. We've got the stuff. But we're pinned in the annexe. Some idiots are loading a truck in the yard.'

'Can you deal, two?'

'I'd say "Bragg" to that, sir. We could take them, but it could get complicated fast. However, we don't want to be sitting here much longer either.'

'Understood, Stand by. When you hear "silver", get out into the alley. One out.'

'Problem?' Cirk asked. She reached out a hand and placed it against Gaunt's chest. He brushed it aside.

'Not now, Sabbatine. We'll talk about this later.'

'What's to talk about?' she asked.

'Stop it.' Gaunt walked back into the parlour. 'Everyone up,' he said. 'It seems to be time for one of those events Major Cirk dreads.'

'A planetary invasion?' she quipped smartly.

'A diversion,' he replied.

'Throne's sake!' she growled, her jaw stuck out pugnaciously. 'Fine, just so long as it doesn't involve your pyromaniac.'

'Bad news part two,' said Gaunt. 'Brostin, you're up. That fething burner work yet?'

'We'll see, sir,' Brostin replied, pulling the harness of the hefty weapon over his wide shoulders.

'Varl?' Gaunt called.

Varl responded quickly, running back into the parlour with his lasrifle ready.

'I'm going out front with Brostin. Gather the team, get out into the alley, and wait for Rawne's bunch. Cirk?'

'Yes, Ibram?'

He ignored the familiarity. 'The next stage is up to you and Mr Landerson. The Leafering cell. How do we find them?'

'Things may have changed, but there used to be a contact point at the Temple of the Beati, just west of here,' Cirk replied.

The Temple of the Beati, Gaunt smiled. *How entirely appropriate*. 'All right,' he said. 'Talk to Varl, explain how to get to it. I want the two of you ready to lead the team through as soon as we rejoin you. If you hear the code word… uh… "Sabbat", let's use "Sabbat"… if you hear that, go on without us. No questions. Varl, at that point, the senior ranking officer has command of the mission.'

'Yes, sir.'

'Stop smiling, Varl,' Gaunt said. 'If things go arse-up now, it could be you.'

'The Emperor protects,' Varl said sweetly. 'And also dumps on us from a very great height.'

GAUNT LED BROSTIN out through the shop front onto the empty street. The public lighting was poor in this area, though streetlamps glowed beyond the street corner, flooding the boulevard that the station house fronted. They could hear motor traffic and, somewhere, a gong beating.

That was all right. There were several sounds Gaunt didn't want to hear, and foremost amongst them was the howling of wirewolves. He never wanted to hear that particular noise ever again.

'What's the plan?' Brostin whispered.

Gaunt was about to reply when a figure came up behind them. He wheeled round, his silenced auto aimed.

It was Eszrah.

'Go back!' Gaunt hissed. 'Go back with the others!'

The Sleepwalker frowned, not comprehending. Clearly his bond was with Gaunt specifically, not with the party in general. Gaunt owned Eszrah ap Niht, and therefore Eszrah ap Niht would go wherever Gaunt went.

'Preyathee, soule… uh…' Gaunt began. 'Ah, feth it. Come on. Aversye wherall!'

Eszrah nodded. Gaunt didn't bother trying to say 'and be quiet'. The partisan seemed incapable of being anything else.

The trio hurried up the street. As they passed the open gateway of the yard, they peered in and saw the troopers loading the truck by the light of the vehicle's stablight.

Gaunt waved Brostin and Eszrah on and they dashed across the opening and up towards the main boulevard.

'That one,' said Gaunt, pointing to another derelict shop that faced the station house across the street.

'That one what?' Brostin asked.

'I want you to burn it down, Brostin.'

A huge smile split Brostin's face. 'Sir, that's the nicest thing anyone's ever said to me.'

They went over to the shop's doorway, and Gaunt forced the door. It was a cloth merchant's – evidently, this was the haberdashers' quarter of the town.

'All right?' he asked.

'Perfect,' replied Brostin. 'Plenty of ignition sources, plenty of wick.'

'Wick?'

'It's an arsonist thing. Don't worry. Just be set to go when I say.'

Gaunt grabbed Eszrah by the arm and pulled him back to the doorway. Brostin circled the shop front, touching bales of cloth and dusty bolts of material as if assessing them for value. He settled on a thick, velvet fabric.

'Here we go,' he said.

He nursed the feed trigger of his flamer so that liquid promethium spilled out of the snout and dribbled the fuel across the bale, and the others beside it. Almost daintily, he dabbed spots of fuel on other bundles, and trailed it down the shop's walls.

Then he backed off to the doorway, leaving a track of liquid fuel across the floor behind him. He pushed his flamer around behind his back, pulled out his tinderbox and crouched down.

'You're not going to use the flamer?' Gaunt asked from behind him.

'A burst of flamer would take this place up like a furnace. I was assuming you wanted it to look like an accident.'

Gaunt nodded.

'Say hello to Mister Yellow,' Brostin murmured, and struck his match. It fizzled between his fingers. 'And get ready to run like hell.'

Brostin flicked his hairy, tattooed arm, not so hard that it would extinguish the match, but hard enough to send it flying. It landed on the prom trail on the shop floor. And took immediately.

Crackling, flames leapt up and raced along the fuel path towards the bales of soaked fabric.

'I'd love to stay and watch,' Brostin muttered. 'But we should go. Running will help.'

They ran back down the street towards the mouth of the alley behind the yard. Behind them, there was a sucking sound and then a hard bang that blew the glass out of the shop front. A swirl of fire engulfed the shop's ground floor, and rippled up into the night air through the broken windows.

Gaunt, Brostin and Eszrah slid into cover behind the wall end. Already they could hear shouting above the crackle of the fierce flames. Figures rushed out of the yard, shouting cries of alarm. Two, three, five. The obese sirdar was the last to emerge.

'Silver,' Gaunt voxed.

Firebells began to ring. Brostin stood at the wall end and watched the conflagration eating into the facade of the old shop.

'Now isn't that just lovely,' he breathed.

'Will you come the feth on?' Gaunt barked.

REGROUPED, THE MISSION team ran through the dark alleys, leaving the furious fire behind them. More fire-bells were ringing now, and the glow lit up the night sky.

'You got it?' Gaunt asked Rawne.

'We got it. But there are three bodies back there that will raise some questions.'

'Understood. Cirk? Where's this temple?'

'This way!' she called.

They crossed two more side-streets, and then ran down an empty boulevard for twenty metres. Abruptly, Cirk and Varl pulled them into cover. They cowered in the shadows, pulses thumping. Half-seen, a glyf drifted past the head of the road, its obscene light reflecting off the polished flagstones. Curth had to jam her hands across Feygor's mouth to stop him crying out.

The glyf was gone. They started to move again, footsteps clattering over the hard cobbles.

'Oh, crap!' said Varl.

Five excubitors had suddenly rounded the end of the street. They blinked at the gang of figures before them and then began to raise their las-locks.

'Cover!' Gaunt cried. Everyone split left and right.

Everyone except Eszrah ap Niht. He'd seen these creatures before. He raised his reynbow and planted an iron dart through the forehead of the lead figure. The excubitor flew backwards and fell down. Eszrah reloaded. The iron quarrel made a clinking noise as it rattled backwards down the bow's barrel, pulled into place by the powerful magnets. He fired again.

A second excubitor tumbled down, its arms flailing. It made a heavy sound as it hit the flagstones, and its laslock snapped under its weight.

Calmly, the partisan reloaded again. *Sklink-ptup.*

The remaining excubitors were firing now. Their weapons cracked and sizzling lock-bolts kissed past the tall grey figure. He didn't even flinch.

Criid and Varl, enjoying the best of the street-side cover, leaned out and let go with their auto-pistols. The stammering, silenced bursts slammed two more excubitors over on their backs.

The last excubitor started to run. Eszrah took a step or two forward, settled his aim and fired.

It was a long shot. The excubitor had all but disappeared around the street corner. The poisoned quarrel smacked into the back of its shaved skull and dropped it on its face with a bone-breaking crack.

'The temple?' Gaunt urged Cirk.

'Down here,' she said.

THE TEMPLE WAS empty and silent. It was the saddest thing Gaunt had yet seen on Gereon. Labour gangs from the local Iconoclave had rendered its icons to debris and shattered the statuary. The murals had been defaced with obscenities.

Guns ready, the team prowled in through the shadows. Ragged bodies, long decayed, lay on the marble floor of the inner shrine where they had been killed months before. Women and children, craving sanctuary from the Saint. Gaunt closed his eyes.

That was exactly what they were doing now.

He walked towards the ruined altar and sank to his knees. The face of the Beati was just visible through the daubings and smears the Occupation forces had inscribed.

'Please,' Gaunt whispered to the defaced image. 'Please.'

'She's not listening,' Cirk snapped, and walked past him. 'I'm the only one here.' Cirk took hold of a battered golden candelabrum, and swung it so it faced north.

'Now we hide and we wait,' she said.

A TEMPLE PRIEST came in just after midnight, to perform his furtive, unconsented worship. When he saw the candelabrum, he made the sign of the aquila and retreated fast.

An hour later, he returned.

'Hello?' he called. He was hunched and old, and his voice was thin. 'Hello? Is anyone here?'

Gaunt rose to his feet and slid out of the shadows.

'Hello,' he said.

TWENTY-SIX

'This is unacceptable,' said Colonel Noth. 'Quite simply unacceptable.'

'Well, I'm sure you're going somewhere with this,' Gaunt replied. 'But I wish you'd get there fast.'

They were in the basement of a municipal store in the north-west of Leafering. The local cell, fifty-strong and surprisingly well armed, had brought them out of the temple into hiding. The mission team was all around, relaxing, sleeping or drinking the broth that had been prepared over the basement's crackling drumfires.

Maxel Noth was a short, well-built man in his late forties. His black hair was long and dank, and tied back in a ponytail.

'You come here with this incredible story. Incredible. And you have the gall to ask me to believe you?'

'You might want to have a word with Major Cirk there,' Gaunt suggested. 'She's cell too.'

'So she says. Of the Ineuron cell. But it's common knowledge that the Ineuron cell was exposed and annihilated over a week ago. You could be anyone. You could be well-briefed informers.'

'Noth,' Gaunt said wearily. 'I need your help. I am here to do the Emperor's work. I need friends.'

'To do what?' the cell leader asked bluntly. 'You claim to be Guard. Are you here to liberate my world?'

'Not this again...' Gaunt sighed.

Landerson came over. 'Colonel Noth? I think we should square this away. The colonel-commissar and his squad are here on a mission of extreme priority.'

'What sort of mission?' Noth asked.

'I have no idea. I haven't been told. But I trust him, sir. Ballerat himself ordered me to bring him and his team in.'

'Ballerat, eh? A good man.'

'He's dead, sir,' Landerson said.

'Is he? Dead?'

'Died getting Gaunt's people in, so that should tell you something of the importance he placed on them.'

Noth shrugged. 'That's not the point. We're on the anvil here in Leafering as it is. We can't be expected to–'

'The Emperor expects, sir,' Gaunt said.

Noth glared at him. 'Understand this, sir. We have been engaged in covert fighting these last months. We have used our anonymity to target grain stores, trackway junctions and power plants. Nothing we have done has been... vulgar or visible. Vulgarity and visibility lead to discovery and death. Now, tonight, you have blundered into Leafering, set fires, killed Occupation officers by your own admission. It's a wonder the wolves are still slumbering. Throne, sir! You'll reveal us all.'

'Maybe he will,' said Cirk, sitting down beside Gaunt. 'Colonel, it's hard to hear... believe me, I know... but you have to understand that the colonel-commissar is here for a reason that's much bigger than you or me.

Much bigger than this cell. Much bigger than Gereon. By the Emperor's will, we might all go to our deaths, and it would still be worth it if Gaunt succeeds. Please, take this seriously. This is about the Imperium, and if Gereon burns to make it happen, then so be it.'

Noth frowned. 'I've been taking things seriously since the archenemy came to my planet. Everything is about life and death. Don't lecture me on responsibility.' He looked at Gaunt. 'What would you need from me?' he asked.

'Some supplies. Rations, field dressings, hard rounds, grenades if you have them. I understand your resources are thin to begin with. After that, transportation. You must have covert ways to move personnel from place to place.'

'Transportation to where?' Noth asked.

'I hope to be able to tell you that shortly,' Gaunt replied.

'Anything else?' asked Noth.

'He'll probably ask you for a diversion too,' said Cirk snidely. 'He's very fond of them.'

'That's quite likely,' said Gaunt.

NEARBY, MKOLL SAT beside one of the drum-fires, carefully sliding the power cells of the team's lasrifles into the flames. Every team member was low on energy munitions, and though cells were simple enough to recharge, the local power supply was less than reliable. Exposing a cell's thermal receptor to heat in a fire was a drastic but effective method of recharging. However, it shortened the life of the power packs badly. Mkoll was resigned to that. He had a feeling their life expectancy was down to days now, if not hours.

Mkvenner came over with the last few packs he had collected up from Criid and Varl. He helped Mkoll feed them into the fire.

'That shouldn't have happened,' Mkoll said.

'What?'

'That nonsense with Rawne. I can't believe I did that. It wasn't me there for a moment, you know, Ven? Not me at all.'

'Curth says we should all expect it. We've been exposed to this world for long enough, and its blight's soaked into us now. She says our personalities will change. Our moods will switch. You've seen it.'

Mkoll sighed. 'I have. I just thought I'd escaped its touch so far.' He looked at his own hands as he dropped the last pack into the fire. Like all of them, his skin was speckled with a rash, and his fingernails had started to mottle. 'We're not coming out of this one, Ven. Our bodies are falling apart and we're losing our minds.'

'But on the bright side...' said Mkvenner.

Mkoll smiled. *That Nalsheen fortitude...*

'I don't think it does destroy us,' Mkvenner said thoughtfully, after a long pause.

'What?' Mkoll asked.

'Chaos. We're warned so often that the taint of the Ruinous Powers destroys a man like a disease. But that's not what it feels like, is it?'

'What are you talking about, Ven? I feel sick to my bones.'

'It's changing us,' Mkvenner said. 'That's what it does. That's why it's so... dangerous. Look at Rawne.'

'Do I have to?'

'Rawne's never trusted anyone. Now the taint's got to him, it's brought that part of him to the forefront. Magnified it. He's paranoid now. You can see that. So jumpy. And Doctor Curth. She was always hard-nosed, but she also always kept her outrage at the cost of war shut away, so she could concentrate on saving lives. Chaos is letting all that hidden anger out like a flash flood. Beltayn too. The lad's always had a cocky streak he works to keep in check. Now he's answering back and wising off. And you...'

'Me?' replied Mkoll.

'You're finally saying to Rawne all the things you always wanted to. Chaos doesn't destroy us, it finds the things that were always there inside us and brings them out. The ugliness, the flaws, the worst parts of us. That's why mankind should really fear it. It brings out the worst in us, but the worst is already there.'

'You could be right,' said Mkoll.

'I could be,' agreed Mkvenner. 'Or that idea might just have been Chaos bringing out the worst in me.'

ON THE OTHER side of the basement, Beltayn was working on his vox-set. Larkin sat down next to him.

'How's it going?' he asked.

'Slow. There's so much stuff to sort through. It's killing my eyes.' Beltayn was scrolling through the transmission log he'd copied out of the archenemy's voxcaster. The set's display screen was small, and he was straining to make out the data. 'It's decrypted, but I'm still having to run everything through the set's translator system, and you know how hopeless that is. Only a rudimentary grasp of the enemy language forms. Loads of words are coming up as *not found*.'

'How much did you get?' Larkin asked.

'Just the last week's worth, but that alone is thousands of transcripts. I'm going through the record of the enemy's primary data-broadcasts first. That seemed the most likely place to start. '

'Want a hand?' Larkin asked.

Beltayn glanced at him.

'Sharpest eyes in the Ghosts, me,' Larkin grinned. 'Go get yourself some of that vile broth and let me have a go.'

GAUNT HAD BEEN asleep for about three hours. The sleep had been dreamless at first, then the pictures had begun to come. He saw ice and snow, which may have been Hagia, the Shrineworld. A silver wolf ran across the snow fields, leaving no trace behind it. It reached a stand of lonely black timbers and looked back. The wolf had Rawne's eyes.

From somewhere, the screaming started up. Distant, but clear. A man's voice, screaming and screaming in such pitiful pain. He knew that voice. Who was it?

The wolf had vanished. For reasons of dream-logic, a door opened in the middle of the trees and a figure stepped out. It was the Beati, but it was also Cirk. The stigma on her cheek was an aquila.

Her mouth moved as she spoke, but the sounds were oddly out of synch with her lips.

She said, 'Under the skin. What matters is on the inside.'

Then she backed away through the door again, like a pict-feed running in reverse, and the door closed.

That was when the screaming began to get louder, until there was no snow, no ice, no door, no trees, no dream at all. Just screaming.

Then Beltayn woke him up, which suited Gaunt just fine.

He yawned and stretched. Larkin was beside Beltayn.

'Well?'

'I think we've got it,' Beltayn said. 'Larkin spotted it.'

'And?'

'It was on the primary command channel. Several transmissions yesterday and the day before. Activity at the Lectica Bastion. As best as I can make out, a lot of senior ordinals are gathering there. The transmissions use codenames for VIPs. Some sort of high level security meeting.'

'Right,' said Gaunt. 'But the bastion is one of the chief fortresses on Gereon. A meeting of senior ordinals would not be an unusual event.'

Beltayn nodded. 'One of the codenames is "eresht". That means parcel or package. Whoever is codenamed "eresht" seems to be there at the bastion already. The others are coming to see him. They've been summoned to see him.

Sir, in some of the early intel gathered prior to the mission, "eresht" was used as a codeword for our target.'

Gaunt stroked his hands down his cheeks and stared at the ground. 'He's still there?'

'Yes, sir.'

'Holy Throne. He's still there.' Gaunt looked up at Beltayn and Larkin. 'Well done, both of you. Let's talk to Colonel Noth. And get Cirk and Mr Landerson too. It's time they learned the truth.'

'OUR MISSION HERE on Gereon is to find and eliminate one individual,' Gaunt said.

The assembled Ghosts sat or stood around Gaunt in a semi-circle. None of what their leader had to say was news to them. This was for the benefit of Landerson, Cirk, Noth and four of Noth's senior lieutenants.

'One individual?' Noth asked. He laughed. 'Who? The Plenipotentiary? I can't think of anyone important enough to warrant these efforts. Not even the Plenipotentiary, come to that. The Anarch would just replace that toad Isidor with another lord...' His voice trailed off. 'Holy Throne, he's not here is he?'

'Who?'

'The bloody Anarch! He's not here on Gereon is he?'

'No,' Gaunt replied. 'Our target is a man named Noches Sturm.'

'A man?' said Landerson. After all his patience and trust, he felt disappointed.

'A prisoner, in fact. He's being held by the archenemy at the Lectica Bastion.'

Noth got to his feet. 'I said this was all a load of nonsense! You're out of your mind!'

'Sit down, colonel,' Gaunt said.

'I want no part of–'

'Colonel Noth, the man I've just told you about has a rank too. Noches Sturm is Lord Militant General Sturm of the Imperial Guard.'

Noth blinked and sat down again. Landerson exhaled a long, whistling breath.

'They've got a lord general?' Noth asked.

'They've had him for many months now. As you can imagine, this represents a critical security risk to the Crusade armies. It's no exaggeration to say that it could change the tide of the entire war here in the Sabbat Worlds. A lord general knows... well, where do I start? Guard codes, cipher patterns, force distribution, army deployment, fleet dispersal, tactical planning, communication protocols, weaknesses, strengths, secrets.'

'How the hell did they get to him?' Landerson asked.

'Accident,' said Gaunt. 'And, to a certain degree, because of a misjudgement I made.'

'What?' Cirk grinned. 'Is that why you ended up with this nightmare mission? To make amends for letting him get captured?'

Gaunt glanced at her. 'No, Cirk. I'm here to make amends for not killing him when I had the chance.'

'I don't understand,' said Noth.

'Sturm is a traitor, colonel. Several years ago, he and I were responsible for the defence of a hive-city on the planet Verghast. It was a close-run thing, hard won. At the darkest hour, fearing for his own hide, he tried to abandon the hive and make his escape. His actions weakened the defence and almost cost us the fight. As senior commissar, I had him arrested for desertion and cowardice. He chose to take the honorable way out, but then turned that opportunity into another attempt to escape. I cut off his hand and put him in detention. I should have executed him, right then and there.'

'Why didn't you?' asked Cirk.

Gaunt hesitated. 'After all he had done, Cirk, I think I wanted him to suffer. I wanted him to endure the humiliation of a court martial, of public disgrace. A simple, summary execution on the field of battle, something quite within my power to exact, would have been too easy. Besides, the commissar in me could see the political value of a court martial. The public disgrace, trial and execution of a lord general would send out a message to any other over-zealous, over-ambitious commander that the new Warmaster was not someone to be trifled with. Sturm was transported for detention pending trial. The trial was scheduled for the middle of last year, but the events of the counter-attack through the Khan Group got in the way. Disastrously, Sturm was en route to the court martial when his ship was captured by an enemy squadron. They quickly realised what a valuable trophy they had accidentally won.'

One of Noth's officers raised his hand. 'Sir, isn't it too late now? I mean, surely Sturm will have already divulged all of his secrets?'

'Especially if they torture him,' Noth agreed.

'Sturm was placed under mindlock by the Guild Astropathicus during his detention. It's standard practice in these cases. The guild would have removed the lock at the trial, so that Sturm could be properly cross-examined.'

'So he can't tell them anything?' Landerson said.

Gaunt shrugged. 'Not willingly, Mr Landerson. But the archenemy has powerful psykers of its own. A mindlock is hard to remove, but not impossible. No, I'm afraid the only way of ensuring Sturm reveals none of his secrets is if they die with him.'

'If it's this vital,' said Noth, 'why only send in a team of troopers? Why not engage the fleet and flatten the bastion from orbit?'

'The same reason the liberation of Gereon has not yet begun, colonel,' Gaunt said. 'The counter-attack is still being fought back. The fleet is stretched to its limits. And besides, there'd be no guarantee. With a bombardment, we could never be sure we'd actually got Sturm.'

'You know the Lectica Bastion isn't the sort of place you just walk into?' Noth said quietly.

Gaunt nodded. 'It's going to take scrupulous planning and a lot of luck.'

'You're sure he's there?' asked Cirk.

'As sure as we can be. Intelligence gathered prior to this mission positively identified the bastion as the place the enemy had sequestered Sturm. There was every chance he'd be moved. But my vox-officer has managed to access and read recent transmissions made on the archenemy command channels.' Gaunt looked at Beltayn.

Beltayn cleared his throat. 'Sturm is referred to by the enemy codeword "eresht", which means a package or parcel. He's definitely still there. In fact, it looks like something big is going down. A large number of senior ordinals is gathering at the bastion to meet with him.'

'Something big?' Noth said. 'Like... the breaking of the mindlock, perhaps?'

Beltayn shrugged. 'Not for me to say, sir. A lot of the transmissions are untranslatable. But we know he's there. Several codes are used to refer to him. Eresht is the main one. They also use "pheguth", but my system can't supply a meaning for that word.'

Rawne nodded across the room. 'Maybe Major Cirk can tell us?'

Cirk glared at Rawne. 'Don't ask me for a literal translation. The word is a slur. Extremely unpleasant. In simple terms, it means "traitor".'

Noth got to his feet. 'I'll assemble what maps and charts I can get hold of, sir,' he said. 'We'll start devising an entry plan. Cirk also spoke of a diversion. It seems to me that's vital. A big noise to draw the enemy's attention. I'll make contact with the other cell leaders in the heartland tonight. Together we can field upwards of six hundred fighters. It wouldn't be hard to cordinate a joint attack on the bastion, especially if I tell my fellow commanders that there's a chance to destroy a whole crowd of the enemy's senior ordinals in one go. That's a target of opportunity the resistance can't afford to miss.'

'Colonel,' Gaunt called out. 'You do realise that's a lie, don't you? Even with six hundred men, the chances of getting through the gate are slim. You're not likely to get anywhere near the ordinals.'

Noth nodded. 'I know it's a lie. But I've got to tell the commanders something if I'm going to persuade them to sacrifice their entire cells just to get you inside.'

TWENTY-SEVEN

'WHAT THE BLOODY hell is that noise?' Sturm asked. At his heels, Humiliti the lexigrapher jabbed out some more keystrokes.

'Don't type that, you idiot!' Sturm snapped. 'Desolane?'

It was late afternoon, but the light outside was already failing, as if a storm was drawing in. Servants with tapers hurried down the long hallways of the bastion, lighting the lamps. There was a general bustle of activity everywhere in the fortress. Transports and aircraft had been arriving all day, and the primary courtyards were swarming with newly-arrived troops. Sturm basked in the knowledge that it was all in his honour. All this fuss, and the formal ceremonies to come. For him.

'Desolane!'

The life-ward was at the far end of the marble gallery, talking with sirdars of the Bastion Guard. The officers were dressed for the evening in extravagant formal uniforms, dripping with gold frogging and silver buttons. The gorgets at their throats were encrusted with gemstones, and the silver helmets they held under their arms were festooned with white feather combs.

Hearing Sturm's voice, Desolane dismissed the sirdars, and hurried to the general's side.

'Sir?'

'That bloody awful noise, Desolane. What is it?'

'It is the martial band of the First Echelon, sir, rehearsing for tonight's reception. High Sirdar Brendel insisted the band played when the Plenipotentiary arrived.'

'This Brendel's an idiot.'

'He is high sirdar of the Occupation army, sir. And he will be one of the senior dignitaries asking questions of you when the formal interviews begin.'

'I'll tell him what he wants to know,' Sturm snorted. 'And I'll tell him his marching band's a bloody disgrace to boot.'

'You must do as you see fit, of course,' said Desolane.

They walked together down the gallery, the lexigrapher hobbling after them. Humiliti had recently cut another flapping swathe of typescript off the printing machine's roll and handed it to a servant to be taken for filing. The lexigrapher had been following Sturm about the bastion all day, recording the general's every comment. He'd had to change paper rolls twice already.

Sturm had been in a magnanimous mood, eager to talk, even though he affected a contempt for the dwarfish servant. Memories were returning now all the time: some small and fragmentary, others long and involved. Sturm took delight in recounting everything that occurred to him for the lexigrapher to take down. He recalled the events of certain actions, uniform details of the regiments he had served with, events from his childhood, the characters of men he had known, his family background, his first battlefield success.

At one point, earlier that afternoon, he had stopped in his tracks and announced, 'Roast sirloin of grox. Bloody, not over-done. That is my favourite dish. I've just remembered. Fancy not remembering that.'

He laughed. Desolane made a note to make sure grox was on the menu for the banquet. Bloody, not over-done.

It seemed to the life-ward that Sturm was desperate to get his memories down on paper. Sturm had speculated about 'composing a full autobiography' as a work of that nature was only fitting for a man of such note and substance. 'History must know me, Desolane. For history will take its shape because of me.'

Desolane had nodded dutifully. The life-ward had no wish to discourage Sturm's urgent recollections, as he seemed to remember more and more with each returning memory. One thought set off another, one idea reminded Sturm of a dozen other new things to say.

But in truth, there was desperation. It was as if Sturm dearly wanted to get everything down in case he forgot it all again. The mindlock had been cruel indeed. Sturm never wanted to feel so lost again.

The general was wearing the plain Occupation force uniform Desolane had found, but he had already insisted on 'something more dignified' for the evening's formalities. 'Something with braid, please, Desolane. A long jacket, a sash. An officer's cap too, or is that too much?'

'I will arrange these things,' Desolane had replied.

Now, as the daylight faded, they wandered out from the gallery onto the wide marble landing that overlooked the double sweep of the grand staircase in the bastion's main hallway. The crystal chandeliers were lit, and huge silk banners decorated the walls, displaying the insignias of various echelon units, the symbols of the High Powers, and, centrally, the badge of the Anarch himself.

Sturm was talking again, something about a formal ceremony like this that he had once attended. Humiliti rattled it all down, pausing only once to re-ink his levers. Down below them, servants and troopers hurried back and forth across the wide floor of the hall, pushing trolleys laden with crystal glasses, bringing food stuffs from the unloading freighters.

Desolane had plenty to think about. Security in the bastion had to be perfect. Apart from Sturm himself, and the exalted Plenipotentiary, three hundred and eight senior ordinals and staff officers were due to arrive before nightfall. Most would have their own life-wards or bodyguards, but Desolane felt ultimate responsibility for the safety of all of them. Since the attempt on Sturm's life, the life-ward had personally overseen every aspect of security. Desolane didn't dare delegate to any of the sirdars, and didn't feel comfortable relying on anyone else to get the job right.

'More seniors are arriving now,' Desolane said, pointing down towards the hall's huge outer doors.

'Do I have to greet them?' Sturm asked.

'No, you will be presented formally at the reception, once the Plenipotentiary has arrived,' Desolane said. 'There. That man is Ordinal Ouflen. He is an expert in lingua-forms, and will want to question you about Imperial battle languages. With him, that is Ordinal Zereth, who specialises in propaganda. He will be interviewing you on Imperial morale, and what methods might be employed to undermine the confidence and motivation of the average Imperial Guardsman. Coming in through the door, that is Sirdar Commander Erra Fendra Ezeber of the Special Echelon. She has interest in tactics and also in cunning and subterfuge.'

'What's that?' asked Sturm, gesturing at a hulking figure dressed in fur-edged robes that had just come in through the door escorted by two silver servitors.

'Aha. That is Pytto, an agent of Flotilla Admiral Oszlok. There will be a lot of questions from him. Imperial Battlefleet tactics, ship weaknesses, possibly even dispositions. It's been a while since you were privy to such information, but the admiral hopes you will be able to pinpoint safe harbours, and secure high anchor points used by Imperial warships. A surprise assault on an Imperial safe harbour could cripple a significant portion of the Warmaster's space power.'

'I spoke about that earlier. Didn't I?' Sturm looked down at Humiliti, who nodded eagerly.

'Earlier today, I remembered some details of hidden high anchor stations in the corewards portion of the Khan Group. The midget wrote it all down. Make sure the appropriate sections of my transcript are passed to your beloved admiral with my compliments.'

'Perhaps you should rest for a while, sir,' Desolane suggested.

'I'll try, if that bloody band agrees to shut up.'

Desolane bowed slightly in consent. 'His highness the Plenipotentiary is due to arrive in three hours, at which time the formalities will begin. I understand he wishes to start by having you swear an oath of allegiance to the Anarch, whose word drowns out all others. After that, I believe he intends to bestow an honorary rank upon you – sirdar commander, I think – and award you a ribbon of merit to acknowledge your efforts and cooperation.'

Sturm nodded sagely. 'Wise. It would be good to reinforce the perception that I am a man of significance to these commanders.'

Desolane was amused. Sturm could not disguise the flush of pride that filled his face. Respect, admiration, power, after all this time, restored to him.

'I will have a bath drawn in your quarters, sir,' Desolane said, 'and send the footmen to lay out your attire. I will come for you fifteen minutes before the ceremonies begin. Now, if you will excuse me, sir.'

Desolane bowed again, and hurried down the stairs, pausing to issue instructions to a group of excubitors. Then the life-ward descended to the hall floor and walked towards the guest most recently arrived.

Mabbon Etogaur was wearing his usual, understated garb of brown leather, but his boots and buttons were polished, and he had affixed a golden badge of the Anarch to his throat button. He wore an expensive laspistol in a belt holster, and a short, curved power sword in an ornate scabbard.

'Etogaur,' Desolane nodded.

'Life-ward. You asked me here early.'

'You understand why?'

'Security, it said in your message.'

'Indeed.'

Mabbon Etogaur turned and nodded at the two men who had accompanied him in. They were both huge, heavily-muscled troopers, wearing ochre uniforms with gold sashes and bone-white helmets that came down in a half-visor over their faces. They stood to attention, rigid, eyes forward, their polished lasrifles crossed in front of their chests.

'It's going to be a fine night,' Mabbon said, 'and I see no reason why it shouldn't be an appropriate time for the worthy commanders of the Anarch's forces to get their first glimpse of the Sons of Sek. I've brought a force of sixty, the best in the camp. I trust that will help you with your security issues?'

'I'm gratified,' said Desolane. 'Most should assemble in the upper courtyard, ready for review. I'd like a few ready to reinforce the front gates and the curtain wall during the banquet. Might you also spare two of the most trustworthy to stand guard over the pheguth's... I'm sorry, over Lord Sturm's private apartments?'

Mabbon nodded. 'You say two of the most trustworthy, life-ward, but I'll tell you an odd thing. Over the weeks of training, I've been speaking from time to time

to the men about the… the pheguth, and how he would
eventually empower them with knowledge and wisdom.
In their expectation, they came to almost worship him.
And then, the other day, when we went to inspect them
on the field, when Sturm collapsed in front of them… I
was afraid they would lose all respect for the man. The
Sons despise weakness, you see.'

'And?' asked Desolane.

'You were there, life-ward. You saw how Sturm recovered, got back on his feet, faced them without a hint of
shame. And the speech he made, just like that. It was
humbling. The man has true charisma. He is a born
leader. No wonder he achieved such a high rank in the
army of the False Emperor.'

'I agree,' Desolane said. 'It was inspirational.'

'It was stunning,' said Mabbon. 'So, you see, when you
ask for the most trustworthy, I'm stumped because I
don't know who to choose. The Sons of Sek adore General Sturm. They almost worship him. And they would
die to keep him safe.'

'The general will be delighted to hear it,' said Desolane.

'Isn't that him, up there on the landing?' Mabbon
asked.

Sturm was still where Desolane had left him. He was
talking animatedly, recounting some new-remembered
detail to the lexigrapher.

'It is. He's been wandering the halls of the bastion all
day, remembering.'

'Remembering what?' Mabbon Etogaur asked.

'As far as I can tell,' said Desolane, 'everything.'

THE BASTION WAS enormous. In the dying light, it seemed
to be part of the giant mountain range that surrounded
it, discernible only because of the thousands of window
lights that speckled its flanks. It was built as a towering
central donjon, flanked by two smaller towers that sat

like broad shoulders against the main keep. There was an upper courtyard, ringed by a bulwark wall, and then a lower ground, encircled by a massive curtain wall.

As they got closer, they could see the defence batteries along both wall circles, enough to see off a brigade-strength attack with the slightest effort. Aircraft were coming in towards the landing fields inside the inner bulwark, their running lights winking in the cold mountain air. Deathships, shuttles, lavish transporters. The cream of the archenemy hierarchy was coming to the glowering bastion tonight.

The single approach road ran up through the deep valley below the bastion, winding around hard turns. There was frost on the road, and only a thin barricade rail defended the sheer drop on one side of the track. A gorge loomed below, so deep its floor was lost in inky shadows.

The wheels of the heavy cargo-10 slithered.

'Keep your eyes on the road,' she said. The hooded driver nodded.

The approach road itself was busy with traffic. Troop transporters, freighters, armoured cars, and the more splendid motor carriages of the ordinals arriving by land, all of them heading up towards the fortress. A tail-back was forming at the checkpoints below the main gate as excubitors and Occupation troopers checked each arriving vehicle.

They slowed down, joining the queue. The transport's big engine sputtered and coughed.

'Don't you dare let it die!' she snapped.

'Enough, will you?'

She glanced in the door mirror. Already more vehicles had bunched up behind them, waiting in line.

'Heads up,' the driver said.

Two excubitors, their breath steaming from their speaking grilles, were crunching back down the line of waiting vehicles, barking orders.

'Voi shet! Ahenna barat voir! Mej! Mej!'

'What is this?' the driver asked.

'They want us to pull over. To the side there. We have to make room.'

'Ahenna barat voir! Mej! Avar voi squen? Mej!'

'Pull it over! Come on! They want us all to make space for something.'

'Trying, all right?' the driver complained. 'This heap of junk is… junk.' He revved the engine and hauled on the heavy wheel, pulling the massive truck over against the cliff side of the road. Ahead of them, and behind, under the shouted orders of the excubitors, the rest of the line was doing the same.

They waited. After a minute or two, a huge transport with four outriders as escort purred past. It was waved on towards the checkpoint and entered the main gates without stopping.

'That was somebody very important,' she said.

'Remind me to find out who so I can kill them later,' the driver said.

The line began to move again, crawling forward. 'Keep cool. Just keep cool,' she said. 'Just do what I tell you and leave the talking to me.'

'And if that doesn't work?' the driver asked.

'Kiss your arse goodbye,' she said.

It took another ten minutes for them to reach the head of the queue. The guards at the outer checkpoint were inspecting every arrival. She saw that at least three transports had been pulled off the side of the checkpoint and were being searched. The crews of the transporters were waiting in the cold, their hands on their heads, weapons aimed at them and fetch-hounds pulling at their leashes to attack.

'If that happens to us…' the driver whispered.

'It won't,' she said, 'because we're going to do this right. Right, here we go.'

They rolled to a halt at the lowered bar. Occupation troopers strolled out to slowly surround the truck. She saw a lascannon emplacement to her left, the barrels trained on their cab. Three excubitors came forward, one of them wrangling a pair of snarling fetch-hounds.

She lowered the window as the lead excubitor came up.

'Voi shet? Hakra atarsa?'

'Consented, magir. I am consented.'

The excubitor switched his speaker to translate.

'What are you?'

'Delivery, magir. From Gornell. Foodstuffs. We have to get them into the kitchens before they spoil. The ordinals will be most displeased if their meat is rotten and–'

'Shut up,' the excubitor said. 'You talk too much, consented.'

'Yes, magir.'

The excubitor with the dogs was walking them round the vehicle. They barked and snuffled.

'Stigma?' the excubitor by the cab asked.

She turned her cheek and showed him.

'Display to me your consent!' it demanded.

She rolled up her sleeve and held her arm out of the cab window.

'Eletraa kyh drowk!' the excubitor said to its companions.

'Chee ataah drowk,' the other replied. It drew the long metal tester from its belt, and placed the cup over her imago. She stiffened as the thing in her arm twisted and seethed. Rune lights on the tester lit up.

'Fehet gahesh,' the excubitor told its companion.

'You may proceed, interceded one,' the first excubitor said.

She nodded to the driver who started to put the vehicle in gear. But the barrier did not raise.

'Wait!' the excubitor commanded.

The pair of fetch-hounds were agitated, growling and sniffing around the back gate of the cargo-10. The hound-master shouted a few words, and the excubitor answered.

Then it looked back up into the cab at her. 'The hounds have smelled something. We must search your transport. Back up and park over there.'

'Of course they've smelled something, magir,' she said quickly. 'The cargo is raw meat. Steaks and brisket, also some chops and four whole grox. They smell blood. It's a wonder they haven't broken down the hatch.'

The excubitor thought about it. It turned and shouted something she didn't catch to the hound-master. An answer came back.

'You may proceed,' the excubitor said.

A nod, and the barrier swung up.

'Thank you, magir,' she said.

The truck gunned forward, up the slope and in under the towering arch of the main gate.

Inside there was a noisy jumble of vehicles, all with lamps blazing. The night shadow behind the curtain wall was especially dark. Excubitors with lighted poles directed traffic to the appropriate destinations. She leaned out of the cab, told her business to one of the excubitors, and was given instructions.

She sat back and closed the window. 'To the right. Up there, where those lowbeds are going.'

'Right,' the driver replied.

They approached the inner bulwark, and entered it by one of several smaller gatehouses. Inside, directly below the massive walls of the bastion itself now, they drove into a smaller courtyard that served the loading docks of the kitchens.

'Pull over there. There, behind those other trucks. Get us in tight, against the yard wall.'

The driver nodded and obeyed. He pulled the cargo-10 to a halt and switched off the engine. They both let out long sighs of relief.

Varl sat back from the wheel and pulled down his hood. He grinned at Cirk.

'That was tight,' he said.

'I know,' she replied.

'Fething tight. For a moment there–'

'I know,' she repeated.

'You were great,' Varl said. 'Talked up a storm to those bastards. Were you born a liar, or does it just come naturally?'

'We haven't even begun, trooper,' Cirk said.

'Yeah, but that was a rush. I could kiss you.'

'Don't,' she said.

Varl did anyway.

Cirk smiled. 'Let's get on,' she said, and rapped her fists against the partition wall behind them.

In the container section of the transport, bloody carcasses swung from hooks and the finest cuts of meat were stacked in trays, wrapped in grease-paper. The stifling air stank of blood.

Gaunt heard the knock.

'Let's get ready,' he told the Ghosts. They got up, gathering their kit, and filed down towards the rear doors.

'All right?' Gaunt asked Landerson.

The cell fighter was carrying a brand new autorifle Noth's people had supplied.

'Sir,' he said. 'I want to thank you again for letting me–'

Gaunt put a finger to his lips. 'You've come this far, it would have been rude to leave you out, Mr Landerson.'

Gaunt looked over at Eszrah ap Niht, the other stranger in their midst. Gaunt hadn't wanted to include the partisan in this, but it had proved impossible to dissuade the Sleepwalker from staying by Gaunt's side. During the journey up through the heartlands, Gaunt and Mkvenner had spent a long time carefully explaining to Eszrah what was at stake and what was expected of him.

'Opening the doors,' said Mkoll.

'Go,' Gaunt replied.

The truck's big freight doors squealed open and the Ghosts dropped out into the darkness, one by one.

Gaunt was last out. Keeping low, they joined Cirk and Varl, and hurried down the dark space between the parked transporters and the yard wall.

It had taken the best part of a day to travel up to the environs of the bastion from Leafering. Noth's people had arranged it. They'd used vittalers' wagons, and crawled through the heartland bocage to a town called Gornell, in the foothills of the rampart massif. There, the local cell, commanded by a woman called Thresher, had taken them in. Going with the details Noth had forwarded to her through the underground network, Thresher had been working hard to design a way into the bastion for the team. A cell contact at one of Gereon's butchery firms had reported that a last minute order for grox had been sent down from the bastion staff, and a truck was being prepared to deliver it.

From there, they had been on their own.

Hugging the wall shadows, draped in their camo-cloaks, the Ghosts edged towards the brightly lit entrances of the kitchen bay. Porters were rumbling in trolleys of food, and they could hear shouted orders and chatter. The smell of heat and cooking filled the cold mountain breeze.

Mkoll and Mkvenner went ahead. They checked one entrance, hands raised for caution, and then snapped off quick gestures to move.

The team raced forward into the bright light of the entrance way. A corridor, stone-built, with doorways to the right out of which steam and cooking smells billowed.

Mkoll waved them on, and they hurried down the corridor to a junction. Left or right, or up the stairs ahead?

Up, Gaunt signalled. Up they went, taking the stairs a turn at a time, silenced pistols in their hands.

Five floors up, they broke left along a draughty hall lit by taper lights. They hugged the walls and moved from shadow to shadow. The diagrams of the bastion that

Noth had been able to obtain had been poor and incomplete, but enough to tell Gaunt that the kitchens were in the base of the right-hand tower, and any guest as significant as Sturm would be secured in the main donjon, probably in the upper levels.

Music rolled distantly from somewhere. Awful, jarring martial music. Bonin ushered them on across the next open junction, staying on watch, pistol raised, until the last of them was across. Was that cheering he could hear?

There were slit windows here. Rawne crossed to one, and peered out.

'We're in the main tower,' he whispered.

Now the hard part begins, Gaunt thought. As if everything they'd been through so far had been easy. The bastion was huge, with thousands of rooms. Sturm could be almost anywhere.

They ascended another series of staircases and came out in a high gallery. The gallery had once been lined with huge oil paintings of Gereon's nobility and army commanders. Only the gilt frames remained on the walls. The canvases had been hacked out. In the centre of each vacant frame, a sign of Chaos had been daubed on the stone wall.

Wind moaned down the long stone hallway. They could hear snatches of the triumphal music again, far away below them.

At the end of the gallery, an arch led through into another broad staircase landing. Gaunt was deciding which way to turn when three patrolling Occupation troopers came around the corner.

Landerson winced. The killing was so quick. He hadn't even registered the enemy troopers before they were dead. The three scouts wiped their silver knives and concealed the bodies in a dingy garderobe off the landing.

The team headed on, across the landing, and down a long hallway lined with doors to private bedrooms.

Mkoll raised his hand.

'What is it?' Gaunt whispered as they halted.

'I dunno, sir. Singing?'

Gaunt signalled the main group to stay where they were and edged forward down the cold hallway with Mkoll. He could hear it now too. Singing, laughing. Voices chatting.

One of the doors was open.

It was a regal bedchamber, lit by glow-globes. Two antlered mutants, household servants, were making the bed. One was singing a tuneless refrain, the other gibbering about something as it smoothed the coverlet of the four-poster. There was a wooden cart near the doorway, stacked with brooms and dustpans, flasks of bleach, nosegays of scented herbs, and piles of laundered sheets.

Gaunt nodded to Mkoll and stepped into view. His silenced autopistol was raised.

'Sturm,' he said carefully. 'Where is he?'

The mutant by the bed defecated in fear and threw its lamp-trimmer at Gaunt. Gaunt ducked, and shot it dead. The other scampered for the door, mewling. Mkoll tackled it, but the beast was surprisingly strong and threw him off. Gaunt turned quickly and his silencer coughed twice. The fleeing servant crashed into the wooden cart and brought it over as it fell.

'Sorry, sir,' Mkoll said, rising to his feet. 'Must be getting slow in my old age.'

Gaunt knew it wasn't that. He didn't want to think about the real reason that Mkoll's reactions were down.

Criid and Mkvenner moved up and helped them to drag the mutants' corpses into hiding behind the bed. Criid also collected up the spilled trolley.

'Sir?' she called. She'd found a roll of parchment that had fallen out of the cart. She passed it to him.

It was a long list of names or titles, and numbers were attached to them. Other than that, it made no sense.

'Cirk?' Gaunt called softly. She came forward.

'Can you read it?'

Cirk studied the parchment. 'It's a room registry,' she said. 'This here is a list of ordinals, dignitaries and senior officers, and this is a chart of the rooms they've been assigned for accommodation. Whoever wrote this wanted there to be no slip-ups. Everything's detailed. Every particular need accounted for. See, here, it says, "Ordinal Cluwge requires a south-facing room". And here, "The high sirdar's bed must be made up with hemp sheets, and a single lamp placed on his night table"'

'Yes, but–' Gaunt began.

'Way ahead of you,' she replied. 'Here. It says that the grand apartment on the sixteenth floor is to be prepared for *the pheguth*. A bath must be drawn. There are some details about a uniform. Blah blah. Seems he wants cotton sheets.'

Cirk looked at him.

'And the sixteenth floor?' he asked.

'According to this, we're on the ninth,' Cirk said.

Gaunt nodded. 'Close up!' he called out. The team gathered round. 'This is where we split up,' Gaunt told them.

LACED WITH STABLIGHTS, the Plenipotentiary's shuttle settled in to land in the upper courtyard. The band began to play, horns droning loud above the thundering kettledrums. An honour guard formed to greet him. Behind them, the long avenues of the Occupation troopers stood to attention, and the phalanxes of the ordinals, heads bowed.

Plenipotentiary Isidor Sek Incarnate stepped down out of his hovering flyer. Two massive Chaos Marines flanked him, snarling, their weapons brandished high, and behind them came four minotaurs, snorting in the cold air, their thick arms supporting the posts of the umbrella shield above the Plenipotentiary's disdainful head.

He waved indifferently at the hallowing crowd, the troopers rattling their weapons. The high sirdar came forward and bowed. Beside him, Desolane made reverence.

Isidor nodded, and allowed them to kiss his hands as another fanfare broke out.

'Does General Sturm await my pleasure?' Isidor asked above the thrashing music.

'He does, magir,' Desolane said.

It took twenty-seven minutes for the Plenipotentiary to walk the length of the long carpet. He stopped frequently to acknowledge the sirdars in the ranks, and then began to greet the ordinals, allowing them to kneel and kiss his fingers.

By then, Desolane had sent a runner to bring the pheguth.

STURM STOOD AND admired himself in the long looking-glass. He shook out his cuffs.

'Not bad. The coat is a little tight, but the sash is glorious.'

The lexigrapher hammered on the keys.

'Don't write that, you maggot!' Sturm snarled.

Humiliti cowered and, taking out his eraser, started to scrub out the lines he had just scrolled back.

'Where was I?' Sturm asked, pacing.

The lexigrapher showed him the sheets that spooled out of his printing machine's clamp.

Sturm read back. 'Ah yes. Vervunhive. So close as it was to my barbaric mindlocking… are you getting this, ape?'

Humiliti nodded, typing furiously again.

'So close as it was to my unreasonable, inhuman mindlocking, I find I have difficulty remembering the details. I had overall command, naturally. Gaunt was a makeweight. He had no talent for soldiering. What he had was a talent for mischief. He was a commissar, you see, as I think I have said. Have I said that?'

The lexigrapher read back quickly and then nodded.

'He was a member of the Commisariate, the discipline division. That's all politics, if you ask me. The man was a self-serving bastard. And the charges? I tell you this, was ever a man so wrongly accused? Desertion? Is it any wonder I hate the Imperium so? All my life, serving the God-Emperor... and then what does he let his minions do to me? Bastards! I was a lord militant general!'

There was a knock on the apartment door.

'Come!' Sturm yelled.

The door opened and one of the Sons of Sek leaned in. 'Magir,' he said. 'The Plenipotentiary awaits your pleasure.'

Sturm put his cap on.

'Let's go,' he said.

IN THE RAGGED slip beyond the approach road, Colonel Noth buckled his helmet in place and looked down the line of waiting men and women.

'On my word,' he whispered into the vox link. 'Three, two, one... go!'

The Gereon resistance stormed towards the gates of the Lectica Bastion, weapons blazing.

'Gereon resists!' Noth screamed. 'Gereon resists!'

TWENTY-EIGHT

THE CHARGING WAVE of underground fighters swept like a
tidal flood through the checkpoint at the head of the
approach road, mowing down the excubitors and the
post guards. The troopers in the roadway weapon
emplacements didn't even get a chance to return fire.
Rifle grenades swiftly ended their contribution to the
occupation of Gereon.

The blizzard of fire from the hundreds of cell fighters
was so fierce that the last few transports waiting at the
barrier for admission to the bastion rocked as they were
riddled with shots. One caught fire.

'Move in! Move in!' Noth yelled above the crackling
gunfire. 'The walls and the gate!'

Hundreds of rifle grenades pelted the steep curtain
wall, drizzling it with explosions. Some lofted high
enough to drop cleanly onto the wall top itself and blow
out manned batteries. But the massive array of wall
defences had now begun to fire back, decimating the

crowds of cell fighters approaching the foot of the wall.
Steam winches were slowly pulling the vast gates shut.

The heartland cells had pooled their resources and
were fielding every last man and every last, precious
weapon left in their combined caches. At least a dozen
shoulder-launched rocket tubes and twenty portable
mortars answered the barrage blazing from the wall-top.
The swishing rockets impacted in savage fire-flashes, and
one actually blew out a section of the battlement.
Chunks of stonework and pieces of body rained down
the flank of the curtain wall.

But if the main gate closed, nothing else counted.
Running forward, Noth looked around desperately. Las-
shots lanced the air around him. A cell fighter just ahead
of him buckled and fell. Another was blown off his feet
by a cannon shell.

Noth saw the truck. Just another supply transport
heading up the road to the bastion. Except it wasn't.

Gaining speed, it swerved around the shot-up vehicles at the checkpoint, splintered through the barrier,
and rattled up the last stretch of road towards the still-
closing gates.

From the top of the wall, the Bastion Guard raked it
with fire, blowing out the cab windows, puncturing the
bodywork, destroying a rear wheel. But it was still going.
Noth saw the driver hurl himself out of the cab.

The transport rammed into the gates with a terrible
wrench of metal. The winches continued to close the
gates, but the mangled transport was now wedged
between them. Its metal hull and chassis twisted out of
shape as the massive gates closed tighter, but then the
steam winches began to struggle and falter.

What's taking so long, Noth thought? What's taking
so—

Nearly a tonne of fyceline-putty explosives – the entire
combined supplies of the heartland cells – at last went
off in the transport's freight bay.

There was a pink haze, bright enough to hurt, and when the hammer blow of sound and shock came a second later, it was so hard it knocked Colonel Noth and many of the cell fighters onto the ground. Some of the underground attackers too close to the truck vaporised with it.

But vast chunks of the bastion's main gates were atomised too.

Wretched, eye-watering smoke billowed all around and the air was full of streaking gunfire. Noth got up.

'Into the gates! Go! Into the gates!' he yelled. 'Gereon resists! Gereon resists!'

THE FIRST EXPLOSIONS backlit the curtain wall like sheet lightning. Then a huge blast spewed flame and debris high into the night air in the direction of the main gate.

On the inner courtyard, the assembled masses froze and turned. The band stopped playing. There was a sudden, general consternation, voices rising, ordered ranks breaking up. Everyone could hear that the bastion's defence batteries had opened up.

Desolane ran forward. The Plenipotentiary's life-wards were already hurrying him back towards the safety of his flyer. Behind them, there was mounting uproar from the assembled worthies.

'Troops to the curtain wall!' Desolane ordered. 'Now! Excubitors, get the ordinals back into the bastion! Get them to safety!'

Men rushed around the life-ward in all directions. Desolane seized a sirdar of the Bastion Guard.

'Assemble your detail,' the life-ward told him. 'General Sturm is on his way down. Intercept him and escort him back to the safety of his quarters. I will be there shortly.'

'HEAR THAT?' BONIN whispered. Mkoll nodded. Even through the massive stone fabric of the bastion, the shudder of explosions was distinct.

'The attack's started,' Landerson said, and made the sign of the aquila. Part of him, his fervent patriotism, wished he was out there, fighting alongside the resistance. But Gaunt had selected him for this greater honour.

'Are we set?' Mkoll asked.

'Almost,' said Varl. He was working carefully to attach a shaped charge low on the wall of the hallway. Criid and Brostin were covering one end of the corridor, Beltayn and Bonin the other. Under Mkoll's command, this half of the team had split from Gaunt's. Their job was to sow confusion and cause as much damage as possible. Colonel Noth had reserved one box of fyceline-putty charges from the giant payload that had gone on the transport, and Varl now carried it in a canvas satchel. Thirty charges, plus detonator pins. Mkoll's team had descended through the fortress as Gaunt's had headed upwards, laying charges at strategic intervals. The satchel was a third empty already.

Varl pressed a det pin into the soft putty. 'Done,' he said. The pins were set on a ten-minute delay. In another five minutes, the first of the charges would start going off.

'Move!' Mkoll ordered. The squad headed down the hall and reached another stairwell. Bonin pulled them all back into cover as a platoon of Occupation troopers clattered past down the staircase. Alarm bells were ringing. The noise of warfare from outside was getting louder.

The Ghosts entered the stairwell as soon as the troopers had disappeared, and silently descended another two floors.

'Here,' Mkoll said to Varl, pointing at a section of wall. Varl got to work as the others stood guard.

'Footsteps,' Bonin warned. 'From above.'

'Varl?' Mkoll asked.

'I'm right in the middle of it!'

'Feth!' Mkoll growled. He pointed at Bonin and Criid and gestured up the stairs.

The pair let their lasrifles swing and drew their suppressed autopistols. Bonin led the way. Criid could hear the footsteps too, now. Boots, several pairs, running.

Criid and Bonin braced their weapons.

Six bastion troopers hurried down around the wide stair-turn. Criid and Bonin thumped rapid shots into them. The enemy troopers went over like skittles. Criid had to side-step as one body somersaulted past her down the stairs.

Five were dead outright. The sixth, fallen and wounded, managed to get his hands on his autorifle before Bonin shot him cleanly between the eyes.

But the man's spasming fingers clawed the trigger and the autorifle blurted out a burst of automatic fire.

Criid and Bonin glanced at each other. Both had ducked and neither had even been scratched. The burst had nailed a long line of craters up the curved wall of the staircase. Smoke drifted.

In the confines of the stairwell, the gunfire had been deafeningly loud.

From above them, they heard shouts.

STURM CAME TO such an abrupt halt that the Sons of Sek who had been in walking step went several paces past him. Humiliti nearly waddled into Sturm's legs.

'What is that?' Sturm asked.

'Sir?'

'Can't you hear it, man? That's gunfire. Detonations.' Sturm threw open the door of a nearby apartment, and strode over towards the narrow windows that looked out over the inner yard. The apartment was unlit and not in use. By the time Sturm reached the window, the amber glow from outside lit his features.

'The bastion is being assaulted,' he murmured in astonishment. 'There is a great fire at the gate, and other explosions...'

He swallowed hard. The sight was kindling other recollections now. Feelings. The apprehension of battle, the
rush of adrenaline.

The Sons looked at each other.

'We should take you back to your quarters, sir,' one
said. 'You will be safe there.'

Sturm nodded. 'That would be for the best, I think.
Until the situation is under control.'

They went back out into the corridor and turned
around the way they had come. Both of the Sons
unslung their weapons and carried them ready.

Humiliti sighed, turned about face, and hobbled after
them again.

ON THE SIXTEENTH floor, far removed from the conflict
outside, Gaunt's squad stole down an almost silent hallway towards the door of a stateroom. Gaunt led the way,
one bolt pistol drawn, flanked by Mkvenner, who carried
an autorifle the resistance had given him.

Behind them came Eszrah ap Niht, his reynbow aimed,
alongside Ana Curth who had drawn her silenced pistol.
Further back, the rest of the group – Rawne, Larkin, Feygor
and Cirk – covered the hallway back down to the landing.

Gaunt and Mkvenner burst through the door,
weapons sweeping from side to side. The lamps were lit,
but there was no one around. It was a handsome sitting
room, with richly upholstered chairs, a card table and a
tall looking-glass. An adjoining door led through to a
bedchamber. Garments lay scattered on the floor. Parts
of an Occupation force uniform. There was also an elegant brass bath tub, full of used water. Mkvenner
touched the side of the tub.

'Cooling. Used not long ago. We've missed him.'

'If this was his room at all,' said Gaunt. 'Let's check the
rest of the floor.'

* * *

BONIN AND CRIID came bounding back down the stairs.

'We have to go! Now!' Bonin cried. Stray shots were following them down the steps, slapping off the curving wall.

'Move out!' Mkoll ordered.

'Done! Done!' Varl yelped, and gathered up his gear.

The squad scrambled down the next long hallway, a wide, panelled gallery. Mkoll was at the back, waving the others on. They were halfway down when the first bastion troopers appeared in the stair doorway behind them.

Mkoll dropped to one knee and opened fire with his lasrifle. 'First and only!' he yelled.

Several of the enemy troopers pitched over, struck by his searing las-bolts. The others began blasting with their rifles.

Criid and Landerson both turned and added their firepower to Mkoll's. Hard rounds and las-shots chopped up and down the great gallery for a few furious seconds, tearing into the wood panelling and shattering lamps. Landerson felt a bullet graze his left thigh, but he kept firing.

A dull bang shook the floor. Somewhere, the first of Varl's charges had gone off.

More bastion troopers appeared. The doorway area was littered with dead, but still they surged to get through.

Firing, hugging the gallery walls, Mkoll, Landerson and Criid backed off towards the rest of the squad, who had now made it to the far end of the gallery.

Beltayn was the first to the exit.

'Check it!' Bonin yelled, but the vox-officer had already gone through.

A sizzling shot from a las-lock hit Beltayn square in the back and threw him down on his face.

'Beltayn!' Bonin yelled. He ran forward, firing his lasrifle one-handed as he tried to drag Beltayn back into cover. Troopers and excubitors were pouring up the steps ahead.

Mkoll's squad was trapped.

GAUNT HEARD THE thump of Varl's second charge come up through the floor from far below. He was about to suggest they might be on the wrong floor, when three figures came round the corner not ten metres away. Two big soldiers, dressed in menacing ochre fatigues, with another man between them.

It was Noches Sturm.

For one nanosecond Sturm's eyes met Gaunt's. One fleeting heartbeat of shocking mutual recognition.

Then the soldiers in yellow were shooting.

Gaunt felt a bullet go through his left shoulder. He crashed against the door of a nearby room. Mkvenner had thrown himself at Gaunt, bringing them both down in the partial cover of the doorway to avoid the withering fire from the strange enemy troopers.

Behind Gaunt and Mkvenner, the others scrambled for cover. By the time Rawne had got himself into some kind of firing position, the two warriors in ochre had expertly backed off around the hall-turn, covering Sturm every step of the way.

'Him! It was him!' Gaunt yelled.

'GAUNT? GAUNT? How could… how could he be here?' Sturm was saying. Humiliti didn't know if he should be recording this, but he did anyway. Guns smoking, the Sons of Sek hustled the general roughly towards the nearest apartment, kicked the door open, and pushed him inside.

'How is this possible?' Sturm demanded. 'How is this happening?'

The Sons didn't reply. Rawne, Mkvenner and Feygor had already appeared around the corridor turn and were firing down the passageway. The Sons slid into hallway doors, using the heavy sills as cover, and replied with quick, calculating bursts that forced the Ghosts back into cover.

'How?' Sturm was yelling. 'How?'

GAUNT REACHED THE corner, ignoring Curth's attempt to dress the wound in his shoulder. Shots were zinging past the end of the wall.

'There's only two of them!' Rawne was yelling.

'There only needs to be,' replied Mkvenner. 'They've got the whole passageway covered. And they're fething good.'

Gaunt knew that already. Sturm's bodyguard had reacted with the speed and tenacity of elite force troopers.

'Two or two hundred, we're taking them now,' Gaunt said.

But suddenly there was gunfire coming from behind him too.

The Bastion Guard detail that Desolane had sent to intercept Sturm had just arrived at the other end of the sixteenth floor. Drawn by the sound of weapons fire, they were rushing down the corridor to engage.

Larkin, Cirk, Eszrah and even Curth had opened fire.

THE DIN OF battle echoing from the outer courtyards was immense. It trembled the cold night air and echoed off the surrounding mountains. A large stretch of the curtain wall around the main gate was ablaze, generating an infernal radiance that lit the vast plume of white smoke rising off the gate itself. Inside, between the curtain wall and the inner bulwark, a flickering mass of flashes, bursts and tracer fire stitched the night.

Desolane reached the bulwark. Reserves of bastion troops, along with visiting companies, were drawn up behind the inner wall, checking their weapons.

Desolane approached the senior officers. 'Report?'

'Somehow, they've breached the gates and got into the outer yards,' said one sirdar.

'We've sealed the bulwark,' another reported, 'but they're hitting it hard.'

'Numbers? And who are they?' asked Desolane.

'Several hundred. Uncomfirmed reports say it is the resistance,' a senior excubitor stated.

'Of course it is!' snapped Desolane.

'This is an unforgivable outrage,' High Sirdar Brendel announced. 'I will of course present his highness the Plenipotentiary with my abject apologies for this miserable failure of security.'

There was a rapid, whistling noise, and a crunch. The officers all flinched. One of Desolane's ketra blades had cleaved the high sirdar's head and helmet in two. His corpse fell backwards.

'I'll save him the bother of accepting them,' Desolane whispered. The life-ward turned to the other seniors. 'That idiot was mistaken. The security of the bastion, the Plenipotentiary and the pheguth is mine to uphold. Mine alone. You will follow my orders and contain this disgraceful exhibition at once. Where is the etogaur?'

'I'm here, life-ward,' Mabbon stepped into view.

'I need a commander I can trust to crush this uprising immediately. Are the Sons of Sek ready?'

'Eager, life-ward.'

'Command of the field is yours. Sirdars and seniors? You answer to the etogaur.'

There was a hasty chorus of affirmatives. 'Prepare to deploy!' Mabbon yelled out. 'In the name of the Anarch, whose word drowns out all others! Now!'

'Life-ward?'

Desolane turned. A junior officer was approaching, panting hard.

'What?'

'Reports of explosions, life-ward,' the junior gasped. 'From within the bastion.'

Desolane pushed the junior aside and began to run across the inner yard towards the keep.

'GET THE FETH down!' Brostin bellowed and squeezed the trigger-spoon of his captured flamer. The weapon gurgled, coughed and then sent a dazzling spear of liquid flame out through the doorway into the stairwell. Voices began to scream.

Mkoll, Criid and Landerson had now rejoined them, still duelling hard with the archenemy troopers coming in through the gallery's far end.

'I'll clear us a way,' Brostin said, firing through the doorway again.

'Make it fast!' Mkoll snapped. Shots were raining down around them, ripping into the walls and carpet. Mkoll saw Beltayn lying on his face, Bonin crouching over him.

'Oh, feth! No!' the scout-sergeant cried.

'It's all right,' said Bonin. 'He's alive.'

Beltayn rolled over, gagging. The potent las-lock shot had hit him squarely in the vox-caster strapped to his back. The sheer force had winded him badly, but he was completely intact.

The same could not be said for his vox-set. Bonin pulled it off him. It was a blackened ruin, smoke wisping out of the shattered cover.

'I need that...' Beltayn gasped.

'Not any more, Bel,' Bonin said. 'It's junked. Come on, on your feet.'

With Criid, Varl and Landerson forming a rearguard, blazing away down the now devastated gallery, Brostin led them through the doorway. The stone stairwell radiated heat from the torching and soot caked every surface. Smouldering bodies, most of them so reduced by fire they were charcoal lumps, littered the stairs. Brostin sent another searing blast down the stairwell for good measure.

'Let's shift!' he cried.

From somewhere overhead, they felt the thump from another of Varl's charges.

THERE WAS SMOKE in the air. It drifted lazily along the empty hallways of the bastion. From far below echoed the sounds of the battle outside, and the pandemonium amongst the ordinals cowering in the main halls.

But this smoke, up here... It was coming from inside the fortress, from higher up. Desolane paused as a tremble ran through the stone floor. Something had just exploded, a few levels above.

The life-ward swept out its ketra blades.

'RAWNE!' GAUNT YELLED. 'Take the squad and drive those bastards back! Ven and I will go in after Sturm!'

There was no time to argue. The hammer of gunfire from the battle with the bastion detail made it almost impossible to hear anyway. Rawne nodded and rolled to his feet. Cirk, Feygor, Curth and Larkin had taken up firing positions along the sixteenth floor's main hallway, and were trying to keep the troopers at bay. The partisan was backing them up, thumping quarrels at the ceremonially-attired enemy soldiers. One of the iron darts hit a man in the face, and he toppled over, his huge helmet-plume of white feathers swishing like a game-bird brought down in flight.

Rawne edged forward. Somehow, Cirk had ended up in charge of the defence, and Rawne had to admit she was doing a good job. She'd arranged the Ghosts into a decent cover formation using doorways and pillars as shields, and they were, for now, holding the enemy back.

Only Curth – inexperienced in combat – was ignoring Cirk's instructions. Curth's anger had broken loose again. She was blasting away wildly with her pistol. It pained Rawne to see the strong, wilful medicae so broken and mad.

'Cirk!' he yelled. 'I want to try and drive them back through the stair head doorway! We can hold that much more securely!'

'Agreed!' she shouted.

Rawne dropped down, and pointed to Cirk, Feygor and Larkin in turn, indicating each position of cover he wanted them to move up to when he gave the order. He and Cirk would move first.

'Larks!' he called. 'Smack a hotshot down through the centre of them and get them ducking!'

Larkin nodded, and loaded a fresh cell into his long-las. The powerful hotshot clips each delivered one super-heated shot before they were spent. He was down to his last three. After that, he'd be using his pistol.

'Set!' he yelled.

'Go!' Rawne cried.

The long-las cracked and the gleaming bolt stung down the passageway. Rawne and Cirk were already moving.

But as he came out of cover, Rawne hesitated. The smoke swirling in the air in front of him had formed the precise shape of the stigma mark, and behind it, the figures of the regal enemy troopers somehow matched it perfectly. The creeping madness was on him again, the paranoia. They were going to fail and die and–

A shot tore through his left thigh and he went down on one knee with a grunt. Confused for a moment by Rawne's hesitation, Larkin wavered too, and was smacked over onto his back by a shot that broke his collarbone.

Larkin writhed on the floor, wailing, blood soaking out of him into the hall carpet.

'Larks!' Feygor bawled, and ran through the hailing fire, head-down. He grabbed Larkin by the straps of his webbing and began to drag him back towards the cover of a doorway, oblivious to his own safety. A shot ripped through his left triceps, another cut the flesh above his right knee, a third glanced off his forehead so savagely it almost scalped him. Blood pouring into his eyes, Feygor screamed out and continued to drag the helpless sniper backwards. At every jolt, Larkin shrieked as his broken bones twisted and ground together.

Rawne crawled into cover, cursing his own frailty. Their effort had been completely unsuccessful.

Worse than that, Cirk had dashed forward ahead, assuming they were all behind her. Now she was pinned down, alone and entirely helpless.

THIRTY METRES BEHIND them, Gaunt and Mkvenner edged back to the corner. The shooting had stopped. Gaunt risked a glance, in time to see the two warriors in ochre rushing Sturm away around the next hallway turn. A curious little hominid in long robes was waddling after them.

'Come on!' Gaunt yelled. With Mkvenner at his side, he began to run after the man he had crossed light-years and risked everything to eliminate.

ON THE NEXT landing, Desolane paused again. The smoke was thicker now. Somewhere in the bastion there was a considerable fire. The life-ward felt yet another vibration. Another explosion. How many was that now? Six? Seven?

Who was doing this? Surely this was beyond the scope of the local resistance. All they ever seemed to manage to do was blow up roads or set fire to granaries.

Desolane thought of Lord Uexkull. He and his band of warriors were now long overdue, along with Ordinal Sthenelus. In his last report, Uexkull had spoken of 'Imperial killers', specialist soldiers who had fought off everything the Occupation had thrown at them. Were they here now? Were they the ones who had so entirely shamed the life-ward and the bastion's regiments?

There could be only one reason an elite squad of the False Emperor's soldiers was here on occupied Gereon. Desolane knew it. That reason was the pheguth. Desolane's beloved pheguth. The life-ward had sworn before Isidor himself to protect the life of the Anarch's precious *eresht*. Other life-wards had refused the duty, spurning it. A traitor, they believed, an enemy, hardly deserved the sort of protection usually reserved for the most high-ranking ordinals. But Desolane had not. Desolane had seen it as a true challenge of its abilities. Life-wards were bred from birth to be the ultimate protectors. Nothing was more important than the safety of the charges they pledged themselves to.

And Desolane was the very best. It had been a mark of pride to accept this task from the Anarch, whose word drowns out all others, and to carry it out faultlessly.

There was another side to it too. Over the months they had spent in close company, often just the two of them alone for days at a time, Desolane had come to care for the pheguth. A bond had grown between them. The pheguth had seemed to Desolane a kindly, sorrowful man, broken down by the harsh hand fortune had dealt him, always respectful of the life-ward, always apprecia-tive of every special attention Desolane paid to make his incarceration more bearable. When the attempt had been made on his life, the pheguth hadn't blamed Des-olane. He'd actually refused to dish out the ritual punishment. It had been then that Desolane had realised the pheguth cared for the life-ward too.

Of course, it had been difficult when the mindlock collapsed, and the pheguth had become Sturm again. Sturm was a pompous, arrogant soul, and he had shown far less respect for the life-ward. But even then, Desolane had been able to see the man it had sworn to protect. The humble pheguth, in his slippers and gown, shackled to a steel bed, smiling as he sipped a cup of weak black tea as if it was the most precious thing in the galaxy.

Desolane would protect its pheguth now. Against anything. The life-ward took a little golden scanner-wand out from under its smoke-cloak. The pheguth didn't know, but early on a tracker had been embedded in his right buttock, so that Desolane would always know his location.

Desolane checked the wand's reading, and then leapt up the staircase, four steps at a time.

THE RESISTANCE WAS at the bulwark. Thresher reported that one of the gates was about to break. Gunfire licked in all directions, most of it coming off the top of the bulwark itself. Around Noth, cell fighters were dying, cut to pieces by the lethal defences.

But they were still advancing. If there had been any time to consider it, Noth would have marvelled at their success so far. There was still a chance. If the bulwark could be breached, they would be into the inner yards of the bastion. In amongst the damned ordinals and the other dignitaries, killing the bastards in the name of a free Gereon.

'Move in!' Noth yelled above the gunfire, his own weapon chattering in his hands as he ran forward. 'Take the gate! Tube launchers! Come on, we've got them! Gereon resists! Gereon resists!'

Noth staggered as the backwash of an explosion struck him from the left-hand side. Grit flew into the air and pattered onto the yard. Through the smoke, Noth saw movement. One of the other bulwark gates had opened from the inside, and troops were charging out to counter-attack them.

They were daemons, dressed in ochre. Noth had never seen anything like them before.

A cell fighter to his left folded as gunfire ripped through her belly. Another man went down howling, his leg shot off below the knee. Still more collapsed under the streaming fire.

'Rally! Rally!' Noth yelled. 'Come about! Line order!'

He turned himself, firing his rifle on auto, and saw at least one of the ochre figures shudder and fall.

'Form on me! Resist!'

The man beside him reeled sideways, as if caught by a whip. A shot had destroyed his jaw. Others ran to take his place. Thresher's cell turned back from the vulnerable gate and laid down fire too.

'Form a line! A line!' Noth yelled. 'Gereon resists!'

To his left, he heard Major Planterson bellowing as he tried to control his formation. Colonel Stocker was already dead. Thresher was trying to re-form her milling troops.

The ochre-clad warriors came on through the smoke like a storm, tearing into Noth's still-forming line. Bayonets lashed and stabbed.

Noth had read the resistance reports on Furgesh and Nahren, bocage towns that had been mysteriously exterminated in the last two weeks. There had been unsubstantiated rumours that the killing had been done by soldiers dressed in ochre, warriors who had howled the words 'Sons of Sek!' as they slaughtered.

Noth's line buckled under the impact of the charge. The colonel saw men and women he'd known all his life cut down, murdered, dismembered as they tried to stave off the feral attack. Thresher's cell was trying to engage, but now the bulwark emplacements were cutting them down in their dozens.

Noth saw Thresher fall.

So close, he thought. One of the ochre bastards came right up at him, and Noth shot him apart. Another smashed his bayonet right through the skull of the man at Noth's side, and Noth put five rounds into the killer's chest.

'Gereon resists!' he yelled. 'Gereon resists!'

Another one was on him. Noth's magazine was empty. He lunged with his bayonet, screaming. The ochre warrior smashed Noth's weapon aside with a supremely practiced flick, as if he had been drilling for months on end.

The enemy bayonet impaled Noth through the sternum. He coughed up blood as it was wrenched out and staggered forward.

He knew he was dead. He tried to make the battle cry of the resistance one last time, but his lungs were full of blood.

The Sons of Sek didn't even let him fall. Cackling like jackals, they hacked Noth limb from limb with their blades.

'DOWN! GO ON!' Mkoll yelled, urging his squad down the next winding staircase. Up was not an option. What seemed like a division of Occupation troopers was hard on their heels, hammering fire down the stairwell after them. Every single member of Mkoll's team, himself included, had picked up at least one flesh wound now, and Bonin had been hit badly above the right hip.

Besides, there was fire up above them. The charges Varl had managed to plant had set several floors in the midsection of the fortress alight. The air was filmed with drifting smoke, and there was an alarming scent of burning. Mkoll wondered if Gaunt had been successful. He prayed so.

Varl and Criid were leading the way down. Blood was running from a cut on Varl's shoulder, and Criid was bleeding from a wound under her hairline.

Landerson was helping Bonin along.

Shots suddenly began to spray up at them. They ducked back. Varl peered down. Dozens of excubitors were lurching up the stairs below.

'We need another way out!' Varl yelled.

Mkoll ran back up the stairs a little way, firing shots up at the first Occupation troopers that poked their faces around the stair bend, and kicked open a door. It led into another hallway. They were crossing back into the side tower adjacent to the main keep.

'Get moving!' Mkoll shouted, blasting up at the troops trying to press down the stairs to get at them. Several fell, hitting the stone steps hard and slithering down, limp.

Varl and Brostin were the last two through the door. Brostin's flamer had accounted for many of the enemy so far, and added to the conflagration in the bastion too. Now his prom tanks were wheezing and almost empty.

'You saving the rest of those charges?' he asked Varl.

'Not particularly,' said Varl. 'But I don't have time to set the det pins–'

'Just fething toss them!' Brostin yelled.

Varl turned and hurled the satchel down the stairwell.

'Now run, Varl. Run like a bastard and don't look back.'

Varl did exactly what Brostin told him to do. Brostin shook the flamer's tanks and drooled up the last of the accelerant. Then he aimed the weapon down the stairs.

'Say hello to Mister Yellow,' he murmured, and belched off his last spear of flame.

Brostin threw the heavy weapon aside and started to run. Most of Mkoll's squad had already reached the end of the hallway. His long legs pumping, Brostin moved fast for a heavy man. He had almost caught up with Varl when the fire in the stairwell ignited the satchel.

There was a strange, drum-like thump. Then a fireball rushed up the stairs and boiled along the corridor, throwing Varl and Brostin right off their feet.

IN THE OUTER yards, the Sons of Sek were beginning to howl out their victory. Mabbon Etogaur moved forward, slapping men on the back, stepping over the butchered dead. Sporadic gunfire still rattled from either side.

He heard something and looked up. Dark against the night sky, the bastion was suddenly illuminated. Some kind of furnace light had split its midriff, spilling flame up into the air from dozens of windows. Mabbon looked at it in astonishment. The right-hand side of the bastion was on fire, and so were the upper storeys of the side tower.

Mabbon keyed his vox-bead. 'This is the etogaur. Primary orders. All units evacuate the bastion. You are charged with the safe removal of the ordinals. Do it now and do it properly!'

He looked back at the vast fortress. Fire was belching from the entire right-hand side. What in the name of the Anarch had happened up there?

'CIRK! CIRK, STAY down!' Rawne cried, trying to staunch the blood gushing from his leg wound. Something catastrophic had just shaken the entire donjon. He could smell burning.

He heard Cirk yelp. She'd been hit. The shot-rate coming from the bastion troopers down the hall was increasing, and some were moving forward.

'Stay down!' he shouted again.

Rawne looked around. The partisan had vanished, and Feygor, last seen maimed and bleeding from at least three hits, had finally succeeded in dragging Larkin into the cover of an adjacent room. The only person in sight was Curth, crouched down in a doorway. She was still firing at the enemy, yelling out her rage. She had ditched her pistol and had grabbed hold of Feygor's fallen lasrifle.

'Ana!' Rawne yelled over the constant fusillade.

'What?'

'We have to get forward! We have to get forward now!'

'Why? What the feth for?'

Rawne staggered across the hall and fell down beside her. 'Cirk's pinned,' he said. 'We have to move forward and drive them back, or she's dead.'

'So fething what?' Curth snarled, firing again. 'She deserves to die. That bitch. She's a total bitch. You've seen the mark on her. She's Chaos filth!'

'I've seen it,' Rawne murmured. 'I see it everywhere.'

'What?'

He sat up and looked at her. She was still shooting.

'Ana. We can't leave her to die.'

'Why the feth not?' Curth asked.

'Because… because otherwise, the archenemy has won.'

'What the feth are you on about, Rawne?'

Rawne coughed the smoke out of his gullet. 'She's helped us, Curth. Every step of the way, without question. She's got us through, risked her life. Feth it, we wouldn't have got in here without her. I don't like her either. I don't trust her. She's got the mark. But then again, I don't think I trust anyone any more.'

'I say we leave her!' Curth grunted and fired again.

'Ana,' Rawne whispered. 'The taint has got us. The poison of this fething world. You and me both. If we leave Cirk, we let it win.'

Curth stared at him. 'That's rubbish!' she said.

'No, it isn't. Whatever you or I think she is, she's got this far. This is our last chance, Ana. Our last chance!'

'Our last chance for what?'

'To prove we're still human. To prove we're loyal servants of the Emperor. Even now. Even though Gereon has done its worst.'

Curth lowered the rifle and gazed at him. Tears welled up in her eyes. 'You talk a lot of feth, you know that, major?'

'You know I'm right,' Rawne replied. 'I won't let this place beat me. How about you?'

'Do the right thing?' she asked sarcastically.

'Because the Emperor protects. And if he approves, he will protect us and let us know he is pleased with our service.'

'You make that shit up all by yourself?' she said.

'No. It was something Gaunt said.'

'All right,' said Curth. Rawne handed her his last fresh clip and she slammed it home.

'For the Emperor, then,' she said.

He shook his head. 'No, for Tanith, first and only.'

They got up, lasrifles blasting, and charged down the corridor side by side into the enemy fire.

THE TWO SONS of Sek had shoved Sturm into another apartment chamber. He was terribly agitated now, pacing up and down, the lexigrapher hobbling after him.

'Gaunt... no, that's not right. As I said, he can't be here. It makes no sense...'

Sturm paused. He glanced at Humiliti, who was still typing, and then walked through into the apartment's bedchamber, throwing the doors wide.

'I remember,' he said, sitting down on the bed. 'I remember now. Throne, I thought I'd remembered everything. Who I was, what I was. But there are deep, dark places in the mind that take a long time to resurface.'

Humiliti tapped and rattled his keys.

'I was a commander of men... did I say that before?' The lexigrapher nodded.

'Men feared me. Respected me. But... oh, Emperor, I remember it now. Vervunhive. The bloody war. We were losing. The Zoican host was right at the gates.'

Sturm got to his feet and hunched down facing the lexigrapher. Humiliti looked up at him with bright eyes, his nimble fingers poised over the key-levers.

'I was afraid,' Sturm said. 'I was afraid for my life. I ran. I deserted my post. I would have left them all to die.'

Humiliti hesitated, wondering if he was supposed to record this.

'Take it down, you maggot!' Sturm cried, rising again. 'Take it all down! This is my confession! This is me! You and your foul masters wanted to know all about me! All my secrets! You wanted to pick my mind clean! Well, how about this one, eh? I thought I was a lord general. I thought I had power and strength. So did your masters. That's why they spent all this time and effort breaking me. And what do they get? What do they get, you little runt?'

Sturm turned and bowed his head. 'A coward. A man too afraid of death to do the right thing.'

Beyond the outer room of the apartment, shots rang out.

MKOLL AND CRIID pulled Varl and Brostin to their feet. Both men had blisters on their skin from the sucking fireball. Behind them, the entire staircase was ablaze. There were ominous rumbles as the structure of the bastion itself began to crumble.

'Nice one,' Criid grinned.

'Time to leave,' Mkoll said.

'WHERE'S THE WOUND?' Curth was yelling. 'Where are you hit?'

Cirk showed Curth her left forearm. A round had broken the bones and exploded the imago in its pus-filled blister.

'It's gone,' Cirk sighed.

'Come on,' Curth said urgently, helping her up. Rawne was behind her, raking las-fire into the doorway of the staircase, pushing the enemy back. Every muzzle flash seemed to form the stigma mark to him, but he didn't care any more.

'You came back for me,' Cirk whispered.

'Yeah, we did,' said Curth. 'How about that?'

THE TWO SONS of Sek turned and began to return fire, but Gaunt and Mkvenner had the drop on them. Gaunt stormed forward, a bolt pistol in either hand, firing at the frantic warriors. One toppled as his skull exploded. The other jerked back, a bolt round striking his right arm

and disintegrating it. The soldier screamed and Mkvenner put a bullet through his open mouth.

Gaunt and Mkvenner prowled forward, their weapons
smoking. The door that the Sons had been defending
was wide open. Gaunt holstered his pistols, and drew
his power sword. It throbbed as the blade ignited.

The chamber beyond was an anteroom, full of opulent
furniture. An empty gilt frame hung on the wall, surrounding a blasphemous symbol. There was a doorway
beyond, open. Gaunt could hear a voice talking.

He glanced at Mkvenner. Ven raised his autorifle. They
crept forward.

And Desolane entered the room behind them.

TWENTY-NINE

THE LIFE-WARD pounced forward, its twin ketra blades scything at the two Guardsmen. Mkvenner reacted first, turning to block, his raised autorifle splintering apart beneath the life-ward's right-hand blade.

Gaunt turned too, bringing the power sword up. It met the left-hand ketra, and the blade glanced away.

He had never seen anything like this creature. A towering, slender, sexless body sheathed in a tight suit of blue-black metal-weave and draped with a gauzy black cloak that moved like smoke. The monster's long legs were jointed the wrong way below the knees and ended in cloven hooves. A smooth bronze helmet covered the thing's head, broken only by four holes: two for the eye-slits and two on the brow through which small white horns extended.

It moved like water, as if the rest of existence had been slowed down.

Gaunt blocked another stab, and another, then danced around to present again. The thing lunged forward, ripping Gaunt's coat with the tip of its left-hand blade, and then swung in a strike that left a long, lacerating stripe down Gaunt's torso.

Gasping in pain, weeping blood, Gaunt leapt back and swung the power sword of Heironymo Sondar around in a savage chop. The powered blade met Desolane's left-hand knife and shattered it.

Desolane lunged again, and stripped a deep gash through Gaunt's right arm with its remaining knife. The sheer impact threw Gaunt over onto the floor. His hands wet with blood, he scrambled for the sword. Desolane knocked it away with one cloven hoof, and then kicked Gaunt hard in the belly. Gaunt doubled up, choking and winded.

Desolane stabbed its remaining blade towards Gaunt's head.

Silenced pistol rounds, spitting like whispers, jerked the life-ward backwards. Mkvenner rose, tossing aside the now-empty autopistol, and picked up the fallen power sword. It hummed and sang in his hands as he crossed and turned it.

Desolane went for him.

Mkvenner parried the first cut, swung wide, deflected the second and wheeled back to stop the third. Desolane snarled, swinging round to attack Mkvenner again. The life-ward scythed in low, and Mkvenner managed to turn the ketra blade away, but Desolane slammed its bodyweight into the Tanith scout, and sent him reeling back. Desolane checked and spun again, fending off the sword and splitting Mkvenner's cheek open from the lip to the jaw-line.

Mkvenner fell, blood pouring out of his face.

Desolane turned nimbly and stepped over to Gaunt, who was still trying to rise. The life-ward raised its ketra blade double-handed to deliver the killing stroke.

An iron quarrel hit Desolane in the ribs. As the life-ward staggered back, another went in through one of the eye slits in its bronze helmet.

Eszra ap Niht walked forward, reloading his reynbow. The partisan fired again, and planted an iron arrow in Desolane's chest. The life-ward staggered forward and smashed Eszrah across the room with one blow of its fist. The partisan lay where he fell, his segmented cloak in tatters. Desolane stumbled round, swaying. By now, the moth-toxin was flooding through its veins. It fell down hard on its face.

GAUNT GOT TO his feet, dripping blood. He limped through the doorway into the bedchamber, drawing a bolt pistol in each hand.

The hunched lexigrapher backed away.

Sturm sat on the end of the bed, staring at the floor.

'Commissar,' he said, without looking up.

'Lord general,' Gaunt replied.

'I'm glad it's you,' said Sturm. 'Somehow appropriate.'

'In the name of the God-Emperor–' Gaunt began.

'Please, no. Nothing so formal,' Sturm protested. 'I remember it all now, Gaunt. All of it. The fear. The... cowardice. It's not a pretty memory. Throne knows, it took long enough to come back.'

Gaunt raised one of his pistols. 'By the power of the Commisariate, I hereby declare–'

'Ibram? Ibram... please,' Sturm begged.

'Not this time, Sturm.'

'Please, in the name of the Throne! Give me a weapon!'

Gaunt stiffened, feeling the blood leaking out of him. 'I showed you that respect at Vervunhive. You turned it into an attack.'

'I know. I'm sorry. I beg you. Gaunt, you have two bolters, for Throne's sake.'

Swaying, Gaunt held out one of his bolt pistols and gave it butt-first to Sturm. He kept the other one raised to cover the traitor general.

'Final request granted. Or... another trick?' Gaunt asked.

Sturm shook his head.

'Final request accepted,' Sturm said. He put the barrel of the bolt pistol to his head and pulled the trigger.

Gaunt took a step forward, not yet believing it was over. Sturm lay at his feet, his skull exploded like a ripe melon.

Desolane burst into the bedchamber, swinging the ketra blade like a sickle. The life-ward howled when it saw the pheguth's corpse.

Gaunt flinched back.

A hotshot round disintegrated Desolane's midriff and threw the life-ward's corpse against the far wall.

Gaunt looked up. Feygor, his face streaming with blood, lowered Larkin's long-las.

Gaunt smiled at Feygor. 'You know,' he said. 'I knew there was a reason I brought you along.'

THIRTY

BEHIND THEM, AGAINST the early dawn, the bastion was burning. The fleeing Ghosts had regrouped in a dim valley below the fortress. Every single one of them was wounded. But every single one was also alive.

Curth was trying to dress Gaunt's wounds.

'See to the others, Ana. The more deserving,' he said.

'That would be you,' she replied.

Gaunt sent her away and limped down through the figures of the Ghosts sprawled amongst the rocks.

Larkin was moaning and seemed close to death. Feygor was now unconscious from blood loss.

Gaunt crouched down beside Beltayn.

'I'm so sorry, sir,' Beltayn said.

'For what?' asked Gaunt.

'My voxcaster, sir. I got it shot up. Now we can't call in the extraction.'

'Bel, we'll be fine. Nothing's awry.'

Gaunt rose, and walked on. Curth was excising the last shreds of the burst imago from Cirk's broken forearm. He watched for a moment as the steel pliers dragged black tendrils from the woman's flesh.

Under the skin. What matters is on the inside. In the heart. In the mind. The Saint used many instruments to guide those loyal to her, even some that appeared to bear the mark of Chaos.

Gaunt turned away. He wondered how he would tell them.

It had been the last thing Van Voytz had said to him before the mission. The one thing Gaunt had not shared with the chosen team.

'Ibram, please understand there's very little chance of getting you off Gereon again. You can transmit a call, of course, but the odds are you'll be left stranded. Getting you in will be hard enough. Getting a ship close enough to pull you back out...' Van Voytz had looked away.

'Are you saying, sir, that if we're still alive at the end of this suicidal mission, it's *still* a one-way mission?'

'Yes, Gaunt,' Van Voytz had said. 'Does that change your mind?'

'No, sir.'

Gaunt wandered down the slope to find Landerson.

'They fought and died with honour,' Gaunt said to him. 'The Gereon cells. They almost had the bastards on the ropes. The resistance did its very best.'

'Yes, sir, it did,' Landerson replied. 'But it wasn't enough, was it? And now they're all gone.'

Gaunt shrugged. 'Then we'll build the underground back up between us.'

'Between us?' Landerson asked.

Gaunt nodded. 'I think I'm going to be here for a while longer. What do you say?'

'That Gereon resists?'

'Gereon resists,' Gaunt replied. He looked up. From the back of his mind came a memory, strong and unbidden. Tanith pipes. Brin Milo, playing the tune he always played when the Tanith First retired from a battlefield. He tried to remember its name.

The mountain wind rose, cold and unforgiving. It blew the smoke from the fortress out across the heartland, another stain upon a wide, disfigured world.

ABOUT THE AUTHOR

Dan Abnett lives and works in Maidstone, Kent, in England. Well known for his comic work, he has written everything from the *Mr Men* to the *X-Men* in the last decade, and is currently scripting *Legion of Superheroes* and *Superman* for DC Comics, and *Sinister Dexter* and *The VCs* for 2000 AD. His work for the Black Library includes the popular comic strips *Lone Wolves*, *Titan* and *Inquisitor Ascendant*, the best-selling Gaunt's Ghosts novels, and the acclaimed Inquisitor Eisenhorn trilogy.